Prologue

Jennifer and I were walking around, and suddenly a storm began. It threatened to sweep everything - people, objects, buildings. I felt confident enough to stay where we were but Jennifer wanted to move on and she left the place. A local told me rooms can be rented nearby. If I didn't hurry, no rooms would be left. The storm was getting stronger and had begun to sweep up everything—people, signs, bins, carts, and children, even parts of buildings were swept away in all directions in a strong, painful din. A huge commotion could be heard from the pained cries of people bumping into objects in their path, carried by the storm. Children were torn from the arms of parents. With great effort, I ran toward the building next door. I had difficulties opening my eyes because of the dust, and the angry blasts of air. From afar, I recognized two multi-story buildings: the Twin Towers. He was there. I had to find him. I started running but was going nowhere. It seemed like I was stepping in the same place. Protecting my face from flying objects, I managed to reach the towers' entrance with great effort and asked if he was renting a room there and if any remaining rooms were left to rent. People were running in all directions and no one paid attention to me. I shouted at them, but no one was listening. The wind's intensity rose, increasing the chaos around. If I didn't hold onto something firm, the wind threatened to sweep me away...

Zero Hour

She took a stool, placed it in front of a narrow gap between the bars and, without further delay, unzipped the belt where she kept all her money. She unfolded the small plastic wrapping where the dollar bills were placed: five $100 bills, five $20s and ten $10s - a total of $700. She spread the bills as if they were cards. His face was looking at her from the bills. Her hand reached through the narrow gap between the bars and, just before releasing her grip, fingers pressed tightly to the bills, she paused, reflecting on the previous moments.

"He isn't here, Madam. I'm sorry, he just left last night!"

It had been two weeks since she and a childhood friend of hers arrived in India seeking him. She flew to Belgium to meet her friend and from there they flew to India. She knew he had traveled to Sikkim – the smallest state in India in both size and population. Sikkim was considered "the Switzerland of India" - clean, comfortable, cool and blessed with high mountain chains decorated with bright snow at their peaks. The weather was lousy all the time, but she couldn't care less. She was sure she would find him there. She only wanted to find him. They tried to track him down, moving from one village to another, wasting time while the clock was ticking and the return flight date looming closer. Finally, on their last day, she received information about the most recent place he was staying. She was not going to miss the chance to see him when she was so close. While her friend was getting ready to leave, she rushed to the airline office to postpone her flight. Her friend left and after she succeeded in postponing her flight, she continued on her own and traveled four hours to finally reach Namchi, the town where she heard she could find him.

When she arrived at the gates of the place where he was supposedly staying, she couldn't contain her excitement. Finally, a frustrating search that started in New York was about to end...only to find out he had left the night before.

Hours later, her fingers were pressing tightly to the bills.

Let go?

She had never experienced such frustration. She remained there for almost an hour, refusing to believe what she had just heard.

How can it be? She asked herself. *Every time I'm so close to him, he's gone. Is it a coincidence or this is also part of the scheme that has been going on?* She refused to accept his absence.

The Indian housekeeper who had delivered her the bad news asked if he could be of any help. She looked hopelessly at him.

"At this point, no one can help. It's all lost."

Struck by this dramatic response coming from a complete stranger, he responded in a soft, sympathetic voice typical in Indian culture, "I'm sorry, Madam. I am very sorry!" while shaking his head from side to side.

Further questioning of the distressed housekeeper revealed that the man she was looking for had left to his home country: Saudi Arabia. This meant he wasn't going to be back to the States anytime soon.

This was the last straw – she was completely devastated. She sat there, paralyzed and lost. When she finally began to process all that was said, she rose heavily from her seat and walked slowly out to the gloomy street, wandering aimlessly. A rickshaw stopped beside her and asked her where she needed to go. It took her a few minutes to recall the name of the hostel where she was staying. What was she going to do now? She couldn't go back home since she had postponed her flight. And what was "Home," anyways? Back at home, all had deteriorated after what had happened these recent months.

If only she could comprehend the events of the past half a year, a time from which she is still trying to recover, still attempting to figure out what had happened and when it all started to go wrong. She is still disappointed, still confused, but most of all, angry. *As angry as hell.* She was so close to reaching him, so close to getting some answers.

Through the bars, the town of Namchi was staring back at her. From the balcony of her room at the hostel, she could see the famous Buddha statue—Guru Rinpoche, the patron saint of Sikkim —a huge figure, 118 feet high, carved into a high mountain, overlooking the city, and beneath it, the mountain range decorated by village houses scattered at different heights. Yesterday, when she just arrived, before going to the place he stayed, the Buddha statue appeared to have an optimistic smile on his face. Now, it seemed that the patron saint of Sikkim was laughing at her.

Five $100s, five $20s and ten $10s—a total of $700. The bills were spread like cards in her hand, and she found herself reaching out through the narrow gap between the bars…

Seemed as if all that's happened lately were leading me to a breaking point. It is as if I am being tested! I can't take it anymore!

Let go!

The bills left her hand, hovering above the valley below the hostel's balcony all the way to the rooftops of the village houses. The Buddha statue seemed to be laughing even harder now. She felt dizzy. Suddenly, she realized what she had just done: the wind began blowing away all her money. There, standing in the balcony of the hostel, she reached the point of no return, with no money, no credit card, and no means of survival.

What madness had gotten into her? She grabbed her head and held it tightly in her hands in complete horror, taken by deep anxiety. *What would happen next? What would she do? How could she leave the room?* Maybe she could run down and try to find the bills, but it was hardly possible – they were scattered across the valley over the rooftops. *Maybe I can find some? Maybe I can go down and track them down and explain what had happened to anyone who picked them up. Will I be able to go home?*

Again, this term. Home. *Home where?*

What the hell made her to scatter her own money into the wind?

Ideas to recover from her point of no return flashed through her mind, but as seconds passed and accumulate to minutes, she realized that the money was lost. Her strength had left her, and she collapsed exhausted into the chair behind her. She'd never know what went through her head during those moments.

She remained motionless for a long time and consciousness slowly started to creep into her as the cold of the night snuck through the balcony bars. She entered the room, crawled into bed. She fell asleep instantly.

She awakened sweating at three in the morning. She had this dream again. The first time she had it was right after… oh!! she couldn't think of it—it was too painful. She wrote the dream down—a habit of hers since the horror that occurred in the States.

I was hanging out with some friends from the training. For some reason, the practice had taken place in the park. I left and walked into some kind of a building, and looked out the window and saw a man walking in the park. Then someone else came out with a gun. He aimed it at the man, demanding money or something—I couldn't quite hear exactly what, it was too far. He shot him and ran away. I followed him to be able to report it to the police, even though I couldn't believe what was happening.

I went downstairs, looking for traces of the killer. A woman passed by, I think with a stroller and a child, and I asked her which direction she had seen the man run. She pointed, but for some reason I didn't understand. In fact, since the beginning, I wasn't responding quickly enough. Something was slow, hesitant in my responses, like some kind of an autistic.

I looked for my friends, but couldn't find them. I've made my way to the crime scene. The victim was lying there, and I approached him carefully to see if he was really hurt. He was holding his hands to his stomach and I could see blood. I looked at his face, expecting to see blood in his mouth, like in the movies, and sure enough, some blood was spilling. He was still alive. He raised his head toward me as if he was trying to tell me something. I brought my face closer to him, and he whispered a name I couldn't really understand. I moved and started to run, shouting for someone to call the police. Someone was in the public phone booth and there was a long line of people waiting to make a phone call, so I ran to my building. Bobby, the super-intendment, was on the phone.

'I need to talk to the police urgently!' I shouted, and Bobby handed the phone over to me, startled.

7

'What number should I call?'

'Zero,' Bobby *told me with a vicious smile. I was sure he is lying but I still dialed, and to my surprise, it was the police.* He hadn't lied, *I thought to myself.*

As soon as the voice on the phone said, 'Police,' I became speechless. I couldn't say a single word.

And that was it.

She set up in bed, feeling sick. She wondered if it was something she ate or drank, or if it was simply her aching soul. A wave of nausea seized her, and with it a sharp abdominal pain hit like a knife. She ran into the bathroom. Was the physical pain growing and strengthening to try to help her forget her madness and stupidity? She experienced an extreme thirst, drank some water. Then, surrendered to the feeling of weakness once more she collapsed into bed.

Minutes After

It was late morning, almost noon, when she awoke. She tried to postpone the moment of truth, but when it finally arrived, it found her sitting on the bed, trying to understand the nightmare of yesterday evening. Did it really happen? Did she really throw away her money, or was she just dreaming? She began to worry. Without money, she wouldn't be able to make any long-term plans. And yet somehow, surprisingly, calmness took over her, a sort of pleasant ambiguity. She was happy not to make long-term plans. She remembered her favorite song, "Comfortably Numb," by Pink Floyd. She wondered whether the songwriter was referring to the same mental condition she was experiencing right then... *Am I physically weak, apathetic, or simply accepting the situation? Or maybe there is nothing more to lose, since it really couldn't get any worse? In moments like this, aren't you supposed to turn to some high being? To a God?*

The Buddha statue stared at her through the window, this time solemnly. She found it difficult to decide if he was on her side. Was he laughing with her, or at her? She stuck her tongue out at him.

She got up and began to pack her bag. Something had changed and she no longer saw her belongings in the same way as before. She was packing them in a somewhat cautious manner, as if she were packing things belonging to someone else. She felt no connection to them. She felt free, liberated from her belonging, from looking for *him*, from pursuing answers to the questions from past events. Free from being herself, free to simply *be*. *Maybe this is what drove me to this act of madness?*

But that feeling didn't last long.

She raised her backpack to her back, ensuring that her bracelet was on her arm. This bracelet, passed down from her mother's side, was the only material possession with emotional value. She grabbed the water bottle. After the bracelet, it was the most important thing on her mind. Not having water in India would mean disaster.

9

She realized that, although she always saw herself as cool-tempered, confident person, being so concerned about water now seemed a bit hysterical. She grasped the bottle tightly, left the room and walked down the stairs toward the exit knowing that the Indian receptionist would stop her. For some reason, this didn't bother her.

The receptionist halted her. "Madam, are you leaving?"

"Yes, I am," she replied laconically.

"Will Madam wish to have late breakfast now? Lunch"

"No, thanks."

"Then I'll prepare the bill for you."

She reflected on the fact that he said "for you". *He prepares the bill for the hostel, not for me...* This seemed to trouble her more than the fact that she won't be able to actually pay the bill.

One of the hostel boys approached the receptionist seeking his attention, and asked him to come with him. The receptionist appeared unsure whether to follow him or not. *Does he feel that if he leaves I will run?* She wondered, slightly amused.

As soon as they left, she quickly snuck out. She felt like she's running away on purpose, a sensation she hadn't experienced since her school days, when as kids, they used to steal candy from the local deli. She picked up her pace, nearly running, but the heavy backpack on her back didn't allow for fast movement. Even a quick walk was difficult, and soon she was covered in sweat and out of breath. For a moment, she was tempted to throw away the bag, but then she would be left with nothing. The thought that she still had something of her own comforted her. She spurred herself and kept walking rapidly through several winding streets, looking for a place to sit. *Once again, physical need dictates the course of things*, she thought, breathing with difficulty. The absence of benches, fences or stones left her with the option of a dirty sidewalk full of local waste.

She animated herself to keep going until she could find a suitable place to rest. Finally, she reached a square with the faded, neglected remnants of a fountain in its center. Several beggars were scattered around the square, engaged in doing nothing. The physical effort had

10

affected her, and she felt dizzy. She sat on the edge of the fountain, breathing heavily.

Her anxiety increased. Troubling thoughts entered her mind. Would the receptionist look for her and report to the police? Could she be arrested? Will her fate be to rot away in an Indian jail without anyone knowing? She thought about her family and felt a heavy weight in her heart. *I've never felt so alone! Free, but alone.*

The beggars nearby stared listlessly at if she were transparent. A strong sensation began to grow along with her feeling of being alone. It was an emotion she was quite familiar with: loneliness. Tears flooded her eyes, and a wave of self-pity enveloped her. Obligated to pay the emotional price of the highs and lows of the last few hours, would she be able to handle what was to come?

Dizziness.

One of the beggars caught her attention. Poor, miserable, and extremely thin, he was sitting on uneasy feet not far from her at the edge of the fountain. His hands and face, his faded and torn clothing were all stained with dirt, and he seemed delirious. He mumbled something unclear and it seemed as if he was not present in the real world. But despite his repulsive appearance, there was something pleasant and soft about him. She had never felt so close to a beggar. Will she, too, look like him in the end?

Horror possessed her and she jerked her gaze away. A little further, there were well-dressed passersby from the upper class. They sped up as they passed the beggar's square. Her feeling of comfort and closeness to the Indian upper class was replaced by a sense of detachment and estrangement. She felt as if she could see deep inside the bottom of their souls, as if they were transparent.

She observed their flashiness, their peacock-like walk full of importance in a world that belonged to them. They did not see anyone but themselves.

Aren't they ridiculous? She thought to herself.

11

A tall woman was standing and talking to a flashy man. She was wearing fine clothes and was holding the hand of a little girl dressed as a doll with matching ribbons in her hair – a showcase display.

She looked at the tall woman and then at the beggar sitting nearby, *No, I'm not like this! I cannot be*! She felt lost. She watched the tall woman and the beggar, the beggar and the tall woman. *I don't seem to resemble either.*

She sat and watched the passersby for a long time. *What do I do now? I have nowhere to go and I can't pay for anything. Where will I get food? Where will I sleep? What will happen when the night falls?* The people were so foreign, so cold and alienated.

Her gaze lingered on the beggar again. The more she watched him, the more human and less repulsive he appeared. He pulled out a small book from his pocket and began leafing through its pages as if looking for something specific. He found what he was looking for. He concentrated on the book, read several lines, scratched his head as if he is analyzing something, and then he returned to reading. Wishing to escape her grim reality, she watched him, completely mesmerized. Her stress decreased and peace and quiet seeped through her once more. The bustle of the busy road and the street noise so characteristic of India faded. Everything happening seemed to be as is projected in a silent film.

Suddenly, he turned his head toward her and smiled at her, exposing a line of broken yellow teeth. *Could he sense that I was watching him?* She began to draw herself back when, all of a sudden, a shadow covered her face. It was the figure of a man. An old man. He sat down between her and the beggar.

She got up as if it was her sign to be released from her frozen trance. She needed to move on. She crossed the road, but something made her look back at the fountain. The beggar had closed his book, risen, and begun walking quickly and decisively. In the absence of any definite goal, she found herself changing her course and walking after him while keeping a safe distance. She tried to imagine where he could have been going with such determination. He passed a row of houses, musty stairs, and another row of houses. She kept on follow him. He reached a street corner and disappeared. She sped up.

Order in the Gutters

She reached the street corner and saw the beggar in the distance. He had just disappeared around another corner. The scene soon revealed to her was a rundown area at the edge of the town, filled with sooty old houses and narrow, dirty alleyways. She continued walking to the corner where he was last seen. There, around the bend, what appeared to be a colony of homeless loomed into sight. She felt like she had stumbled upon an entire city. People were sitting between improvised tents and wooden beams. Electrical wires, rags, and ropes tied blankets together as tents. Laundry hung in front of some tents and an improvised kitchen could be seen in front of others. A baby cried.

The homeless watched the foreign guest who had accidentally come across their homes with puzzled eyes. She debated whether to retrace her path or keep moving ahead. She appeared to already be in the center and the way back didn't look any better. She quickened her steps, but would have to pass among the tents. She thought about turning back again, but a great number of people had already started to gather behind her and she feared they were after her backpack. She felt her entire body tense, threatened by a possible clash. Would she be able to put her training to the test, if needed? She decided to move forward.

One of the homeless people—a man in his fifties—crawled out of his tent and, upon noticing her, rose and walked toward her. She froze. Was there going to be an attack? But he simply greeted her.

"Hello, Miss!"

She had no idea what to do. Should she ignore the greeting, as if it never happened? Respond politely? But maybe that would be considered an invitation for further interaction. *I'm definitely not interested in that, and they are definitely interested in my backpack,* she thought.

"Hello, Miss!" he yelled again to her face, almost indignantly, as he noticed her lack of attention. Her eyes quickly scanned him— shabby, faded, dirty clothes, an untrimmed beard and gleaming, frightening eyes.

"Hello," she replied in a quiet voice, indecisively and almost inaudibly. But he heard her, gently nodded and passed her by. She turned slightly to watch him and to make sure the danger really passed. Indeed, he kept going.

She realized what had happened. All he wanted was attention, nothing more.

She moved on while trying to maintain eye contact with the homeless people surrounding her, nodding to each one. Such direct eye contact was a new experience for her. In New York, she intentionally would pass people quickly, deliberately avoiding eye contact. This close contact was intimidating. Perhaps they would make demands of her and she wouldn't be able to placate them; she would be forced to say no, to let them down, but more importantly, would lose her freedom to move without obligation. The homeless women and men nod back at her. She thought she could see a smile raising the corners of their mouths. Her confidence increased.

Suddenly, she felt someone touch her arm. She stopped and turned around. An old man with a long beard had made a huge effort to take an additional stumbling step to catch up with her and beg for change. She wasn't expecting that. She paused and stood in front of him, uncertain of how to react. Everyone appeared to be watching curiously and intently, waiting for her response. The silence in the air became loud. The baby's crying stopped.

Ironically, she thought, *even if I want to give something, I don't have it. What do I do?* She had the feeling that she couldn't move on without giving him something. It would be a disappointment, after all, now that she carried the burden of proof that rich, successful, lucky people are human beings and have human dignity. *But what to do?*

Thoughts ran through her mind. If she looked for some clothes or anything else in her backpack to give him, she'd need to remove the pack to the ground and open it. That would be calling for trouble – it would mean spending more time in this unsafe area and her open backpack may tempt them to attack her after all. *What to do, then?*

But her salvation came from an unexpected direction—an old woman approached the man and pulled him away, teasing him while reminding him that it was not proper to ask for change from guests who appear in the neighborhood, right at their home.

With the backpack on her back, she then continued walking and passed by the last tent while looking at the faces of the people. They seemed to approve of her leaving. No one was moving toward her and soon enough the homeless colony was behind her.

To her right, broad steps appeared. Their generous width invited her to climb. She moved up the steps heavily and stopped twice on the way to catch her breath. *This heavy backpack.* When she reached the top, a deserted path appeared. She needed to use the bathroom. It was a good location and she quickly took the opportunity, hovered among the bushes and moved on. A house could be seen in the distance. She kept going and reached the beginning of a street full of rural houses.

Maybe I'll continue even further? But what am I looking for, anyway? She could not answer that. *Where will I spend the night?*

The sight and the smell of Indian streets - with filthy sewer canals and their stench spreading into the air - had become cleaner. The houses looked pleasant and flowers and plants could be seen on their tiny porches. The evening began to fall and she wondered what to do. Tired and worried, she collapsed heavily on a large rock on the side of the road. She leaned on a dirty fence, no longer willing to fight for a clean territory given the dirt and squalor of India. It was cleaner than most fences.

Homeless

Her thoughts wandered to the events of the homeless neighborhood, attempting to escape harsh reality. She tried, as usual, to analyze what had exactly happened. How had she managed to leave unharmed? Why didn't they mug her? What was with that bearded old man and the woman pulling him away— maintaining the dignity of homeless people declaring no begging should be done in their own territory?

A distant noise brought her back to reality. It was starting to get cold. North India was characterized by warm, clear days during this season. It was autumn, but nights were cold. What could she do now? What if she needed to spend the night outside? Once again, the temptation to leave the backpack behind rose. It seemed that without the backpack she would be able to move around quicker and perhaps find a way out of the situation more easily. *But what if I can't?* Without the backpack, she would be left with no warm clothes and no sleeping bag. And where would she sleep? I can't sleep on this filthy sidewalk.

What the hell have I done to myself? Am I crazy? What is going on with me? What, do I want to die? I might as well just end it all right now; throw myself from some high place, finish the day...

An image of her mother rose and tears began filling her eyes uncontrollably as she sank into self-pity. Images of people close to her appeared, as if her mind were trying to hold onto something warm and caring in the lousy situation she had brought on herself.

The cold increased and it began to darken. Her tired, aching body would not handle it. Her fears began to intensify. In the dark the village thugs will appear, will mug, abuse, and murder her...

She could imagine the headlines in both the U.S. and Israeli newspapers: "Israeli traveler murdered in India October 15, circumstances unknown."

Will they say Israeli or American? Which am I? She wondered. She agonized on that question until the image of her mother mourning her death came to her mind. She tried to picture her own funeral. *Who will come?* She wondered. *Well, there is the immediate family and the distant one I usually only see on special occasions.*

There are also those relatives in England, but no - they wouldn't bother to come, she determined flatly. *What about my friends in New York? Which of them would come? Who, if any, had remained after all that happened?*

I don't want to think about New York. The friend she was traveled with and had already left would be surprised to hear that this is how the trip they had started together ended. *So what if I missed him? It is really the end of the world? Is it?* She was always perceived by her friends as someone rational, pragmatic—a woman with both feet on the ground. So how come she had suddenly become so irrational? *No one who I know would have done something stupid like that ... Will they find out the circumstances that led to my death? Should they find out?* She grinned for a moment at her tinge of self-consciousness. It was shortly followed by distress and anxiety at the thought of a possible change in her image in the eyes of others.

Why the hell should it matter? But it does! To me!

A loud noise could be heard down the street. It sounded like rolling tins followed by an explosion. She remembered it was the "Diwali," a national holiday in India.

Silence.

She wondered what was going on and again, the sound of tins arose. This time the noise intensified, and with it came the voices of shouting children. From afar, their figures could be seen. The children ran down the slope of the street while rolling big metal tins, hitting them on their covers and creating a huge din. The group quickly passed her by. Behind the big children lagged the youngest children of the group. The kids passed, nodded and shouted in English with a local accent.

"Hello, what is your name? How are you?" they repeated these questions several times, not expecting any answer, while passing her. Local children did this a lot with tourists, eager to show they could speak English.

A little girl who was lagging behind and was trying to keep up stopped in front of her, looking at her with curious eyes. She smiled, her grin revealing a line of bright, shiny teeth. Although it seemed she was shy, she could not conquer her curiosity. A shout was heard coming from up the street as a waving woman suddenly appeared. The girl looked back. It seemed that the call was directed at her, but she refused to reply. The woman quickened her steps down the street, approaching. When she arrived, she scolded the little girl in the local language —Nepali, while carefully exploring the sited foreigner from the corner of her eye. She was about to leave with the little girl, but had changed her mind when she thought she saw distress in the foreign woman's eyes. The woman turned back to her with the greeting.

"Namaste."

The foreigner weakly replied "Namaste."

The woman seemed somewhat perplexed and observed the stranger more closely. The little girl, who now more confident with her mother by her side, asked, "Where you come from?"

She debated how to reply.

"Israel." she said, weakly. It did not seem that the answer left an impression on either of child and mother, and it was not surprising. Unlike the rest of the continent, not many tourists visited this region of North East India, and even fewer Israelis.

The girl continued, "What is your name?"

"Yael," she replied.

"What does that mean?"

As previously done when asked about the meaning of her name, she started to bleat like a sheep. The woman and her daughter looked at her in astonishment, then back at each other. Yael dropped to her knees, mimicking walking on all fours, while repeating the sound "Baa." The shock expression on the faces of the woman and her daughter changed to laughter. Maybe they didn't understand what she wanted to say, but they understood that she was trying to communicate what is the meaning of her name. And the ice was broken.

In broken English, the woman asked, "You go hotel?"

"No, not hotel," Yael replied, she was embraced to say that she had no money because she feared that the woman would think she was asking for handouts.

"No hotel?" the woman insisted.

"No, not possible" Yael replied. The girl pulled at her hand, curious about the bracelet on her arm. For a brief moment the idea of paying for food and shelter with the bracelet popped into in Yael's mind, but no—she couldn't. It was too precious to her.

The woman waved with her hand as if gesturing for her to follow.

Yael was surprised. Again, the woman called out and indicated for her to follow. Then she placed the palm of her hand on her chest and said "Yael." The meaning was immediately understood. Your name is close to my heart. Yael was flooded with joy.

Rescue

Yael got up and followed the local woman and her daughter. They passed by modest but pleasant looking homes until they reached a small house that about the size of a room. A yellow gate was in the doorway. For a moment she hesitated, and disturbing thoughts came into her mind. How could she know that the woman was not going to harm her? Could it be that the woman had realized that she didn't have anywhere to go and invited her home, just like that? The woman stood in the doorway, signaling her impatiently to enter. Yael dispelled the fear and followed her into the little house.

When she entered, she was amazed—the house looked even smaller from the inside. She stood in a small room. In the center of the room rested a bed on which an old man was seated. He appeared to be blind and held a stick in his hand. He immediately felt the presence of the stranger and muttered something in Nepalese or Hindi. The woman responded and he silenced, as if digesting what had been said. *She probably told him she collected some deserted stranger from the street*, thought Yael. Beside the bed stood a table and next to it, a chair. A book was on the chair and an open notebook with a pen rested on the table. Some vegetables—potatoes, tomatoes and onions—some dishes, and neatly folded clothes were also laid out on the table. It was an organized disorder.

This child is studying on a table that's also a wardrobe, kitchen cabinet and a storage place for food, thought Yael. *Where does everyone sleep?* She wondered. The bed on which the old man sat was a little bigger than a single person. In the West, it would accommodate one person. Images of her apartment, friend's apartment, and other peoples' apartments she saw, the grandeur of her job and the place where she came from surfaced in her mind. These were two worlds that had nothing in common.

The woman interrupted the flow of her thoughts by pointing to the chair while clearing away the worn, shabby book. Carefully, without adding to its tears, she placed it on the notebook. Yael removed her

21

backpack. Now, more than ever, her backpack seemed huge compared to the tiny room. She felt embarrassed. The old man, as if sensing her confusion, pointed the end of his stick at her stomach like a weapon. Yael looked into his eyes—blind, bluish gray, expressionless eyes. For some reason, she could tell he saw her despite his blindness. The woman, upon seeing the stick pointed at the visitor, smiled in embarrassment as if apologizing for his action, and gently diverted his stick away. She smiled again, a soothing smile, reassuring that everything was okay and that there was nothing to be worried about. Yael sat down uncomfortably without removing her sight from the old man.

"Food?" the woman briefly asked. Yael nodded, trying to smile in gratitude. The woman turned to the girl, said a few words, and the girl quickly left for outside. Yael continued to explore the house with her eyes. Across the room rested a small chest beside a door that perhaps led to a bathroom. Or was it the kitchen? Or maybe both?

The house was clean, considering what Yael had seen in India. The old man asked the woman a few questions and she replied in a low voice.

I wonder if they're talking about me, she thought.

Yael directed herself towards the woman. "What is your name?"

"Sabitri," the woman replied with a big smile, and disappeared behind the door next to the chest. The sound of a fire being lit was heard, followed by water filling some kind of a container. After a few minutes, during which the old man continued staring at Yael with his blind eyes, Sabitri came back to the room carrying a bucket and placed it to the feet of the old man. She then turned to the closet and pulled out a bottle filled with brown liquid, went back to the old man, took off his socks and dipped his feet in the water.

Yael noticed that one foot was very swollen, probably suffering from some kind of illness. Sabitri opened the lid of the bottle and poured a little bit of the oily liquid into her hands and rubbed them together. She then pulled a small stool from under the bed, sat down, pulled the swollen foot of the old man onto her knee and started massaging it expertly and gently. The old man groaned in pain.

After a few minutes, the little girl returned with a pot and a plate in her hands. Some kind of a metal cup was the plate. Sabitri gave an order to the girl, and the girl, smiling, placed the pot on the table in the narrow gap between the notebook and the clothes. She then took the notebook and the book and placed them on top of a plastic bag on the floor, assuring they would not get dirty.

A pleasant steaming smell rose up the pot — rice with lentils. Beside the hot dish, Yael received a cool yogurt. She held herself back from digging right into the food and ate in moderation, sure that this kind of food would be good for her upset stomach after yesterday night's hardships. She drank some water and soon felt that all she needed was to sleep. To sleep and wake up and know that all that had happened was only a dream. Her eyes began to close following the sense of fullness that had spread in her stomach. Through veiled eyes, she saw Sabitri rise. Panic gripped her for a moment. *Maybe she will send me back out into the cold night? After all, where could I sleep here when there is no room?*

But Sabitri said something to the little girl and the latter rushed to the chest, pulled out a rolled-up blanket, spread a large cloth on the floor and then spread the blanket over the cloth. Sabitri looked at Yael, pointed to the blanket, and said something to the girl again. The girl bent over and pulled out a thin blanket under the bed. Yael shook her head and pulled out her sleeping bag from the backpack, pointing at it as if saying she would need no blanket to cover herself. Now she was happy that she didn't leave the bag behind. Fatigue and a sense of relief knowing she was not going to be thrown out on the street overcame her. When she slipped into the sleeping bag, she sank into sleep as the voices of her hosts could be heard accompanying her in the background.

Images from the past few hours rose in her mind—the flying money, the colony of the homeless people, the beggars —all mingling with images from her previous life. Now, thanks to her new situation of being penniless and subject to the mercy of her host, the horrible past began to fade.

When did this whole mess even start?

Ready Stance

Starting position. A shout was heard.

"Hajime!"

The attack followed with no delay. Despite the attempted dodge, a fist met flesh just between the eyes. The joint between the index and middle finger hit precisely above the left eyebrow.

It hurts enough, but the shock, the shock that you are being hurt, takes you out of balance more than the physical pain — the surprise, the inability to accept that you are not able to pull an evasive maneuver, yes! And the insult... the humiliating insult..

"Yame!" The leading senior yelled to stop and firmly instructed her to leave the battle compound, using his hand to signal. She returned to the bench, straightening her white Karate uniform.

How did this happen to me?

Zoe – her rival – was shaking her legs and bouncing a bit, waiting for her next opponent.

She's not human. None of her facial features even moved. Maybe that's why she's undefeated?

The leading senior instructed one of the trainees to enter the compound. This trainee wore a white belt.

He's got no chance against her, she thought.

"Hajime!"

Zoe switched the position of her legs with a quick jump, but she didn't attack. The first few seconds were for reviewing both the mental and physical state of the opponent in order to study him or her. Zoe seemed observing him carefully —what was he projecting? How determined was he to win? How much danger does he have in his eyes? What does his body language say? Is he slow or quick to move? Is he flexible, athletic, heavy, fast? Zoe stopped jumping and switched legs, waiting for her opponent to make his first move, and then she began tempting him to attack. Unconsciously, he was driven to attack; his right leg rose up in the air for a kick — a beautiful, powerful kick, precise by the book. Zoe moved away just the right distance to allow his toes to graze her uniform, and only the rustle of cloth friction could be heard.

Surprisingly, his left leg rose without returning his extended leg to the floor. This time he attacked with the knee. It seemed that Zoe was taken by surprise, but she instantly diverted his knee with her left hand. She sent her right hand to his chin, cupping it from below while lifting it up. His head was jerked back. He was helpless and instinctively stepped backwards. Zoe continued forcing him to retreat. He took another two steps backwards. He was going to fall.

"Yame!" the leading senior yelled for them to stop.

Zoe released her hold. The leading senior signaled the trainee with his hand to return to his seat. He then gestured for the trainees to rise up from their seats and perform a *Kata*. This series of movements ended the class.

"Want a drink?" Daniel smiled at her as she walked toward the bench as she takes off the upper part of her uniform. He handed her a bottle of water.

"Thanks" she said with a warm smile.

Daniel had been practicing with her for some time now and seemed to like her a lot. She took a sip of water from the bottle, thinking that it was a bit like kissing whoever previously drank from the lid.

"Don't be upset about the spar with Zoe," he said gently.

"Why do you think I'm upset?" she handed over the bottle to him, removed the rubber band tightened around her hair, and shook it loose.

"I saw it in your face right after her fist..." his voice weakened as he tried not to go into too many details.

"She's already a *Yodan* with her high black belt rank, you know," He attempted to console her.

"Yes, I know."

Peter approached.

"How are you, Blondie?" he'd always called her that. Peter was a training mate and a close friend of Daniel. All three had been trained for more or less the same amount of time and had the same rank and because of it, a strong sense of camaraderie.

26

"You can wring out my *Gee*, there's so much sweat," Peter proudly declared, taking off the upper part of the Karate uniform and revealing his naked upper body.

Not bad, she thought to herself.

"Well, did you start preparing for the Special Training coming up in three weeks?"

He stood in front of her, hands on his hips. *Is he deliberately standing like this? Shirtless?* She forced herself to look above his neck, but her eyes traveled down.

"What's going to be there, exactly?" she asked, concerned. She'd only heard intimidating things about the upcoming "Special Training." Daniel also took off the top of the training suit and immediately turned his back on her. *The complete opposite of his friend— gentle and modest*, she thought.

"Come on, Daniel, tell her," Peter giggled as he searched for his shirt in his bag.

It was going to be the first "Special Training" for the three of them, in which all three will be tested for their black belts. Daniel turned back to her with his shirt on, and explained that the program would be spread over four days and that it resembles a military training. There would be running every morning and then they will have two to three hard practices each day, with each practice taking around two hours. The practice everyone feared the most was the *Kiabadachi*, or horse stance. In this practice, everyone must stand completely still with bent knees, and no movement is allowed for a full hour and a half.

"Sounds like real fun," she said, trying to light things up.

"Yes, Blondie, laugh indeed," Peter replied, and then added "the veterans tell stories of fainting. The *Kiabadachi* is considered to be mentally the hardest."

"Well," she sighed as she tried to internalize what she was hearing, "I got to go."

"That's it! She's quitting Karate after what she just heard," Peter joked.

"Where are you rushing?" asked Daniel. Usually, the three of them left the class together since they all lived somewhat close to each other.

"I've got to run and bring food to the cat. Sorry, today I won't go back with you." She lifted her training bag to her shoulder.

"Shouldn't we set time to run together?" asked Peter.

"We'll talk later on the phone," she replied.

"Okay, bye now. Take care" Daniel smiled at her.

She walked toward the exit. One the way out, one of the trainees stopped her and said, "So are you 'Down' but not 'Out'"?

Puzzled, she stared back at him. He chuckled, finding some pleasure in the fact that she didn't understand. Maybe she'd return to Daniel and Peter and ask them what he meant... But they looked deeply immersed in a conversation with two other guys from the group.

It's not a good time, she thought, *I'll do it some other time,* and she kept going. This was not the first time she'd missed meanings associated with the local culture. On the way out she saw Zoe talking to Malcolm, the leading senior, from the corner of her eye. It was too far to hear what they were talking about. Zoe shook her head from side to side in a gesture of total refusal. Malcolm looked upset.

What are they talking about? Now she was close enough to hear what Zoe was saying.

"There is no way I'll do that."

"But you have to, before you leave," Malcolm replied.

That's all she could hear as she passed. The exit of the gym was already in front of her. She stepped out of the training hall and walked up the stairs to the curved corridors of Columbia University, reflecting on what she had just overheard.

Zoe is leaving? Did I hear right? Leaving what? Karate? The city? Can't be! She is one of the best practitioners and teachers.

She left the training hall at 116 Street, on the upper west side. It was late evening, almost ten o'clock.

Class was longer today, she thought to herself. A decline in commotion on the streets could already be sensed. A few individuals looked at her as they rushed passed on their way.

We have nothing at home, she thought and debated whether or not she should stop at the deli in front of her, but she decided to do it near home instead of having to carry the groceries on the subway.

Then she debated whether she should take the subway or just walk. She'd need to walk 11 blocks to get to her home on 105th Street from the gym. The subway station was on 103rd Street. *Always the same dilemma...* but tiredness and laziness after an exhausting two hours of practice and the chilly weather tipped the scale in favor of the subway.

Climbing the stairs to the station on 103rd just before entering the subway station, she heard some shouts. A man wearing rags and waving a banana in his hand was standing in front of the subway station. The banana's color seemed to match the color of his long hair: once golden blond, but now a dirty, faded gray. It took her a while to catch what he was shouting and why some of the passersby had concerned and amused expressions on their faces.

"This is a robbery! Give me your money or I'll shoot!" he shouted as he turned in circles and aimed the banana at passersby like a loaded gun. "I warn you, I'll shoot!"

This is so typical of this crazy New York city, she thought as she boarded the subway.

In the fifties and sixties, the government's policy was to release a large percentage of mental patients from hospitals and test their ability to become integral parts of society. By the eighties, this policy had already failed. Those who were categorized as mentally ill due to drugs, Vietnam veterans who never regained their sanity and the people with no family and friends whose minds had been devoured by loneliness were all marginalized on the edge of society, a searing reminder of an alienated capitalistic society.

The subway stopped at 103rd. She got off and walked up to 105th Street. She could already see her building. It was not pleasant to walk around this area so late at night, particularly in her neighborhood and street. Amsterdam Street was often the hangout for homeless, beggars, and junkies. There was a reason this street was referred to as "the injection street" by locals.

Suddenly, a noise came from the end of the street. The sound of running footsteps could be heard. A man was running towards her, looking back. She tensed. All her instincts were concentrated him. If he attacked, she would have to muster all what she had learned in the two years she had trained. Would she find out that, in reality, her ability to fight would be revealed as a fiction? The man quickly passed her, and three heavily-built men emerged from around the corner in pursuit. All three passed her and quickly disappeared, leaving a trail of their pounding footsteps and evaporated, heavy breathing behind.

A disturbed city... she thought and hurried home. Finally, she was in her building. She buzzed the intercom.

A voice responded, "Who is this?"

"Me, open up!"

He's home.

The buzzer sounded and she pushed to open the door, quickly slamming it behind her. An immediate sense of relief followed. Another buzzer and she pushed the second door. Ahead were three stories of stairs leading to the two-bedroom apartment they shared. He came to New York about a year before she did. Before he left, they were not very close. Only after he left did she realize he was more emotionally involved with her than she thought. He tried convincing her to come with repeated calls, attempts to persuade her to come, and seductive stories about the place. She always knew she would come back one day to the States, but only after she graduated from the university in Israel. Only when she finished her studies in the department of Economics and Business Administration did she feel it was time to check out life in the big city. That was two and a half years ago. When she finally came, she crashed at his apartment. That was a year ago.

"Oh! The door," he hadn't opened it for her, as usual. She always felt that he was living his life too cautiously. "Don't open the door! Are you crazy?" he had yelled at her one evening when she heard that one of the neighbors was shouting in the corridor and she was curious to know what had happened. Maybe someone was injured... "This is not Israel," he said firmly, "it's dangerous."

When she wanted to talk about it, he refused.

"That's all I'm saying on the matter," he ended the discussion.

She knocked on the door, and it opened. There was Eyal, standing at the door, with a small smile on his face and Spike— the cat, in his arms.

"Hey, how's it going?"

"Alright. How about you?" she entered and took off her coat.

"Well, so, so. Another long day!" he sighed.

He always grumbles. Everything is always so terribly difficult for him. She focused on his dimple, the same dimple that had won her heart when they first met, and the dimple that could redeem his grumbling.

"Did you bring the food for Spike?" he lowered the cat to the floor and Spike howled briefly as if confirming he knew they were talking about him.

"Oh, I forgot," she winced. "There was a lunatic next to the subway. I'll tell you later, after I take a bath…"

She turned to go to the bathroom, but was able to catch his look of dissatisfaction from the corner of her eye. As she started walking down the hall, she heard him grumble "What will feed him? He doesn't like the dry food..."

She entered the bathroom before she could hear out the rest. She turned on the bath faucet, undressed and stood in front of the mirror to check how many bruises she had gotten this time in training. A tired person stared back at her with her round face still slightly red from the practice. Her fair hair was still wet from sweating. Here and there dark spots emerged on her arms, bruises from hits. She rubbed her eyes and sat down on the toilet seat, which he had finally gotten used to putting down.

The bathtub was full of warm water. She dipped her hand in to check. Too hot. She added a stream of cold water. The bathroom started to fill with steam. *Warm water is good for the muscles, but it*

31

won't be good for the bruises. One foot followed the other and she let her body slowly sink into the water. She rested her arms on the edge of the tub to avoid touching of the water on her bruises. A light drizzle of rain had started and the raindrops gently knocked on the window.

It still feels like winter sometimes and it's almost May, she thought. She could never quite get used to the weather in New York.

The water in the bath was warm and relaxing. She leaned her head back. A pleasant feeling enveloped her. She closed her eyes...

The subway man with the banana was walking on a tightrope in a circus show. He was using a stick made out of a huge banana for balance. He laughed, stumbled and fell into a huge circus net. He leapt up few times, landed on the net, up again, and landed. The circus announcer's voice boomed, "Up, Down, Up, Down!" Suddenly the man jumped across the net to the stage floor. "He's out, he's out! Beware!" I didn't understand. Zoe, Daniel, Peter and a few others from training are sitting in the audience with me. The banana in his hands turned into jagged bayonet handlebars and he started threatening the crowd. Zoe emerged behind him with a stick. I thought she could be able to stop him - but no! She became his ally and I wondered what business she has with this homeless lunatic? I was looking for my friends, but I couldn't find them—all the people in the audience were gone and I was the only one left. When did they leave and why did they leave me alone?

There was a knock on the door.

She awoke with panic.

"Yael, what's going on? Are you okay?" Eyal asked, "You've been in there for a while now." She didn't know how long it had been since she fell asleep.

"Yes, I'm fine," she hastened to reassure him, her mind still walking the thin line between reality and dream.

As they sat eating, she joked about the supposedly armed robber, but Eyal, with a hard, scolding voice, warned her that she had to be very careful in New York and, soon enough, it turned into a whole lecture on crime and violence.

"While the current mayor managed to skew the statistics for the better, still ..."

But she was no longer listening. She was reflecting on the training. Eyal rose from his seat and began clearing the table as he continued his lecture. When he noticed she wasn't listening to him, he put his hand on her shoulder and leaned toward her. Spike, sensing the impending intimacy, hurried to come too, rubbing against her feet. She picked him up and put him on her lap.

Eyal moved closer to her. She started to lightly stroke the sensitive skin of his neck. He groaned with pleasure. Then she moved to behind his ears. *It might help him stop talking....* Moans of pleasure. He was still talking between moans. She moved her hand to his genitals. Immediately he stopped talking and grabbed her hand.

"What are you doing?" he laughed.

Their sex was amazing. True, it was probably not as amazing as it was at the beginning, when they had just met. But considering that they had been living together for about a year, the bedroom kingdom had remained a kingdom. It was probably the only area that remained with a crown.

He pulled her after him into the bedroom. *And why not right here?* The thought crossed her mind, but soon the thinking part of her brain stopped working. Eyal held her tightly. With him she always felt like she was on the edge of something, and if he had ever dared to cross it, it had been just with words. She always knew he had a lust to tie her down. Only once had she caught his eyes wandering the room, trying to find something to exercise his fantasy of tying her down. His hands sought the tail of her bandana at the edge of the bed. As soon as she realized what was happening and decided to let her curiosity overcome her reluctance and let him try, he withdrew.

Foreigner in New York

Morning had broken. She awoke heavily. Light drizzle on the window. *Have to get up for work.* Spike sensed the subtle morning movement in the bedroom and jumped up on the bed.

She grumbled. Eyal, knowing she didn't like Spike on the bed, sacrificed his slow awakening to get up and remove Spike from the bed.

"Down! Spike! Down!" he said firmly but the latter —as befitting a cat who took a lot of pride in his feline identity - didn't show any sign of obedience. He was looking for a suitable place for his paws in order to walk to their heads. He snuck through the narrow gap between them without notice. They were dozily fluttering between wakefulness and sleep.

Spike sensed his moment, jumped, and landed on Yael's shoulder.

"Spike! Get the hell out of here!" she waved her hand in the air to shake him and sent a distress call to Eyal. Spike, panicking from her shout, displayed an impressive acrobatic flip in the air and landed right in the depths of the dirty laundry basket at the other side of the room.

Silence. Both rose at once to see what had happened. No movement. Eyal got up first and went to the basket. He looked down into the basket with indiscernible gaze.

"Lalush!" he called with the nickname he reserved for her, "Come! Quickly!"

She went over to him. Looking anxiously at the bottom of the basket to see if anything was damaged, she suddenly burst out laughing. Eyal tried to pull Spike out while the cat, terrified, was still trying to figure out how he had gotten there in the first place. He looked up at them. A dirty pair of underwear lay across his tiny head, covering his ears symmetrically. Eyal joined in her laughter. Spike expressed his displeasure for this situation and howled. The poor expression on his face, accompanied by his snarling howl, only increased their laughter. Spike shook his head. Yael bent over, pulled him out from the bottom of the basket, and removed the underwear from his head. After a few quick strokes, Spike relaxed.

The race of the work day began. Each of them was well-practiced in preparing for departure. They usually would leave at the same time, take the subway in the rush hour, catch the express line and travel together to 42nd Street where they separated. Eyal would walk up to 42 Street and then continue for two more blocks, finally reaching Final Cut, a video clips production company. Yael would transfer and travel downtown to Manhattan's financial district. There she would walk to World Financial Solutions, one of the most highly respected and prestigious investment consulting firms on the east coast.

The subway was extremely crowded. Their attempt to stand close to each other failed when the crowd rushed into the subway car and separated them. Eyal was only a few feet away from her and a crowd of people stood between them. Everyone was packed in like sardines. *Farting isn't even an option here*, she thought, trying to make light of the situation. The doors closed and the subway started moving. All hands extended to grab the subway handlebars.

Transportation by the subway was very efficient. Every morning, millions jumped in and out the cars. It was the core of the city's commotion, filled with an infinite number of people — all running, rushing, pressed to be on time, trampling and fighting against the subway doors threatening to close on them. From the outside, they looked like hundreds of rats running through stale tunnels.

My shoelaces are untied, damn it! There's no chance I'd reach them now. Yael looks around. *Gosh, it's so crowded. This infinite quantity of faces of people seen every day stared back at you with a lack of singularity and unrecognizable uniformity. People are sharing a car together for a minute or two— ten minutes at the most. They are sitting in front of each other, and then moved to another corner, then to another car, and then they got off— all in a matter of minutes.*

Not far from her, a seat became vacant. She rushed to occupy it. After all, an empty seat on the subway was like a small, fresh breath in a suffocating sea.

35

The station. People piled out to the platform like a giant wave. Yael quickly managed to tie her shoe laces before a new wave of people flooded into the cars.

A beggar maneuvered his way through the crowd while reciting verses from the New Testament. He sounded as if he was hallucinating and brought a strong wave of unpleasant odor with him. Most of the passengers – mix of White, Blacks and Hispanics —were reading newspapers or magazines. Some read books.

Are they all so intellectual here or is it just a way of escaping the suffocating crowd during the ride? She wondered.

A beggar approached the bench where she sat, asking for spare change. Other passengers were hiding behind their books or newspapers. Yael also pulled out a newspaper from her bag. The beggar continued with his attempts to win the hearts of the passengers. Only one black woman was willing to pull a coin out of her purse and hand it over to him. He bowed his head slightly, "God bless you." Encouraged, he made his way through the people, now praising God even more.

42nd Street. Yael separated from Eyal and made her way through the subway tunnels. She had to switch stations. She walked down to the platform. The subway had just arrived and she got in. It was so crowded and in each station, it seemed that as soon as the car emptied, it filled right back. While driving, some passengers moved to the front cars while others shifted to the rear cars.

The current subway driver — as opposed to the previous one — was in a light-hearted mood and when they reach the station he announces, "Next stop— 34th Street," and after pausing for a second continued, "Dear passengers: please do not pass by your driver's car but get off on the platform. If you have passed the car driver, it means you went off the rails. Thank you! Stay clear of the closing doors and do not forget to take your belongings…this is New York City, so don't count on getting anything back." His words, though, managed to put a smile only on some passengers' faces.

A few more stops and it was her station. She left the subway and walked up the street. Wall Street. A surge of people flooded the sidewalks and someone accidentally bumped into her, apologetic. *This city should have traffic lights for pedestrians.* As always, she walked into the neighborhood Deli and got a coffee and a chocolate croissant. Although she'd asked for the same thing every day for the past year, the Chinese Deli's owner still always asked what she wanted, wrapped the croissant, took the five-dollar bill and, without even looking, returned the change: one dollar and forty-nine cents. No, she wasn't looking for a friendship with the deli owner, but the lack of a personal touch was extreme even for her.

The doorman in the reception of the grand, ostentatious building owned by Leona Helmsley nodded at her. *Is this a "Nice to see you" or a "Move on" gesture?* Neatly dressed men and women were entering the elevator with her. Someone had pressed the button for the 31st floor. The elevator was extremely fast, and before she knew it, the doors opened.

The firm's pompous name hung above the receptionist desk: World Financial Solutions.

"Good morning." The receptionist smiled at her with her usual fake "industrial" smile, as Yael liked to think of it, and immediately went back to her affairs.

Yael walked into her office. Her busy workday would be full of meetings with so called "heavy" financial clients, mostly the New York City elite and, among them, high-profile companies and individuals coming from outside the city. A lot of math, formulas, and tables full of figures would accompany these meetings. She ran simulations that were supposed to illustrate the high profits these customers would make. A lot of money rolled between banks and companies every day. Her work in front of the computer was not particularly fascinating, but the encounters with the high-profile elite could be interesting. Rarely would there be a talk in which no personal aspects of the client would surface, but usually more was hidden than visible. In the short time she had been working there, she managed to

37

gain the trust of her clients and served as their confident holder. During her year there, she had already learned that a client's financial decision was almost always influenced by personal matters. Although her salary was certainly among the highest, she still hadn't gotten used to the idea that she made good money and she still lived modestly. She also tended to dismiss a flashy lifestyle when it came to money and wealth. When she looked at those who had lost their money, she reminded herself that it was easier to dismiss lifestyle that could be within one's reach.

Kristen, her boss, entered the office. Kristen was a sharp and witty woman, excellent manager, and one of the partners in the firm. She was away for business meetings quite often, sometimes days. Yael was surprised to see her —she was not supposed to be in the office today. Yael always felt some fear of her and stood up immediately when she saw her enter. Kristen approached her desk. A manila folder was in her hand. She remained standing.

Any other manager would either set an appointment or ask me to come to her office, but not Kristen, Yael thought. Despite the fact Kristen was well-practiced in formal manners; one of her strongest qualities was breaking the rules when necessary. Because of this duality, she succeeded to build a successful company with Jane, her-long time friend from years back at Yale university and to recruit a third partner, Max – all in a very short period. Before recruited, Max was the head of the World Bank of the International Finance Corporation in Washington. The three of them established what became to be one of the most prestigious and successful consulting firms in New York.

Kristen, as usual, went right to the point.

"Chris-Daoud Khan," she said, tossing the folder onto Yael's desk and continuing, "We got to him through Max. He's a very important new potential client and I'd like to assign you to his profile." It was clear by her tone of voice that this was extremely significant. She continued, "He is an oil tycoon from Saudi Arabia. Although Muslim, his mother is Jewish. He is very close to the political leadership in

38

Washington as well as to the government in Saudi Arabia. This is all the information we could get on him, so we'll have to dig more since..." Kristen pointed her finger to the folder "...what we have is not enough." Yael listened carefully.

"Cancel all your least important meetings this morning, study his file, and, if needed, use some outside sources." She pauses for a second, "Questions?"

Yael shook her head, "No, no questions, I'll read the portfolio," she said in a decisive tone and opened the folder.

"Excellent, we will be meeting him sooner than later, I hope, and I want you to be on top of it."

Kristen was about to turn to leave. She paused for a moment and then turned back to Yael, "I understand next week it will be exactly one year since you've joined the company. I heard the guys are taking you to celebrate after work."

"Yes," said Yael, and closed the folder, as if giving great importance to the subject at hand, "We'll go to the bar down the street."

"Excellent." Said Kristen "By the way—" she continued "—the bar is just the foreplay – yes?" she winked.

"Foreplay?" Yael questioned, insecure and embarrassed. Kristen, realizing that Yael didn't understand. She was too pressed for time to explain vocabulary to foreigners so she just muttered "never mind" and left the office.

Best Friends

Yael sat back down. *Again, I appear stupid,* she thought, frustrated. *I'll call Jennifer. She'll explain what Kristen meant.*

Jennifer was a photographer and a childhood friend of Yael's but they had lost contact for years. When Yael arrived to New York, during her second week, she had gone to an opening of a gallery which had featured, among others, Jennifer's works. The topic was "Disabled in the City". Jennifer's tremendous talent was to merge the human aspect with the environment in which it had been photographed. One photograph in particular had caught Yael's eye: a blind girl standing in a 360-degree colorful graffiti painting. In the photograph, Jennifer's sharp eyes managed to capture the reflection of the graffiti painting in the gray-blue eyes of the girl.

Yael had been desperate to know how the artist did it. She looked for the photographer and, when she found her, they realized they knew each other —they use to be childhood friends when Yael lived in New York as a child. The thrill was overwhelming. They immediately re-connected and Jennifer had become Yael's best friend since then. Jennifer was also the one who got Yael the position in her current company. Previously, Yael had worked in various random and meaningless jobs. The job at the firm was a significant breakthrough and enabled her to get closer to the local culture. Jennifer was also the one who was responsible for helping her fit into the social life. There was no doubt that she would have accomplished very little without Jennifer.

A siren went off. She looked through her office window at the view of the spread city.

Wow, it's now a year I've been with the company. How time flies, and how much things change in so little time... she reflected. *A great job in a prestigious company...* She looked out the window again. *And yes...I still feel so useless in a way... but I shouldn't think like that... I should be grateful for what I have, and it's all thanks to Jennifer...*

A phone call interrupted her thoughts. It was Jennifer. It was a mystical thing that sometimes happened between them. Almost every time Yael was thinking about Jennifer, Jennifer called.

"Hey sis, how are you?"

"Good, good." Yael replied.

"Did you think of me again just before I called?" Jennifer checked on the recurrence of the phenomena.

"Yes! It's unbelievable. So weird!"

"What were you thinking about me?"

"I'll be celebrating a year here soon, and I recalled who was responsible for it."

"Yes, your 'Guardian Angel'" said Jennifer with laughter.

"You remember that you were the one who fixed me up with the job here?"

"Nonsense!"

"No nonsense!" Yael protested.

"Well, okay... Maybe I had my reasons..." laughed Jennifer.

"Yeah, right."

"Is it fulfilling?" Jennifer asked, "You've kind of said in the past you still feel useless and you do want to be involved in something greater than this..."

"It is okay for now...it does allow me to get some power, integrate in the culture, and learn more..." Yael smiled to herself. *It's funny how Jennifer just brought up what had been on my mind.*

The fact that Jennifer had gotten her that dream job had prevented Yael from bringing up the fact that she wasn't quite fulfilled too often.

"Yes," said Jennifer, adding," That was the intention. It'll be a springboard for you!"

"But for what?" asked Yael with a chuckle.

"Oh! Only time will tell..." Jennifer replied in a sweet, secretive voice.

"Ok! We are being skeptical now!" said Yael, smiling. She continued, "Listen, I need your cultural guidance... an English clarification."

"Shoot!"

"What does 'Foreplay' means in this context?" Yael told Jennifer what had been said.

"Oh, she wanted to know if you have planned a big party on that night so the bar would just be for a drink before the real party," clarified Jennifer.

"Shit, I came out looking dumb again," Yael said, frustrated.

"Sorry," said Jennifer, and added, "Listen; it takes a while to be a part of what is happening here, to actually belong."

"And maybe it will never happen and I'll never be one of the gang," replied Yael with a hopeless tone, and asked, "Any chance you can join for the drink next week?"

"No, sorry, I can't," said Jennifer sadly.

"Going away again?" Jennifer was frequently traveling out of the city for her work. These trips were sometimes long.

"This time it's short, nearby ..." said Jennifer, "I have a photography project in Harlem, something for the community. You know, I was asked to do it as a favor. I'm not even being compensated for it."

"As always - Jennifer to the rescue," Yael smiled.

"Well, you know... I couldn't say no..."

"What exactly are you going to shoot?"

"Some kind of an event at a school in one of the poorest areas in Harlem. As usual, I'm planning to get out there a little early and shoot any interesting portraits I see."

"Say, it is not dangerous, is it? How do you get there?"

"I'll take a cab, don't worry. I know my way around. I was born a tough New Yorker bitch."

"Unlike me. This we know."

"Not like you? You're tougher than me," said Jennifer. Yael couldn't quite figure out if she was joking or serious. "You just don't know that yet," a serious note sounded in her words.

"Yeah, right!" Yael replied in self mockery.

"So how's it going with the Karate?" Jennifer changed the subject.

"And who brought me there as well? It was also you!"

"And how is Daniel, actually? You know I haven't spoken to him for ages..."

"He's fine," said Yael warmly.

"Is he still tutoring at the university?"

"Indeed he is."

"One day he'll become a teaching professor there, I'm sure," said Jennifer with determination.

"He does sure love it there," Yael agreed.

"Come on, leave this anal-retentive of yours and go for Daniel — a golden, no-nonsense boy. And I'm not saying this just because he's my nephew."

Yael was speechless. Sometimes, Jennifer's direct approach was too much for her.

"Well? I hear no comment!" Jennifer teased and continued, "That means I hit the target, right? You know that with me it is better to be up front."

"Yael, your meeting is here!" the secretary's rescuing voice was heard over the intercom.

"Jennifer darling, I must go to a meeting with a potential investor."

"Saved by the bell."

Yael laughed and said, "Maybe this meeting is foreplay?"

Jennifer laughed. "Well, I don't think that quite fits here..."

"I know, I know. Just playing around with words," Yael responded quickly, a little embarrassed "But we'll meet this weekend as planned?"

"Yup, sure will," confirmed Jennifer.

"See you then!"

"Later!"

She hung up. She wondered how different her life would have looked without Jennifer.

Too bad she left Karate, Yael thought. *Daniel said she was very good, the highest rank, and it would have been so much fun together...*

But Jennifer had chosen to go in another direction. She often announced that photography was her life. She was considered a valued and highly talented photographer. She kept relationships with most people and clients from her previous jobs, although Yael couldn't figure out from her vague answers what she was actually doing before she became a photographer. In any case, with Jennifer's assertive personality, Yael was convinced Jennifer was able to achieve anything she desired.

After returning from the meeting in the conference room, Chris-Daoud Khan's portfolio was staring at her. She sat down and opened the folder. There wasn't much information on him, as Kristen had said. There was a list of his financial assets and financial institutions he was related to, and a picture. In the picture was a good-looking man in his fifties: Daoud Khan, or in his Western name, Chris Khan. He was dressed in a completely Western style, but the mustache that decorated his face disclosed his cultural affiliation. The fact that he was a Muslim and his mother was Jewish fascinated her. She could feel the sense of non-belonging in his big smile under the mustache.

I'll have to get more info on this guy...

Scenes from a Marriage

"Lalush, quickly! We're late," he warned her, naked, looking for his underwear.

It was Friday evening, the beginning of the weekend, and they were supposed to meet Jennifer and friends to hang out downtown in the Village and then go to a jazz performance. She stopped looking for her own underwear and looked at him with an expression on her face as if saying, *what? Sex wasn't more important?* But he was already busy fulfilling the role of the serious, responsible man.

His voice took on a harsh tone. "What's with the beating you're getting in training? Look how many bruises you have!"

She laughed. "Yes, Dad! Where did you throw my underwear?"

"Here, over here," he immediately knew where they were and pulled them out from under the bed. He had this amazing ability to sweep her to a world beyond reality while making love, and yet was able to stay so connected, so aware of what was happening in this world. He approached her and handed them over to her.

"I was careful with the bruises, right?"

"Absolutely not! It was painful, I suffered the whole time!" she joked sarcastically. He smiled.

A few rushed minutes of preparation and they headed out.

"Oops! We forgot our umbrella," he said and grabbed her hand, pulling her as a drizzle started. "Quick, to Broadway Street – we'll have the best chance of getting a cab there."

By that time in that neighborhood, far from the center, most cabs were already inhabited.

"Subway?" Eyal asked.

She grimaced with an unsatisfactory expression. When leaving for a night out, the subway was an option only when there was absolutely no other choice. Every morning they used the subway to get to work. It just wouldn't feel right to leave on the subway at night. It would spoil the weekend's special atmosphere.

45

"The taxi's coming!" Eyal declared, waving as hard and excitedly as if it were a boat come to rescue them off an island. The taxi stopped. Another man, also seeking a taxi, tried to edge in front of them. Yael was not going to let him pass — no way was she going on the subway. Her persistence paid off and they were inside. In Israel, they might have been able to share a cab. In New York, they'd share a cab with a stranger only in the most exceptional cases.

The taxi pulled away. Views of the city that never goes to sleep were reflected through the windows and she began to be filled with energy and vitality. The fatigue she felt was slowly abandoning her. This city was a wonder in her eyes. She recalled her early days there.

She took a lot of pictures in the first few weeks she was in New York. Streets, buildings, the subway, lights, commotion, day sights, sights at nights, heat and frost, different people, different characters, different cultures, different manners. The camera caught it all. Her initial impression was a dirty, gray city, with no halo, nor long-term historical affinity. Despite the wide streets, the tall buildings hovered over and spread an atmosphere of narrowness and suffocation. One can rarely see the strip of road between the tall buildings since it was always full with streams of traffic. It seemed to her there was no guiding hand in planning the city. Modern buildings were being constructed right next to old buildings and somehow this mix went hand in hand with all and any other extremes that were so typical of New York. Extreme. This was the core, the essence, the magic of New York. The cloudy weather only brought out the concrete. The city inhaled and exhaled smoke and smog while running with stress and panic during the day in a mad chase after time.

But at night... at night a whole different city snuck up. The dirt, concrete and smog are visibly gone and replaced by a dark cover. It is a darkness that is dressed up in the colors of traffic lights, the neon lights of street bars, headlights, projectors illuminating the squares, buildings —an amazing show. A wave of creativity overflowed the river's street creeks. Concerts, movies, music, standup comedy shows --there was always a huge cultural celebration. Yellow cabs were passing as raindrops fell and cascaded off the heated windshield and onto black road. White smoke rose from the steam holes, reminding of an entire life that was conducted underground. And below the city, just at the lungs of the subway, the smoke merged with the rain drops and reflected the changing traffic lights in a celebration of motion, lights, colors, and contrast. The radio played a Billie Holiday song about some impossible love in a big city while the taxi driver navigated skillfully between the wide lanes of the road, heading south towards the Village.

They were going for a night out with Jennifer, Lorenzo, and Jeff. Yael hadn't seen Jennifer for quite some time. They were both so busy lately. Lorenzo, Jennifer's boyfriend, was a terribly sexy Italian young man that smoked pot and sniffed at every opportunity. He was an unemployed guitar player not doing anything with himself. He was fifteen years younger than Jennifer. Eyal was recently recruited to examine the possibility of having Lorenzo as an actor in the video clips he produced, but it seemed that Eyal didn't want to go out of his way to help him. Photos of Lorenzo that were passed on to Eyal so he could pass them on to the appropriate people remained on his desk since the last time Yael questioned him about it. Jeff was a friend of Lorenzo and a tall American nerdy stock broker. He was the type that had difficulties with social relationship in general and particularly the intimate ones. Yael had never seen him with a woman. He clung continuously to Lorenzo and it seemed to her that one of his reasons for doing so was the unbearable lightness of Lorenzo's being and his accessibility especially to women.

At the beginning of their relationship, Jennifer was annoyed and grumbled a lot about the constant presence of Jeff. Finally, she gave up. Jeff was, for Lorenzo, everything he couldn't be: a serious, mature, responsible, financially knowledgeable, politically active WASP. Lorenzo could never have those white, Anglo-Saxon roots, and would always feel like an outsider to American culture — his faltering English, casual jobs as a musician, poor, with no financial means. He looked like a child from the sixties with his long black hair, and dark skin. Colorful necklaces always adorned his muscular chest and showed through his airy, colorful boutique shirt and light Bermuda pants. Lorenzo opened endless possibilities for Jeff with people in general and especially with women. Upon realizing this symbiosis, Jennifer had no chance and she came to terms that if she wanted Lorenzo, Jeff was part of that package deal. She decided to harness herself to the mission of finding a girlfriend for Jeff, knowing it was the only chance to escape his boring and tiring presence. But it wasn't as simple as it sounded, because it seemed that Jeff wasn't particularly interested in women, or maybe he just feared them. She couldn't hook him up with any of her single women friends since she knew his demeanor would not permit him to date someone older, even if he felt attracted to her.

"Say! How is she coping with the age difference between them?" Eyal asked Yael.

"If he was older, would you also have asked how he was coping with that?" she fired back. It annoyed her that people were always amazed about the age gap only when the woman was older.

"It's 2001 — the beginning of the 21st century. Now it's our time. It's time for the women and you — you men, must pay back your dues," she said.

Eyal smiled with satisfaction. As a man with a modern and intelligent self-image, such a girlfriend only benefited his image.

"But they don't want kids or anything?" he persisted annoyingly.

"So what? What's wrong with that?" she retorted.

"The age gap won't be perceived well," he said firmly.

Since when did he become the establishment's delegate? She thought to herself.

"Say! So when are we going to have some kids?"

Terrified, she threw at him a puzzled look. There was a serious tone in his voice and she always felt that "a man who wanted to breed you was to be avoided."

"What kids? Why this all of a sudden?" she replied wide-eyed.

"Look, you're not so young anymore." There seemed to be a small degree of satisfaction in his voice.

She understood that his words were only said as a means of pressuring her, but they also carried a patronizing undertone. She remained silent.

"It is happening with everybody else." he added, "Why not us?"

"So you want kids just to be like everybody else?"

"Yael, don't distort what I'm saying. It's part of our evolution. It's a natural process."

"Sounds more automatic to me than natural."

"Well Yael, really!"

"Really!" she answered back stiffly.

"Hey, Girl!" Jennifer joyfully approached her as soon as she saw them get out of the cab on West 4th in the Village. "Long time, no see!"

Lorenzo approached behind Jennifer, all smiles.

"You saved me from an annoying conversation, my dear," Yael whispered in Jennifer's ear while they hugged. Jennifer was much taller so Yael had to stand on her toes to reach her ear.

"Is the anal retentive is bothering you again?" whispered Jennifer back as she tapped Yael's shoulder to comfort her.

Yael released her hug.

"What? Jeff isn't here?"

"Not to worry." Jennifer didn't hide the cynical tone in her voice, "he's here. He went to buy cigarettes."

"Oops." Yael muttered with a sympathetic tone.

Yael enjoyed a pleasant kiss on the cheek from Lorenzo while Eyal did the same with Jennifer.

"Hey Yael, when did we say we'll do couples' exchange?" Jennifer joked.

"Whenever you want, dear, whenever you want!" said Yael with a silly wink.

These last sentences were what Jeff heard as he got back from the newspaper stand and a pack of cigarettes in his hand. He stopped in his tracks, completely lost.

"A joke, amico, a joke!" laughed Lorenzo.

"Of course!" Jeff was quick to answer.

"That's how quickly you are replacing me?" Lorenzo hugged Jennifer tightly, trying to draw a declaration of love out of her. She passed her hand gently through his long hair.

"You think?" she asked softly.

"Here are your cigarettes," Jeff interfered. Lorenzo released his grip of Jennifer.

"There were no Camels, so I bought you some Winston's. I hope that's ok?" Jeff looked somewhat fearful. Jennifer rolled her eyes and looked at Yael.

"Shit, I don't smoke those! Why didn't you ask?" Lorenzo looked upset.

"Well, I'll go back and return them..." Jeff trailed off and turned around, despondent.

"Drop it. Never mind. I have to smoke something," Lorenzo interrupted, grabbing Jeff on the shoulder in a hastened grip. "Let me have them…"

Jeff looked relieved— the small drama was over. He rushed to give the cigarettes to Lorenzo before he changed his mind again, and turned to greet Yael and Eyal.

"Strange relationship," Eyal had said once when defining what was going on between Lorenzo and Jeff. Back then, Yael found it difficult to admit, but wondered if there was maybe something more to it.

Lorenzo urged them to move on and led them into a dark alley. The alley led to a descending staircase behind which they would have never imagined to find a jazz club. A sign in flashing lights hung above the door read "The Fourth Note Club."

"Where are you dragging us, Lorenzo?" asked Eyal.

"Not many know this place," Lorenzo bragged while knocking on the door.

50

The door opened. Light Jazz music played in the background, welcoming them. The club was small but crowded. The smell of cigarettes and alcohol filled the air.

As they entered, all eyes were turned toward Lorenzo. He looked beaming and shiny. The hostess smiled at him with a huge grin.

"Could you get us a good place to sit?" he turned his charm on her.

"Yeah, sure," she smiled. "Haven't I seen you somewhere before?"

"It may very well be," he replied with a crooked smile.

"Why don't we just sit down?" grumbled Jeff. It was clear he wasn't happy with the attention Lorenzo was getting. Jennifer, on the other hand, didn't show any sign of unease.

The hostess led them across the room while sending smiles at Lorenzo, finally placing them at a round table of five.

"Is this alright?" she asked.

"Excellent," said Lorenzo with a broad smile. They sat down. The hostess continued to stand near him.

"I think we're fine," Jennifer said with a threatening tone. The hostess seemed to shrink in half and quickly evaporate.

"She didn't like the blatant flirting, that's for sure," whispered Eyal in Yael's ear.

Yael raised her eyebrows skeptically. She was actually inclined to think that Jennifer was very secure in her relationship with Lorenzo. Jennifer was the one who served as a safe place for his extreme mood swings and covered up for his inability to function as an adult. She didn't seem bothered about how he conducted himself with people in general and women in particular, and perhaps that was part of her charm in his eyes.

"She's nice," said Lorenzo.

"You'd need beer goggles for her," muttered Jeff.

Everyone laughed. Yael smiled slightly; she didn't understand what the joke was and asked Jennifer for a clarification.

"When you go on a blind date and you see that your date isn't particularly attractive, you drink before having sex so your date seems

51

sexier, more appealing," explained Jennifer, while playfully mimicking the shining facial expression of the hostess.

They had arrived just in time. The stage hosted a band of four players—three African Americans and a white—on a trumpet, bass, piano and drums. They barely had enough room on the small stage.

During the next hour, the audience was taken along with the four musicians in a wave of blues. The excellent performance was accompanied by dinner and drinks. One thing was certain: you didn't want to miss any performance recommended by Lorenzo.

At the end of the show, however, they were surprised when they received the bill, which also included a big fee for the show. Lorenzo had missed that little detail when he made the reservations. He had thought the cost was only for dinner. He was so embarrassed that Yael and Eyal, despite their displeasure, thanked him without making a fuss. He beamed again.

Hidden Lust

Yael and Eyal were wondering where would be the best place to catch a taxi back home, but Lorenzo had other plans. There was an S&M club he wanted to see for a while. He heard it was fascinating—"Not to be missed," he claimed. Unable to resist his charm and whatever possible fascinating place he had in mind, the group squeezed into a cab. Lorenzo and Jennifer sat in front with Yael, Eyal and Jeff in the back. The cab rushed them across town until they ended up near the port downtown.

Lorenzo didn't have the exact address, but just a poor description of where it was. Soon, they found themselves circling around and around a radius of three blocks within the industrial area. According to Lorenzo, one of the buildings had to hide the club. All of them were getting tired except Lorenzo, who always seemed to be on an endless high. Eyal suggested to maybe give up, but Lorenzo guaranteed he would find it soon.

"Stop, stop right now!" he shouted to the driver.

The driver, startled by the sudden yell, stopped in screeching halt.

"Wait here a moment!" he said as he jumped out of the car. "I'll be right back!"

"Lorenzo!" Jeff called after him, "Where are you going?"

Jennifer rolled her eyes as if to say "This Jeff is such a leech", and turned to Eyal. "Well, is there a chance you'll find some kind of a role in a video clip for him?"

"It's no longer in my hands; I passed his photographs over to the producer."

What a liar, thought Yael, *not even blinking.*

It seemed that Jennifer didn't buy Eyal's lies.

"Make sure she really got it," she turned to him and said with a commanding tone.

To add to Yael's annoyance, Eyal added, "Amazing photos, Jennifer, you managed to capture him at his best."

"Definitely," Yael agreed. She adored Jennifer's photos, and whenever Jennifer had new ones she sent Yael the low-resolution version for her to enjoy them. Sometimes, she consulted Yael regarding which photos to choose.

"She was a modeling photographer before, you know," Yael said, hoping that the quality of the photographs would spur Eyal to do something.

"If he's not accepted as an actor here, I have no doubt he'll be accepted somewhere else," Yael added.

"I do hope so, since he's already going crazy from doing nothing." Said Jennifer, her tone had turned serious and then worried, but then she continued somewhat humorously, "Eventually he'll hang out in clubs like that all day long."

"That won't happen," said Jeff firmly.

Despite the fact Jeff grew up here, he doesn't really understand when people are joking, thought Yael.

"Can you guarantee that?" asked Jennifer. An angry undertone could be heard in her voice. Yael realized that Jennifer wasn't joking.

"Where is he, anyway?" Eyal asked impatiently. They looked out the window. Lorenzo seemed to be speaking with two blacks on the street. He ran back to the taxi and ordered the group to get out.

"We're really close," he said excitedly. "We'll walk."

He led them through several dark alleys from which the stench of urine was rising and they reached a building that looked ready to collapse. A flight of stairs could be seen at the front of the building, leading down to a dark iron door.

Where does he find out about these places? Thought Yael, her heart pumping. The door opened as if they had been expected. The bouncer scanned them quickly. His gaze rested on Lorenzo and he nodded his head, allowing them to enter.

It's amazing he let us in. Don't we look too nerdy for the place? Yael wondered. She felt some kind of rising excitement. She had never been to such a club and was curious to find out what was going on in those dark places. Lorenzo, in contrast to everyone else, was rushing

54

forward as if it was his second home. Jeff followed, not leaving Lorenzo out of his sight.

Eighties music played loudly in the background. Yael immediately recognized her favorite band, Depeche Mode, in a song suitable for such a club: "Masters and Servants". A dark hall welcomed them as ultra violet lights flickered on the floor and on the dark walls. Machine-made smoke —the kind that is used in dance clubs and rock concerts—clouded out from time to time from hidden openings in the floor. The sound, the lighting, the smoke and the design of the place all created the sensation of a bizarre and mysterious scene. When the smoke dissolved, a bar appeared in the distance. Several men and women were seated next to the bar. Once again, everyone's eyes were directed toward Lorenzo.

This guy is magnetizing, thought Yael. A couple passing right next to them caught their attention. A young man, slim and athletic, dressed in a tailor-made suit walked by confidently.

"He doesn't look so bad," whispered Jennifer in Yael's ear.

An executive-type briefcase was in his one hand, and in the other there was, to their surprise, a leash attached to the neck of a woman. The woman, dressed in a traditional S&M style, was covered head-to-toe in chains. Her nose, ears and lips are pierced. She wore a black tank top and tight leather pants, black leather boot. The man led the way and her purple-haired form walked behind him at a distance permitted by the leash. A half-naked man being led by a woman dressed in gothic-black drew their attention away from the first couple. The semi-naked man and gothic woman disappeared into a doorway.

"I wonder what's going on there" whispered Eyal in Yael's ear.

But where had the man and leashed woman gone to? Yael looked around only to spot them approaching an armchair next to a table. *What's on the wall behind them?*

A huge wheel was connected to a wall, and in its center hung a completely naked man, tied by his arms and legs to the wheel's edges, waiting for something. All of them except Lorenzo, of course, were embarrassed and curious at the same time and didn't know where to look at first, given the flood of people and their shocking activities. Yael returned to watching the man and the leashed woman. Lorenzo said he had to have a drink. Jennifer and Jeff, of course, joined him at the bar.

Yael and Eyal watched the man with the briefcase and the leashed woman with interest. The couple approached the armchair and the man sat down. The women knelt at his feet like a properly disciplined pet. The man set his briefcase on the table and turned it over so it faced him. The actions were completed with a slow-paced attention as if he wanted to demonstrate his seriousness, knowing that he was being watched. Other people were gathering around the couple. Yael observed the people, mostly men of various ages. She wondered how different they looked from the ordinary male on the street.

She wondered if those who went to the club were the marginalized, the low or the middle classes. She was left with no answer.

The man opened his briefcase. Its contents were surprising: various sizes of whips, chains, handcuffs, and other accessories difficult to identify stared up at him. He took out a small whip. The woman turned her back to face him. He pulled the top layer of her leather pants down, revealing her buttocks to all. He caresses her buttocks as if preparing it for the future action and then - slash! The whip is lashing. The woman cringes from pain. A few more strokes and then he pulls out a feather from his briefcase. He taps his knees twice and she—the pet—sits on it. The audience gets even closer. The man pulls the top layer of the front of her leather pants down, revealing her genitals. He pulls the leash and she spreads her legs. A few of the men in the audience are getting even closer. The man gently passes the feather between her legs. She moaned, flirting with the men in the audience with her eyes. Eyal and Yael exchanged looks and Yael sensed that Eyal was uncomfortable with the whole scene. So was she.

After a few more minutes, the show ended. Next, the scene moved to the wheel and the naked man. A woman approached the wheel and turned it. The naked man stretched and stretched.

Curious, Yael whispered into Eyal's ear that she wanted to see what was going on in the private rooms.

"Well, let's go," he urged.

"No, that's fine, I'll go alone." She didn't feel comfortable watching these bizarre sex activities with him.

He looks at her quizzically.

"Don't worry, I'll be fine."

She turned toward the private rooms, searching for Jennifer and the guys. She located Lorenzo and Jeff seated at the bar, but not Jennifer. Could she be in one of the rooms?

Yael walked down into a rather dark hall, illuminated by narrow beams emitted by colorful halogen lamps through a transparent floor. She arrived to the doorway of the first private room she passed. She glanced in briefly. Four men and three women were inside and appeared busy in some sort act–– she wasn't sure if it was sexual, but it looked like a private party. She moved down the hall where there were entrances to the private rooms but none of them had doors installed. A naked man, a bit older with a hanging belly crossed her way and winked at her. A half-naked woman, also a bit older walked out from another room. The woman threw at her somewhat curious look. For some reason she didn't feel threatened in a place so full of dark lust. It seemed that this place only housed weirdos. She began to wonder what it meant to be ordinary in such place.

The third room looked a little more spacious and inviting and she dared to enter. A few people, some dressed, some wore few cloths, were inside. She sensed nudity becoming more and more of a norm. In the center of the room stood a young, painfully beautiful blonde man with blue eyes, and handcuffs wrapped around his arms, which were hanging over his head. His legs were spread apart. He was wearing a pair of jeans and his upper body was bare naked. An elderly looking woman with eyes covered in a black scarf was standing next to him and, beside her, sat an elevated stool. A mask and a bottle of oil rested on the stool. She passed the mask to a beautiful dark-skinned Indian man who was standing next to her and was dressed only in brown lederhosen highlighting the genital area. On his feet was a pair of brown boots with silver buckles. The dark-skinned man put the mask over the blonde man. The woman took the bottle of oil, squeezed the liquid out and rubbing it over her hands.

What is she going to do to him? Yael wondered, intrigued.

The woman approached him. She let her finger travel over his body—forehead, nose, lips, neck, chest—creating an electrical sensation in his body. He trembled. His lips spread apart. She returned to his lips, tracing over his upper lip, lower lip, and then inserted her finger into his mouth — in and out, in and out, very gently. He complied. She traveled down along his body, this time with two hands, massaging and kneading. He trembled again. The dark-skinned man grabbed the blonde guy leather belt and started to slowly unzip his pants while the woman caressed blonde guy upper body. His pants are shed off, followed by his underwear. She pressed his buttocks. He moaned and his head drooped. She grabbed his hair and pulled his head back. The room was quite dark and a white-yellow beam fell right onto him and with this particular décor he seemed as if he is Jesus tied to a cross, as if there was something almost religious to what was happening. It was more than just a sexual scene; it was ceremonial, ritual. It wasn't a wild brutal act, but rather gentle and under control.

The woman moved down to his penis. He moaned. Yael wondered what makes such a man participate in such an activity. Perhaps he was implanted by the club and all of it was just an act to get more people? After a few minutes of caressing his penis, the show finished. Everybody cleared the room. *Clearing it for the next show?* Yael wondered as she left the room.

She returned to the bar and noticed Lorenzo. He was ordering another drink. Jeff was at his side. Lorenzo seemed to be quite drunk. A woman approached and said something to him. Jeff raised his hand in a gesture asking her to leave. She refused and moved closer to Lorenzo. Her body touched his knees, but somehow it didn't look like a sexual gesture. She said something else to him. He seemed to be listening.

Suddenly, without warning, Jeff raised his hand and laid a ringing slap on her cheek. The woman pounced on him. Right at that moment, a sturdy man emerged toward them and it seemed that a fight was going to break out. The sturdy man separated Jeff and the woman. He grabbed Jeff and appeared to be threatening him.

Jennifer arrived and tried to separate the two of them. A hand comes up, and she's punched in the nose. Yael ran to her. The woman was being pushed away and the inflamed atmosphere started to cool down.

Lorenzo could barely stand on two feet. Jeff hugged him around his shoulders, steadying him. Jennifer and Yael headed to the bathroom to pour some water on Jennifer's bleeding nose. Jeff led Lorenzo to be seated on the sofa. Jennifer walked out the bathroom first. Yael remained to use it, as well.

When Yael walked out, she looked for Jennifer. Her eyes caught Lorenzo and Jeff. They were sitting on a sofa for two, while Jeff was hugging Lorenzo tightly. From the corner of her eyes, Yael could see Jennifer standing further away looking at Lorenzo and Jeff, carefully watching what was happening. Something in Jennifer's gaze made it clear that what she saw bothered her. Yael shifted her gaze to Lorenzo and back at Jeff. Jeff was still holding Lorenzo. He passed his arm over his back, caressing him, and pulled him closer. Jennifer, not noticing Yael, continued to stand in the distance, staring at them.

Yael approached her. "Jenny?"

Jennifer didn't respond. Her eyes were still fixed tightly on the two.

Then Eyal approached Jeff and Lorenzo. Jeff noticed him and immediately disengaged from Lorenzo. Eyal sat on a small table in front of them. He inquired as to what had happened.

"Jennifer?"

Jennifer recovered herself.

"I want to get out of here!"

"Okay, let's go," Yael agreed and they walked toward the boys. Eyal noticed them, and rose up from his seat.

"I think we should get going."

"Yes, we should," agreed Jeff.

They left the club. Jennifer and Jeff were supporting Lorenzo from both sides. When they said goodbye, Jennifer seemed detached, troubled.

Jennifer and Lorenzo, who lived in Soho, the southern part of the city stopped a taxi and soon disappeared. Jeff, who lived not far from Yael and Eyal, shared a taxi with them. While headed home in the taxi, Yael tried asking Jeff what had happened at the bar, but Jeff seemed withdrawn and didn't say much. Eyal pressed Yael's arm, signaling her to drop it. Jeff was the first to get out of the cab and they continued for a few more blocks.

"That woman was actually from the club, maybe even one of the managers..." explained Eyal."She offered Lorenzo, believe it or not, a job there. I assume she flattered him a lot and told him he could make a lot of money."

"Oh, I see. Well, I'm not surprised."

"I am!" said Eyal with a disgusted expression. "I think Lorenzo was actually interested in the offer and Jeff tried to push her away. She didn't comply and a fight broke out."

"Hmm," said Yael. The sight of Jennifer's gaze fixed on Lorenzo and Jeff on the sofa resurfaced in her mind, but she kept her thoughts to herself.

"Did you see the differences in the responses of Jennifer and Jeff?" Eyal said, panting lightly as they climbed up the stairs to their apartment "You'd think that Jeff and Lorenzo are the couple. While Jennifer didn't seem bothered by this scene, oh gosh did it bother Jeff. He reprimanded Lorenzo for agreeing to talk with the manager—or whoever she was—and for allowing her to degrade him."

"Yeah," Yael nodded, but in her mind thought, *this evening Jennifer looked very shaky, and it was not because of the woman.*

"Jennifer's been always so indifferent. It's no wonder Lorenzo is so wild." Eyal continued.

"So that's how you see it?" she retorted. "But Lorenzo is wild regardless. You said it yourself. Now blaming his perverse behavior on Jennifer?"

"That's my opinion." He said concretely with a tone that didn't leave a room for further discussion.

How did you become so scared? Wondered Yael. Recently, whenever there was a disagreement between them, this was how it ended. Eyal concluded it aggressively. For some reason, it became less and less important to her to confront him.

"Thank god tomorrow's Sunday. This city's wearing me out!" he said, still breathing hard after climbing the stairs.

61

Downtown, Uptown

Her cell phone rang. Despite the late hour—eight o'clock on Friday evening—the day at the office—and the week—had passed quickly. Eyal called to inform her that his efforts in this past week inquiring about a condominium on the East side had been fruitful. He thought it was time to move out from the "disgraceful"—as he called it —neighborhood where they were living.

Yael was reluctant to hear that.

"This means some astronomical costs," she replied.

"But both of us are making good money," said Eyal, adding reproachfully, "Shouldn't we get ahead in life? We have to keep up with the Joneses."

"I don't understand that last one," she said.

"It doesn't matter, Yael, it's an expression. You see? Your attitude isn't appropriate to the place. Whoever isn't getting ahead quickly here will soon be left behind. The fact that you also hold an American passport doesn't mean you belong here. If you really want to belong, then go with the flow...ahead. It's time to move forward!"

Yes. She did really want to belong. He was right about that, as usual. The fact that she was an American citizen was thanks to her parents, who were diplomats in the States when she was a baby. At that time, citizenship was automatically granted to babies who were born on the mainland. When she was a young girl, they were called again for a second and last diplomatic service and she lived in the States again for a short time.

Her past contributed to her constant feeling of being an outsider. Living in two countries for a short period of times had only contributed to the feeling of being foreign. She scanned her lovely office, looked through to the view that could be seen from her window, and then at the computer monitor that was displaying figures and financial forecasts.

Yes, we must move forward, she thought, but found herself saying, "Let's wait with this."

He sighed. Knowing her, he dropped the subject for the moment. He noted that he had actually called to remind them both—"Not necessarily you," he emphasized—"that at some point, food cans for Spike must be bought. If you've forgotten, he doesn't like dry food!" His words are accompanied by a borderline provocative tone.

The cat's his, after all. For god's sake, he should buy it.

She sensed that Eyal was using Spike's food to demonstrate his dissatisfaction in her unwillingness to move ahead, to integrate with the local culture, not having command of the local dialect and not taking steps to institutionalize their relationship. He never said anything directly, but she knew.

"I don't know if I have time. I have an important meeting Monday morning and I've got to stay here a bit longer to prepare. Worse comes to worse, we'll buy it tomorrow."

"Hmm," she heard him grumble.

"Are you meeting with Lorenzo?" she asked, attempting to change the subject. Eyal was already in the café, waiting for Lorenzo and Jeff. A week has passed since their memorable evening at the S&M club, and Lorenzo wanted to show Eyal more pictures, hoping it would make a difference. Eyal wanted to know if Yael would join them because Jeff would obviously be coming as well and after the last hangout in the club, Eyal was even less comfortable hanging out with them by himself.

"No, I'll pass. You'll have a boys' meeting." As soon as the words came out of her mouth, she realized it wasn't the right thing to say.

"I'd better get back and go for a run," she added as an excuse.

"Alright. See you at home later," he said with disappointment in his voice.

Yael was alone in the office. Everybody had already gone. She had to prepare for Monday morning's meeting. Kristen had informed her that day that she had finally managed to arrange a meeting with Chris-Daoud Khan. She asked Yael to be well prepared. She left another manila folder holding information about him earlier. It was marked "confidential" and Kristen had asked her to take it home and bring it to the meeting since neither of them would be at the office before the meeting.

"Keep it safe!" she said "He's a very important client, or will be, hopefully, after the meeting with us."

Yael hadn't managed to find any more information on him during these past two weeks using the company's regular resources. However, Kristen had managed to do so—god knows how. The new information was in the manila folder. She opened it. Again, the picture of him in his Western cloths with the giveaway mustache stared up at her. Reading his portfolio, she started to get an impression of the extent of his businesses, of his actions, and no less important, his personality. Oil, casinos, diamonds, horses and a surprise: no women, but a rather strong affiliation with the ASPCA.

How come the ASPCA? A rich man regrets, perhaps? Conscience problems? She wondered.

The report in the portfolio showed that his financial situation had been good over the years with impressively high revenues, especially from oil and casinos.

She looked at the portfolio for some information to help her diagnose what his future plan. Again, she could see a trend of investments in green energy industries. *Hmm...Is it to balance the green dollars he gets from creating oil pollution?*

His biography demonstrated a unique miscegenation: a Muslim father and Jewish mother. He had only one brother. *Not a very typical Arab family*, she thought, wondering about the possible reason for the small number of offspring. *Is it because the mother was very dominant and had dictated her will against the orders of the Muslim society, or maybe she couldn't bear more children?*

It didn't say much about the circumstances of the intermarriage. *I wonder how he—Chris—perceives himself. A Muslim? A Jew?* According to Judaism, he was a Jew, even if his mother converted to Islam. He carried a very Hebrew name: Daoud, or David. According to Islam, he was a Muslim. And at the same time, he was clearly trying hard to integrate into western society. He was living in New York, had taken on a Christian name, and not just Christian, but Chris—Christ. So which was he? Who was he? What was he aiming for?

In the absence of sufficient information, she would have to use her intuition in the meeting on Monday.

Done with her preparations, she left the office. It felt late. Very few people could be seen in the office area. The subway was delayed. It would be late when she would get home. She still wanted to go for a run. She wondered whether to call and invite Daniel and Peter to join her. *It's too short of notice. I'll run alone*, she decided.

When she reached the station on 103 Street, she heard a shout while climbing the stairs. It was the crazy banana man again. This time, he was without his "impressive gun". He was waving with some kind of an object.

I wonder what he is holding this time. As she got closer, she saw that he had no shoe on one foot and he was holding his other faded, worn shoe in his hand.

As she approached her street, his shouts could still be heard echoing in her mind. She thought about the huge difference between where she worked and where she lived. The financial area was one of the most prestigious areas in terms of Real Estate investments as well as residency, as opposed to where she lived—Amsterdam Street was the complete opposite. Here, in her neighborhood, she constantly encountered the unemployed, the beggars, the druggies. *The locals used to call this street "the Injection Street," and for a good reason. It isn't for nothing that Eyal wants to leave this "colorful" neighborhood he often calls "the slums."*

Spike was happy to see her after being on his own all day. He begged for attention, but she knew that if she didn't go out at once, laziness concealed in all sorts of excuses would prevent her from running. She had to run and prepare the upcoming Special Training. She had to be at her best for four days of intensive training from morning until night with few other hundred trainees. She was going to be tested in her first test for the first rank of a black belt, or Shodan. It would also be her first Special Training and she had no idea how or if she would get through it, especially after what she heard from Daniel.

She took off her clothes quickly and put on her jogging suit, lightly apologizing to Spike as she left. She headed to Riverside Park along the Hudson River. After three blocks along "The Injection Street", she found it hard to move her body after sitting all day.

She wasn't the only runner in the Park. She used the other runners as a reference point; she was motivated by those who were passing her by and found comfort when she succeeding in passing others. In the "Special Training" that will be held in Amherst, Massachusetts, a morning run of about five miles would begin every day, she was told. Immediately after that, the practice would begin.

She ran along the river on the esplanade, heading north. The more north she got, the more of the gray concrete of the esplanade would disappear, and the park would get wilder and wilder. Residential buildings could be seen further away from the park. It was getting dark already. Night was falling. An improvised tent of a homeless was perched in a small opening in the middle of the wilderness of the park. The concrete esplanade was gone, so she ran along a sandy path.

"It's not wise to hang around the northern side of the park in the dark," Eyal had once warned. He had been right, as usual.

She remembered last winter. It had been pouring rain that day. She was on the other side of town. It was night time, and she was returning from a meeting. The streets were completely deserted. She hurried to the bus stop in order to cross the city back home. She stayed under the cover of the fronts of buildings, hoping that the pouring water would miss her. She clung to her umbrella.

Suddenly, from the corner of her eye, she noticed a shifty character. She couldn't tell if it was a man or a woman. It walked a measured distance from her. A cigarette was carelessly placed in the corner of the figure's mouth. Its clothes were worn and its walk was nervous. She felt that she had become a target. She looked around in all directions —she was alone on the street. It was a small street and no cars were passing through. And even if they would, no one would stop

—it was New York. The tall buildings and the pouring rain only strengthened her feeling of being trapped. There was nowhere to run.

The suspicious character got closer. It was a man. He crossed the border of what could have still been considered a reasonable distance. She felt her muscles contract. She decided to make the first move, fearful of being with her back to him as he approached. She suddenly turned towards him, hoping to be the one to catch him off guard.

As soon as she turned, he immediately leapt toward her and grabbed her bag. She held tightly to the bag, not letting go. The man pulled even harder. The strap slipped from her shoulder. He tried to take one step further while continuing to tug at her bag. She pulled it back.

He made another attempt to tear the bag from her.

"Give me the bag!" a hoarse voice ordered. Fear turned into anger and she found herself replying firmly.

"I will not give you my bag!" she asserted while continuing to pull back the bag.

"Give me the bag!" the shifted man ordered again, but his tone of voice tone was more hesitant this time.

"I won't give it to you!" she said determinedly, feeling that the balance was changing in her favor. They stood face-to-face for a few seconds, examining each other. The decisive moment was about to come. The man reached one hand toward his coat pocket.

Is he going to pull out a knife? A gun? The shifted man examined her, and she examined him. Both tried to assess their chances against each other. After a few more seconds, he released his grip from the bag.

She's got away quickly, but unconscious senses were triggered to check if he had followed her. While crossing the road, she looked back quickly. He was standing still, watching her moving further away.

An Incident

The park was dark. *I better turn around and go back home by the subway.* She turned around and continued running until finally reaching a more populated area. She left the park and continued to run along the streets, passing by the neighborhood Deli. Again, she had forgotten to take money with her to buy some food for Spike. Eyal would be upset.

She had only an ID with her. "It is advisable not to walk around this city without it - you never know what can happen!" Eyal used to preach to her until the words sank in so she took it but she had a reason for not taking anything else. She enjoyed the sense of lightness, to be able to move around freely without anything that gave away who she is, with no commitment, with no obligation. She missed this sense of freedom. Every day she felt like she was in a constant struggle to remember the tasks for that day, and to take care of both personal and work-related things. Every day she had to carry so many items with her, whether it is money, a credit card, a metro card, or an entrance pass to work. If there was a meeting with new clients, she needed her laptop, the appropriate folder, presentation, portfolios, etc... Even the clothes she needed to wear were dictated by the schedule for that day. If she had Karate practice after work, she would carry, her training bag containing her training suit, her ranking belt and all the accompanying accessories: protective gloves, a hair tie, an elastic sock for her ankle in case the foot inflammation decided to kick in again.

So she was thrilled to travel light when she could. Such freedom! She would never give up her thirty-minute illusion of freedom, something Eyal could never understand.

The subway station was on 125th Street. It was on the border of Harlem. It was better not to hang out there at that time of night, especially alone. *But how will I get into the subway without a metro card?* She thought as she reached the station's stairs.

A tall black man with dreadlocks, dressed in a long, flapping faded red coat, pushed past her while running down the stairs. She could see him jump lightly over the subway station's revolving door, while his left palm, which was missing a finger, grabbed the railing for support. *Was he one of those who never paid? Was he running away from someone? Or was he just one of the regular New York psychos?* She wondered.

Two policemen armed with clubs and guns passed by her in pursuit, leaving the subway station door open. She felt excitement. Her curiosity had awoken.

She had seen and heard about criminal pursuits in the news quite often, but to be present for such an event seemed like something she would actually experience. The subway station door left open. It was a sign to enter.

She went inside, searching after the police and the man with the dreadlocks. The officers could be seen at the far end of the long platform. Apparently, the man had entered the tunnel. One of the officers talked into his radio.

Maybe they want to wait for reinforcements at the next stop and catch him when he gets out of the tunnel?

The police officers returned and stood in the middle of the platform. One was short with a bit of a belly and a thin, black mustache. He looked Hispanic. The other was tall and blonde—a cold, Irish-looking man. The few people who were waiting for the subway didn't seem eager to know what had happened. She couldn't hold back and went over to the police officers.

"Excuse me, what happened?"

Still panting from the chase, the short officer gave her a quick glance as if saying, "The last thing we need now is nagging questions!"

However, to abide their duty and induce a sense of security in the residents, the blonde replied.

"Everything is under control, Miss," he said with an artificial, compulsory smile.

The rumbling of the approaching subway could be heard. She understood she wouldn't be getting more information from them. The subway arrived at the station, producing a huge screech from the

69

breaks as it started to slow down. It reached a full stop. A pressured blast of air could be heard as the doors opened. She was about to enter the car when the blonde officer stopped her.

"Miss, did you see the man we were chasing?"

"Yes, I did. He passed me on the stairs."

The officer sharpened his question.

"His face…did you see his face?"

She made an effort to remember his face.

"Not really, he came from behind me and passed me running."

The officer seemed to have noticed her heavy accent and scanned her as if trying to categorize her or guess where she was from.

"Okay, thank you." He concluded.

She stepped into the car, paused for a second, and turned around.

"There is one thing…"

The doors were about to close. The Hispanic policeman was quick to insert his foot to stop them from closing.

"Yes?" she could sense a skeptical tone in his voice.

"His left hand...it looked like it was missing a finger."

"Do you remember which finger?"

"I think the index finger," she pointed to her corresponding finger.

"Miss, I would like to ask you to leave me your contact details in case we need you."

"Yes, certainly," she said and quickly wrote down her name and number. He asked to see her ID.

Lucky I took my ID…Why must Eyal always be right? They wouldn't have taken her seriously without her ID, especially as a foreigner, she thought. He checked her card, thanked her, and removed his foot from the door.

The ring as the doors closed was heard. She remained by the door, standing. The subway started to roll. The lights in the car had turned off and the platform lights penetrated the moving car in flashes, creating a unique light show. The subway entered the tunnel. There was complete darkness for a second, and then the light has returned to the car.

But then the subway stopped. She looked around. There were only three other people, two men and a woman, scattered throughout the car, and each was occupied in his or her own business. The subway didn't move. She wondered if it was somehow related to the man in dreadlocks who had run through the tunnel. Maybe his presence was preventing the subway from continuing.

She was tired and eager to get home. She wanted the subway to get going, but it wasn't budging. A beggar entered from another car, humming something that sounded like a prayer or maybe a folk tune. He was expecting a response from the passengers. The other three passengers pulled out newspapers.

They really do hide behind it, she thought as the subway forged ahead. *They're in their own bubble, their way to hide from those who were on the margins of society.* The marginalized were manifested in several forms: beggars, AIDS patients, fortune tellers, music players, singers, vets, the bitter ones, the violent ones, drug attics or those who simply had mental problems. Each had his or her own agenda. For one it could be money; for another, recognition, and for a third, pure attention. When the passengers didn't wish to comply, they simply pretended to be reading. It helped. The image of "I'm busy in my own world. Don't bother me, don't approach me. Don't ask me for change, charity, or tell me that you are infected and that the Lord Jesus told you today that you will gain salvation by us!"

The beggar, disappointed by the lack of responses, moved on to the next car. Maybe he would find salvation there. *From what? In what form?* She wondered. *A slice of bread? Dope? Booze? Will the money even bring him salvation at all?*

Remembering her conversation that morning with Eyal about the condominium he wanted to move to, had raised more thoughts about it. *People are actually living in the gutter and we're discussing moving into a condominium in a wealthy neighborhood. What a difference between these worlds...and how much is the world I live in really my world?* She didn't feel like she belonged in it.

Then a man entered the car, limping slightly. He sat close to the doors where she was standing. It has been almost ten minutes now and the subway continued at a stand-still. He was watching her carefully. She felt uncomfortable. It wasn't acceptable to stare at someone so boldly. She suspected she'd gotten his attention because she had been talking to the police officers. Something in the man's gaze felt wrong. She wanted to move far away from him, but if she went too far, he might notice.

Finally, she decided to sit several seats farther away from him. She snuck a glance at him to see if he was still watching her, and try to figure him out. He looked to be of mixed origins, in his mid-thirties, and from the working class. She still had a hard time categorizing most Americans, even after two years in New York. The continent's vast size in addition to the huge number of immigrants created an enormous variety. Even her American friends couldn't always guess the origin or background of strangers correctly.

The man continued staring at her, almost restlessly. She tried to fix her gaze on the floor and the advertisements along the walls to avoid making eye contact. A few more uncomfortable minutes passed and suddenly, the subway started moving. His gaze turned toward the tunnel, as if it seems as if he was looking for something there.

Is he looking for the fugitive? She wondered. His gaze returned to her. As soon as he did so, she quickly withdrew her eyes. *Oh! I wish we would have reached the station already,* she thought, feeling her nervousness increasing. *Is he still looking at me?*

She raised her eyes from examining the floor and cautiously turned them toward him.

Something is really wrong.

He was persistently staring at her and not even trying to hide it... In a split second, thoughts began running through her head. *Should I look directly at him as if saying, "Don't mess with me!" Or play it safe and ignore him? Will ignoring him be interpreted as weakness?"*

Despite her fear, something in the power game gave her a thrill. His eyes were still fixed on her. The subway continued speeding through the dark tunnel. Light and shadow were alternatively falling on his face, increasing the intensity.

"The next stop is 103rd Street," the driver announced over the speakers. The screech of the subway brakes increased. *My station,* she thought, relieved.

The train reached the station, and suddenly the lights in the car went off. Now, in the absence of lighting, each face appeared and disappeared repeatedly. Her discomfort increased. *Now he can take advantage of the darkness.* Her instincts told her to move far from him, and usually her instincts were right. She rose from her seat and stood by the doors while supporting herself on the subway bar. A final, loud scream of brakes resounded. The train stopped. The doors opened.

She got out, but he was right behind her, limping slightly. Suddenly, he stopped. She continued. She managed a backward glance, but couldn't believe her eyes. The man with the dreadlocks had appeared. He had emerged, out of nowhere, but this time without the long coat. It seemed to her that he and the limping man knew each other.

Within seconds, the station filled with police officers and the chase after the man in deadlocks began again. The limping man immediately changed directions. She continued walking, searching him tentatively with her eyes, wondering if he would continue following her. *Does he want to harm me? Is there a point in asking one of the officers to accompany me?*

The man limped towards the second subway exit. She continued walking through the transit gate, then up the stairs and to the street. Immediately, she looked around, checking to see whether he was there. He was nowhere in sight.

She proceeded cautiously only one and a half block further and she would be home. Right then, it seemed too far. A police car was parked across the street. The street light flashed red, and then green. She crossed. The man with the limp was nowhere to be seen. After another half a block, she reached Amsterdam Avenue. It was completely deserted. The next building was hers.

A homeless man jumped out at her out of nowhere. Her heart leapt. For a moment, she thought it was him.

"Change! Can you spare some change?" he begged.

"Sorry," she replied weakly, and rushed into the entrance of her building, quickly ringing the door intercom to be let in.

Invasion

Eyal was already at home.

"You wouldn't believe what just happened," she said, breathless, and sat down on a kitchen chair while untying her right shoelace, "but I'm dying for a bath, I'll tell you everything when I get out."

"How was your meeting with Lorenzo and Jeff?" she asked while untying her left shoelace.

"It was ok," he replied, an unsettled expression on his face.

"You seem reserved," she said and wondered if he was comfortable being alone with Lorenzo and Jeff.

"I don't know," he replied thoughtfully, "there's something strange about them, and I can't seem to put my finger on it..."

"Can you help him?" she took off her second shoe. Eyal seemed lost deep in his own thoughts." With a job," she added.

"They sometimes behave like a couple, and it's making me nervous," he said, ignoring her question.

"A typical Israeli!" she teased him, "a little intimacy between two men and it already threatens the image of the macho man." But even she had to admit that something in their behavior was bothering her. She kept her thoughts to herself.

"Very strange," he added.

"So can you help him or not?" she took off the top of her sweat suit.

"Look, there's a problem. He's interested in an acting career, and we examined the possibility of him participating in some of our music videos, but do I know how long he'll stick with his desire to be an actor? How long had he seen himself as a musician?" he said with hauteur.

"It's not fair," Yael rushed to Lorenzo's defense, "He still plays well, but it's hard to find your place when you're a foreigner."

"What's hard? What's so hard about it? I did it; you did it —it's just an excuse!"

"Well, not everybody got as lucky as we did. And even if you've made it in your career, it doesn't mean you've made it socially, and that you feel you belong, right?" she felt compelled to defend Lorenzo.

"That's nonsense! If he would've found something meaningful to do, he'd feel like he belonged!" Eyal's voice rose.

"Well, maybe you're right…" she said, but was interrupted.

"Of course I'm right! He should make an effort to belong!" He jumped ahead with increased vigor.

"Still," she tried to explain, "not everybody was born to be mainstream like you."

He looked at her, assessing whether or not she had meant it as a compliment or an insult, and replied, "Do you really think that the reason he isn't focused is because he doesn't want to be mainstream, or is it because everything is too hard for the spoiled, charmer lover boy?"

Is it jealousy, or just him growing into his arrogance? She thought angrily to herself. But again, despite his arrogance, she felt he had a point, and this irritated her even more.

"Listen, I'd be very happy if you helped him." She took off her sweatpants.

"I don't know. I don't think I want to get involved with him."

"But you used to like him," she turned to the kitchen and opened the refrigerator.

"Yea, he has his charm, but I don't wish to mix a personal friendship with my work."

"But after all that Jennifer's done for me, it wouldn't be right not to help." She poured herself a cold glass of water.

Eyal remained firm.

"No."

"Your decision," she muttered disappointedly with a dry voice, took a sip of water, and set the glass down determinedly in the sink.

"Well, now what? Are you angry?"

It had already been some time now since she recognized the man she had fallen in love with no longer existed. The most irritating part was that he usually was right. But the man she lived with had slowly become a man who wasn't showing her any sympathy, who was fearful, weary, preserved, and…she searched for the right term in her mind… mainstream. He was once so unique, so different, so unafraid to go against the crowd, and now either age or desire to be liked or for what he called 'getting ahead' had made him an ordinary guy, a conformist, he was even boring. Sex was the only part that remained good, intriguingly enough. There, he was interesting; he had diverse —and sometimes even dark—sides that attracted her. But could their relationship survive only because they had good sex?

"Have you bought food for Spiky?" he interrupted her thoughts.

"No, I went out with no money on me. Why didn't you buy any?"

"I thought you would." he grumbled. "I'll go out and get it now."

"I'm going to the bathroom," she replied laconically, and headed down the hall.

She turned on the tap water and slowly filed up the tub. The room filled with steam. *It'll relax the muscles,* she thought, and gently massaged her legs. *Wow, I'm tense.* She turned her head in slow circles to loosen the stiffness in her neck. She stepped another foot inside and then slowly let her entire body down into the tub. The water was warm and relaxing. She felt calmness slowly spread throughout her body. Light raindrops gently knocked against the window. She leaned her head back and closed her eyes.

There was the noise of a door being slammed and an indistinguishable bang coming from the living room. She jumped up, alarmed. Heavy rain was sharply pounding against the window. She heard furniture being dragged across the wooden floor. Banging. Unrecognizable voices. The bathroom was full of steam and stuffy heat. She pulled away the bathroom curtain but couldn't even see the door because of the steam. The rain was getting stronger. The knocking increased. A real storm was raging outside.

What's going on? Where's Eyal?

Suddenly, from behind the door, she heard an unfamiliar male voice shouting, "Where is she?"

She had just about risen and grabbed a towel when the door crashed open. Two men burst into the bathroom. Before she understood what was going on, they grabbed her and dragged her into the living room. There, she was amazed to see Eyal tied up to a chair, head dropping back.

Is he hurt? He seemed unconscious. She looked for blood. There wasn't.

A tall man wearing a long coat was standing in front of him with his back facing her.

What is he doing to him? Is he hitting him?!

The man turned around to face her.

It was him.

The dark, black dreadlocks stood out over his red coat. She tried to release herself from the grip of the two other men, but with no success. Upon twisting around, she discovered that one was skinny little Bobby, the building's maintenance man, who had emigrated from Mexico.

How the hell did he know the man with the deadlocks, and how the hell did he find me? Through Bobby?

Bobby's tight grip began inflicting pain. Was he taking some sort of revenge? Why? Hadn't they treated him nicely? Had they troubled him too much? Was this some sort of strike against feeling like a second-class citizen in his country? Perhaps some way to get even, since they, too, didn't belong?

All of a sudden, someone came out of the bedroom. His face is covered with a dark mask leaving only his mouth visible, but he limped as he walked.

Her heart beat faster. *It's got to be him, the lame from the subway,* she thought to herself, frightened. He gripped Spike tightly by his neck.

She focused on his face, where only his mouth could be visible. She noticed that his upper lip was slightly torn. He limped forward

78

mockingly and then suddenly and effortlessly begins walking evenly. The limp disappeared.

He was pretending to be lame.

He reached the corner of the room where the kitchen was located and, as if he already knew the exact location, opened the silverware drawer and pulled out a fork.

"What?" he asked with a sinister laugh, "Are you surprised I know where this is?" His language caught her off guard. It was surprisingly elegant.

"Earlier," he added, "I used your thoughts squeezer," he gestured towards the juicer.

Shocked by his bizarre choice of words, she felt her legs begin to shake. The masked man was approaching Eyal, aiming the fork at his neck and lifting Spike up high while the cat howled and twitched, trying to escape his grip.

"Well, which one would you rather have alive? Hmm?" the formerly lame man shook his head from side to side, pleased.

"You took a fork, you idiot!" The man with the dreadlocks ruined his fun and tore Spike from his hands.

"Get a knife! Let's cut the boy…a finger or two…" He lifted his hand, showing his missing finger, "...or a limb." He pointed between Eyal's legs and winked at her.

"What would you rather we cut?" the masked man chimed in with the corners of his mouth drooping. She could imagine a dark, evil gaze behind the mask. A huge smile spread across the face of the man with dreadlocks and remained frozen there as his eyebrows moved up and down, up and down.

"What do you want"? Yael dared to ask trying to use a firm tone, but it ended up coming out very weak.

"Where are the documents?" demanded the masked man.

"Documents? What documents?" asked Yael, puzzled. He appeared angry.

"I won't ask again! Where are they?" he aimed the fork closer to Eyal's neck.

"Yeah!" confirmed Bobby, tightening his grip on her. "He's not gonna ask again!" Something in the way he said it made it seem as if he were acting out.

"I have no idea what documents…" she replied, completely confused and fearful.

"Search the bedroom!" the masked man ordered. The man with the dreadlocks quickly disappeared into the bedroom.

Then it hit her.

Could he possibly have meant the confidential documents I brought home from the office? But why would they need them? Who are they? Should I say anything? As long as they're not harming Eyal, I'm not saying anything.

Two long minutes passed and the man with the dreadlocks returned with a manila sealed folder in his hands. The lips of the masked man could be seen turning up with a smile of content.

There was a knock at the door. Silence. The men looked at each other, anxious. The one with the dreadlocks brought one of his four fingers closer to his mouth, instructing everyone to be silent. The knockings were getting stronger. She attempted to turn to the one she had known throughout the past few months.

"Bobby" she whispered. The masked man tightened the fork to Eyal's neck and pushed his head backwards, warning that he would not hesitate to go further if silence wasn't maintained. Bobby looked anxious, but it seemed to her that it was because of the knocking at the door and not because of worry for Eyal.

Silence. All were waiting. She didn't dare to say anything or call for help while the fork was close to Eyal's neck. Then a shout was heard from behind the door.

"Police! Open the door!"

Heavy thumps followed. The masked man and Bobby looked at each other quickly and then sent a questioning glance at the man with the dreadlocks.

So he's the boss in this bizarre triangle, she thought to herself.

"Bobby! You idiot." The leader whispered between clenched teeth, "The fire escape?" he proposed while gesturing with his eyes towards the escape.

Bobby paused for a short moment. He looked as if he had been struck by lighting.

"Hurry!" the leader whispered again, still holding Spike by his neck skillfully paralyzing him without harm.

She couldn't help but wonder if he had his own cat at home...that was, if he had a home. Bobby ran to the window near the fire escape, opened it, jumped over the windowsill, and disappeared.

"Leave him! Quick!" The leader whispered to the masked man. The latter released his grip on Eyal, rushed to the window, and disappeared. Eyal's head drooped forward. He still looked unconscious. *Or was he dead?* Terrible thoughts began to cross her mind. She looked around frantically. *I've got to do something.*

The man with the dreadlocks seemed to read her mind.

"If you'll be quiet until we all disappear, you'll get him and the cat back in one piece. If not, I'll butcher him on the spot," he whispered, sticking his tongue out and signaling to the cat still in his hand.

He then ran to the window and disappeared, Spike with him. For a moment, she remained frozen, in shock, unsure of what to do.

The banging on the door tore her out of her terrified trance, but what to do first? Run to open the door? Check on Eyal? Run to the window to see if they were really gone? Eyal's head moved slightly— *He is alive,* she thought.

A strong blow reverberated through the room, and suddenly the door is being uprooted. Three policemen armed with guns burst into the room like a whirlwind. Two of them were wearing helmets; plastic shields were covering their faces. Everything happened in a heartbeat. Guns were aimed at her and at Eyal, whose head was still down. She was supposed to raise her hands in a sign of surrender, but, unwilling to pose nude for the officers, clung to the towel with one hand and raised the other hand slightly in a gesture of surrender. Eyal's head moved slightly.

"Don't move!" the police officer who was pointing the gun at Eyal shouted hysterically.

She was astonished. *Can't he see that Eyal is unconscious and tied up? That we are the ones that were being attacked?*

The two officers were scanning the room, searching. A third officer entered the room at a moderate and quiet pace. He did not hold a weapon in his hand and wasn't wearing a helmet. He was older than the others, with a strong, gray patch of hair resting over his forehead. A strong surge of tobacco scent accompanied him, clearly the scent of a pipe, not cigarettes. He walked into the room with a kind of carelessness with which one would enter one's own house or a social event.

He has to be the senior officer, she thought.

He examined her and Eyal and nodded to himself as if unsurprised and, in a calm and steady tone so contrary to the chaos that had just occurred, asked, "Where are they?" it was as if he were inquiring after invited guests.

She couldn't speak. The situation was becoming more and more surreal by the moment. *Is this really happening?*

She waved her free hand towards the fire escape window as a response to his question.

He nodded with his head to the policeman who was still pointing a gun at her, instructing him to lower his weapon, and gestured to the fire escape with his eyes. The policeman jumped out the window and disappeared down the escape. The senior officer then instructed the second officer to go into the bedroom. As he turned into the bedroom, the senior officer, with a nearly intolerable indifference, turned towards her.

"What happened? Get a little too scared?"

Yael swore she could see the peak of a smile on his lips. Shocked by his question, she followed his gaze to the floor beneath her. A small puddle of water rested on the floor between her legs from the bath she had taken.

What on earth is he even asking? Has the world gone mad? This can't be real. I must be dreaming.

The other policeman returned from the bedroom, nodding with his head from side to side as if saying he hadn't found anyone.

"Sit down! Sit down!" The senior officer shoved a chair under her. "Check over there again..." he continued to instruct the policeman, and as the later disappeared, he shouted, "...and bring me a robe or something."

Eyal's head started to rise. The shout had probably woken him up. He slowly opened his eyes, blinked, and began looking around, clueless.

He's OK; she let out a sigh of relief.

The policeman returned from the bedroom with a robe in his hands. He handed over the robe to her, turned his gaze to the senior officer and shook his head again from side to side. He hadn't found anything else.

"You can lower your hands now and get dressed," the senior officer said. Again, it seems to her that he was amused. He ran a finger through his hair proudly and rose.

His eyes were grayish-blue and his facial skin was very wrinkled, too wrinkled for his age. *He must be younger than he looks*, she thought. He stared at her with examining eyes.

"Release him!" he instructed to the policeman, nodding toward Eyal. Eyal mumbled a few unclear words.

"So what can you tell us?" he turned to her.

"Shouldn't we call an ambulance first to check Eyal?"

"Who is Eyal?"

"Eyal! The one sitting right here," she raised her voice angrily. *This guy is unreal, completely unreal. Is he really a policeman?*

The senior officer signaled with his eyes to the policeman. The policeman muttered something into his radio that sounded a lot like "The target is found."

What target was found? They didn't find anything...Are we the target? She wondered, even more puzzled.

83

He continued to speak using unclear codes in which the word 'ambulance' slipped in once. *How kind of them*, she thought cynically.

The third policeman who had jumped to the fire escape appeared at the window, shaking his head.

"Nope!"

He didn't catch them, she thought. *What about Spike?"*

As soon as the thought entered her mind, a howl could be heard coming from the window. A second later, Spike appeared in all his glory, a bit wet, but still in one piece.

"Lucky devil!" she took a deep breath.

The conversation between her and the senior officer while Eyal was gradually regaining consciousness would be a conversation that would accompany her ever since then. In that questioning scene, it seemed that something was not as it appeared.

Ashram

She woke up to the shrill call of a rooster. It didn't take long before the little room was in turmoil. The young girl was getting ready to go to school. The old grandfather continued to grumble as he had the evening before while Sabitri swung a whining baby in her arms.

Where had the baby come from? It was not there yesterday.

So worried she was being a burden to her hosts, she got up, feeling she shouldn't stay there another minute. She asked politely to use the bathroom.

With a big smile, Sabitri pointed to a doorway covered by a piece of cloth opposite the kitchenette. Again, Yael was struck by the simplicity. The toilet was a traditional, simple hole in the ground. However, it was sparkling clean.

When she came out, everyone sat around the small table for a modest breakfast. Sabitri invited her to join, instructing her to sit down. On the table, there was Chapatti, a traditional Indian bread, and Bag'ee, fried vegetable patties. Even though she wasn't hungry, she debated whether to join them or not for a moment—she feared she wouldn't be able to eat much later since she had no money. This reminder tilted the scale and she joined them at the table.

Sabitri wrung her hands. It appeared that they were all delivering a blessing for the food. Yael was struck by how the blessing had much significance, given the lack of abundance in the little house and her fear of what was to come. After they expressed their gratitude for the food, they began eating, quietly and moderately.

The baby stopped whining when it realized that all were engaged in an important task. The smiles Sabitri and her daughter her way during the breakfast warmed her heart. After the meal, without a word, the girl cleared the table quickly and efficiently.

Feeling like a burden again, Yael turned to Sabitri.

"Thank you for everything. I really should be going now." She turned to pack her bag, searching for something she could give Sabitri for her hospitality and rescue.

Sabitri looked at her with a suspicious expression.

"Going to hotel?"

Yael quickly considered whether she should lie and say yes, but decided against it and responded with an honest "No.'

Sabitri shook her head from side to side and said in a manner that either expressed a question or determination.

"No possible?" she questioned.

"No, no possible," Yael replied reluctantly, afraid she would put the generous woman in an uncomfortable situation. She rose from her seat and faced the door. There was a heavy silence. She realized she had done something wrong. It was evident from Sabitri's facial expression that she was offended. Yael realized the magnitude of the mistake she made by her eagerness not to continue to be a burden. She asked for her forgiveness. Again, it seemed that Sabitri understood what Yael was going through and made a gesture with her hand, instructing her to sit down again.

She turned to her daughter and said something. Her daughter looked at Yael and rushed out. After only a few minutes, she came back with a young boy who took the baby away. Sabitri gathered a few things into a tattered plastic bag that had known better days, and signaled Yael to get up, saying hurriedly, "Come, come!"

They left the house. Sabitri waived to a rickshaw and after about a twenty minutes' ride during which the scenery gradually changed to a wealthier neighborhood, Sabitri ordered the driver to stop in front of a large house, which looked richer and more well-maintained than the other houses in the neighborhood. It featured a strange architecture—there was something colonial about it. Sabitri ordered the driver to stop, and they got off the rickshaw. They passed through a big gate and walked along a stone path lined with flowers. A sign at the entrance, rather faded, read "The Ayurverdic Ashram."

The front door of the house was wide open. Sabitri told her to wait outside and went without hesitation.

I don't understand how such a poor woman could be connected to this place, Yael wondered.

A few long minutes passed. A Westerner, dressed in an Indian traditional male Dhoti and Kurta suddenly appeared at the end of the stairs, greeted her while passing, and disappeared into the house.

Vera

Yael decided that she waited enough, and went in after the Westerner, in search of Sabitri.

There might be more Westerners like the one she just saw, and they might be able to help her.

But what the hell would I tell them? They'd probably think I've gone mad...No. I've got to make up some kind of story instead of telling them what really happened.

Yael took off her heavy backpack and left it on the floor as she began to walk around. She entered a big, long room. In it, there were wooden benches and tables. Tableware adorned the tables. It was apparent that a breakfast had taken place there not too long ago. An aged woman and a young man entered the room. Both appeared to be Westerners. The woman spotted her, nodded a "hello," and sat down. It looked like she had come back to finish her breakfast. She seemed to be in her late sixties or early seventies. Her hair was white and gathered in a long braid that fell down past her neck. She was tall and slender and sat tall and upright. There was something about her that reminded Yael of Kristen, her boss—her ex-boss, actually.

The thought of Kristen shook her a bit. It brought back scenes from the past she didn't want to remember. The young man, short with long hair, looked troubled and his behavior seemed edgy and nervous. It appeared that they were in the middle of a conversation and he was questioning the woman about the place. They spoke in English. The woman had an Australian accent and the man had a heavy Russian accent.

A beggar entered the room. She asked for alms in Nepalese. The Australian woman ignored her demonstratively. The man watched the Australian woman's reaction, or rather, her lack of reaction carefully. The beggar didn't back off and persisted with her requests.

After a few long moments, the Australian woman turned to the beggar and said filmy in English, "Please, go!"

The beggar stopped and scanned the Australian woman for a moment as if she checking to see how determined the she was, and then without a word, turned and walked away.

"She understood," the Russian commented.

"Of course she did. We must send them away. Otherwise, the place will be full of beggars."

The young man, as if jumping at the opportunity, eagerly asked, "But isn't this place supposed to be a place where charity is given? Doesn't the guru preach about it?"

"Master gives plenty to those in need," the woman responded coolly.

"What about people who need money? Like me, for example?" he protested, continuing, "I'm stuck here with only fifty rupees and I asked several people for money, but nobody wants to give me anything."

The Australian looked at him intently and replied, "You don't need to beg! You can work if you have no money!"

The Russian appeared to be getting angry.

"But I have no money! I'm stuck!"

"Then you shouldn't have reached a situation in which you are stuck," she responded coolly.

Wow, I wonder what she would have said about my circumstances, thought Yael as her stomach twisted.

"But it wasn't my fault," he defended, agitated, "I transferred money into my bank account, but the bank made a mistake and now I have nothing!"

The woman looked at him suspiciously.

"Are you kidding me, or what?" she said, but he stood his ground.

"No, it's not my fault," he continued defiantly, "I'm stuck and no one here will help. What do you say about that? I need five hundred rupees!"

"How will five hundred rupees help you? They'll also disappear, no?" she asked with a curious glance.

"With five hundred rupees, I could get to Calcutta, where my bank is, and resolve the problem!"

The woman looked at him for a long moment, as if trying to figure him out, clearly debating whether she bought his story or not. Then, without a word, she opened her bag and pulled out a money belt. From the belt, she took out several bills and counted six bills of a hundred rupees each. She then placed them on the table, in front of the young man.

"Here, this is for you to get to Calcutta, where you can sort out the problem."

The young man looked stunned.

"I am completely honest; I'm not lying. I can show you my bag!" he said as if wanting to assure her that he was telling the truth.

"No, you don't need to," she said firmly, shaking her head.

The man seemed hesitant for a moment.

"But how will I repay you?"

"Next time we see each other, you'll return it," she replied.

Still hesitant, he continued. "I can give you my CD player, it cost me six hundred rupees."

She shook her head incessantly. He insisted.

"It won't work anywhere else, anyways, since the power adapter is good for here only."

Again, she shook her head, refusing. He didn't give up.

"You can hear the CDs."

"I don't listen to CDs. You can pay me back when we meet again."

He was about to say something, but she cut him. "Use the money to get to Calcutta!" Her firm tone left little room for debate.

Then the Westerner that Yael had seen before entered the room.

"We must put all the chairs aside," he said to the young man.

"All of them?"

The man affirmed, and left.

"Well, that's my last SEVA," the young man said significantly, and turned to put all chairs aside in his last selfless act at the Ashram, as he was asked. By the time he finished, the Australian woman had also finished her breakfast.

He asked for her name. "Vera" she replied.

He then asked if he could wash her plate and cup. His voice became softer, no longer arrogant and defiant as if he was trying to please her. She answered in affirmation. He took the bills and folded them into his pocket and cleared her dishes off the table. He waited patiently until she arranged her things and rose from her seat. He offered to carry her bag. He seemed to be going out of his way to please her, and when she left the room, he hobbled after her, her bag on his back, maintaining a respectful distance.

Master Buphendra

Pondering what she had just seen, Yael's thoughts were interrupted.

Sabitri appeared and instructed Yael to follow her. They passed through a wide corridor decorated with pictures of Hindu gods. The corridor led to a staircase. At the end of the stairs, there was a wide, wooden door. The door was half-open. Sabitri knocked lightly. A man's loud and deep voice was heard:

"Yes!"

Sabitri opened the door cautiously and instructed Yael to follow her, entering the room in a respectful manner. Yael followed her into a large room that featured a huge window. Facing the window, a male figure stood before a big desk. His man's back was facing Yael and he appeared to be examining the view outside. Sabitri was hesitant, as if debating whether or not to disturb him.

"Master?" she finally spoke in a weak voice. The man turned around. Yael noticed that he was tall and with an intense presence. He looked to be in his mid-fifties. A thick beard decorated his face. He was dressed in the traditional orange clothes of the "Sados"—the ones who dedicated themselves to spiritual work. An orange cloth was wrapped around his head, reminding her of the first Hebrew pioneers who came to build the country and had similarly wrapped coercion around their heads for protection against the hot sun.

Sabitri then introduced Yael to him. "Master Buphendra" she said in a weak voice. Master Buphendra looked at Yael curiously. She felt that he was examining her, trying to figure her out.

"I am Master Buphendra", he introduced himself, as if he had not trusted Sabitri's introduction.

Yael remained silent, unsure of how to respond.

After a short pause, he prodded with a defiant tone, "... and?"

"I'm Yael Finkelstein."

Somehow, she felt the situation required introducing herself with her full name.

Master Buphendra waved with his hand to Sabitri, instructing her to leave. Clearly, Sabitri was his inferior. Without delay, Sabitri disappeared from the room.

"Sabitri has told me you were a guest in her house and that you are not able to go to a hotel..." he stopped as if expecting to get an explanation from her.

She was silent.

"Well?" he added in a dissatisfied tone.

She found him very pretentious, which made her reluctant to comply. But she was in no position to express her views.

"I lost my money," she finally said.

"How?"

"It was stolen."

He watched her for a long while.

"Do not lie! How did you lose your money?"

Having no choice, she found herself telling him about how she had been standing on the hotel balcony when she scattered her money. It was the first time she shared the puzzling experience with anyone, and she was anxious to hear how he will respond. He did not blink once as she spoke. When she finished, his facial expression remained the same.

She wondered if he believed her. His reaction was so cold. Did he have any empathy?

"I will not ask you why you did it. That is your private business," he finally said with a harsh expression.

Despite of what he said, she sensed he desired to know what had driven her to do so.

"We'll have to find you some kind of work here. What do you know to do?"

His immediate offer caught her off guard. Shocked, she remained silent, unsure of how to respond.

"You want to work, do you not?"

"Yes, of course! Sorry, I didn't expect this," she replied, amazed. She realized it was an invitation to stay. Intrigued by the place and by him, she couldn't think of a better getaway. She wanted to stay.

"Well, life is full of surprises…" he smiled "…as are our actions," he added with a cynical tone. She knew full well which actions he was referring to.

"So, what can you do? Can you cook? Clean?" he asked.

"I don't know how to cook," she admitted.

"How do you eat if you do not know how to cook?"

For some reason, the obvious answer that she ate in restaurants didn't seem to fit, so she found herself keeping silent.

The Western man had seen before entered the room and talked to Master in a language she did not understand. It was evident that he felt a great respect, even a slight fear, from his manner of speaking. He constantly referred to him as "Master".

Master turned back to her.

"I must go, someone has come for treatment."

Noticing the questioning look on her face, he added, "We treat sick people here."

"Sabitri!" he called loudly.

Sabitri entered.

"Take her." he ordered. "What's your name again? Oh yes, Yael," he said emphatically and turned back to Sabitri.

"Take Yael to the room on the ground floor," he said. Then, he repeated it in Nepalese and looked at the both of them.

"She'll stay here and we'll find her something to do, yes?" he turned again to Yael and repeated his words in English so she could understand.

"Yes, thank you," Yael responded.

"Don't thank me! Thank her!" he responded, pointing to Sabitri. He then left the room, followed by the Westerner.

Sabitri signaled her to follow, and led her through a hallway to another hallway and then to a staircase and a small room. The room had a twin bed and a window over which a stretched canvas was hung as an improvised curtain. Attached to the room, there was a small bathroom with simple shower, sink, and toilet. Everything looked clean and modest.

Utilizing gestures, Sabitri signaled her to leave her backpack in the room and follow. She led her to the kitchen and showed her the dining room.

"Where is Master Buphendra?" Yael asked.

Sabitri pointed up with her finger and said "up floor". She then grabbed a bucket and rag that were on the floor by the dinner table.

"You work here?" asked Yael.

"Yes, work here, Master, cook, clean," responded Sabitri in broken English.

"Long time?" Yael asked, trying to figure out how well Sabitri knew Master, but Sabitri hadn't understood the question.

Science and Religion

During the day, Yael did her best to comply with the cooking and cleaning instructions Sabitri gave her while familiarizing herself with the Ashram. Work side by side with Sabitri was enlightening. It was a pleasure to be next to her. Yael was moved by her devotion to each and every task she completed. All her attention was focused on the job at hand, whether it was cooking, ironing or washing. The attention, the tenderness, and serenity accompanying her actions were so foreign to Yael in the world she had come from.

In her world, there was endless running, stress, and a lifestyle that required dealing with a number of things simultaneously. It was a world in which achieving a goal quickly as possible was the supreme value, in which countless objectives were affixed in a rigid timetable; a lifestyle that required raising endless energy. In her world, the means had no value and the only thing that counted was the end results. In her culture, people were measured by the number of trophies they have accumulated, by their conquered achievements. Those who weren't lucky or who worked even harder without achieving their goals didn't count. Sabitri, supported by the local cultural environment, offered Yael saner and satisfying way of living and working.

At the end of the day, Yael retired to her room to rest. As she lay on her bed, she reflected on the past two days that had brought her there, to that point. Was that what she wanted? A place that offered her a new view of her goals, of how to approach, prioritize, and feel a deep satisfaction without the materialistic victories?

Was the sequence of events that led her there only possible because of a brief moment of insanity and a sudden point of no return? It is really true that one had to lose in order to gain? And what exactly was the strange place she had landed herself in? An Ashram of patients? People who got stuck with no money? Guru's followers?

During the day, she could hear people coming in and out and a commotion upstairs, where treatments were given. She was very curious to know what kind of treatments Master gave, and who the people were who were coming. Dinner was expected at seven. Maybe then she would learn more about the place.

After taking a shower, she walked tentatively to the dining room. As a guest in the place and with no money in her belt, she felt that she was at the mercy of others, a situation that, in fact, had not been experienced since she was a child. Since the age of twenty, after serving in the army, she had earned her own living for her own well-being. Economic independence provided her a mental independence, a release from the need to be like everyone else. As long as she minimized her dependence upon others, she was not bound to think like them or behave like them. She could be truly free. But that freedom had its toll. She didn't belong.

Several people sat down at the table and presented themselves to her: Susie, an American, Mohan, an Indian, and John, another American. The Australian woman she had seen earlier was not present, and John informed them that she would be late.

Everyone had come for treatment. Susie and John were a couple in their mid forties, from California. Suzie worked in real estate and John worked in high technology. Mohan, the Indian, came from Calcutta and was volunteering and teaching English in an orphanage there.

Master Buphendra, she learned from them, treated the patients using one of the ancient methods Indian healing: Ayurveda. Ayurveda was based on drinking herbal remedies and staying in a booth full of created by boiling herbs in water. Some medicinal plants grew in the Ashram's garden and others were brought from outside. Treatments were usually accompanied by a medical massage done with oils brewed on site.

Susie was recovering from breast cancer, Mohan had heart problems, and John had knee problems. He was also a devotee of Master Buphendra since he saw him seven years ago in California while Master was there giving a lecture on Ayurverdic treatments . Since then, John came regularly, at least once a year.

The Westerners were staying in nice-looking rooms in the Ashram. Later, she learned that they paid a considerable sum for their stay and treatment: about one hundred and fifty dollars per day, a huge amount of money in local terms. For the poor local people who come for treatment, such as Mohan, an appropriate amount of money is charged, and sometimes not charged at all.

She wondered whether that duality of values was derived from a set of values Master Buphendra believed in: taking from the rich and giving to the poor?

On the surface, it sounds good, she thought.

They waited for Master to arrive. He was still giving treatment. She wondered about the nature of the people who were sitting at the table. Susie was restless and with little peace of mind. She never stopped talking about this, that, or any other unimportant and uninteresting subjects. It was evident that she was crying out for attention from her husband, who refused to give her what she wanted. John, her husband, looked cold, alienated, and rather dorky, but full of self-importance. He held a senior position in one of the world's largest technology companies. It appeared that they played a regular game: she acted as a child in need of attention, and he played the bored, indifferent parent.

Yael was happy sitting next to Mohan. He revealed himself to be a fascinating conversation conductor. He was relatively young, thin, short, and shy, but his face gleamed with a constant smile. He was simple in appearance, but his manners were surprisingly educated and intelligent.

She asked him if he could explain to her more about the Ayurveda. He said that it was a healing method that had been practiced for over five thousand years, and was considered the "Mother of all healing methods." It was based on Vedic philosophy, which claimed that the entire universe was comprised of actions of energy and a mutual reaction of five major elements: space, air, fire, water, and earth.

"Have you heard the terms 'Vetta', 'Pitta' and 'Kapha'?" he asked, with an anxious, hopeful expression.

She had heard the words before. She answered affirmatively. He was thrilled to have found someone who was somewhat familiar with the subject and willing to listen.

"These three—Vetta, Pitta and Kapha—are different combinations and transformations that act on the five big elements. They appear as different patterns in each work of creation and can be attributed to the body's biology. For example, Vetta is a movement, Pitta is a changing metabolism, and Kapha provides the structure and lubrication needed by the body. A healthy person," he explained, "is a person in which these energies are balanced. Once the balance is broken, meaning, there is an over-dominance of one of these energies, a disease is formed," he said with a grin, "You see?"

Yael wondered if he really expected her to understand the concept just from his short explanation, but given his enthusiastic expression, she could not allow herself to let him down and she nodded her head positively. Encouraged, he went on to tell her about the place of Vethathiri Maharishi in Aliyar Pollachi. In this place, one could purchase Bio-Magnetic healing skills. Using these skills, he said, one could regenerate body cells. "There are saints", he said, "that by using mental power, could produce a substance in their brain that allowed them to sit in meditation for a long time without food and water, similar to the substance produced by a snake with a double tongue".

"The philosophy of this place", he then said, "is to get science closer to religion."

With even greater enthusiasm, he went on to quote Einstein. "Science without faith is lame; religion without science is blind."

He went on to argue that Einstein moved the Vedic philosophy toward science through his unified field theory, while Maharishi had merged science and philosophy into a single system of Jnana which portrayed how the primordial cause evolved into the present physical universe.

"This primordial cause", he explained, "which Maharishi calls 'pure space' or 'God', is both energy and consciousness, with an inherent quivering and a self-compressive surrounding force. The concept of a self-compressive surrounding force is missing in science, resulting in incompleteness in both".

It's hard to understand exactly what he's talking about, she thought and wondered how much Mohan was a man of science and how much of faith.

She always had an interest in physics and, and at the same time, in spiritual theories. She had some notion that human beings didn't use their full potential and abilities most of the time. This opinion was based on her own experience. When she was facing mental and physical challenges, she managed to concord them only when she was at her peak. The peak was characterized by a very high motivation, a lack of fear and full synchronization between body and mind. Her purpose in life, as she saw it, was to make things better, to get better, and constantly improve herself at whatever she could. It made her wonder if her current lifestyle was the right one for meeting her expectation.

Master Buphendra entered. Everyone stopped their conversation and got up from their seats, eyes turned to him. She was puzzled in light of their rising, but as a guest, she acted the same, albeit with a minor lag.

He invited all to sit down. He had come straight from a treatment; his clothes were still stained from the massage oil. It was clear that he was tired and drained, but along with it was very present and radiating vitality. He went to the sink on the side of the room, washed his hands, turned to the guests and, while wiping his hands asked, "Hello, Hello, how are you?"

He looked around the room at them. His gaze lingered on the new guest, Yael.

"How was your day?" he asked in a loud voice.

"Very fine," Yael replied.

"Did Sabitri work you too hard?" he joked.

"No, it was fine," she replied with a smile.

"Well, we must then speak to her so she will work you harder tomorrow," he said with an emphasis.

Everyone laughed. He sat, played with his beard, and corrected the cloth on his head that had granted him somewhat of an exotic look.

All sat back down.

Sabitri came in and out several times, bringing the pots, and set them in the center of the dining table close to Master Buphendra—too close, in Yael's opinion. He lifted the pot covers and checked the food. It was clear that he was pleased. He filled his plate generously, gave a brief greeting and started to eat.

With an open mouth, he bellowed "Sabitri! Where is the bread?"

Sabitri emerged quickly from the kitchen with a loaf of bread in her hand.

West – East, East – West

Yael felt uncomfortable that Sabitri didn't join them to eat. *I do, and she doesn't*, the thought bothered her. But being just a guest—a guest who wasn't paying for her stay—she didn't dare to ask why Sabitri didn't sit with them.

The castes in India were something that had occupied a small corner of her mind since she arrived here. She knew there were four main castes: the Brahmans, usually priests and teachers, the Kshatria—warriors and rulers, the Vaisia—farmers, merchants and artists, and the Sudra, who were usually the common workers. Under it all were the untouchables —the lowest caste.

Sabitri probably belongs to those who serve, the common workers, she thought. She had never felt so bothered by this system until now. *This woman saved me last night, and here I am, seated like a queen, while she's being treated as an unworthy inferior.* Her anger increased.

"What are you angry about?" Master's voice startled her.

For a brief moment, she was shaken. *How does he know I am angry?* She debated whether or not to speak openly.

"Well?" he prodded, "Are you going to share your thoughts with us or not?" his attitude and the tone of his voice pissed her off even more, and she decided to confront the issue.

"Well… I was wondering why Sabitri doesn't join us while we are eating."

All were silent. Master Buphendra stared at her.

"Well, seems to me that you have a lot to learn, young lady," he said quietly and then added, "You will have your lesson soon."

She wondered about the double meaning of his words, but not for long.

A strikingly attractive young Indian man had entered the room, catching everyone's attention, including Master's. She saw a spark in Master's eyes.

"Arjun!" he called with a loud voice.

The Young man approached Master. His soft, flexible and refined pace testified the body of an athlete. He carried himself with a confident stride, and although he demonstrated awe to Master, it was different from the awe of the others. Master stood up and hugged him.

"This is Arjun, my son!" he said with unconcealed pride, directing his announcement toward the Americans couples and especially to Susie. This was apparently her first time in the Ashram.

"I'm so happy to meet you. I've heard so much about you...that you are excelling in school and have high scores and that ..." Susie would have continued with in artificial smile if not interrupted by Master.

He turned to Arjun and asked with a soft voice, "You will eat with us, right?"

Arjun thanked him, but said he had already eaten, and he had to study for his exam.

Master assented, and then they exchanged a few sentences in Nepalese or Hindi that Yael could not understand.

The beauty of the young man fascinated her. He was absolutely stunning. Usually, when man captivated her, she avoided looking at him. But since all were following the conversation between father and son, even if they didn't understand what was being said, she felt it would be presumed as bad manners not to look at him.

Suddenly her heart started to beat faster. The son stole a glance at her while talking with his father. For that split second, she couldn't determine what he felt. His expression remained impassive. After talking briefly with his father, he turned to go, but not before politely saying goodbye to everyone. His gaze skipped her.

Master sat down and everyone went back to eating. Now she was even more curious about the father, after seeing the son. She was anxious to know more about Arjun, but Master Buphendra set the content and tone of conversation. He was going on about districts he wanted to talk about in impressively fluent English. He did not spare them his political and social opinions about the developments in India, the corruption, the accelerating economy and the lack of values among the younger generation, a generation that was pursuing the faulty Western culture.

"No offense—" he turned to John.

The American techie looked puzzled.

"None taken," he replied.

The conversation then turned to the younger generation. Suzie was interested to know how much time was left until Arjun graduated. Now seemed the appropriate time to ask about him.

"What is he studying?" asked Yael.

"Arjun is studying conventional medicine..." said Master, and added with a firm voice, "But it won't be long until he acknowledges the value of the Ayurverdic medicine, the traditional one." He continued, "In general, he is too much like me..." His words were said with an unconcealed pride, "...stubborn as a mule, and he has his own mind; nothing can be done."

He returned to talking about social issues while presenting a strong opinion regarding the modernization that only served to alienate people from spirituality. He turned to Mohan, as if he the latter represented the spiritual sector, and asked for his opinion.

Mohan, with a slight whimper voice, dared to say that Hinduism left plenty of room for adaptation and therefore he didn't see a conflict between tradition and modernization.

"Materialism is becoming more and more in demand and it is a byproduct of modernization, so can't you see the conflict?" Master Buphendra replied with a patronizing tone. He went on to argue that, "It is a destructive mistake, and because of this mistake, the pluralism in Hinduism evolved while false spiritual teachers had become corrupted, and they corrupted all in the name of religion."

He's so vain, Yael couldn't help but think.

But an interesting psychological issue was hidden behind his strong opinions: a generational gap and the struggle of the old to preserve itself against the new. He began to count the names of well-known spiritual teachers as well as less famous ones while passing criticism on each of them. Some of it sounded accurate, while others seemed to be more personal criticism than concrete. Again, being a guest in his Ashram, she didn't feel comfortable expressing opposing opinions. She realized that in front of her was seated someone who thought he knew better than anyone else does. He felt he knew what was good, what was right and wrong, and how the world should be conducted, and somehow her instinct—which later turned out to be true—told her not to challenge him.

The conversation was gradually taken over by politics and religious topics. Master Buphendra protested that, "The war between religions creates religious identity at the expense of the Indian national identity, and that all religious flags must be removed and only the national flag should remain. The government is pushing to eliminate the definition by caste, and that is done by omitting the caste indication from the name of the citizen."

"Also," he continued, "In universities and in workplaces, a quota of places is reserved for the lowest caste, but the sad result is that people do not meet the minimum requirements and still get in, while upper caste people do meet the requirements, and do not get in."

Vera entered the dining room. Yael was surprised to see that Master rose from his seat. Vera did not seem moved by the fact that he stood up. She apologized for being late and sat down. Master waited for her to sit and only then seated himself.

"How was it in the center?" he asked.

Now that she's gone, much better," Vera replied.

"I'm glad to hear that. You made the right decision, then."

"Apparently so," said Vera and added with a decisive tone, "Western aggression is sometimes useful in a place like India."

Yael looked at Master, curious to see what his reaction would be to a statement that contradicted his strong opinions about the East's faulty pursuit of Western culture. His answer surprised her.

"Sometimes, yes, you're right, it helps," he agreed in a moderate tone.

"For every job, one must pull out the right tools from the box!" Vera replied.

Yael was curious and wanted to know what they were talking about.

Master Buphendra then introduced the two. Vera was a seventy-three-year-old yoga instructor from Sydney, and had been there for several months. It was her third visit to Master. She, like the others, also suffered from medical problems of which she avoided to specify any details. She said she was volunteering at a center for girls in distress, and that it turned out that the woman who ran the center was corrupted, and abused the girls. Vera had exposed the problematic conduct of the principal and had begun a series of actions to kick her out. Master had served as a consultant in this matter and had also pulled some strings when he could.

Well, thought Yael, *his personality is more complex than I thought.*

Vera seemed like an impressive character to Yael—a tough woman without an easy personality, but very remarkable. Her cool conduct with the young Russian man that was questionably penniless had been very impressive.

When they finished dinner, Yael suddenly remembered Sabitri, who she hadn't seen during the last hour, and she wondered where she'd gone. When she asked about her, Master replied that she had already left for home and she would return the next day. Yael wondered if, in light of Sabitri's absence, she had to clear the table.

Master Buphendra, as if he can read her thoughts again replied, "Tonight you are free to go to sleep."

"Ravindra!" he called loudly.

An Indian man entered the room. He looked to be in his thirties, short, but with a very strong and solid body. He was slightly balding, what was very unusual in India, and a black mustache decorated his face.

"This is my assistant, Ravindra," said Master and then said something in Nepalese to him. He then turned back to Yael.

"Ravindra, meet Yael," Ravindra nodded. "Hello, nice to meet you…you go now to sleep?" he asked in slightly broken English.

"I will retire to bed as well. Good night!" said Master Buphendra. He said goodbye to everyone and turned to leave. All rose from their chairs when he left. Again, she lagged slightly behind in rising. All remained standing as he departed. She didn't like the gesture one bit.

Ravindra began clearing the table. Everyone approached her and said good night and expressed their pleasure in meeting her.

She retired to her room, reluctantly. There, alone, she would have to deal with thoughts about the past again, with all that had happened when all she desired was to forget, to escape for a while...

Imagine an Opponent

"Hajime!" Zoe's voice boomed.

Two by two, the trainees entered the display area to present their Kata. They would be tested on this series of movements in the upcoming "Special Training."

"Peter and Yael," Zoe's voice yelled. Yael looked at Peter and took a deep breath. They entered the room. It was very stressful to perform the Kata while everyone was watching. The other trainees were sitting on the benches around the area and waiting for the "show."

Yael found it difficult to concentrate after the incident at home. At least they hadn't been hurt and Eyal was fine.

"Yael and Peter will now perform Basai," Zoe announced, This Kata, translated as "penetrating the fortress," might earn them their black belt in 'Special Training', if performed well.

They bowed and began. It was very helpful to perform the Kata with another person, but all of a sudden, Peter had a black out, forgetting some movements.

Concentrate on the Kata, Yael thought while continuing, *and be precise in your movements...*

Peter pulled himself together and they completed.

"A Kata is not just a collection of defenses and attacks," explained Zoe, and, in response to the puzzled expressions on the trainees' faces, she added, "A Kata is the choreography of a battle against an imaginary opponent."

She turned to Yael. "It's not a dance class!"

"Hai!" assented Yael in Japanese, a bit embarrassed.

Zoe then turned to Peter. "With you, Peter...Something in the technique is lacking. If you stand like this during an attack—" she reproduced an instable stance, "—the opponent doesn't need much to get you off balance or take you down."

Hai!" responded Peter.

"Attack me!" Zoe turned back to Yael.

With what? Yael asked, "A punch? A kick?"

"With whatever you want, go ahead!"

Yael stood in starting position and then aimed a kick at Zoe's stomach. Zoe calmly and lightly stepped aside

"Again! Imagine a real opponent," she egged Yael on, "someone whose ass you'd like to kick. Then come at me again."

Yael returned to starting position. This time, she was in a battle stance. A feeble image rose in her mind and transformed to the senior officer, followed by the masked man. She wasn't sure whose ass she would like to kick more.

The masked man was frightening and threatened her existence, but the mocking officer, who was almost even more surreal than the actual gang who broke in, was completely incoherent when questioning her and Eyal later on. There had been something was careless and uncaring about him...

Could she have done something to prevent them for hurting Eyal?

Zoe, interrupting her thoughts, signaled her to attack. The image of the masked phony lame took over, and this time, armed with raged, she forged ahead with a stronger kick. But instead of the expected impact, her body mass had bumped into nothing. She was so determined to hit Zoe that she had miscalculated the distance. Zoe's evasive agility had helped her avoid Yael's kick, and Yael lost her balance and landed on the ground. Zoe was already on top of her with a fist to Yael's face—a fist that stopped before the edge of Yael's nose with amazing accuracy.

"Excess of motivation and uncontrollable anger is often our destruction," Zoe explained and reached out with her hand, helping Yael to rise up, "When we strike the opponent, we must channel both the motivation and the energy that follows the strike accurately."

She signaled to Yael to return to the rest of the trainees and continued, "An attack with no control is doomed to fail. We do not want to win the battle; we are interested in not losing. Do you understand the difference? When you concentrate on not losing instead of winning, you develop a less agitated attitude and you can read the opponent facing you correctly."

She turned around, pausing for a moment. It seemed as if she was considering how to continue the lesson. Again, memories of the incident surfaced into Yael's mind. She thought about her reactions.

I had no agitated attitude...However, my motivation was maybe too little, but what the hell could I do when a fork was aimed at Eyal's neck? And how had they gotten in?

The police had explained their theory. When she went into the bathroom, Eyal had left the apartment to buy food for Spike (*The food I did not buy,* she thought with guilt) and they had followed Eyal back.

"I want to do an exercise," Zoe interrupted her thought. "Line up in two lines facing each other and then kneel down in Seiza."

The trainees squatted down. "Seiza" was not well-liked in the West. The pelvis rested with all its weight on unnaturally-stretched feet. It was a pose that created both pressure and enormous pain. Most Westerners, if any, were not able to sit more than two minutes in this position.

"Inhale and exhale slowly, take another breath, and then let the air out. Now look carefully at the person in front of you," said Zoe "and keep on looking; do not let your eyes stray."

Yael was facing Daniel. There was something a little embarrassing in having to look into another person's eyes. It felt too intimate, she thought. After about thirty shaky seconds, Zoe's voice interrupted the silence.

"Close your eyes!"

She turns off the lights, leaving the room in darkness.

"Now, with your eyes closed, each check what you still see about the person facing you," she said. Yael was surprised – in the dark, the outlines of Daniel figure continue to appear very clearly in her mind, despite her closed eyes.

"The opponent is there, even if you do not see him or her; you need to know how to feel it, not just by relying on your immediate senses," Zoe explained, and instructed them to continue for a few more seconds.

Questions about the break-in continued to haunt Yael. *There, on the stairs, they ambushed Eyal. Were they waiting especially for him? Or would any neighbor who had happened to be there been ambushed?*

The indifferent senior officer hadn't had an answer.

"Now, all of you facing the windows, get close enough to those facing you and extend your hand towards them just enough so the tips of your fingers are touching them."

Yael felt Daniel's hand brush the tip of her nose. Zoe instructed them to adjust their position until their hand could reach the other person's face.

"This is the exercise. As soon as you feel that the person facing you is going to attack, indicate it by letting out a soft shout to stop the attacker," instructed Zoe. "This will be done in the dark and with eyes closed," she added.

And how will I know when the hand is coming out without seeing? This is crazy! Thought Yael.

"Ready? Each of the attackers will start at his or her own pace, but take your time. Allow enough time for the defenders to study your stillness and the coming change."

Silence.

Yael thought back to the break-in again. *They attacked him and stunned him with an anesthetic. Eyal had said that anyone that worked with this anesthetic had to have a higher level of sophistication not common in everyday street criminals.*

One of the trainees rushed into an attack and a shout was heard. It sounded like the shout of someone being injured, not of someone who had managed to prevent the attack.

Concentrate, Yael, she reprimanded herself and breathed deeply, trying to oppress thoughts about the incident unsuccessfully. But since that event, whenever silence was present, or it was dark, or it was bedtime, she played the entire event over and over in her mind, attempting to crack it, to clarify what was going on.

What had happened, and how? Why? Why didn't it add up? *They found the key which they probably couldn't have done without Bobby's help, dragged Eyal back to the apartment, and tied him up.*

Whoosh!

Daniel's hand landed on her chin. A moment's lack of concentration and she had missed the coming attack. Her chin throbbed with pain.

Silence.

The pain did its job. Soon all of her senses were sharpened and focused. A rustle of fabric was heard in front of her.

"Aahh!" she shouted softly, signaling Daniel that she sensed he was about to attack.

Stillness.

Around her, the movements of the fabric of other trainees could be heard, followed by soft shouts.

What could I have done? Could I have attacked them? Who could I have attacked? The phony lame in the mask? The man with the dreadlocks? Why didn't I do something? Anything?

A rustle could be heard again, immediately followed by the blow. An agony poured into her. She had completely lost her concentration and was hit again.

Black Out

"Yame!" yelled Zoe to stop, and the lights turned back on.

Daniel wanted to assure that Yael was okay. Yes, she was fine, she assured. A small stream of blood flowed from her upper lip.

"On your feet, everyone!" ordered Zoe. Everyone rose, blinking because of the lights. Some trainees found it difficult to stand after kneeling for so long. Zoe, with a thundering voice, reprimanded them.

"Guys! You should be doing exercises to increase your flexibility. We'll squat a lot in Special Training."

Daniel and Peter, who were among those who had difficulties standing, didn't seem encouraged by her words.

"We're finished for today!" announced Zoe, "And remember, imagine an opponent!" she added.

"How's it going, Blondie?" Peter exuberated while approaching her, limping slightly, still not recovered from the prolonged kneeling.

"Fine, what about you?" She smiled weakly at him, "Did you recover from the Seiza?"

She looked down at his feet.

"It sucks!" sighed Peter, "but great practice, wasn't it?"

"Definitely!" Yael agreed as they took off the tops of their training suit, "And where did Daniel disappear to?" she asked, scanning the practice hall from end to end, looking for him.

"Maybe he went to the bathroom to wet his knee. The poor guy probably didn't have fun in Seiza either with his knee problem," Peter responded.

Daniel could be seen approaching with something white in his hand from across the room. It was a wet bandage. He handed it over to Yael and asked her how her injured lip was doing.

"It's okay, I'm really fine, just a bit of lack of concentration," she said.

Daniel nodded as if to say that he understood. He knew about the incident. She had immediately called him that night after the police left and told him what had happened right after calling Jennifer.

"Well, how did you like the exercise?" Peter asked Daniel.

"I liked it a lot," replied Daniel while looking at Yael as if trying to assess her well-being.

"And your knee didn't bother you?" asked Peter.

"A bit," admitted Daniel, still looking at Yael.

He was quick to change the topic and started telling them about a time when the entire class, led by Zoe, was done in the dark and they had to deal with an attack coming from behind. The methods Zoe used were not always methods that were accepted by the organization. She was different, unusual, but in spite of her out-of-the-box methods, she was much appreciated.

"Say, how did we manage to get her?" Yael asked, and as she looked at Peter, added, "I thought she wasn't going to teach anymore."

Peter was always the one who knew everything about everyone.

"Why do you think so?" he asked.

"Because I overheard her conversation with Sensei Malcolm in our last practice, and she said something about leaving."

"No! That's not it," Peter rushed to explain, "Zoe was asked to sit at the examiner's desk in the upcoming Special Training, and she doesn't want to."

"Oh, they were speaking about that?" Yael was relieved.

"Yeah, and are you prepared for Special Training next week? Did you know we get up at 4:30 every morning and run five miles just to warm up?" asked Peter, as if provoking.

"Well, you know, it doesn't sound as much fun. I'm not really into running," she admitted.

"That's why you didn't call to schedule running together?" Peter teased.

Yael and Daniel looked at each other briefly again. As opposed to Daniel, Peter knew nothing about the incident.

"Well," she said, a bit lost for words, "Not because of that...I was pretty busy."

Daniel rushed to rescue, respecting her decision not to say anything. "Anyway, we should all get into a running mode, otherwise it won't be easy," he said.

They left the training room and walked to the subway station. They agreed to run together on Sunday during the coming weekend at River Side Park, the day before Special Training.

"I'll walk with her tonight," said Daniel to Peter.

Peter said goodbye to them and left. As soon as he was gone, they found a bench and sat down to talk.

"The police found out," she told him the latest news, "that the burglars acted in a similar way to a gang who is responsible for a series of thefts. The gang always had the same method: they hooked up with the Super of the building who knew who lived in which apartment, and he let them into the building. Then, they would ambushed tenants in the stairwell, blindfolded them, forced them into their apartments and threatened them to give up their valuables, money, etc. Then they would disappear down the fire escape. By the time the tenants could call the police, they would already be gone."

"But it makes no sense," said Daniel. He agreed with Eyal's argues that the use of anesthetic substances was too sophisticated for petty street crooks. "If you go through all this trouble, why an apartment on your street, the 'Injection Street', and not in a more prestigious place? What is there to take, after all? Bobby must've known you guys didn't keep diamonds or anything like that. And in the end, they only took some documents?

"Right. Not to mention that Eyal was threatened with a fork...they didn't even have a proper knife," she added.

"Maybe they're on drugs and don't always think clearly," Daniel suggested. "Maybe they're nervous about something."

He was interested to know if she thought that the phony lame had followed her from the subway just before the break-in. Yael said that, contrary to the senior officer who insisted he did, she was quite sure he hadn't followed her and that he never saw which building she entered.

115

The officer also said that several undercover police officers were after the phony lame.

"So what took them so long, for these policemen to get to your apartment? You could've gotten hurt, meanwhile," insisted Daniel.

"Yes, the senior officer said we were luckily we got off the hook, and that if it is indeed the gang he was thinking of, they often harmed their victims."

Daniel seemed puzzled.

"On top of it, another thing is weird," said Yael, continuing, "You see, when I gave their description, it didn't completely match the description of the phony lame they had from other victims. He didn't have a cracked lip like I noticed, and there were no reports of him wearing a mask"

"Did you notice the cracked lip in the subway, too?"

"No, there was a problem with the lights on the subway, so it kept switching from light to dark, and he was too far away," she said, "but the work method of hooking up with a local super and the presence of the dreadlocks guy—these do match" she added.

"Hmm ...very strange," Daniel was thoughtful.

"Yes, there are a lot of questions, it's puzzling, no doubt about that," she agreed.

"What did they say at work about the documents?" he asked.

"Oh! Nothing really. Apparently, my boss had a copy of the folder and the important financial information was encrypted, anyways," she paused, "You see, in a company like the one I work for, they don't take any chances..."

"Did the police investigate a link to whoever you were supposed to meet with the next morning? Maybe these crooks were looking for information on him?"

"That was exactly my thought, but no! Neither the police nor my company thought there was a link. The police think that since they didn't find anything valuable, and this was the only thing that seemed of a value since it was labeled 'Confidential' and had plenty of financial information, maybe they thought to intimidate me with it."

"Yeah, right." said Daniel, a cynical tone in his voice, "That's a bit stupid, don't you think? Eyal was in chains, unconscious, with a fork to his throat, and a folder would have intimated you?"

"Yes, exactly. It's weird," Yael agreed.

They sighed lengthily, rose up from the bench and walked toward Yael's street.

They ran into a beggar asking for change at the corner. Despite her firm protest, Daniel insisted on accompanying her to the building's entrance. There, before they parted, he unexpectedly spread his hands to embrace her, maybe to ease her sense of security. His embrace felt good. They stayed locked together for a minute. Then they said a rather confused goodbye.

She entered the apartment hesitant to see Eyal. The way she saw it, he was in danger that night because of her. She felt guilty. And now, she also felt guilty because of Daniel. She felt it had been more than a casual, friendly hug.

Psychology of a Steam Sauna

The next day, she woke up very late. She jumped up in panic from her bed, wondering why Sabitri didn't wake her up to help with the work. She recalled hearing a rooster crow while still asleep at dawn. She dressed quickly, washed her face, brushed her teeth, and went to look for Sabitri. But Sabitri was nowhere to be found. In the back garden, she ran into Ravindra grinding plants and putting them into a huge tank. She greeted him with the blessing of a good morning and he returned her greeting with a big smile. She asked him if he had seen Sabitri. With broken English, he replied that Sabitri didn't work that day, only the next.

"Is something wrong?" she dreaded hearing the answer.

"No, no!" he reassured her, "she comes only three times a week."

"So what about the food? The cooking?" she asked.

He signaled her to follow him into the kitchen and showed her that there was plenty of food. She discovered that she and Sabitri had cooked for two days. Obviously, he was surprised in light of her question because he knew that she had helped Sabitri with the work.

I'm not coming across as very bright, she thought.

"Where is Master?" she changed the subject.

"Upstairs, treatments." Ravindra replied with a smile.

She liked him already. *What a pleasant guy*, she thought. She asked him if she could help.

"No, no. Kutan is helping me," he said, and pointed with his finger toward another Indian man who had just entered the kitchen. "He is one of the staff," he explained.

"Okay," she said, "I'll just watch."

Ravindra had to prepare a steam sauna of medicinal herbs for Suzie. She sat next to him while he ground plants and prepared the big tank for boiling. He began preparing the wood for kindling. She was intrigued by the simple, basic means he used—work that in the modern world could be done with a simple turn of a knob—and watched with a renewed amazement.

The idea that the drugs were made there from scratch was very appealing to her. She remembered shelves upon shelves loaded with drugs packed in plastic containers being picked up like fresh rolls in a pharmacy. There was something very soothing about the natural preparation process. The experience of seeing the whole process, the formation from start to end, the use of the most basic, most primary means to perform the requested tasks, filled her, for some reason, with calmness and joy. It was the complete opposite of what characterized the States: efficiency, rapid processing, no delays, the shortening of the gap between supply and demand. All of these were reflected in every consumer experience she had back at home, from ordering coffee to buying or returning electronic goods, furniture, computers, or clothing. In New York, she felt this was the only way things should and could operate. It was funny—or rather sad—how any slight deviation from the time-pressed norm used to bring her stress, frustration, and even agony.

For making oil, which was used by Master in his treatments, they gathered the relevant medicinal plants and squeezed their juice by hand. In order to do so, they took a number of wooden logs, lit a fire, poured water into a huge pot that resembled a Chinese wok, and placed this pot over a fire to boil. They put the plants in the boiling water and continued to boil until the plants turned black and they shrunk. Ravindra then put a white cloth, used as a filter, on top of a metal bucket. He held the fabric in such way that it was stretched at the edges, but has a little belly directed toward the depths of the bucket, where Kutan spilled the black mixture previously boiled in the pot. After pouring the mixture extremely carefully so as not to leave anything on the sides of the pot, Ravindra and Kutan took sort of a device, composed of two parallel boards tied up with a rope as a kind of improvised clamp. Ravindra held the side that was tied to the rope in his left hand and the cloth with the mixture in his right hand. At the same time, Kutan pressed the two boards against each other and a magnificent juicer was revealed at work. Black oil filled up the bucket. After they extorted the last drop, Ravindra created a ball made of the cloth that contained the mixture that remained after the extortion. He tied a rope at the edge of the cloth ball and tied it to another rope hanging from a tree. They then laid the metal bucket under the cloth-ball, allowing the remaining oil to drip into the bucket.

There was an opening in the lower part of the big tank from which a pipe, which was inserted into the tank, came out. They tucked a towel and nylon to seal this opening around the pipe. The pipe was later inserted into the steam cabin, a cabin built out of branches.

It was all so simple, so basic, and yet very effective.

Susie arrived an hour later, apparently after a massage and oil treatment. Only a colored cloth that absorbed the oil on her skin covered her body. On the exposed parts—her face, neck and arms—Yael could make out the remaining signs of the massage in spots of red skin. She was concerned about entering the sauna cabin, and with a nervous tone she said that she suffered from claustrophobia and that she wasn't going to go in the sauna but would rather wait for Master.

When Master Buphendra arrived, it seemed she asked for more than just encouragement, but rather for a deep mental support. Master Buphendra was willing to provide what she wanted and somewhat tenderly encouraged her to enter the sauna, convincing her the good it would do her. Her hysteria intensified. For all, it was quite embarrassing to see a woman in her mid-forties acting like a scared little child.

Master Buphendra turned tougher and tougher. It became more and more dramatic and surreal as the minutes passed. In a yard somewhere in northern India stood a grown Western woman, weeping and hysterical, wearing nothing but an oil-soaked cloth. A tall Indian man wearing an intense orange color traditional dress was trying to calm her down while the entire scene was being watched by two locals and one foreigner—Yael. The weeping didn't ease and Master decided to try another strategy. He raised his voice and demanded she pull herself together. When that didn't help, he cursed and finally moved to heavy criticism about the way she was conducting herself, both in the present moment and in life in general. Yael found herself watching a scene that the greatest psychologists would have been happy to take part in it.

It was clear that he felt very comfortable being in that position. Susie, in turn, tried to make excuses for herself and defend her tear-soaked behavior. She brought up traumatic events from her childhood and tried, without success, to justify why a rational person should not go alone into a stuffy, dark cabin. As time passed, she seemed to give up her resistance, retreating one by one from the reasons why she couldn't go into the cabin.

This is a slap in the face to all psychoanalytic therapy, cognitive or even symptomatic, Yael thought to herself.

The tactic adopted was so simple and primitive, but it proved itself. A tough hand, charisma, and the application of an unquestionable authority seemed to do the trick.

Susie gradually became relaxed and agreed to enter the cabin as long as Master stayed nearby. She had to stay inside for about forty-five lengthy minutes. Master promised to stick around for those forty-five minutes. Susie went in.

He then began to talk about Ayurveda medicine. He praised the treatment of the herbal sauna.

"Why do you go into the sauna smeared with oil on your body?" asked Yael.

He replied that the idea was to sweat hard, to the point that the skin pores were opened, so the steam of the medicinal plants could seep into the body with ease.

"The Patient," he explained, "is covered with hot oil and enters the sauna sweating. The sweat cannot permeate the skin since it's blocked by the oil, and the result is that it forces the body to sweat even more. As the body sweats more, more toxins leave."

Despite his promise to Suzie to stay nearby while she was in the cabin, he left after several minutes. Yael turned to Ravindra and Kutan and asked in a whisper what would happen when she found out he had left. They responded dismissively, and it seemed that they were used to see him leaving in similar situations.

He promises one thing, but allows himself to break the promise, she thought, and no one seems to be bothered by it. It's probably typical of him.

Yael wondered if this scene had contributed even more to the bad image of the spoiled, anxious and hysterical Westerners Master had already had. The thought made Yael feel even more embarrassed than before.

She spent the rest of the day primarily writing. She kept a travel diary documenting experiences and thoughts. The trip started to feel more like a journey. She found great pleasure in going back to simply writing on paper. Back home—if it was still home—everything was done digitally. Right after the collapse of the towers, she was sitting for so many hours every day in front of the computer, designing a web site for Jennifer, writing a story for her, hoping to give it to her as a reconciliation gift...

But I can't think about Jennifer, now, she thought. *What the hell had happened? Was she involved?*

No. She couldn't think about it, didn't want to think about it...

She looked down at the scrambled words on the page. Images from the past had surfaced into her mind. She tried to remove them. If there was something she didn't want to deal with, it was the past. But it was hopeless, as she kept returning over and over again to her own Ground Zero—the scattering of bills.

How could she have managed to miss him - Chris-Daoud Khan, the only person, except Jennifer, who could have given her the answers and solved the mystery? These questions tormented her, and attempts to concentrate on the 'here and now' were unsuccessful. Events from the past kept surfacing, although scattered, but connected to each other. However, she failed to understand the common ground, to hit the essence—the core of all the events. She sensed something was linking them, but couldn't find the missing link. She felt she was going around and around in circles. She got tired.

Bedroom Secrets

"We're going down in a few minutes! Ready?" one of her colleagues peered through the door to warn her.

"No problem, I'll start to wrap things up," Yael replied, smiling. There were about to go out and celebrate a year of her being a part of the company. It was supposed to happen two weeks earlier, but was postponed every time for other reasons.

I think I'll allow myself to drink a little bit tonight, especially in light of recent events, and the fact we got lucky and unharmed, Yael thought.

Kristen, who had just returned from one of her business trips, entered Yael's office.

"How's Eyal?" she was interested to know.

"Fine, thank you! He's already been back at work for the past week since it happened," Yael informed her. "How did it go with the police investigation? Any news?"

"Nothing much," said Kristen, "They were just looking for something that will help them to catch those guys,"

"And…? Did they find anything?"

"Nope!" replied Kristen, not elaborating, as usual.

"I'm glad to hear Eyal is doing fine," she said and added, "The meeting with Chris-Daoud Khan is this coming Thursday. This time, I hope it won't be cancelled." She smiled, "We are so lucky he cancelled that day, aren't we?"

Yael nodded in agreement. *We're more lucky Kristen had a copy of his file,* she thought.

She was a bit surprised that Kristen had taken it so well. After all, confidential data about a client was stolen.

"Be prepared!" advised Kristen, and continued with an apologetic tone, "Yael, unfortunately I can't join you and the guys tonight. Jane and I have an important meeting with clients and we can't move it, so we'll go out just the three of us on a different night. Is that alright?" she asked.

"Of course," Yael replied, hiding her disappointment.

"Ready?" her colleague called from across the hall.

Kristen left and her colleague's head peaked out from around the door.

"Is your friend coming?"

"Who? Jennifer? No, she can't."

As she spoke, her cell phone rang. It was Jennifer, of course.

"This is her on the line! Give me a second, I'll be right there!" she told him, answering the call.

"Ok, but hurry up, they're all ready to go," he said before his head disappeared.

"Hey Jennifer!"

"Yael, what's up? How's Eyal?" asked Jennifer in a weak voice.

"Recovering, but ok."

After the incident, she had immediately called Jennifer and told her what had happened. Jennifer offered her sympathy, but Yael felt that she was somehow distanced and not as supportive as usual. Could it have been because of the evening when they went out to the Village? And what had actually happened in the club?

"Jenny, is everything all right?"

"Yes, yes ..." Jennifer replied weakly, and added, "I'm going away for a few days."

Yael could sense Jennifer's usual eagerness to travel wasn't present in her voice.

"Yael, we're going down now!" her colleague called her.

"Jenny, I got to go, they're all waiting for me. Call me, will you? Let's meet when you're back!"

They hung up and she joined her colleague, slightly annoyed by being interrupted in her short conversation with Jennifer. The boisterous group was heading to a nearby bar, where they would raise a toast to Yael.

They were seated and making quite a lot of noise. Everyone had arrived already with the exception of Kristen and Jane. She was a bit hesitant to join the conversation. Among all the bustle and noise at the bar, she would surely miss a lot of what was being said. She'd have to make a very big effort to understand the conversational slang. Too often, she felt left out. She waited a few seconds and then elegantly rose from her seat, taking her empty glass with her, "I'll be right back guys," she said and went to the bar. To her surprise, Max stepped into the bar.

Max, the third partner, was a New York Jew, originally from Brooklyn whom, although non-orthodox, had attended a Yeshiva like most Jewish children. The greater his financial skills and ability to acquire new clients were, however, the greater his personal problems. Max was single, but not by choice. It had been a while since he turned forty and this bothered him. He was heavy, with a belly that grew every day, lived alone, and found it very hard to develop friendships and, more over, a romantic relationship. The few friends he had were from work, Work filled most of his time and his world. With no other choice, his dating life had thinned to phone conversations with call girls. Once he even dared to invite one over. It was both the first and the last time, probably due to the echo of his mother's voice in his mind that chided how improper it was for a Jewish boy from a good home to be in contact with a "Shiksa" who sold sex for "greens."

Yael's friend Joy, a Canadian law student, had told this to her. Joy worked evenings as a dispatcher in an escort agency. Through her friend's work in the agency, an entirely unknown world was revealed to Yael. Yael also knew exactly what had happened during Max's rendezvous with Anna, the bleached-blonde Russian escort who had gone to his apartment. She had shown up in her usual attire: black leather lingerie, high red boots, equipped with a whip and all the appropriate accessories. Anna said that Max had requested that she dominated him. Her scolding and repetition that he was a "bad boy" had probably reminded him of all the times he had run away from the Yeshiva to the school of the Gentiles, all those times he had stared through the tree branches at the "Shiksa" girls studying side-by-side with the boys, all the times he wished he could be with them, full of envy, lust, frustration...So she pulled out a whip and warned him that if

125

he didn't speed up, she'd use it. Exhausted, he couldn't crawl any longer. And maybe he wanted her to whip him, after all. The first lash landed on his back. The second lash landed on his exposed, naked butt. He asked her to order him to take off his clothes. She had ordered him to take off his shirt, but he pretended as if he did not hear it. Maybe because he was embarrassed by his big belly, maybe it was because the office-style buttoned-shirt was the only reminder of his professional success, despite his personal failure.

Yael had begged Joy to stop telling her the details of the evening. True, her curiosity was great, but it was too much and too humiliating.

"He's one of the partners in the company I work for. He's my boss. How can I take him seriously after hearing all of these despicable descriptions?"

Joy, eager to tell the whole story with all its juicy details, insisted on continuing and told Yael that she had asked Anna how it ended, if there had been any "action" or not.

"No, the evening ended with some whip caresses on Max's groin..." She quoted Anna.

"Enough! I don't want to hear anymore of it!" protested Yael. The image of the whip on Max's genitals was not particularly pleasant for her. Joy had burst in laughter.

"What are you thinking about so much? Work?" Max's question shook her back to the present.

What timing...Now, of all times, he decides to talk to me?

"Yeah, right!" she replied sarcastically, "All work and no play, and Jack becomes a dull boy." she fired out, happy to remember the saying. But then a fear sunk her enthusiasm. Maybe he would assume she was referring to him as Jack, knowing that he had no life outside of the office? But his reply relieved her.

"All play and no work makes Jack a mere toy," he added with a smile.

"And what is the only other Jew in the company working on? Is it Chris-Daoud Khan's case?" he wanted to know.

126

"Yes. It looks interesting. I understand we got to him through you. How do you know him?"

"Well, actually, it was Kristen's lead," said Max, looking a bit disappointed he couldn't take the credit himself.

"Oh! I thought Kristen said we got to him through you!" said Yael, surprised.

"Well, Kristen arranged that I will attend a financial conference of oil companies about a year ago. She told me about him and that he can be a heavy client we should get, so I met him there and we talked about professional matters. I was trying to get closer to him, but it wasn't successful, and then we ran into each other in a Seder organized by the Anti-Definition League for all kinds of supporters of Israel. I was quite surprised to see him there. Although he didn't really want to reveal any personal details, he mentioned his mother was Jewish, but Kristen thought you'd be a better choice to handle his case since he was somewhat distanced with me."

"So how did Kristen get to him to begin with?" Yael was curious; maybe she would learn something new from his reply about spotting new potential clients.

"I have no idea," he said, smiling, "Kristen is full of surprises," he paused for a second and added, "and secrets."

"An excellent business woman and a great partner, despite of the fact she is a Christian," he grinned and continued, "She knows how to smell business opportunities from afar. If we can have him as a client – it'd be awesome!"

"So, from what you know about him, it wasn't problematic for him being an Arab whose mother was Jewish?"

"He was able to harness it for his own benefits," said Max and waved to the bartender to fill up his glass. "In his country he's a Muslim, and in the West he's a Jew. Just think about it. It opens many doors and a lot of business opportunities on both sides of the globe."

"So how does he see himself? A Jew or Muslim?" she asked.

"Like I said, depends on where he is."

"Interesting," said Yael, thinking about how she could use that information to their advantage.

A woman in her forties approached the bar and sat in the empty seat next to them. She was heavy and looked educated. She ordered a red wine and smiled at Max. It seemed that she was trying to understand the nature of the relationship between Yael and Max. The age difference between them seemed even bigger because of his size and his belly. Max smiled back at her, noticing that Yael had spotted her and that she spotted Yael. Yael thought that it was a good time to clear the area and re-join her loud co-workers at the tables.

In the short intervals in which she allowed herself to rest from the effort of listening to her colleagues, she watched Max and the woman. They looked like they were groping each other. Effort, mixed with embarrassment, was evident on Max's face. Beads of sweet ran down his beat-red face.

Oh, No. This isn't pretty... Let's hope for his sake, she won't run away...

Chris-Daoud Khan

She and Kristen were waiting for Chris-Daoud Khan in his
luxurious Han Oil Ventures office located in the Twin Towers. From
the window of the forty-seven floor, the entire city spread out below.
The city looked like a multi-armed monster, cold and calculated. All of
the streets branched out and met at 90-degree angles, street to an
avenue, street to street, alley to alley, as if built by a gigantic machine.
The symmetry, straight angles, and constant construction of huge
buildings with such inhuman dimensions was astonishing.

So many transactions were being formed at that very moment.
Financial forces drove the wheels, the stock market rose, money
exchanged hands, thousands of transfers of real or fictitious properties
were occurring. In the world she lived in, it seemed that everything is
driven by financial wheels. Among the monstrous arms of the concrete
jungle, there was a constant movement of people, cars, trains, buses,
planes, gatherings in galleries, theatres, restaurants, halls,
schools—organized chaos tucked away in drawers of a rocking,
metropolitan closet. She had the feeling that any day something might
explode. It couldn't be that such a small island could tolerate all the
abuse. Every day, sophisticated machines were digging and turning
roads and streets inside out. The clods of revealed earth reminded her
that, once upon a time, a true land had been there, a land of sand and
dirt. Now, it was covered with gray concrete, and beneath it, an entire
world existed—pipes spread across the length and width of the island,
streaming water, electricity, steam, sewage, and all types of
communication lines. It was a world that had only one purpose: to
answer to all of its growing, expanding needs.

At some point, some time, something is going to happen. Every day
her sense of fear intensified.

"Good morning, ladies," the multi-millionaire tycoon, Chris-Daoud
Khan, entered the room.

Both Yael and Kristen rose from their seats and exchanged
handshakes with him. He seemed quite short standing next to Kristen,

who was blessed with generous height. They complemented his beautiful office, and he said that it was too expensive and that his brother was determined he would leave it before summer. He then invited them to sit in a spacious sitting area near the window, which Yael thought was a good sign. Seated, relaxed corners that resembled private living rooms created a less formal and more comfortable atmosphere. It was a sign that he saw their meeting on a more personal level.

Chris-Daoud Khan's appearance was very meticulous. He wore a custom-made expensive suit, the light, refined scent of an expensive perfume wafted off of him, and his black hair and mustache were carefully trimmed. All of his appearance and scrupulously polite conduct indicated that he was among the social elite. However, he chose to continue the informal atmosphere even when they discussed the investment options available to him. He seemed like a considerate man, not in a hurry to jump into high-risk financial ventures, even if the potential profit could have been huge.

But despite his relaxed mannerisms, Yael found it very difficult to figure him out. Eventually, the informal atmosphere he had created played into his own hands. It created a sort of safe haven for him where he allegedly revealed a lot but hid more than what he revealed. Even Kristen, who had demonstrated a remarkable ability to read potential clients during many meetings and had become a role model for the rest in the office, seemed to be groping in the dark this time.

Yael wondered if the fog surrounding Chris-Daoud Khan was connected to the fact that he was such a cultural mixture of Muslim, American, and Jew. She felt that there was something divided about him. When Kristen asked about his hobbies, he seemed to draw back, as if afraid to be caught off guard. Then, when Kristen threw out the fact that Yael was both Israeli and a Jew, he showed an increasing interest in this matter and wanted to know more. Kristen, who always went straight to the point, didn't seem to mind that the conversation was drifting away from the business, but also seemed to encourage it.

Yael recalled that he was interested in investments of more of a "green" nature from his personal portfolio. She had done her homework and brought up some suggestions. He seemed interested—that was the signal for Kristen to come into play, and from that moment on, he was hers. She managed to get him interested in a startup company that dealt with research and the development of technology that would generate energy using environmentally friendly means.

"No," she said when she felt his hesitation, "it will not contradict your conventional energy business in oil. It will, eventually, however, help to break into markets that are interested in green energy that today you have no access to."

"My brother, unfortunately, is not interested in environmental awareness companies," Chris-Daoud Khan admitted, almost complaining, "but I will try to persuade him, if you provide me with the economic data statistics".

Yael was interested to know how he had become more environmentally conscientious. Kristen seemed a bit concerned that it might be too much of a personal question, but this time, it seemed he was willing to share. He went on to say that a few years ago, he had a kidney problem that conventional medicine couldn't fix. Searched everywhere for an alternative until his search took him to India, where he went to a particular place for an Ayurvedic treatment.

The meeting ended on a positive note. After exchanging handshakes, he requested they kept in touch, and gave his regards to Max. He was sorry that Max could not attend, but he had an enormous pleasure in meeting them both, and foresaw a fruitful collaboration with them.

"You did a great job!" Kristen complimented her as they stepped out, "It looks like he might hire us!"

On their way out, Yael's gaze stopped on a semi-hidden poster hung in the hallway leading to his office. It read, "If you think sex is a pain in the ass, try a different position!"

A Job Offer

At dinner, the conversation evolved around the rapid development of India's technological power. Master Buphendra had strong opinions, of course. He was not in favor of technology. Continuing his previous views, he said that technology was alienating people from noble values. However, it was apparent that he was proud of the fact that Indian engineers and technicians were staffing key positions in the technology arena in India and overseas. Finally, he even admitted that he bought a computer and would like to publish his treatment place on the Internet. He said he was looking for someone to help with that.

Of course, thought Yael, *when it serves him, it becomes ok...*

"You were asking where Yael can contribute..." Vera suggested. Vera seemed to be much more than just a patient, and Yael could see that Vera and Master shared thoughts. *He also fears her a bit,* Yael thought, *she's older than him and in his culture, and paying respect to the elderly is one of the highest values.*

She noted a resemblance between their personalities; it seemed they broadcasted on the same wavelength of charismatic personalities, teaching conduct, and authoritative demonstrations. Being with both of them together seemed like a meeting between evenly matched opponents who decided to unite when faced with an inferior, shoddy world. When they voiced their opinions, both were very careful not to trample over each other. However, both never spared their views, either.

Master turned to Yael with a sharp gaze and a glint in his eyes. She felt his joy in discovering something for her to do so she wouldn't be eating for free.

"Is that so?" he asked.

"Well, it's not really my profession. I've started doing it only recently, so I'm not so familiar with creating a web site," she admitted. *This website for Jennifer,* she thought, a painful thought.

"See?" he turned to Vera, reveling in his small victory, "she can't help!" he stated flatly.

"She certainly can!" insisted Vera, turning to Yael. "You can try, no?"

The united front of them both had pushed Yael to a rebellious spot, but, on the other hand, she had her pride. She couldn't admit that she was completely incapable, but she also didn't want to give Master any more satisfaction. Her response was directed to Vera, ignoring Master completely.

"Yes, I can."

Master as if he is reading her, grinned, and said loudly, "Your pride is too big, eh?" and with his finger tapped her nose lightly. This gesture was quite embarrassing for her in front of all the other guests. She couldn't find anything to say, so she remained silent.

"Then it's settled!" Vera concluded with satisfaction.

At night, before falling asleep, Yael tossed and turned in bed. For her, it was a challenge on his part.

In the morning, she woke up to the sound of Sabitri's voice. She was very happy to see her. Today, she would do housework again. Working besides Sabitri felt so pleasant. She felt filled with motivation and desire to perform tasks that, back at home, she had hated. Maintenance work, she used to call it—little duties whose only purpose was to maintain her daily life so she could reach the real thing: ego-flattering visionary projects full of big ideas and creativity. And now, here, in this place, that work was finding a respected place. It became the important task, the main project.

Strange how your perspective on things changes, and how it depends on the people you're with, she thought. *Or maybe something changed in me. Are there really no people like Sabitri in the West? Why does the perspective only change here?* She wondered. Images from her office in downtown New York emerged in her mind. *A well-oiled money machine, running crazily, at an unbelievable speedy pace,* she thought. And here? *There's a common denominator between today and yesterday. Yesterday, I was sitting besides Ravindra, gleefully watching him as he prepared the steam sauna. I enjoyed the entire process, the joy of the process, the slow pace. Maybe it's the uniqueness of India; maybe that's why the west is drawn here. Who knows, maybe eventually I'll find a home here,*" she thought, and then felt a pang. Jennifer.

Was it her?

What is Love

"Two coffees with two chocolate croissants," she said to the person at the cashier.

"Three and a half dollars, please," recited the cashier, and with an amazing agility, the tray of goods was already in her hands. Yael was always so delighted when faced with the efficiency of service in this country, the complete opposite of the constant delay and bureaucracy that characterizing her homeland and other places she had seen. From ordering coffee to buying or returning electronics, her costumer experience in the States had been far from the shoddy, inefficient service back in Israel. The customer was a queen in America. Competition streamlined and shortened the gap between the demand and supply. *This is the way things should operate*, she thought.

When there was any slight deviation, she became stressed, irritated. The world seemed to her like was doomed. No, she had never been in therapy, but it was clear to her that if she would have gone to a shrink, he or she would have focused on the excessive sensitivity she had with this issue. There was more to dig up from her appreciation of the American order, but she never paused to analyze it and just took it as it was.

The last two hours of the yoga class worked wonders for her body and soul. The Indian-style yoga practice allowed her to learn about a culture that she could only assume was very different from the one she lived in.

Jennifer was waiting for her. Yael approached the table where she was seated in the neighborhood coffee shop uptown. She hadn't spoken to Jennifer since the day of the break-in, and hadn't seen her for two weeks since their night out at the club. Jennifer had been traveling out of the city again on a work project.

Yael was keen to share her excitement with Jennifer regarding the "Special Training" coming in two days, but Jennifer didn't look her best. In fact, she looked quite upset, mournful and despondent. In view of her state, Yael sat and kept silent, waiting for her to speak up.

"He's going through something," Jennifer shot the opening sentence without preamble.

"Lorenzo?" Yael asked for clarification, although she already had an inkling who she was referring to.

"Yes, he's already deep in it; in the last couple of weeks he went deeper and deeper. I'm beginning to believe he won't snap out of it."

Yael knew Jennifer was referring to Lorenzo's drug problem. His "high" wasn't only derived from his personal charm and charismatic personality, but was also a direct result of the drugs. Yael had no idea how deeply involved he was, however. Jennifer stated that in the past, when he was on coke and there was a shortage of "material," he used to smoke grass, but soon he couldn't go a day without it and it was on a regular basis.

"I'm losing him. He spends more time with Jeff, and you know who got him into this drug scene in the first place—that asshole. And that son-of-a-bitch is also buying the drugs for him and keeps feeding them to him. I'm trying to keep them apart, but I've been gone a lot, as you know, so it's quite hard to prevent him from seeing his supposed 'best friend." Jennifer looked desperate.

Yael realized the severity of the problem, and kept silent. Jennifer continued.

"Lorenzo was supposed to go through rehab, but I'm not always around looking after him, and they spend hours together, smoking pot and coke and then going out to the bar for a drink. He returns home when it's already a morning, completely done in." Jennifer responded, lost.

"And there's something else", she continued, pausing.

"What?"

"No... Never mind. It's nothing," her face was anguished.

"Jennifer, dear, it seems to me you suffer too much from this whole thing."

"Absolutely! I'm tired of it! It's not doing me any good!"

"Then leave him."

Jennifer looked at Yael as if Yael was pointing a gun at her.

"I can't," she said firmly.

"Why?"

"It's simple! Because I love him."

"Then stop loving him."

"I can't. We've found true love."

"What is true love?"

"Unconditional love!"

"Jennifer, what's this bullshit? What's unconditional love? Love without conditions?"

"Unconditional love means when there are difficulties, you stick together, not just when it's all happiness and roses," she said firmly.

"Unconditional love is love for fools," Yael retorted, "Obviously, there should be conditions. If he were beating you and you suffered, would you also call it true love?"

"You've just never felt the same," Jennifer shot at her.

"Why not?" Yael was getting irritated, "I've experienced very intense feelings."

"Yes? Like what?"

Yael paused for a second.

"I have experienced intense fear! You know how it feels when a giant man attacks you and you know you won't be able to escape in time to flee the blow?"

"It sounds more like the feeling of preparing the ground for the coming failure, an excuse you use when you haven't managed to avoid the attack," Jennifer stated coolly.

"Okay, then. So, on the same level, you also use love to explain the failure of your relationship," Yael returned.

Jennifer was silent.

"Look, it's really more simple than it sounds—when the bad's greater than the good, that's the sign you should leave," Yael said, thinking that this was a saying she might consider applying to her relationship with Eyal, but Jennifer looked back at Yael, and it seemed as if she hadn't even heard her.

Lorenzo was Jennifer's weakness.

A loud commotion was heard coming from the direction of the cashier. Two men were fighting. One's fist had knocked out the other.

In a second, Jennifer had recovered from the oblivious state she was in and jumped at them. Everything that followed happened quickly. She approached the attacking man from behind while snatching a wooden napkin holder from the closest table on her way, and she came up behind him, striking a blow between his ribs, apparently in a very precise spot. He immediately fell to the ground, paralyzed.

Astonished, Yael recalled that in the highest level of martial arts, there were what's called "vital points," to which a strike could cause anywhere from light to severe damage, even death.

"Jennifer, how did you manage to stun him in a second?" Yael asked, shocked.

"Just got lucky," answers Jennifer in a dry tone, and she walked nonchalantly back to their table. All other onlookers appeared to submerge in their own worlds to have even noticed or commented on the scene.

What dull lack of caring...each in his or her own world. Yael tried to share her astonishment at their ignorance with Jennifer when she got back to the table, but Jennifer had gone back to brooding and showed no interest in dealing with what had just occurred.

"That was something, what you did there," said Yael, not hiding her admiration, "So come on! How did you do it? You should have been with us in that evening when they broke into our apartment!"

But Jennifer was completely withdrawn.

After several silent minutes, the paramedics arrived to load the attacked man on a stretcher and left. The man struck by Jennifer had slowly recovered, and police brought him outside, restoring order.

"Sorry, Jennifer, I snapped out of the issue. What will you do?" Silence.

"Jenny, are you with me?"

But Jennifer had already boarded a ship of deep thoughts, as was embarking on her own journey for a solution.

"Jenny, I'm simply watching your back as you always watched mine," said Yael, adding, "Since we were small..."

Silence.

"Jenny?"

"I know you mean well, let's drop it now. I'll be fine," she replied coldly.

The Man at Home

On her way back home, Yael accidentally ran into Daniel and Peter. They were returning from a job fair. Peter was unemployed and had asked Daniel to accompany him to the fair.

Daniel wanted to know how she was doing. They both knew he was interested in knowing her condition due to recent events. She said she felt fine and told him she had just returned from seeing Jennifer—his niece—and that Jennifer was the one they should be worried about. Yael pointed out that she thought something was going on with Jennifer.

Daniel looked surprised and worried at the same time. Although they weren't close, he couldn't remember Jennifer ever being in bad shape. He asked Yael if she had any idea why.

Yael wanted to share with him what happened at the club, but felt it was somewhat personal and that she'd be betraying her friendship with Jennifer if she told.

Then Peter asked if they wanted to speak in private.

"No! I don't have much to say beyond the fact that I'm worried," Yael explained, a little embarrassed that Peter had been listening in.

"Probably issues with the man at home" joked Peter.

He hit the nail on the head, Yael thought to herself.

Daniel kept silent as usual, examining Yael. He felt something was bothering her.

"I hope she doesn't have major problems with him, like that one girl in our class," added Peter, not revealing the person's name on purpose in order to create a thrilling effect.

Yael and Daniel looked at him quizzically.

Peter, who enjoyed the attention, continued, "Well, see if you can guess."

Both Yael and Daniel looked at him impatiently for a few seconds.

Peter finally gave in, unable to hide his satisfaction at their puzzled faces.

"Michelle, remember?!"

Michelle was a relatively new student to the Dojo where they trained. Yael was facing her once and felt that she couldn't trust her. The odds of getting injured by her were too high, similar to young male trainees who were too frantic, too out of control, and overly zealous to prove they could do it. Michelle was the same.

"Over motivation can dazzle your eyes and may thwart," Zoe had once explained to them.

"So what about her?" Daniel asked impatiently. Sometimes Peter's efforts to acquire attention were tiring for him.

"She's married to an asshole who beats the shit out of her," said Peter nonchalantly.

Yael was shocked.

"Are you serious? You sure? How do you know?"

"I know! That's the truth!" Peter said haughtily.

Both Yael and Daniel were startled by the information. Daniel changed the subject. The three of them confirmed they would meet at Riverside Park the following day to run together. On her way back home, she jogged her memory regarding Michelle's conduct to find some hints regarding her situation, but couldn't recall anything unusual.

Eyal was already home when she returned and was busy packing. In the morning, he would be flying to the West Coast to shoot a commercial. He would stay there for three days. When he saw her, he stopped packing and, once again, spoke enthusiastically about the condominium he had found. He checked out the tenants, and said they would only benefit if they moved. The potential relationships with "heavily rich people" could help them move up the social ladder very quickly alongside both of their salaries, the prestige of Yael's firm, and the connections he had with famous actors. They were already making good money, he reminded her, and they should take out a mortgage to buy it. Money would buy them the status they needed as immigrants and would make them accepted.

Yael attempted to listen positively and to agree, but she couldn't. For some reason, his confident plans upset her, and she drifted away from the conversation. She wanted him to stop, but she didn't dare express it. He'd be offended.

Since the incident, he hadn't stopped talking about leaving the "shitty neighborhood," as he continuously called it. Yael could tell that in his heart, he blamed her for what had happened. She had gotten them into that mess by being careless and because she never heeded his repeated warnings. She knew he had been affected by the whole scene that night. His manhood was compromised after being sedated and helpless. Somehow, she also knew that as far as he was concerned, none of that shameful incident would have even happened if she had just bought food for Spike.

Worst of all, she knew he was right. He was just as right in his warnings as he was about her not wanting to institutionalize their relationship. Nevertheless, or perhaps just because of this, she felt she was drifting apart from him more and more. The guilt she felt only increased her anger.

Peter's words continued to echo in her head. *She's married to an asshole who beats the shit out of her.* And Jennifer—her entire shaky state was a result of Lorenzo. Eyal seemed to represent just one more of the world's controlling men.

Who needs these men, anyway? They're only making a mess, she couldn't help but think. Eyal seemed redundant and pointless now.

He continued speaking, but could feel the conversation closing as he turned slightly as if he were going to the other room.

Good, he's going away, she thought, *I want to be alone.*

A phone call interrupted him and came to her rescue. It was Barbara, his colleague. She had called to finalize a few last minute things before their flight in the morning.

It had always seemed that Barbara has a crush on Eyal. Despite this, Yael felt relieved that Barbara was the one who had called, since she'd keep him busy for a while. She actually found herself hoping the call would be long enough and that she'd be asleep before he got done. They'd see each other again only after she returned from Special Training.

As she slowly drifted asleep, she could still hear him on the phone, speaking about the potential earnings from the commercial.

"Big money..." she heard Eyal happily exclaim.

Big money, prestige, heavily rich, condominium, don't want it...want to sleep... She mumbled to herself while she is falling asleep In her dream, she was sinking down into a huge, dark, gloomy rabbit hole.

A Troubling Rendezvous

"Eyal's already gone?" her mom asked on a Trans-Atlantic phone call.

"Yes, this morning."

"Work?"

"Yes."

"For how long?"

"Several days."

"So he won't be at home while you are in this thing, what's it called ...?"

"Special Training, Mom, Special Training!"

"Yes, the special madness!" her mother said cynically.

"It's not crazy; there are going to be hundreds of people over there."

"And you can't be reached there, so how can we talk to you to know that everything is okay?"

"I'm not taking my cell phone, Mom; I prefer to concentrate on what I'm doing there."

"Getting beaten?" her mom asked with a cynical tone, "When are you going"?

"Tomorrow, Mom."

"All right, Yael," her mother sighed with resignation, "Please be careful out there, don't do anything foolish, and call us immediately when you're back to tell us you're okay!"

The lawn in Riverside Park was waiting for her. Whenever she could, and unfortunately not as often as she would have liked, she came there with a blanket or a folding chair, reading material, and, most importantly, music. The round lawn stretched over a sort of hill, sloping down into a small hillside of bright green grass surrounded by lush trees, creating a cozy circular lawn. There, she could escape from the city noise, the bustle, work, and Eyal—it was her private place. She spread the blanket and lay down. Blue skies floated above her. An occasional breeze caressed treetops, creating a gentle murmur against the branches and the leaves.

She lay on her back with the headphones of the music player jammed in her ears. She pressed "play," let the sounds start relaxing her, and slowly began to calm. She felt her body weight dropping to the ground. Being close to the ground made her feel safe. She closed her eyes. The electric guitar playing interwove its way into her mind, making her relaxed and at peace.

A cool breeze arrived and the sun disappeared behind a patch of clouds. She opened her eyes. Light white clouds moved above her against the blue backdrop. The music turned to tuned, airy tones. She closed her eyes again, letting her imagination take her wherever it desired. She let herself be carried up into the clouds and was no longer on the lawn on the hill in a little park in that crazy city but watching from above. Her mind wandered around and she started flowing between sleep to consciousness.

Jennifer and I were walking around, and suddenly a storm began. It threatened to sweep everything - people, objects, buildings. I felt confident enough to stay where we were but Jennifer wanted to move on and she left the place. A local told me there were some local girls who ran to the nearby building to seek shelter and they were renting rooms there. If I didn't hurry, no rooms would be left. The storm was getting stronger and had begun to sweep up everything. People, signs, bins, carts, and children, even parts of buildings were swept away in all directions in a strong, painful din. A huge commotion could be heard from the pained cries of people bumping into objects in their path, carried by the storm. Children were torn from the arms of parents. With great effort I ran toward the building next door. I had difficulties opening my eyes because of the dust, sand and the angry blasts of air. From afar, I recognized two multi-story buildings: the Twin Towers. I started running but was going nowhere. It seemed like I was stepping in the same place. Protecting my face from flying objects, I managed to reach the towers' entrance with great effort and asked if any remaining rooms were left to rent. People were running in all directions and no one paid attention to me. I shouted at them but no one was listening. The wind's intensity rose, increasing the chaos around. If I didn't hold onto something firm, the wind threatened to sweep me away...

In her semi-conscious state, Yael passed by provinces where no words could be spoken. The sunlight, in flitting yellow spots, moved around her blinking eyes and beams of light flashed against her eyelashes, followed by shadows and dark spots. The cool breeze picked up. Cold and trembling, the music reached its peak and then silence. Raindrops began to fall. Gradually, she shifted from the simplicity of deep relaxation to the waking reality of the world around her. She opened her eyes and several tears slowly glided down her cheeks, accompanied by raindrops. It was the transition between the end of the spring and the coming summer.

Someone touched her arm. She jumped in alarm. It was Jeff. He looked sullen and exhausted.

Something is wrong with him, she thought, but didn't feel comfortable enough to ask. Jeff's apartment was also uptown, not far from where she lived. She had never seen him at the park before, however.

"Have you seen Lorenzo lately?" he asked eagerly.

"What do you mean? I saw Jennifer yesterday."

"I just saw her," he mumbled with a distressed tone.

Yael was puzzled, unsure if she heard him right. He avoided her request to repeat, and nervously continued, "Lorenzo isn't returning my phone calls. Is everything ok with him?"

"I think so. Why? Did something happen?" she asked, wondering if she should reveal Jennifer's concerns about Lorenzo's drug use and Jeff's part in it.

Jeff looks like an addict who needs his fix right now, she thought, examining his frazzled state.

She had never been particularly close to him. She couldn't find anything about him to like, and, naturally, she was biased because of the issues Jennifer had with him.

She also had to get home and change to her running gear since she was scheduled to run with Daniel and Peter in about twenty minutes, so she couldn't continue talking with him. Something was definitely wrong, and he seemed desperate to get attention and talk, but she had to dismiss herself. Special Training began the next day, and she couldn't be late for their training run.

"I have to go, sorry! I'm really late," she said to Jeff, gathered her belongings, and left in a hurry, leaving him alone to his despair.

One Mile Too Far

She arrived five minutes late. Daniel and Peter were already at the location they had agreed to meet for a run, bouncing from one leg to another.

"Sorry I'm late," Yael apologized, "someone grabbed me for a talk."

It was the night before Special Training, and considerable excitement was evident in all three.

A long line of high school students, all dressed in uniforms, passed them. Daniel and Peter exchanged a few words about their own high school times. Yael found it difficult to understand the specific vocabulary they used, but in the company of Daniel, she somehow felt comfortable enough to ask for clarifications. As they warmed up, they exchanged pieces of information each of them had collected regarding Special Training. The program, which would be spread over four days, sounded like a military training. The practice that everyone most feared was the Kiabadachi, or horse stance. In this practice, everyone had to stand still with their knees bent with no movement permitted for an entire hour and a half. Yael remembered stories about people's breaking points, people fainting in the middle, people going crazy and other unpleasant things. This was considered to be the most difficult mental practice. Although they were advised not to attempt this stance before Special Training, the three of them decided to try it out for ten minutes at the park before leaving for their run.

They didn't make it beyond three minutes, a three minutes that felt like an eternity. Yael began to understand why they were advised not to do so. Most failed in the attempt outside of Special Training and the failure could permeate into doubt regarding whether or not they should even attend the training.

Daniel was the first to clear the air of the doubts and direct the atmosphere to encouragement. Yael and Peter joined him, animating each other, and the three began to lift each other's spirits. They reminded themselves that they must maintain a fighting spirit; they would keep on fighting, and they would withstand it.

148

In this spirit, they started jogging. The destination was a blackened bronze cast statue of an eagle at the very far end of the park. As they start moving, Yael spotted a figure at the edge of the park out of the corner of her eyes. It looked a lot like Jennifer.

Probably just someone who kind of looks like her, she thought to herself, dismissing it. It was getting dark and was difficult to see clearly, anyways. It was probably just her overactive imagination after her encounter with Jeff. Besides, what would Jennifer be doing there, anyways?

Twenty minutes passed to the sound of feet pounding against the trail. It was a long way. Yael concentrated on the run, encouraged by the group support, urging herself to continue. She didn't like running and never had, but in the past couple of weeks she had trained her body to get into the cardiovascular shape that would allow her to physically cope with the difficulties in the upcoming training. Both Sensei Malcolm and Zoe repeatedly stated that physical fitness was a necessity for participation in Special Training.

"Without it, you have no business being there, period!" Sensei Malcolm had firmly stated.

However, physical fitness wasn't enough. The mental spirit was no less important. This depended on the individual personalities of each of the trainees. It was the outcome of everyone's unique experience in life, their previous experiences, and their desire to overcome obstacles.

They neared the edge of the park, next to the brown waters of the Hudson River. There were no nearby buildings and vegetation had taken over. It was the last few minutes of twilight before darkness.

Suddenly, a thump was heard.

"Shit!" Peter exclaimed as he collided against the earth.

Yael and Daniel stopped, waiting for him to get back up.

"Come on, you can do it," Daniel urged.

But Peter can't move.

"It's probably a strained tendon," he winced, trying to move his leg.

Daniel helped him lift himself off the ground.

149

"This can't be happening...not the night before special training..." Peter limps against Daniel, devastated. Daniel drags him to a bench and turns to Yael.

"There's just a mile left. I'll stay with Peter, but you should keep going. Finish it for all of us."

Yael hesitated.

"We can wait for you right here," Daniel urged.

"Go on, go on!" Peter joined in, pain evident in his voice.

Both Daniel and Peter knew it is important for her to complete the run without a break so she could know that she could do it.

Yael gave up her resistance and continued. It was more difficult to be in motion again after the break, as short as it had been. She ran forward, her feet striking against the gravel path, breathing heavily. Despite the burning in her chest, she's determined to reach the goal: the bronze statue. Silence surrounded her. She was alone. Only the rustle of her feet on the ground could be heard. Leg after leg, breath after breath.

She increased her pace, when suddenly she heard voices. She looked over her shoulder. There was no one. She scanned from side to side, but there wasn't enough light to see from the distance. The voices approached in front of her.

Something made her stop. Something sparkled in the twilight. She could barely see two human figures, one tall and one short. A hand could be seen raised in the air, and something was shimmering. She realized what it was and froze. It was a knife. The hand with the knife pierced it into the body of the tall figure.

Yael remained frozen until she came to her senses and jumped behind a bush, hiding. A glimpse back at the scene revealed that both figures had disappeared. Yael leapt behind the bushes. Gripped with a fear that paralyzed her legs, she felt her heart beat faster than it ever had during a run.

Where's the guy with the knife? Did he see me? Is he coming to me?

Her heart couldn't stand the intensity. Suddenly, she felt a sharp pain between her ribs. Her world turned upside down and darkness covered her instantly. She fell.

"Yael, wake up! Wake up!"

Although she couldn't see much in the dark, she recognized Daniel's voice.

"What happened?" he asked concernedly, helping her to stand.

"Did you also starch a tendon?" he joked, but he couldn't hide the concern in his voice.

Yael was slowly recovering.

"I'm fine," she calmed him down, "I only have a terrible pressure between the ribs and a terrible headache." She replied, and suddenly it hit her. Had she just witnessed a murder?

She told Daniel what she saw excitedly, and dragged him several feet toward where she saw the figures.

"We must see if someone is hurt!" she raised her voice, and then stopped. "Wait! But where's Peter?"

"He's waiting on the bench. You were gone too long, it's getting dark, and we started to worry. I thought I'd come make sure everything was alright," Daniel explained.

"We must go back immediately. If there is a killer, Peter is alone in the dark. Shit! What do we do? Keep on looking to see if someone is hurt, or go back to Peter?" Yael's frightened voice pierced the darkness.

They scanned the area but darkness had already taken over, and they couldn't see anything. Daniel reassured her that probably, in the dark things looked different and there really was no murder.

"Yeah, it's New York, but the mayor's created some order here, hasn't he?" he said.

He must think that my mental state is shaky because of the incident at home and that I'm probably imagining it, Yael thought, stressed.

She shared her debate over whether to keep looking or whether to go back and find Peter.

Daniel encouraged her to return. It seemed that, despite his lack of trust in her words, a certain degree of fear had overcome him.

"Come on, let's go, it's already dark and really not pleasant here; it's too isolated and dangerous!"

Yael insisted on making another round, but it didn't reveal a thing about what she thought she had seen. Doubt began to creep into her heart. Maybe she hadn't seen what she thought. Maybe it was just a mind game, and the two normal people had gone home and no murder had taken place after all. As time passed, her doubt increased.

She sighs with relief when they found Peter on the bench. Neither of them shared of what had happened with Peter in an unspoken agreement. They helped him to get up and, with a remaining sense of uncertainty blended with some fear; they plodded slowly out of the park.

Special Training

Amherst University, Massachusetts: Special Training had begun. There was one building for women and four for the men. They were the residential buildings of students that were on summer break. It reminded Yael a bit of being in the Girl Scouts. Curious to know her roommate, she hurried to get there. It was a simple room with six narrow beds and one closet for all. All bed linens and towels were folded on each bed. There were shared toilets and showers at the end of the corridor on each floor.

To her surprise, she found Zoe in the room. It was a little embarrassing for her. She was used to seeing Zoe from the distance, even with a certain admiration, and she knew her only from the practices that Zoe usually lead. Now, she would be able to get to know her more closely, and Zoe would be able to know her better.

Yael was happy to share a room with a familiar face and have someone senior and experienced with her to watch her back. Zoe greeted her warmly.

Two women enter the room: a tall, older woman and a young one who was small and slim. Despite the difference in height, there was a similarity between the two.

"Hey Cheryl, how are you?" Zoe turned to the older one.

Apparently, Cheryl and Zoe knew each other from California, where they used to live and train in the past. Zoe trained there before she arrived to the East Coast a few months ago. They exchanged greetings and hugs.

"I want you to meet my daughter, Eleanor," said Cheryl.

Zoe shook Eleanor's hand with a smile. The mother and daughter were then introduced to Yael.

"We brought someone with us, as well," Cheryl added.

A tall, heavy-looking girl entered the room. Zoe immediately turned to her.

"Hey, Charlotte, you've decided to come on time this year, eh?" she said humorously.

Cheryl replied instead of Charlotte.

"It's because she came with us."

Zoe smiled. Charlotte was also from California and had relocated to the East Coast. There was something odd about her—her gaze was not focused, and she had a nervous tic in her eyes. She scanned the beds in the room, occasionally blinking one eye.

"Which bed? Hmm...I don't know..." she said to herself, either joking or serious, and abruptly jumped on one of the beds.

"Shitty mattress," she determined, and jumped over to another one. "What a drag! What a drag! How do they expect us to sleep here?"

At the sight of Charlotte's jumps, Zoe and Cheryl looked at each other, amused.

"She'll never change," said Zoe.

"I wonder who the sixth girl that is staying with us is," Charlotte questioned, and continued, "I hope it's not someone who snores, or I'll break her bones!"

Michelle entered the room. She carried a number of bags on her shoulders and she was rolling a medium sized carry-on suitcase. Her coat's sleeves were loosely wrapped around her waist and its edge was almost trailing to the floor.

Michelle? The battered one from class? She's in this room? This will be interesting, thought Yael.

Charlotte took one look at Michelle and, without greeting her, started counting the bags Michelle brought.

"Oh! We have a real diva here!" she teased.

It seemed that Michelle didn't like what she heard, and she frowned at Charlotte. Zoe noticed and was quick to welcome her to the room. Yael followed her greeting, and so do the others.

Someone yelled from the corridor that the first practice was about to begin. Zoe beat everyone in putting on her training gear and rushed out.

They all quickly donned their Gees and wrapped their belts around their waists. All were curious to see from the color of the belts who was senior and who was junior. Cheryl had a black belt; Eleanor, her daughter, was junior, wearing a white belt. Charlotte and Michelle—like Yael—were brown belts and, like Yael, they were also expected to be tested for black belt. They all went out to the gathering place.

The first day of the four days of Special Training had begun.

Trainees of different schools from the East Coast and also a few from the West Coast had all come to the event. All were dressed in white training suits and were lined up in rows in the order of their ranks: white, brown, and black belts.

Quite a big group, thought Yael while starting to feel the excitement. She wondered if, at the very end of those scary four days, she would be granted the honor of wearing the desired black belt and join the prestigious group of this ranking. But the road to the black belt seemed so long, if at all possible. She looked for Daniel and Peter among the rows of people and found them. They noticed her and waved. She pointed to her ankle in a gesture asking if Peter's foot was okay. He lifted his thumb up. She smiled back and returned the gesture.

The seniors divided the trainees into groups. Each group would go through a different practice.

A short walk and her group reached a sports hall. It was noon and hot and Yael was glad they would be practicing in a relatively cool, shaded place.

The practice began. They would be performing a large number of Katas, or series of movements. It seemed endless. A momentary lack of concentration and Yael made a false move with her foot. The toe twisted badly. A sharp pain cursed through her and she failed to strangle her howl. The senior leading the practice heard the yell, but continued to lead the practice while searching from the corner of his eye for the source. Yael didn't turn herself in. She continued despite the pain; after all, she couldn't stop now in the first practice. She hoped it was a temporary pain and that it would pass. During certain movements it appeared, and in others it didn't. She felt anxiety and it did have an effect on her technical performance. As a black belt candidate, she was also being watched for technical performance, so not only the test would determine if she was going to pass. They would observe her with examining eyes during those coming four days. They wanted to see mental strength, technical ability, precision, and durability in the hard training. The pain began to be unbearable and she wished the practice would end. She hated herself for the fact that she had managed to get injured right in the first few minutes of the first practice.

A lack of concentration, and in a second it'll happen again if you don't stop thinking about it! She scolded herself.

The leading senior shouted for them to stop. "Yame!"

The first practice had ended. She released a sigh of relief. Everyone bowed, and it was over. She found it difficult to step on the injured leg. Her limp captured the eye of the leading senior. He stopped her and asked what happened. She told him, and upon examination of the injured foot, he found no external sign of injury. He asked her to report to him regarding her condition right before the evening practice.

All trainees were scattered everywhere and returning to their rooms.

"There are three of us from the same Dojo. Is that on purpose?" Michelle asked Zoe in the room.

"Absolutely not! This is a coincidence," said Zoe. "Beyond the separation between women and men, of course," she added.

"There will be quite a lot of women here, right?" asked Michelle.

"Yes, all the practitioners from the entire east coast are here, so you will not feel like a minority," laughed Zoe.

"How is it for you being in New York after California?" asked Charlotte. Yael found the question a bit intrusive. Based on Zoe's response, it appeared Zoe felt the same. She looked hesitant as per how to respond.

Charlotte continued, "Over there you were close to Sensei Yoshida, whereas here there is no real central figure."

Cheryl intervened.

"Zoe is already a central figure. Perhaps she will formally become one for the East Coast."

"It would be wonderful," said Eleanor.

"I'm all for it," added Charlotte.

"They won't let her!" Michelle exclaimed.

"Who won't?" Cheryl was interested to know.

"Men! This is a masculine world in general, and particularly in Karate."

"Slowly, slowly things are changing," responded Zoe calmly. She didn't seem moved by the fact that the discourse was revolving around her.

"Who has time to wait? When?" Michelle said defiantly.

Yael wondered if they knew about Michelle's horrible background.

"Meanwhile, we must put our trust in God," continued Michelle.

"In God?" exclaimed Charlotte, "How the hell does God have anything to do with this?"

"God is the one who will save us in the end. Without him, all the shit in this world won't go away!"

"A lot of shit—" Charlotte emphasized the final word, "—is in the world thanks to this God of yours, who is, by the way, also a male, if you haven't noticed," she stated in a mocking tone, continuing, "Only people can change things."

"Then why don't things change?" asked Michelle.

"Because most people are weak!" Charlotte hissed between her teeth.

With a bit of fear, Yael examined how this last statement affected Michelle. *Will she argue it?*

But, to her surprise, Michelle didn't undermine Charlotte's opinion, but, on the contrary, nodded her head in agreement.

"It's true."

Then Zoe intervened. "I don't entirely agree. People choose to be weak; they're not like that by nature. People, in their most difficult situations, can find extraordinary courage and spirit."

"Thanks to them and not to this damn God," added Charlotte.

"It doesn't really matter," responded Zoe, "from where you draw your strength to stand against difficulties or evil."

157

"God does give you the power to change when necessary, to be strong. Right?" Cheryl turned her question to Michelle.

"No, he disappoints me," she admitted weakly.

"Great! She also believes in him and he is also disappointing her!" Said Charlotte cynically.

"But you're here, no? You got to carry the ball!" said Zoe to Michelle.

"Yes, I'm here, and you're right." Michelle nodded.

"This is a start," added Zoe.

Silence. They stretched, each in her own bed. Although the first practice did not require too much, fatigue was already evident in all of them. They tried to sleep but apart for the veterans who already knew what to expect from their Special Training, all they could manage was some restless turning.

Is she here because of her horrible situation? Yael wondered. Is that why she started to practice martial arts to begin with? And what the hell did Zoe mean by 'carrying the ball?'"

Zoe's alarm clock woke them all up from their rest. They quickly dressed and left for the evening practice. Yael was having trouble with her leg, but she wasn't going to let it stop her.

Outside, evening fell.

Gates of Heaven

"Brown belts only, inside the hall!"

Yael, Daniel and Peter looked at each other as if wondering out loud what they were planning for them. The large group was then divided into two.

The practice hall was small and it seemed it had not been used for a while. The windows were closed and it was stuffy inside. Seven seniors among the black belts were joining the practice. Yael was happy to see a familiar face among them: Zoe.

"Align in seven rows, and stand one after another!" the voice of Sensei Marlon was heard. "Each row must face one of the black belts!" he added.

"Can you open a few windows?" asked one of the students. She received a reproachful look from the seniors, but they did open a few windows that screeched as they were pried open.

The seniors stood at the end of the hall, each facing the first student that stood at the head of the row. About fifteen feet separated the practitioners at the head of the row from the seniors facing them. Before they started the practice, two seniors would demonstrate what needed to be done. One of the seniors, Hamid, faced another senior by the name of Kenny.

"Hajeme!" was heard. It was their sign to begin. Hamid walked straight with a determined and confident step toward Kenny, who was facing him. When he reached him from the distance of an extended arm, he stopped. Kenny attacked with his fist straight into Hamid's face, stopping an inch from his nose. No movement at Hamid was apparent. His body remained in place and not a muscle moved in his face. He didn't blink or flicker.

"This is the "Gates of Heaven" practice."

Inhumane! Determined Yael.

Then they began. Each did the same on his or her turn, with the senior in front. No movement was allowed, no blinking. All were watching everyone else out of curiosity to see how the others were doing, if they were conquering the fear, if they were successful in overcoming the instinct to shift the body or to move their heads away from the oncoming fists.

After all, they had to rely on the skills and experience of the black belts, the seniors. Inaccuracy on behalf of the seniors, or their failure to precisely measure the distance to the brown belt trainee's face, in addition to their ability or inability to assess the force and the momentum of their punch, could easily cost someone a broken nose, a broken chin, or eye injuries.

Yael wondered if the ability to remain still was a matter of skill or personality. Her colleagues lacked the skill of the highest ranks, but still there were those who moved less, blinked less and flinched less.

She was last in the row, after Peter. Daniel was in another row.

Peter stepped out. She followed him. He did not do very well. He moved too much.

It was her turn. Just before she stepped forward, she wondered to herself. *Do I have it or not?* She moved toward the senior.

When she reached him, she stopped and took a deep breath. All eyes were on her. How would she do? Her eyes met with those of her opponent's. For her, all the surrounding sounds went quiet. She was fully concentrated. She heard her own breath.

Suddenly, a fist came at her. She felt the blow of air created by the movement of the fist, right under her nose. She could smell the body odor emanating from the fist. The senior lingered with his extended fist and then withdrew. She did not move. She got a pat on her shoulder. Apparently, she did alright despite a small blink. It was inevitable.

She returned to the end of the line. From the corner of her eyes, she saw Michelle, just stepping out. Her gaze followed her.

Michelle walked toward Kenny. The way she stepped out of the line already demonstrated insecurity. She hesitated, clearly standing too far from Sensei Kenny. He instructed her to move closer. She moved slightly. He instructed her to get even closer, and she did. He looked into her eyes and she avoided his gaze. He signaled her to do so, and asked her to take a deep breath to calm her down. It seemed that she was loosening up a bit. He instructed her to return to the row and start again. Zoe approached Michelle and whispered something in her ear. Michelle began again, stepping out. This time, her steps seemed more determined, more confident. She stood facing Kenny. A fist went out. She threw her head back in defense. Kenny told her something. Again, she returned to the row.

Not cool that everybody is witnessing your failure, thought Yael, her heart with Michelle. Another failed attempt. Kenny gave up.

Next was Daniel, and he did quite well. *Why am I not surprised?* Thought Yael.

In another line, she located Charlotte. It was her turn. Her steps toward the senior were quite determined. There was something frightening in the way she walked toward him. She had the look in her eyes of someone that would go all the way, no matter what. She did not avert her head, but just blinked slightly as the punch came. *Nice!* Though Yael.

However, the next time it was Yael's turn again. This time she didn't do as well. This time, the impact of knowing what was to come had taken its toll, and she moved more
I don't have what Charlotte has, she thought, but after a few more times facing the "Gates of Heaven," she felt better.

Red Skies

The practice ended. There were few injured trainees.

Daniel and Peter approached her, and Daniel asked how she was, and she said she was just fine. Peter was upset—he felt that he didn't do well in the practice and it would lower his chance of receiving his black belt. They were being carefully examined by the seniors throughout the practice; clearly, the seniors were beginning to make judgments about who had better potential for passing.

Daniel tried to cheer him up. Yael said that one would need a certain degree of madness to be able to stand motionless in front of such an attack. She uses Charlotte as an example. She described her overall attitude, how Charlotte had stepped out of the lines and boldly approached the senior. Yael told them that she was sharing a room with Charlotte, and that she appears to be a bit of a "wacko" to her.

"Is that the right term?" she asked Daniel, hoping to get an affirmative answer. Daniel nodded, and Yael continued, "I most likely don't have this madness Charlotte has or the ability to give up my fear of getting hurt."

"Just by practicing martial arts, you must be giving up on your fears, no?" asked Peter firmly, but doubt was evident in his voice.

"Well," said Daniel, "I don't think we're giving up our fear of being hurt, but rather learn as we go how to live with and how to control it." He thought for a second and continued, "I think it will always be there; it never goes away."

"But look at Charlotte! It seems like she has none, with this crazy look in her eyes and her 'ready to kill or die' personality type," argued Yael.

"But you saw Hamid—he's far from being crazy. One of the stable, quiet, and confident people we have in the organization, and he is a very skilled trainee," said Daniel.

"That is a good point," said Yael and added, "I wonder if it's a matter of personality or skill."

"Maybe both," said Daniel.

"And if you don't have either?" asked Peter with disappointment on his face.

They talked a bit longer, but the short time that had passed between the two practices soon became evident. Physical tiredness started to overtake them. The mental stress regarding what was to come and the fear of whether or not they would be able to go through the next practice was decreasing.

"I'm heading off," said Peter, despondent. Yael hoped Daniel would stay for a bit longer with her.

"See you later," Peter said.

"Bye, Peter. It'll be fine," said Daniel to her delight, meaning he was planning to stick around with her. They watched Peter walk away.

"He's upset," Yael noted.

"It's not easy for him. You know, it's very important for him to get black belt," added Daniel.

"It's important for all examinees, no?" said Yael, thinking that for Daniel it must be important as well, even if he didn't make a big deal out of it.

"For some reason, I think it matters more to him than to others," he stated, adding, "Peter has nothing at the moment. He doesn't have a job, his girlfriend recently broke up with him...he's quite cut off."

"I see," said Yael empathetically.

"Want to sit on the grass?" asked Daniel.

"Yeah, sure," she smiled.

They turn into a pitch. She tried to hide her limp. Daniel asked what had happened.

"Nothing, just a twist of the toe," she responded.

He looked concerned and instructed her to sit. They settled among the trees in a green meadow. The sun was setting and the skies were red. A light breeze created a pleasant rustle among the leaves. All were scattering to their rooms to get some rest before dinner. The pastoral setting was a complete contradiction to the hard practice, and to the emotional stress of the coping trainees. Daniel asked to see her foot and checked it gently, careful of inflicting pain. Seeing her wince, he gently massaged her ankle by moving the joint.

"Daniel, what does it mean 'to carry the ball'?" she asked out of nowhere. He smiled, already used to her questions and need for clarifications.

"It means taking responsibility," he said, adding, "It's taken from soccer." He paused and then continued, "Why?"

"Oh, someone in my room used the phrase and I didn't understand the intent," Yael said. "Say, is soccer popular here? Did you play when you were a kid?"

Daniel smiled, "No, baseball is more popular."

"And you played?"

"No. Actually, I wasn't on any sports team, to be honest."

"You? Of all people, you weren't?" She was surprised because Daniel was considered to be one of the best trainees.

"Me of all people," he said with a small smile, pausing slightly and continuing, "As a child, I suffered from a paralysis and was totally not into sports, so I was never assigned to any group or team."

Yael was stunned. She kept her silence for a short while and then said sheepishly, "You don't show it at all."

"I managed to get over it. It wasn't easy," Daniel smiled sadly. "Also, since my father was a diplomatic ambassador, we had to move all the time because of his work. We drove a lot from one place to another, so I never really had the chance to be one of the guys. But, in the end, when I was a teenager, I got over the paralysis and decided to run a marathon."

"Really? And did you do it?" she was interested to know.

"I practiced diligently for months, and when we moved to New York, I finally did." He paused, clearly debating whether or not to continue. Finally, he added, "I was among the first to finish."

"Wow!" said Yael, impressed. "Good for you!" She did not hide her sympathy for him. She wanted to know more, but he preceded her.

"What about you?"

He's so private and so modest, she thought to herself.

164

"As you already know, my parents were also in diplomatic service, and, like you, it was difficult to feel like I belonged. I also was not good at anything specific," she said, "I remember that at the end of the year, just before primary school graduation ceremony we were being examined for a number of things to decide where to place us in the ceremony—athletics, dancing, singing, etc. I wasn't accepted to anything."

"Bummer!" he said warmly.

Encouraged by his sympathy, she continued, "All my friends got accepted into something and I felt so left out, like I wasn't good enough for anything. I was really depressed." She laughed lightly with embarrassment.

"So what did you do?" he asked.

"I joined the drill team, those people who march with flags. It seemed to me all those who were not accepted into anything else went to the drill team."

"Ah," he said, "but you need good coordination for this."

Cute, Yael thought, *he's trying to make me feel better.*

"Sort of," she agreed.

"How is the foot?"

"Better," she smiled, thinking of how lucky she was to have him there. Everything would have been so different if there was no Daniel.

Outlaws Room

It was dinner. Yael and Daniel joined the other trainees and were walking to the dining room. It was a big dining hall and a long line was formed by the self-serve food facilities. It was their turn. They filled up their plates and found vacant seats by a big round table. Soon, Peter joined. He looked tired but better. Zoe and two unfamiliar young men joined as well.

Feeling responsible as their senior, Zoe inquired if Daniel and Peter had settled comfortably in their room, making sure everything was okay with the boys. Peter tried to extract information about the practices that were waiting for them later, but Zoe refused to cooperate and give any information. From time to time trainees approached Zoe and greeted her. Some even stopped to chat. Zoe had been training for a long time in California and was well known among trainees from the west coast. She was very close to Sensei Yoshida, the head of the organization, who had come from Japan and established the organization in the West two decades ago. They said that he had raised her, in a way. She had begun training at a very young age and was considered a prodigy from the start. Sensei Yoshida was very proud that such a talented practitioner came from his school.

Peter asked Zoe what it had been like practicing with Yoshida. Immediately. Zoe corrected him.

"You must call him, or, for this matter, anyone of a higher rank, 'Sensei,'"

She continued to say that he was an outstanding man. Sensei Yoshida was approaching seventy and still lead practices with great talent and strength. He was adored by all members and students.

Zoe's face lit up when she spoke of him. "Sensei Yoshida was able to make the Japanese martial art attractive for the West. His charm, vast ability, and charisma have brought tens of thousands of Western trainees to the organization."

"We heard he had something to do with Bruce Lee," said Peter.

Zoe did not seem to rejoice in hearing the passion in his words, and responded calmly, "Some say he grew up at the same time Bruce Lee did, and when Bruce Lee started his first steps in the movies, Sensei chose to implant the philosophy of martial arts in the West."

"And it's a good thing he has." said Yael.

When they finished dinner, Yael, Daniel and Peter left the dining hall together. Again, Yael found it difficult to hide her limp. Peter was interested to know what had happened, and she told him.

"What a drag that it happened in the first practice," he said dramatically. She knew he was trying to comfort, but his choice of words was unfortunate.

"It's okay. It's not as bad as it looks; it'll be fine," said Daniel with a calm voice carrying a little comfort.

They parted ways. Limping, she dragged herself to her room where she found the other women already getting organized for the night.

"If I snore, throw shoes at me," stated Charlotte. She continued to tell everyone how she woke up from her own snoring to her great fortune once when she was driving too fast and being followed by a police car on Route One between Los Angeles and San Francisco. No, she was not drunk; it was just after a stormy one-night stand with a guy she had met, and she fell asleep at the wheel. When the police stopped her, she told them, with no shame or hesitation, that she was almost raped and ran in panic from the rapist and this was why she was not aware she exceeded the speed limit.

"And they let you off the hook?" asked Zoe.

"Sure!" said Charlotte with an unconcealed smugness.

"Why am I not surprised?" said Zoe, shaking her head.

"Wow!" exclaimed Eleanor, and turned around to her mother, "Mom, it reminds me a bit of what had happened to you, right?"

"What, what?" Charlotte seemed eager to know.

"Well, I'm not sure this is educational for you young girls," said Cheryl, somewhat embarrassed.

"I'll tell!" Eleanor volunteered and continued, "Mom was stopped once by the police for speeding, and how do you think she got out of it?"

"How? Tell!" everyone prodded.

"By the time the officer approached the car she had managed to quickly tuck a small blanket she had in the car under her dress. When the officer got to the car she told him she was in labor and was rushing to get to the hospital."

All, except Michelle, laughed loudly.

"We got a room full of outlaws!" Zoe exclaimed.

"You know what had happened to me once with the police?" Yael began, and as soon as she said the word "police," the incident at her house entered her mind covered by a black cloud. She pulled herself together, and continued.

"Once, I went with my boyfriend, a friend and her boyfriend and his friend who is sort of a—" the appropriate word had slipped her memory— "how the hell do you call someone who is a bit...oh, yes! A nerd," the word came to her, "and we were getting really tired and it was getting late and, since there was no other choice, we laid our sleeping bags out in the median of a cross road. A police car arrived an hour later."

"And what happened?"

"They told us it was dangerous and illegal to sleep there and asked us to leave."

"So what did you do?"

"We reached a compromise with them that we'd leave right at dawn."

"And?"

In the morning, right at dawn, the nerdy guy woke us up, all frantic, saying 'We must leave, we must leave, we promised!'"

"And?"

"Nothing. The three of us didn't move. We were blown away by the fact he was freaking out about leaving the place."

All were silent. Yael felt that her story didn't have a good punch line like the other stories.

"Someone could have gotten hurt," said Michelle suddenly with a quiet, serious tone.

All were silent. Again, Yael wondered if the others—or at least Zoe—knew what Yael knew about her.

"We won't be woken up tonight, right?" asked Cheryl, diverting the attention from the embarrassing moment.

"You never know," replied Zoe shortly.

"What? It can happen even on the first night?" asked Eleanor.

"Anything is possible," Zoe replied knowingly, "Be prepared for everything." After a brief pause, she continued.

"I suggest we go to sleep."

They all started to prepare for the night. Yael watched Michelle as if trying to find some difference in her behavior to indicate her condition, but failed to do so.

But what did I expect to see? She asked herself.

She prepared her Gee in case there would a practice in the middle of the night. Because of her foot, her greatest fear was running the next morning. How would she do it?

There better not be a practice tonight, she thought to herself, *so I can rest my leg.*

They all said goodnight and the last one to go to sleep, Michelle, turned out the lights. Darkness invaded.

Yael tried to fall asleep, but with no success. *Are they all finding it hard to fall asleep or it's only me?* She wondered.

Disturbing began to flood her mind: the incident at home, the murder... oh, the murder in the park—was it even a murder? Up to that point, she was so busy with the strict regime of Special Training that she hadn't had time to reflect upon the latest occurrences.

Yes, Special Training had come just in time. It was a great break from all of the recent events and the next day would soon be approaching. She found comfort in dealing with the burning matters of the moment—the training, the practice. Her concerns were replaced again with the morning run. The voices of Daniel, Zoe and Michelle blended in her head.

"It will pass," she heard Daniel's words repeated. Zoe's voice added: "You never know." And Michelle's voice echoed: "Someone might get hurt...get hurt...get hurt..."

Sabitri

Yael was very curious about Sabitri, but Sabitri did not speak English except a scattered word here and there, so Yael decided to look for someone who could translate.

Ravindra entered, as if sensing an invitation. It was also a good time to talk because they were on a break. She asked Ravindra if he could translate, and he obliged with a big, white smile. She asked him to ask Sabitri to tell about herself. It was hard to tell whether Sabitri was fond of the interest in her, since she was always smiling naturally. He translated.

"I lost my husband, who was a soldier sent to quell the riots in Gujarat about a year ago," she said, and for a brief moment, a slight expression of turmoil showed across her face, and then the regular big smile returned and she continued, "I have a seven-year-old daughter and a sick father that I take care of," There was a slight change in her facial expression.

"Her mother died six months ago from a serious illness. Since her husband was killed in a car accident in Gujarat and not while he was on duty, the military is delaying the payments she should be getting," Ravindra explained, "She cannot afford a lawyer or someone to represent her, so she had to leave home and move to a little house where she is paying rent."

He clarified something with Sabitri, she nodded in agreement, and he added, "Weekly rent."

There was a silence for a few moments. Yael wanted to know if there were any other family members that could help.

"She has a brother that got in trouble with the law," translated Ravindra, "A few times she even had to pay to bail him out of jail."

Yael also learned that the brother had a baby; his wife could not function since she was diagnosed as mentally ill, and so Sabitri was dividing her time between taking care of her family and her brother's infant. Yael started to feel a bit dizzy. It was too much to bear. But Ravindra continued.

"The parents of her brother's wife are also sick and she takes care of them, too." For a long time Sabitri and her family were starving for bread.

Yael felt sick and that she could hardly bear listening. It seemed that all the evil of the world had fallen on this woman, and in such a short period.

She asked to be excused and went out into the garden to get some air, anxious. Images of a homeless woman she had once seen on the subway in New York floated into her mind.

Maybe she also had a child, like Sabitri...

And then she had another thought.

Damn! The money! The money I threw away...Oh my god...It could have helped Sabitri so much, and I threw it away just like that! Damn me!" Yael tortured herself, *why on earth did I throw it away?*

Tears came to her eyes, but were quickly replaced by embarrassment.

Now people here will see me cry and won't understand why. She didn't want to have to deal with all their questions.

She quickly wiped the tears away as if she was wiping all the accompanied troubling thoughts, and so, with heavy guilt, she returned to the room just to find Ravindra and Sabitri already busy in daily matters. She found herself avoiding looking directly into Sabitri's eyes during the entire day. She performed her work quietly, secluding herself.

A Black Toe

Yael found it difficult to fall asleep. Her body ached. She slowly drifted off, then would wake up and fall asleep again several times, changing position to ease the pain of her body.

There were some noises in the room. She opened her eyes. It was completely dark outside.

What happened? She wondered to herself.

But she soon realized that it was already early morning and time to get up for the morning run. Less than five hours of inconsistent sleep and now they should go out running. She got up slowly and heavily.

What on earth am I doing here? She dragged herself, limping and bruised, to the bathroom. The convenience of home is gone. Girls with red eyes were piling into the shower rooms and the toilets to wash their faces, use the bathroom, and brush their teeth. One was throwing up. Yael also felt a little sick.

Back in the room, Michelle passed by. Yael nodded a greeting, but Michelle was either too sleepy to notice her or ignoring her.

Charlotte and Eleanor were in the room. Charlotte was still getting organized. Eleanor was about to leave the room and noticed that Yael was having troubles with her leg. She asked what happened, but there was no time to discuss it. Zoe came in and pushed everyone to leave. Everyone lined up outside in the usual gathering compound. All were standing barefoot and shivering from the morning chill, lined up in rows, with their legs shaking and shoulders hunched to keep warm. It was still dark, but the sun was slowly rising. The senior about to lead the practice was not familiar to Yael. He waited a few seconds until all were lined up and asked if anyone had any problem that would prevent him or her from running. Yael debated whether to declare her leg—the short walk to the compound had already bothered her. Eleanor, standing next to her, encouraged her to say something.

With a heavy heart, she left the row and joined a small group of trainees that could not run for various reasons.

The Sensei led all the rest on the run. The group of non-runners was led by several seniors into a hall.

"Why can't you run?" The trainees were being questioned one by one by the seniors that Yael referred to as "The Tribe's Elders," or the older men of the highest ranks. They were the ones pulling the strings behind what was going on in the organization and were leading all special trainings.

Her turn came. As an answer, she pointed to her foot and the blue toe that since the previous day had begun to turn black. The instructors all gathered around her to observe the toe. Each of them was compelled to press slightly on the injured toe, causing her pain every time.

"Hmm," Marlon, the most senior among the elders, muttered to himself as he slowly stroked his beard, "This does not look good!"

"Yes," agreed Joseph, another senior, "it seems it should rest."

"No doubt," Kenny agreed, scratching his head. And so, with general consensus, the Special Training Council ruled that Yael had passed the validity test and she would not need to run. To her surprise, a number of trainees that sought an exemption were sent back to join the runners.

Her group, the few trainees that remained, would perform Katas while the others ran. When the runners returned, all were led to a field and scattered to begin the morning practice. It was going to be a practice of kicks. It was a physically exhausting practice.

The counting began in Japanese: "Ich! Ni! San! Chi! Go! Rouk! Sitch! Hatch! Qou! Ju!"

Yael found it hard to perform the technique properly because of her injury and, with no choice left, she continued with her good leg when the Sensei yelled to switch, hoping it would pass unnoticed. The seniors walked between the lines, observing the kickers, memorizing who was giving all they had and who was withdrawn or showed weakness.

In Special Training the technique was less important. However, sometimes the seniors corrected the trainee's technique. They were primarily looking for a fighting spirit and for trainees that could cope with physical and mental difficulties.

"Don't give up!" the senior yelled, "Tighten your mind! Go on! Forward! You didn't come here to rest! This is a war! A war with yourself! Who will win the battle? The weak or the strong?"

The sun had risen. Yael felt that her physical strength had already left a long time ago. She kept going in some sort of unexplained state of inertia. She looked around her. The majority was in the same state. The kicks released were not in any way worthy of a Bruce Lee movie, and the legs were thrown forward tiredly and heavily.

Yael heard a commotion behind her. Someone had fallen. It was far behind her, so it was hard to see what had exactly happened. Several seniors gathered together, but the counting continued and the lines of legs were still kicking.

"Ich! Ni! San! Chi! Go! Rouk! Sitch! Hatch! Qou! Ju!"

After a short pause, the seniors yelled "Kaite!" and the lines changed direction.

One of the trainees stepped out of the line and ran toward the scene behind. *Who is she?* Yael wondered, *why is she running there?* The practice continued, but something was definitely happening. After twenty minutes of uncertainty, the siren of an approaching ambulance is heard.

The counting continued.

"...Ni, san ... Kaite!"

Paramedics jumped from the ambulance with a stretcher and ran toward the scene. Still, the counting continued.

"...Rouk, sitch...Kaite!"

Several minutes passed and soon the falling trainee was carried on the stretcher and disappeared into the ambulance.

"...Hatch! Qou! Ju...Kaite!"

The ambulance drove away.

"Ich! Ni..."

The training continued.

"Yame!" the leading senior yelled to stop.

Thank god, thought Yael. They lined up again in rows and squatted down in a "Seiza," or meditation for the closing of practice. The rapid breathing of the man to her right side blended with the rate of the breathing of the woman to her left. Breathing heavily as well, she tried to figure out where her breathing was in comparison.

"Five minutes to breakfast!" announced the Sensei.

There was no time to change. Although time was limited, all crowded to find out what had happened and who was the one taken by the ambulance. Apparently, the man who fell was in his mid forties. "A real beast," some had said, as he was in a great shape, very athletic, and had also previously raced and won a triathlon. Apparently, he had a heart attack. Luckily, there was a doctor among the trainees who kept him alive until the ambulance arrived. The doctor shook her head. His situation was not good and she said she was hoping for the best.

How fragile we are, thought Yael. Everybody walked in silence toward the dining hall, exhausted.

"No, I'm not going for breakfast. I'm going straight to bed!" Yael overheard a man say to his friend as he left. Someone could be heard vomiting. She looked for Daniel and Peter and located Daniel.

"Peter had to go to the bathroom," Daniel told her, "He felt nauseous after running this morning and barely managed to get through the practice."

"I saw someone vomiting on the way, and there was another in the ladies' bathroom this morning," said Yael.

"Yes, many feel nauseous," said Daniel, "Tremendous mental and physical effort, stress, and also the process of the cleansing of the body's toxins." His gaze moved downward toward her foot, "And what about you? How is your foot?" he asked, adding, "I didn't see you running this morning."

"Yes," she admitted, "I got exempted by the council of the Tribe Elders," she giggled, "It was pretty funny how they poked at my toe..."

Daniel smiled. "You did the right thing."

"What about you?" she asked. Daniel was always concerned for everybody else and he never complained. It always seemed that

176

everything was fine with him. He didn't make an issue out of anything and no one ever bothered to ask him how he was, Yael had noticed.

"Just fine," he replied laconically, and went back to talking about her foot. "Use a bandage to wrap the injured toe with the toe next to it. It will help avoiding twists and will ease your pain."

"Good idea," she said, grateful.

In the dining hall, seated at the table, they shoveled down the simple but nutritious food. Charlotte began to tell about someone who complained about the food in the previous Special Training, but it seemed that right then no one was interested in hearing about it. Everyone was talking about the Kiabadachi, or horse stance, practice to come, fearful. There was a gamble going among the trainees whether it would be the next practice or not. Most bet that it wouldn't be. It's too early, they said; it was only the second day and the kicking practice was too exhausting for the Kiabadachi to follow. Everyone then scattered to rest. There were only a few hours until the next practice. The seniors encouraged getting sleep as much as possible between practices, but Yael knew she wouldn't be able to fall asleep. There was too much adrenaline. She grabbed her music player, tucked the edges of the headphones to her ears, and lay down on the grass, listening to music. Music, as always, was uplifting for tough times.

She lay down for a while and then went back to the room. There, she found the women lying or sitting on the beds and chatting. The high adrenaline had caught them all. It seemed that Michelle wasn't really participating in the conversation, but Yael noticed that she followed Zoe's words closely. She nodded in agreement after almost every sentence.

Michelle had gotten a thorn in her foot while running. The running, as Yael learned, was done barefoot in a field that had thorns and thistles.

Not pleasant, she thought.

Michelle asked Zoe if she could help her to pull out the thorn. Zoe rummaged through her bag, pulled out a first aid kit and took out a tweezers. She asked Michelle to bring her foot towards her and started to pull, apologizing for any inflicted pain. Michelle tightened her lips, clearly hurting.

Charlotte took the opportunity to return to her story that had been cut off in the dining room.

"In a previous year there was a guy who didn't like the food and complained through the entire Special Training. He complained and complained for four days, and it wasn't just about the food. He also complained and whined about the hard practices, his snoring roommates, the conditions of the lodging, that there were no showers and private toilets...in short, he complained about everything."

She said she had had enough of it, and on the last day, while they were having breakfast, and she was sitting next to his table and he started complaining again, she couldn't restrain herself, and she snapped. She got up, walked to him, grabbed his plate, and turned it upside down, spilling the food all over him. He was as shocked as everyone else. She then went back to her seat and continued to eat as if nothing had happened. Then she felt a tap on her back. She turned around. He was standing behind her, covered with his breakfast, waving with his hands to get her attention with a look of confused anger on his face

"You're crazy! What the hell did you do to me, are you completely nuts? This is a new Gee, and you've ruined it!"

Charlotte felt as if smoke were coming out of her ears. She got up abruptly and took her fist to his face. He collapsed on the floor. People rushed to him. She was reprimanded and was warned that she would be dismissed from Special Training and from the organization if it ever happened again, but she knew that everyone felt he had deserved it, including the senior who scolded her.

Eleanor listened eagerly, thirstily drinking in Charlotte's entire story. Michelle, however, seemed to be uncomfortable, and it was not clear if her discomfort was a result of Charlotte or the recently-removed thorn.

"Yes," Said Zoe, "it's true, he deserved it, but it was unacceptable, disrespectful and could even be considered contradictory to the behavioral code that we undertook when we joined Karate."

"Which is?" asked Michelle.

"Never start a fight!"

"Meaning?" grumbled Charlotte.

"If you see a fight, get away from it. If you are provoked, don't respond."

"He didn't provoke me personally, but his whining was presumed provocation to all—the practice, organization, and all what it represents," Charlotte interrupted her, agitated.

"This is your interpretation, which seemingly justifies violent behavior," replied Zoe. She continued, "To each violent person, there's always a hidden reason, but does it justify the violence?"

"So when are we supposed to react?" asked Michelle.

Zoe pulled out iodine and began disinfecting Michelle's wound.

"When there is no choice. When you're being attacked and cannot escape," she paused, thought a bit, and continued, "or when someone is being attacked and needs protection."

Yael observed Michelle carefully. The entire discussion couldn't have been a coincidence. It had to be hard for her to hear. Zoe pulled out a bandage from her kit. Michelle looks like she wanted to say something, but Cheryl preceded her.

"You came here well organized," she said to Zoe.

"Yes," said Zoe, "There's always someone who gets injured."

"Were you ever injured in your previous Special Trainings?" asked Michelle.

"Sure, but nothing serious," Zoe replied.

"What is not serious?"

"Nothing that made me stop," she scanned them all while saying it. *Was she looking differently at me, or did it just seem like it?* Yael wondered to herself. *Is it because I didn't run? Is that considered quitting? Is she trying to imply something?*

179

Emotional Arithmetic

The rooster crowed. Yael woke up the next day with a headache; she felt that each task, even the easiest one, was executed with lack of motivation. Even the basic action like brushing her teeth drained the energy from her.

Today's definitely a sick day, she made clear to herself.

As the minutes passed, she felt her physical state deteriorate along with her dark mood and the pain in her back increased and she found it difficult to sit. Her body agreed to stand or lie down, but when she tried to sit down, she felt like a metal pole was stuck in her back and wasn't allowing it to bend. She shortened her morning visit to the toilet.

Grumbling, Yael climbed back into her bed and lay down. Her eyes fixed on the ceiling. There was a spot there that caught her attention. Over time, the longer she concentrated on the spot, the more features of an uncertain shape started to form. Then a face appeared: Sabitri. It was a screaming face, contorted with pain. Then Sabitri's face transformed into the face of Michelle.

Abruptly, Yael turned her head, looking away. A sharp pain like a knife sliced across her head. She closed her eyes. The image of her emerged as if seen from a flying bird. She watched herself sprinkle the money through the bars of the balcony in the hotel.

How could she have said that to Jennifer? After all she had done for her?

Yael's figure on the hotel balcony moved away, further and further, and the balcony looked more and more like a jail. She appeared so small behind these bars with her hands outstretched through them.

A sharp pain shot through her head again. She opened her eyes, tried to sit up straight, but her back refused.

I have two choices, she thought to herself, *either run away from what I'm going through or stand up to it.*

She clasped her head in her hands. She shook her head from side to side, took a deep breath, and tried to sit up.

180

No, I'm not in a condition for mental negotiation, she thought, there's no choice, but to run away from it. But...how?

She tried to sit up again, but each movement, as small as it may be, caused her immense pain. She managed to stand up and felt somewhat of a relief. She dressed slowly and left the room, heading toward the kitchen.

Maybe a cup of tea will help, she thought. It was a day off for Sabitri, so helping her was not required today.

This is the worst: being sick on a trip, on a journey like this, Yael thought. She took the kettle and filled it up with water. *I hope I don't see anyone today. I don't really want to have to communicate with anyone.*

Ravindra entered, carrying a big sack. Immediately he noticed she was not at her best.

"Are you sick?" he asked.

"Yes, I feel sick," she replied curtly, trying to steer him out of a conversation. "Are there problems?" he asked, as if he knew she was not really sick.

"Yes," she admitted weakly.

"Here," he said, raising the sack, "I bring it this just for you." He said with broken English.

Surprised, she looked at him, questioning.

"Put all your troubles into this bag," he said earnestly, and opened the sack. "Quickly, hurry" he prodded, "No time!"

Trying to figure out whether he was joking or not, Yael watched as he waved his hands toward her as if lifting something very heavy, and threw it into the bag.

"That's it! Now I have your troubles, I go and throw away," he said with a grin.

She couldn't resist his playful attempt to cheer her up, and she smiled back at him. In doing so, she already felt some relief.

"What's wrong?" Ravindra insisted.

"My back's hurt," Yael replied curtly.

"Why not you go up for treatment from Master?"

181

Ravindra's proposal came as a surprise to her. She recoiled at the idea. She was the only guest in the Ashram who had not been led there by medical circumstances. Addressing to Master as a therapist did not suit her.

Ravindra stood quietly, still awaiting her response.

How can I tell him no? He wouldn't understand, Yael thought. I wish I hadn't left my room...I'll make something up and go back to bed."

Vera came in and immediately noticed Yael's state.

"What happened to you?" she asked with an expression filled with both worry and suspicion.

"I'm a bit sick," Yael replied weakly.

"Well, then go up to Master!" she ordered, and turned to Ravindra, "He's here, no?"

"Yes," he said.

"Well?" Vera turned back to Yael.

"I'm not sure" Yael pulled her shoulders back, trying to gain time. She thought for a moment that it might not be such a bad suggestion after all, but the idea of asking Master to take care of her when she was in a weaker position than she already had been didn't seem so appealing.

Vera, having realized the root of her dilemma, stated flatly, "Don't be a little girl. Go up to him!"

"No, really, there is no need. I'll do some yoga on the roof, it would do me good." Yael relentlessly insisted, and without allowing Vera to respond, she rushed out to the roof, still able to hear her words to Ravindra.

"Pride! Foolish pride!"

The roof was spacious and pleasant and had an overlooking view of the city roofs from it. In the center, there was a small pool of water made of concrete and above it, two huge black plastic tanks.

So this is where we get our water supply, Yael thought.

A cool morning breeze caressed her face. In light of the absence of other people, she felt a little better.

A small room at the end of the roof caught her eye. Curious, she approached it slowly. A heavy wooden door partially blocked the entrance. She pushed the door, widening the crack a bit and peered inside. It looked like a meditation room. Mats and mattresses were laid on the floor around the walls and pillows were scattered on them. At the end of the room stood a small round table, covered with dark red-velvet cloth. On it, there were incense and candles surrounding a picture of one of the Indian gods with a face reminiscent of a monkey and a thick long tail. She searched for an appropriate mattress for her exercise when she heard someone coming up the stairs. As if by invitation, Vera's figure appeared in the door carrying two yoga mattresses.

"I thought it could help you," she said.

"I was just looking for a mattress," Yael explained.

"If you want, I'll show you some special exercises to release the tension and pain," Vera offered. "I mean," she added sarcastically "if you agree to get help from me."

Her comment raised a smile on Yael's face, and she nodded in agreement.

Vera laid down her mattress and ordered Yael to put her down, and the two started practicing.

Vera chose to start with a Pranyama breathing exercise.

"Breathing exercises," she explained, "allow the troubled mind to relax and help synchronize the body with mind. Breathing exercises, as difficult as they may be, will benefit you in your condition."

Yael followed Vera's instructions and slowly relaxed her breathing. Indeed, she felt calmer. Vera listened to the sound of Yael's breathing, and when she determined her breathing had slowed down sufficiently, they started to practice Asanas, or yoga positions. She chose to start with simple and straightforward positions that warmed up the body and then she gradually increased the degree of difficulty. Yael felt that Vera had an extensive experience, since, without even touching Yael, she sensed when to raise the difficulty and when to back off. She felt that the charismatic presence of Vera, her confidence, and her ability to lead the way in both challenging and safe manners were taking their toll. After about an hour and a half of practice filled with sweat and maximum concentration, only a dim memory of her headache, aching back and soaring soul was left.

They folded their mattresses and Yael thanked Vera. Vera smiled.

"You may allow yourself to get help from others when in distress, you know."

Yael returned the smile.

The Demons of Kiabadachi

"All forty years old and over, with me!" ordered the Sensei. She led the forty year old plus trainees a few feet further into the huge grass football field. Yael didn't understand why they were being divided into two separate age groups.

"Black belts! Form two circles" ordered the Sensei. "White and brown belts, form a circle in between the black belts. There should be three circles formed with black belts in the exterior circle, brown and white belts in the next circle, and then black belts again in the most interior circle."

The seniors walked among the trainees and changed the position of some with other trainees, at a discretion that was known only to them. They moved Michelle next to Charlotte.

Why? Wondered Yael. *What is this practice going to be?* Looking around, everyone else seemed to be wondering the same thing. Suspicion arose in Yale's mind that it was going to be the Kiabadachi, or horse stance, practice, which was soon confirmed by whispers passed among the other trainees. A heavy tension invaded the air. All began anticipating what was to come.

Yael felt a thrill of excitement in her stomach. She searched after her other roommates—Cheryl and Eleanor. Cheryl had been moved to the "forty plus" group. Yael turned her head slightly back. Eleanor was behind her, but not in a comfortable angle to see. One of the seniors approached Yael.

"Have you lost something behind you?" he asked with a hard tone and moved on.

Zoe was approaching her. She wanted to confirm that everything was alright. The thought that Zoe was be spreading protective wings upon her was a comforting one.

"Hajeme!" shouted the Sensei suddenly.

All black belts trainees spread their legs and bent their knees. The rest – brown and white belts hurried to do the same. For some trainees, the bend was massive and they squatted quite low, while others did less. They interlaced either their arms or their hands, placed them on their stomachs, and shook their shoulders to release any coming tension. Kiabadachi, the practice everyone had feared, had begun.

They had to remain with their knees bent in that position in complete silence for an entire hour and a half. No movement, even the slightest, was allowed. Yael felt the excitement, something that wasn't negative, but actually quite positive. It was a curiosity, an anticipation to see how things would turn out and how it would be. A comforting thought passed into her mind.

Now, ironically, no shifting and no movement should be a blessing for the injured toe, she thought, but her body seemed to think otherwise. After only a minute, she began to feel a terrible, aching discomfort and a strong desire to get out of the prison-like position. She scanned the crowd for Daniel and Peter. Peter looked more uncomfortable compared to Daniel, whose facial expression conveyed calm.

Opposite her, in the white belts' circle, there was a woman trainee who looked young, doll-faced, fair-haired, and a bit plump—a figure that didn't seem to fit the scenery of Martial Arts.

Another minute passed. The position became more and more unpleasant. Her body wanted to move, to change positions.

"Look forward!" the Sensei shouted.

Yael stole a glance back at the fair-haired young woman. Her facial expression was constantly changing: her eyebrows were going up and down, her mouth opened and closed, her shoulders moved up and down and it seemed she found it extremely difficult to stay in her stalemate position. Yael wondered what would happen to her if she couldn't keep still after only three minutes.

How treacherous is the body, she thought to herself. *When it's asked to do something, it rebels...*

Thoughts continued to pass through her mind.

When there is no synchronization between the body and mind, it seems it hurts more. The discomfort became so strong she didn't know if she could stand it.

"Tighten your mind!" the Sensei yelled, as if directed straight at to her.

The advice arrived just in time. She decided to "tighten her mind" and stare straight into the eyes of pain as if it was an opponent she must defeat. No, she would not lose this battle. From that moment, she knew that no matter what, the battle was hers to win. She started concentrating on the breathing she exercised in yoga practices and used the breathing as a weapon to defeat the pain. And sure enough, slowly, her mind gradually calmed down from the pressure and the fear that she could not handle it began to diffuse. The pain, although still remaining, was no longer a threat. The stress in her body decreased. The first five minutes, those few minutes that had felt like an eternity, had passed, and a small splash of relief swept over her. After the first round of her battle with herself, she was free to check what was going on around her again.

The seniors were moving among the trainees and, as if it were not hard enough to stand still in that impossible position, the seniors made it harder by standing behind the trainees and pushing their thighs with their knees or foot to deepen the bending. Then they stood in front of the trainees, faced them and tapped on both their shoulders to encourage them to go further down and lower.

Another five minutes had passed. Yael lost her rhythm of breathing for a second and felt a small panic. She focused again on slow, deep breaths. Her yoga training seemed to be of the most use in this practice. Her body remembered the sensation of being in one position for a very long time without moving.

These minutes are adding up, she thought, *after ninety minutes, it'll all be over.*

"Soften and drop your shoulders!" shouted the Sensei.

Half an hour had passed. Some people were having a very difficult time. As soon as someone showed signs of falling apart, it had an immediate impact on the person next to him or her, a sort of wave that affected and weakened the entire group.

Suddenly, a shout was heard.

Who is it? Yael wondered.

And then another shout. It came from the direction of the black belts. Similar cries resembling a Kiai, or a yell used during basic techniques, began being shouted around the room. It seemed that the black belts and the seniors were using the shout as a release of energy when they felt the group was in crisis and getting weaker. The release enabled them to gather strength to defeat the most threatening enemy: themselves. The opponent, this time, was their mental weakness, and their lack of faith in themselves. For a few moments, while Kiai shouting were heard, curiosity overtook their mind and they were distracted from the harshness of the practice.

At this point, the power of the group was being discovered. The wave of cries strengthened everyone for a few minutes, but then the Kiai stopped, and an oppressive silence resumed.

With the restored silence, everyone's breathing could be heard again along with the uncomfortable sighs. The senses were sharpened so that each grimace, each shortness of breath or sigh, testified to the mood.

Yael recalled Zoe's words from the conversation earlier that day.

When are we supposed to attack? Michelle had asked.

When someone is being attacked and needs protection, was Zoe's answer.

Yael's mind started to return to the incident at home.

They attacked Eyal—she felt her knees tremble a bit—*Could I have done anything? Jumped on the man with the dreadlocks? On the damn phony lame? Could I have prevented it? I didn't protect Eyal well enough...*

Suddenly, she noticed that one of the trainees was moving too much. From where she stood, it seemed to be only a few inches a movement.

Immediately, one of the seniors approached him. He forced him to deepen the bend, tapping hard on his shoulders. Then he stood facing him, raised his right arm and pointed with two fingers to his own eyes, instructing the trainee to look into his eyes. He stared right into the eyes of the trainee. He did not offer comfort. His gaze was harsh. It

188

was not only a disciplinary gaze, but a demonstration of power, an instruction to the trainee as to where his mind should be. The trainee stabilized and only after the senior saw that he could stand still on his own did he leave.

Yael glimpsed the fair-haired woman moving slightly from the corner of her eyes. A few seconds passed and the young woman started to twitch. After another few seconds, her body began going into spasm. A terrified expression passed across her face. There was no doubt that she was going through something bad, very bad. Yael felt anxious, concerned.

After a few more seconds, Zoe arrived. She stood facing the young woman. Like the previous senior, she instructed her to look and focus right into her eyes. The girl, still terrified, stared into Zoe's eyes. Zoe instructed her to breathe deeply together. The tics gradually decreased, and the girl relaxed and stabilized.

After a few seconds, Zoe left her. But the tics started again and then, all of a sudden, she disappeared from Yael's sight.

What happened? Did she fall?

It was hard to see since the trainees next to her, not daring to move, blocked her view.

A senior hurried over, and Yael, through the corner of her eye, saw him bend down.

Then it hit her. *She passed out.*

Another senior arrived, followed by Zoe. Nervousness mixed with cautious curiosity could be felt spreading across the practice area.

"Remain in your positions! Look straight ahead, not sideways or anywhere else! You are in a practice! Concentrate on your practice! What is happening around you is not of your concern!" the Sensei's instructions were heard.

Three minutes passed by and the young woman got back on her feet again, as if nothing had happened. She returned to the position. The seniors stabilized her and made sure she was fine a number of times. Then they left her, still watching from afar. Zoe stayed in close range, watching her back.

189

A few more minutes passed and it seemed that another trainee on the other side of the circle passed out. The seniors rushed to him.

These are not good signs, thought Yael. The fainting began to affect the group and a wave of nervousness rose again. The group was weakening. The black belts felt it, and they started another round of Kiai shouts.

This time, the brown and white belts joined in. It moved like a wave of energy through the group and everyone filled with the spirit of battle. The group could be felt getting stronger.

Yael didn't join the shouts. She suddenly felt like she was in a psychiatric department of a hospital.

What the hell am I doing here? It's one big madhouse...is this really happening?

But along with these thoughts, she felt the power of the Kiai began coursing through her. It lifted everyone's state of mind.

And then silence.

Another five minutes have passed. Then, images from the strange event in the park surfaced in her mind. Again and again she saw the glint sparkle of what she believed a knife. She tried to recall what had happened to make her pass out just like that.

Is it possible it had happened by itself? Or had she been struck down, and that caused her to fall? But she had not felt any pain anywhere when she awoke, just a slight pressure below her ribs and in her head. If indeed someone had struck her, this someone must have been very skilled, had known the weak points of the body, and had managed to cause her to pass out without her even being aware of it.

The pain of her body brought her back to reality. It hurt. Her body ached. The position was intolerable. It was miserable. Yael tried to concentrate and calm herself down. But again, her thoughts wandered to that evening in the park.

And what did Jeff want? He had wanted to talk about something with her; it seemed it was important and that he wanted to talk particularly with her. And she had refused, turned him down, and turned her back on him—how embarrassing.

What if I imagined the whole scene of that murder in the park? Maybe my mental state isn't entirely alright after all that happened with Eyal, but why? What happened? After all, we were left intact and I am strong, right? Or maybe not? The sight of Eyal unconscious with the fork aimed at his throat hit her repeatedly. *Everything is my fault. If I wouldn't have gone to the subway...me and my curiosity. If I had paid more attention, I might have noticed that the phony lame was following me and if I would have bought that damn food for Spike, it wouldn't have happened,"* she agonized.

An hour had passed. Everybody ached with discomfort, and the room was full of bodies that sweat without having moved. The amount of the physical and mental energy required for the practice squeezed the practitioners up to the point that they were standing in a pool of water caused by their own dripping sweat.

I wonder what Eyal is doing right now, she mused, *with the production now on the west coast."* She wondered if Barbara was also traveling with him. For some reason, the thought that Barbara would use the opportunity to hit on him didn't bother her.

This is a sign that I really don't care anymore about what's going on with us, she reflected. She embraced her mind to understand how and why things had started to deteriorate. She failed to find a proper reason. *Relationships are such fluid things. A friend becomes an enemy, an acquaintance becomes a friend, and a friend becomes a lover.*

Suddenly, she heard a yell.

"Yame!"

"Is it over?" she wondered.

But it wasn't. To her surprise, no one from the black belts in her group had moved and, as a result, neither the white nor the brown belts were moving either.

The only apparent movement was in the forty-plus group. Now she understood why they were divided into two groups: the forty-plus trainees were doing the practice for only an hour.

Only an hour, she thought, amused. It did seem to make much of a difference.

Yael watched them from afar. She located Cheryl. It seemed it was very difficult for Cheryl, like the others, to move and walk. They rubbed their legs, shaking them out.

I also want to move, she thought.

Apparently, Yael was not the only one. The finale of the above-forty group made it psychologically more difficult for the under-forty group. Again, the group spirit broke.

The black belts felt it and a series of Kiai started again. This time, Yael joined. In fact, it seemed that this time, all were joining and yelling. *Wow, this is powerful*, she thought

Another fifteen minutes passed. The situation became unbearable. This last half an hour seemed the most difficult of all. Kiai cries were heard more often.

Then, out of nowhere, the call came.

"Yame!"

Everyone was shocked that it was finally over. Yael's body, as everyone else, found it hard to snap out of the position it had gotten so used to for an hour and a half. She managed a small movement and, all of a sudden, moving seemed so unnatural. The pain involved in the movement was unbearable. Her muscles were terribly tense. The seniors instructed them to walk a bit and then divide themselves into pairs and massage each other. Everyone breathed a sigh of relief. It was over.

The Opponent Within

"What else do you know about her?" Yael couldn't refrain from attempting to get more details about Michelle.

"Nothing," he shrugged.

"Are you even sure that what you heard is true?" she prodded, hoping he would say no.

"Yeah, I'm sure," said Peter emphatically. Daniel remained silent. They sat down for dinner. Yael located Zoe at the seniors' table.

"This evening Zoe's with the tribe elders," she observed out loud.

"They must be exchanging stories and opinions about us from the Kiabadachi practice." said Peter as he watched Zoe, "Finally she's agreed to join the clique."

"What do you mean?" asked Yael, curious.

"Oh, there was a big argument between her and Malcolm."

"Our Malcolm?" clarified Yael.

"Yes. He wanted her to undertake the responsibility of a senior in Special Training."

"So what's the problem? She didn't want to?"

"Malcolm got in trouble politically with Sensei Yoshida. Zoe, as Sensei Yoshida's favorite, didn't want to be a senior acting from Malcolm's Dojo as long as the relations between Malcolm and Sensei Yoshida weren't a bed of roses. She even thought about leaving. I think she's still thinking of leaving and opening a Dojo of her own."

"It wouldn't be bad at all," Daniel said.

"Yes, many would join," Peter agreed.

"That's why it was probably important to Malcolm that she would be here, representing his Dojo, so he could keep her under control and prevent her from spreading her wings," said Daniel.

Yael recalled the debate between Malcolm and Zoe she had witnessed. Now, the little mystery was solved.

"The politics are pretty gross," she said to the two, and added, "You wouldn't expect this in a martial arts organization, would you?"

"You can't prevent it. It exists in every organization that has some kind of hierarchy, any chain of command," Daniel said with a sad expression on his face.

Michelle approached the table. She seems indecisive as per whether to sit with them or continue to another table.

"Hi!" Peter said loudly, welcoming her.

"Hey," She replied.

His greeting tipped the scales in favor of their table, and she joined them. Peter, smooth as usual, asked Michelle how the Kiabadachi practice was for her. Michelle paused a moment before answering.

"Not easy, but it's good it's behind us..." she laconically replied.

"How do you feel now?" Peter pressed.

"Just fine, and how are you?" Surprisingly, Michelle replied with an assertive tone.

Peter, failing to recognize that she realized he was trying to talk her into telling more about herself, tried another technique and began sharing experiences. He talked about his moments of crisis, the thoughts that passed through his mind, and how others standing next to him handled it. Surprisingly, the conversation turned intimate and swept them all into sharing.

Michelle appeared like a real fighter. During the practice, she nearly fainted several times and suffered from terrible nausea and even hallucinations, but she didn't give up.

These, thought Yael, *are the strongest ones, since whoever experiences such great fears and is able to overcome them is really the strongest.*

Yael was unable to understand how the features that were discovered in Michelle could coincide with being a battered woman.

It'll be really interesting to see the true nature of people during these few days of special training, Yael thought to herself.

She scanned the others. Daniel was listening carefully with interest and, as usual, didn't talk much.

"What about you?" Peter asked Daniel, as if reading Yael's thoughts.

194

"Not an easy practice," Daniel said in his typical quiet manner.

"But surely for you it was unbearable with your knee."

Daniel had a serious knee problem and the flexing his knee was particularly difficult and dangerous for him.

"We all have our demons," said Daniel, adding, "I tried to ignore the pain, sometimes more successfully, sometimes less..."

"And you, Yael?" asked Peter. Yael said that the practice was less difficult and scary than what she originally expected. Maybe the yoga and meditation she was practicing had helped.

"How is that?" Peter was interested to know. Daniel also seemed curious.

Yael thought for a moment and explained, "In Yoga and meditation, you are training both body and mind to be in a static, quiet state for a long time. I guess being in a posture so long was not foreign to me."

Peter seemed to have troubles understanding her last misspoken sentence, but Daniel clarified it for him while Yael continued to reflect. She knows her weak points: speed and agility. But in slow and static scenarios, she came out strong.

Michelle, on the other hand, found the static state to be very difficult, but for her, like the others, it had mainly been a mental struggle. She said that she felt at times that she wanted to scream and run, breaking all the rules. She barely kept herself from doing so. Everyone nodded in agreement, completely identifying with what she had described.

The girls departed, chatting on the way back to the room. It seemed that the ice broke a bit. Yael asked Michelle if it was her first Special Training.

"Yes, and you?"

"Yes, mine too."

"Were you nervous?" Michelle seemed curious.

"Yeah, sure, it didn't sound easy, but it seems to me it'll make us stronger," Yael said.

Michelle raised her eyebrows skeptically, "Maybe yes, maybe no."

Yael went on to say that she began to understand that it was about more than the physical effort; it was about forging their minds. To her surprise, Michelle replied that she didn't believe in forging the mind.

"The mind is weak and vulnerable." She stated flatly, "Everything to do with emotions is weakening you."

Yael, surprised by this blunt statement, didn't know how to respond at first.

"So what? Do you believe that a strong body is enough?" she inquired.

"Whoever has physical strength, muscle..." said Michelle, "...is the strongest!" Determined, she continued, "Nothing else matters." Michelle mused a bit to herself, and then added, as if trying to convince herself, "This is why I'm here—to forge the body! To become stronger!"

Yael thought about how to respond. She strongly disagreed.

"But isn't the Kiabadachi practice we went through a proof that, without a strong mind, you will fail?"

"Yes, but there you were facing yourself. What would happen in a fight or if a giant man attacked you on the street? What's a strong mind worth then?"

It was seemed there was mocking tone in Michelle's words. Yael knew where it was coming from, and she wanted to try to understand, but they were already about to enter the room where all the other girls were getting ready for the night. The scenery changed, and with it, the topic.

While trying to fall asleep, Yael returned to pondering Michelle's words.

It's complete nonsense, she thought, "There is so much evidence that a strong mind wins." But doubt entered her mind, and she hesitated. "But maybe she's right... from her perspective, maybe she has to face a violent giant every evening... "

1000 Punches

Troubled, Yael couldn't fall asleep for a long time. By the time she managed to fall asleep, it felt like she had just closed her eyes and it was already time to wake up. It was a drill—a night practice.

It was 1:30 AM, and cold. They went out barefoot, blurred, and half-asleep. The whiteness of their Gees gleamed occasionally in the complete darkness. There was no moon, just starlight twinkling above.

They were led quietly, without speaking, to a field. They stood in lines and began the night practice. They had to do a thousand Oizuki front punches. They were to step ten steps forward and, with every step, throw a punch. Then, they were to turn around and do another ten steps, and so on, until exactly thousand punches were performed.

A thousand Oizuki sounded endless. I doubt I can do it, thought Yael.

"Hajeme!" shouted the Sensei.

Here we go, she thought.

"If you do each of the Oizuki well and imagine an opponent, it will be to your benefit!" the Sensei advised.

Darkness. It was clearly not a practice of showing off. No one could see the technique. Her body was waking up slowly, and she felt that the shock after the drill was slowly starting to fade. The moon rose up in the sky. The white uniforms gleamed in the dark, and the soft rustle of cloth friction merged harmoniously with the touch of the dew-soaked earth. Again, the atmosphere seems surreal. Yael imagined herself in ancient Japan, practicing a secret Samurai regiment going into a battle to protect the king.

This time, all trainees lead the practice in turns. Each counted from one to ten in Japanese, and punched at every count. *Ich! Ni! San! Chi! Go! Rouk! Sitch! Hatch! Qou! Ju!* After a short pause, they shouted "Kaite," and changed directions. The counting baton passed from one to the next.

Soon, it would be her turn. They had to count loudly enough so that everyone could hear, expressing confidence and inviting a warrior spirit to come out.

Yael's turn arrived. It was a special feeling to lead hundreds of people moving all as one body, one spirit. Again, she felt the recognition of the strength of the group. But even here, despite of the magical atmosphere and the special scenery, she experienced moments of crisis. Her body was tired and sore. They all would have to pull together as a group to get through it.

The practice ended relatively quickly. It had lasted one hour—half the time of a normal practice. They scattered to their rooms. All climbed back into her bed, longing for the comfort and relaxation more than ever. Yael wanted nothing more than to sleep.

A thought entered her mind: half of the Special Training had already passed. Had she really given all she had in each practice?

Feelings and fears of what was to come possessed her mind, especially regarding the upcoming test. She managed to fall asleep, but her sleep is continuously uncomfortably interrupted. The physical and mental efforts were leaving their mark. She felt twinges in her knees and stomach like stabs of knives and some are quite unbearable. She found herself occasionally waking up due to a punch or a kick she delivered into the air while asleep.

Whip and Carrot

One day Master instructed John to volunteer his camera so Yael could take some pictures of the Ashram and upload them to the website she was working on. Master left the Ashram, and Ravindra told Yael he was expected to return that evening because a local family was coming for counseling.

He works hard, she thought, *to be constantly available to treat illnesses as well as acting as a psychotherapist. He treats mental and deceptive aching souls as well as handling the world's problems, providing practical advices, plus he runs a small school where he teaches the Ayurverdic medicine to those chosen students - not simple at all!*

The family arriving that evening was a very limited group: a teenage boy with an older man whom Yael later learned was his uncle and a police officer. The boy looked detached from what was happening. His uncle, on the other hand, seemed excited and agitated. Master exchanged a few words in Nepalese with the uncle while the boy was standing in the middle of the room, his head down and his hands interlaced on his lap in a defensive pose. It was clear that they were talking about him, but all this time Master did not look at the boy even once. When they were done talking, they turned to the boy and started roaring at him. He burst into tears, crying even more while their attacks on him intensified. At one point, it seemed that they were playing the roles of a good cop, bad cop.

After several long minutes, the uncle and Master spoke again with each other, ignoring the boy completely. Then, the uncle looked at the boy with a harsh glare and left without saying a word. Master, who now had the stage for himself, has switched to a "show" mode. Yael, Ravindra, Kutan and Partab – who was Master's student – were his audience. He told everyone in the room in English why the boy was brought to him: he used to go out drinking in bars, disobeyed his parents, hung out with hooligans, brought these hooligans to school and picked up fights. After discussing it with the uncle, Master decided to have the boy over for few days; otherwise he would have to be quarantined in India's so-called "Correction Center."

The show began. Master sat at the table and told the boy in a loud voice to approach him. The boy approached the table and immediately started to cry. He was afraid. Yael did not understand what was said between Master and the boy since it was said in Nepalese, but at some point, Master asked Ravindra to do something and the latter went out and returned with a knife and fork in his hands. He handed them over to Master. Master told the boy to put his left palm on the table and spread his fingers. He asked the boy a question. The boy shook his head, panting heavily. Another question was asked. This time he shook his head and began crying again, his palm still on the table.

Yael missed a heartbeat when, all of a sudden, she saw Master holding the fork high up in the air, waving it and landing it with an amazing precision in between the boy's two fingers. The boy kept on crying but his hand still did not budge from the table. "What would have happened if he would have missed it?" Yael thought, 'This is crazy!" After saying a few more sentences to the boy, Master threateningly waved the knife again. The boy removed his palm in fear from the table. Master grabbed the boy strongly, said something else, and then released him. Then he rose up from his seat and left the room while muttering just loudly enough to be heard by the audience, "Some boys do need strong discipline!"

Still in shock, Yael turned to Ravindra so he could clarify the scene for her. Ravindra said that sometimes, when there are severe disciplinary problems with youngest that had left the right path and their families no longer can cope with them, they are brought over here. Then, Master exercises his different disciplinary techniques on each of them. With the boy who was here he had threatened to injure his finger's nerve and cut his balls off with a knife.

"What?" exclaimed Yael, astonished.

Ravindra continued, "Often, at the "Puja" ceremony—a ritual for honoring the gods—, he deprives the wayward boy of all of his jewelry and pride in front of everyone and slaps him, causing him to pass out

200

outside and in front of a group of strangers. He embarrasses him again and again to break his spirit. Then, when the young one expresses genuine remorse, he returns him back to his parents. Sometimes the process takes a day or two, sometimes more. There was a hard case that lasted two weeks."

The next day she went up to the roof to the quiet, peaceful meditation room. She sat and reflected about yesterday's extreme event. She sat there for a while. Later, as she was leaving the meditation room, she saw the disciplined boy sitting at the end of the roof, crying. The boy did not dare to look into her eyes.

Three more days had passed and to her surprise, when she saw the boy again he seemed smiling and joyful. Something looked different with him. He was helping with the works at the Ashram and seemed eager to please everyone. He even dared to look into her eyes. A day later, she no longer saw him and when she inquired about him, it turned out that the treatment was successful and the boy has returned to his home.

Combat

It was dawn. The alarm clock sounded. Yael sat up, immediately experiencing a flash of terrible nausea and a strong headache. She attached her injured toe to the one next to it and tied them together with adhesive tape as suggested by Daniel.

They were lined up in two lines for the Kumite combat practice. Each of them stood facing an opponent.

"Hajeme!" shouted Sensei Zoe, who led the practice. The match began. Yael was tired, her head ached, but something in her was awakening in light of the fight. Facing her was a woman who wore white belt. Yael attacked strongly, but carefully. As a senior to her by rank, she must be careful not to injure her. Being too cautious, she immediately got hit in the arm.

"Yame!" shouted the Sensei.

The lines moved a step to the left. Facing her, then, was a man - she recalled his name being Don. Like her, he was a brown belt and would be tested for his black belt. He was more skillful. He examined her carefully. He noticed her injured toe. Would he use it to his advantage? How skilled opponents looked at each other could determine who would win the fight. The facial expression, the body position, and the initial scanning of the opponent were already a part of the battle. How one projected oneself to the opponent and what she or he projects back was crucial. She felt he was an even match.

"Hajeme!" shouted the Sensei.

This time, the other side must attack first. She received a strong hit on her arm, in exactly the same spot struck by the previous opponent. She brought her protectors with her, but had seen that no one was wearing them, so she was reluctant to use them. She didn't want to be an exception. Now, she regretted it. She almost didn't manage to evade the attack.

That was close...I've got to pull myself together.

"Yame!"

The opponents alternated. Next, she faced Hamid. Hamid was known to her from previous practices. He was a man in his forties, clearly a handsome man in the past—tall and sturdy but, at the same time, thin and flexible—one of the most self-controlled practitioners in the organization. He never panicked and was very calculated, cold, and very fast. He had the capability of accurately estimating distances and adjusting the intensity of his attack and body momentum. She had seen him in real fights. He could defeat her in a single attack, if he wanted to. It was clear to her. There was a lot to be learned from Hamid. He was a combat veteran. He had been in Karate almost forty years, starting as a child. He emigrated with his parents from Lebanon to the States.

Yael, however, had only been in Karate for less than three years, and started at a considerable old age. She felt complete inferiority up against him.

However, his confidence, quietness, tranquility, and the energy radiating from him ironically calmed her. The likelihood of getting injured by him was very low because of his superiority, and she knew there was no point in trying to defeat him. From him, she only had to learn, learn and learn.

"Hajeme!" shouted the Sensei, and the dance of combat began.

Yael revolved around him, looking for a breach to burst through. He was generous. She felt that sometimes he gave her an artificial upper hand, but she wouldn't accept charity from him. He closed the breach, understanding she wanted to play a fair game. She decided to attack when he was distracted by closing the breach. Her attack was bad, the timing was wrong, and the speed and the intensity of the attack did not match the distance between them. His evasive maneuver to avoid her attack was effortless. He tried to correct her, to stabilize her shaky stance, and to demonstrate how she should have attacked. She regretted having to switch opponents. She would have liked to learn more.

She faced Michelle next. She tried to get a sense for her as a rival. After Hamid, the difference was huge. In contrast, Michelle radiated nervousness and insecurity. Yael knew she should be even more concentrated now since the likelihood of being injured by Michelle was higher—her ability to control and her skills were low, and that made her a dangerous opponent.

It was Yael's turn to attack. Michelle was not successful in blocking the attack, but Yael halted it just before making contact, so Michelle is unharmed. It seemed that despite Michelle's nervousness, she acknowledged that Yael had halted the attack.

Although they weren't allowed to talk, Michelle muttered, "Don't spare me! I won't spare you!" in a tone that sounded a bit threatening.

"No talking!" a shout came from the Sensei.

Yael didn't know what to do. *Did Michelle feel I was patronizing her by sparing her, or that maybe I was doing it out of mercy? She probably didn't take it as a goodwill gesture,"* thought Yael.

It was Michelle's turn to attack. *I won't spare you!* Was echoed through Yael's head. Yael spread apart her legs, bent her knees, and raised her fists, one to protect her face, and the other slightly lower to protect her abdominal. She anxiously awaited the attack, trying to calm herself down by breathing deeply. The dance began. Both started to prance in front of the other, circling. Yael tried to guess where the attack would come from. There was always a small hint, a gesture that indicated the moment the opponent chooses to attack—it could be a small headshake, a slight movement in the body, hands, or foot, a blink of an eye—there was always something. It could hardly be noted in the seniors thanks to the years of practice that had taught them to suppress the small hint that could tilt the balance between winning and losing. But skills and experience were also required for identifying the gesture and take advantage of it.

Yael examined Michelle carefully. Where was her center of gravity? Would she attack with a punch or a kick? Would she attack once, or would she perform two attacks one after another? Michelle hesitated. Yael's self-confidence rose. She decided to "invite" her to attack like Hamid had to her. She would position her body where her rival would feel she had a breach to burst through.

Michelle didn't accept the invitation. Instead, she continued to prance around, bouncing, switching legs—once to the left, then to right, and over again.

Maybe it's her tactic to wear me out, thought Yael while constantly performing evasive maneuvers to accommodate Michelle's, *or maybe she is afraid to attack.*

She decided to try a different strategy, and got closer to Michelle instead of moving away from her. It was already much more than "an invitation" to attack. This was "pushing the opponent against the wall." Now, in this situation, the opponent had no choice. She must attack. The safe distance opponents mutually maintain before the attack was broken. When one of the opponents got too close, the other had to either get away or attack immediately. The instinct was to attack right away without thinking too much.

The trick worked. Michelle had to attack. Yael, thinking she had the upper hand and she was controlling the game, was surprised to get a punch in the nose.

A sharp pain spread through her face. She grabbed her nose. It was bleeding—high price for her arrogance. Michelle continued to bounce back and worth, unsure whether the combat was over or if her opponent would attack back. Zoe rushed over. Yael was removed from the combat area. She would be examined by the physician.

The physician was one of the trainees, the same woman who treated the man who had a heart attack. She hadn't participated in the practice and was busy with handling all sorts of injuries. After a brief inspection that confirmed that no serious damage was caused, she ordered Yael to lie on the ground with her face upward so the nose would stop bleeding. A few minutes after the bleeding stopped, Yael returned to the combat area.

In the following combats, she was already less arrogant and more careful. The practice ended without additional injuries. She had gotten off easy this time with just a bleeding nose and a bruised arm. Other trainees were also injured. One sprained his foot, another broke her finger, and another's shoulder dislocated; some had a few stretched tendons or were hit in their faces.

Yael went out onto the lawn and spread a piece of cloth on the grass. There were several minutes left before breakfast, and she lied down to rest a bit. She found it difficult because of her injuries. While lying on the grass, she recalled the fights, analyzed how they went and what her state of mind had been during the fighting. Accuracy was only a barrier until it would be achieved. The desire to be accurate undermined the fighting spirit. Because they were being watched by the seniors, each attack was done thinking of how it should be done, and how it would appear.

She continued reflecting as she walked to breakfast. Zoe noticed her and was interested to know what was bothering her. In the dining hall, seated at the table, Yael asked how a person could be clear-headed in a fight, and how one could acquire the ability to see things as they were, without putting the ego ahead, and without the need to impress.

"How can you reach the 'no will to lose' instead of 'desiring to win'"? She asked.

Zoe waited patiently until Yael was through with the flood of the questions and replied.

"It's much simpler than it seems. It just works from the gut, intuitively. To defeat an opponent is possible when working in a vacuum, not engaged in the fear of being hurt and not being pre-occupied with how to break the opponent so it will look good. You don't think about victory. One must move from point A to point B without any disturbance and without even understanding what had happened on the way. This is being clear headed."

Yes, thought Yael, *with the seniors and the highly skilled trainees it does seem so. That's the difference, the state of mind I must adopt to become a good fighter.*

Yael suddenly felt her stomach turn upside-down. She had to get to the bathroom quickly. She apologized to Zoe and left the dining hall.

A bout of diarrhea was the last thing she wanted during Special Training, but unfortunately, luck and her body was against her. She emptied her bowel and slowly walked to her room, rummaging through her bag to pull out a pill. She blew her nose, and a little bit of blood showed up in the tissue.

It is really not broken? She wondered.

Michelle entered the room. She asked how Yael was doing.

"Everything is fine," Yael replied.

Michelle apologized, and Yael responded that it was alright. Michelle asked if she wanted to go out to sit in the sun a bit. Yael nodded in affirmation. They left the room together, and Yael couldn't help but think that, for some strange reason, the fight brought them together. They sat down on the edge of the stone fence that surrounded the building, enjoying the warmth of the sun. Each of them began to point out their injuries.

"I got hit in my arm!"

"I completely twisted my finger!"

"My back and shoulder blades are so tight!"

"Yeah! Me too, and that's usually more characteristic of the men!"

"Why?"

"Because they put their ego ahead more than women, and they find it difficult to soften while fighting," Yael explained.

Then Michelle shared her experiences from the Kumite practice with Yael. The conversation that began with talking about their physical state took on an interesting twist.

Michelle admitted that she had been terribly frightened for the combat. It was a lot harder for her than Kiabadachi. She felt that she wouldn't be able to attack or defend properly and, as she faced more and more opponents, she felt she had to succeed. She had already failed once in a test for a black belt and it was very important for her to succeed this time. She had to pull herself together.

Yael listened quietly, thinking about the fact that, for Michelle, this particular combat practice meant so much more. Michelle told her how, for some reason when she stood facing Charlotte, something had changed within her, and she became very determined. There was something about Charlotte that caused her anger to rise. Most likely, it was Charlotte's prideful arrogance. The anger took her to another place; it transformed her to another state of mind, a state which she had realized all of a sudden that 'all is in the mind'. She had gone head to head with Charlotte, and said that, if it had been a real fight and not a practice, she would have bit her.

Yael noticed when Michelle said it her eyes were sparking. And then, Michelle continued to share more experiences, saying she faced another trainee – a giant one, and also felt she could have bit him. She claimed over and over that something had changed and it seemed to her that defeat was all in her head.

Black Belt

The last day was physically very hard. Yael's body was completely worn out, but knowing it was the last day and seeing the coming end made the physical pain more bearable. However, a huge tension replaced the relief of being nearly finished: the tension before the final test.

Yael would be called after Daniel, Peter and Michelle. The excitement for the test was apparent on the faces of those who were about to be tested. They replayed the two forms they were about to demonstrate in their minds. The anxiety of going into oblivion in the middle of the test while everyone was watching was huge. It could be so embarrassing. Yael hoped it wouldn't happen to her.

"All examinees please enter the hall!" announced the Sensei.

The seniors directed them to the corner of the hall. It was the university's basketball court, and it was big enough to have a large audience, which included all of the trainees who participated in Special Training, their families and friends, and visiting trainees from all over the east coast who came just to watch the tests. Some people in the audience were equipped with video cameras to capture the test of their loved ones. At the edge of the big hall, there was a long desk and behind it, a row of chairs for the examining seniors. There were pens and papers, soft drinks, and refreshments on the desk.

Nice set up for the seniors, she thought.

The examiners stepped in, Zoe among them. They sat in front of the long desk. It seemed it was not clear who was supposed to sit where, and Yael watched how they shifted between being polite and being pushy with a bit of amusement. Finally, the hierarchy was settled and each found his or her appropriate place. On the paper laid in front of them, they would put down their remarks and would rate each of the tested.

There's someone on my side at the table. At the sight of Zoe, Yael was encouraged.

The level of tension and nervousness among the examinees was at its peak. Most of them were busy warming up—bending, stretching, or jumping. The formal test began, and the first two examinees were called to perform their Kata.

The two examinees received instructions from a black belt Senior. The other examinees were watching the examiners, trying to guess what they were thinking, what they were looking for in the examinees. Was it speed, confidence, or accurate technique? Maybe it would help them to understand what they should do in order to pass.

Time slowly passed by. Yael was called to the arena with an unfamiliar trainee, and her stomach churned with excitement. She sensed that all eyes were on her.

Don't screw up, she thought. She and the other trainee walked to the center of the arena, and bowed.

"Hajeme!" announced the instructor.

She felt a weakness in her knees.

They performed the first Kata, and it felt like it was over before it even started. They bowed.

Bad postures, she thought to herself, *I think I showed some degree of insecurity.*

Daniel patted her on the shoulder, encouraging her. So did Peter. The sparring would soon start.

The tension and excitement rose again. Who would she face? She had to demonstrate her abilities, and who her opponent was mattered. She debated whether or not to wear her guards again, but repeated blows to the same spot that had resulted in layers of bruises and a swollen arm tilted the scale. She put on the protectors. Not wearing them will not only hurt, but would make her mentally inferior in combat.

Her name was called. She entered the arena and bowed. The instructor showed her where to stand and she waited.

Then Michelle's name was called.

Her, of all people?

A disturbing thought crossed her mind. Michelle entered and they faced each other with a nod. The signal to start had not yet been given. The examiners talked amongst themselves. They appeared to be in consultation.

The Sensei signaled with his finger for the instructor to approach their table. Both Yael and Michelle were closely following what was happening. The instructor bent over toward the Sensei to listen. He then nodded and returned to the contestants. He instructed Michelle to leave the arena.

Yael and Michelle bowed to each other before Michelle left.

Thank god, thought Yael, *It's good she'll be replaced. It could have been tremendously uncomfortable to be tested facing Michelle.*

Don is called to the arena, the same guy who faced her in the Kumite practice. He seemed very tense. It was obvious that if she was very good, it would be at his expense and would hurt his chances of passing the test. A few seconds passed and "Hajeme" is heard, signaling the start.

As soon as it began, Yael forgot all dilemmas she had and intended to attack in full force. She did alright in her first attack. Each of them must attack and defend three times. Her second time was less successful, and in the third round, she did well. They bowed.

She received another nod from Daniel and a wink from Peter as if to say, "You did fine!" The test was over for her, but her adrenaline was still high.

She observed the examiners, hoping that something in their facial expressions would reveal their impression of her, but they were already busy with the following examinees.

Michelle captured her attention and it appeared she also offered her support. Next Michelle was called up to the arena. Yael watched her carefully. She hoped she will do well.

It seemed that something had changed. Michelle demonstrated much more confidence. When they started, it appeared almost as if she was fighting for her life. An intimidating energy flowed out of her.

211

Whether it would be enough to pass the test remained to be seen, but she looked extremely determined to pass.

Next, it was Daniel's turn. Yael watched him. He was doing well, really well, demonstrating strength, confidence and calm. He would pass for sure, she thought, happy. Then came Peter – he was alright.

Another long hour passed and the tests finished. The results would be announced the next day, on the last day, right after the tests of the high-ranking black belts.

Yael felt she had done her best. Now, there was nothing left to do but wait. What an unbearable suspense. The rest of the evening would be passed discussing the fights, gossiping about the examiners, and finding it extremely hard to fall asleep.

The next morning, the high-ranking black belt's tests were completed. Finally, the time had arrived: the announcement of the names of the examinees that had passed the test. The suspense was unbearable. Yael, Daniel and Peter stood next to each other with anticipation.

"Berry Lock," the Sensei's voice is heard. He continued.

"Don Gilbert!" he announced a Don different from the one she had faced.

"Yael Finkelstein!"

She had passed. Daniel and Peter patted her on the shoulder. Her relief was now replaced by eagerness to hear if Daniel, Michelle, Peter and Charlotte had passed. The Sensei continued.

"Cindy Stern!"

"Daniel McCloud!"

Yes! He did it! But of course he did, she thought to herself, *this isn't much of a surprise.*

They smiled to each other and she and Peter patted him on the shoulder.

"Charlotte Erwin"

I'm not surprised. Yael congratulated Charlotte. And with that, the announcements finished.

Yael got a sinking feeling in her stomach. *Peter and Michelle didn't pass.*

Those who had passed had begun encouraging the ones that did not. It was embarrassing and unpleasant to witness, but fortunately, the announcer interrupted.

"We must clear the rooms! All leave, please, and get your things out of the room. Linens and towels should be wrapped in your bed sheets and placed at the end of the corridor!"

The girls climbed up the stairs to the rooms. Laughter and sighs of relief were heard all around. The tension had diffused, and they were all relieved to be finished. They hugged, shook hands, and said goodbye to each other. Yael said her goodbyes with a joy mixed with a sadness. Michelle is the last.

"Next time with me it's going to be a black belt," said Michelle assertively and bowed to Yael as a gesture.

"Definitely!" Yael returned a bow and smiled.

"A strong mind or not?" Michelle yelled behind her as they departed.

Puja

It was a Friday and Yael was told that the next day, in the evening, Master would conduct Puja, a Hindu ceremony in which offerings to the gods would be given. Local residents from the neighborhoods were expected to arrive for the ceremony, to receive blessings, and give their offering.

In a coincidental encounter with Master in the kitchen, he asked her how her back was. Surprised by his question, she was eager to know how he knew about it.

"Oh, I know everything that is going on here!" he replied with an arrogant tone, and continued, "Well? How it is?"

"A lot better," She replied and clarified, "the Yoga with Vera helped."

"So it did...excellent." He muttered and turned his way.

Interesting. He's not offended by the fact that I didn't come to him for a treatment. Yael wondered if he really didn't bear a grudge against Vera, and concluded that he didn't. It seemed he had a great respect for her that nobody else had managed to earn.

Saturday passed sluggishly and she waited in anticipation for the evening event. No one approached her regarding uploading the web site, and she wondered if everyone had forgotten it or it was again the manifestation of a typical Indian conduct in which 'no rush' was the status quo.

In the evening, she wore the Salwar, or traditional Indian women's clothing, she had purchased in the market. By wearing it, she felt she was honoring her hosts, the guests to come, and the local culture and place.

At 6:00 o'clock, a flood of people entered. Women and men, young and old, families and individuals all sat on mats spread especially for the occasion. The Puja shrine at the corner was located at the end of the hall, neither too fancy nor too modest. The Puja corner was decorated with colorful flowers, red cloth, oil pitchers, incense, a pile of flowers whose stems were removed, and a picture of one of the

Hindu gods hanging over the canvas. It was the same god she saw in the room on the roof: the monkey-faced one with the thick, long tail.

The people who came to the ceremony were dressed festively. Their faces were glowing. Several of them appeared as if they had some kind of illness.

Are they coming to seek a cure? Yael wondered. After a half an hour of being fashionably late, Master Buphendra arrived, dressed in a kind of Dottie for Indian men folded between his legs. His upper body was bare and a red piece of cloth was wrapped around his waist as a belt. A long, white stone necklace rested around his neck.

Everyone stood up and pressed the palms of their hands against each other when he entered, assuming the welcoming gesture of "Namaste", or customary greeting. Then they all bowed their heads, expressing respect. Master Buphendra sat down in front of the Puja shrine. All sat after. He started his prayers and one by one people stood up and walked over to him. Then they squatted on the mat in front of him, adding their offering to the growing offering pile and bowing their heads down until the head almost touched the floor. While plotting circles over his head and above the person's bowed head in front of him, Master mumbled a blessing for a half a minute.

Yael didn't find this affable in the least bit. Although she tried to hold on the rationale that customs and conduct in society were dependent on the culture, her belief that there were still universal rules that were beyond culture or religion was stronger and therefore she had difficulty accepting their submission with equanimity. When he finished, the blessed one raised his or her head, put his hands together, and then opened his or her palms to receive a flower. Master rummaged in the pile of the stem-less flowers, as if he was selecting a flower especially for each devotee. He then put the flower in the hand of the blessed one.

It was her turn to receive blessing, and she made the decision to 'play the game' without any protest. *You're a guest here and you are fed by the goodness of his heart right now*, she thought, *act according to the place's custom and keep your thoughts to yourself."*

215

Yael repeated this to herself as she was walking toward him, as she was bending, while she was listening to the blessing, and while receiving the flower. But when she attempted to make eye contact with him in order to nod her head as a sign of thanks, she discovered that he was avoiding her gaze and his attention was already given to the person next in line. She felt a burning insult. Not only had she sacrificed her honor and played it by his rules, she hadn't even received proper attention from him and she was just another product in the production line of the guru-devotee system.

After the ceremony, most of the attendees remained in the room. The majority of them requested a personal word with Master. Ravindra told her that some were traveling from far places to share with Master their family problems, difficulties they had in business, financial issues or any other personal matters, seeking his advice.

Yael watched him curiously with mixed feelings. He looked tired, but seemed to be trying to accommodate everyone, listening to their stories and providing advice.

After some time, only a handful of people remained and they, too, had begun to get ready to leave.

Suddenly, Master Buphendra's son Arjun entered the room. Master Buphendra's face immediately lit up, and all his exhaustion seemed to dissipate.

Yael felt a thrill go through her body when she saw Arjun. As she helped Ravindra to organize and clean the room, she squinted at him constantly. He was wearing a white Dhoti cloth tied from the waist down and a long Kurta tunic. He was slender, and his walk was graceful. His long, straight hair, carbon black, was gathered in a rubber band and fell gently on his neck and back. The Dhoti clung tight to his slim form, making it very hard to hide what Yael considered a very sexy form. She had always considered Indian men to be among the most beautiful men in the world. She had found beauty in them regardless of what they wore or their caste. They could have been either homeless beggars or from the upper class.

216

But Arjun was something special. He seemed like an Indian prince to her. She could not take her eyes off him while he exchanged a few words with his father. To her misfortune, he left too quickly.

She asked Ravindra if Arjun lived at the Ashram. Ravindra said that he did, but he was usually staying with his grandparents not far away since they lived closer to the university where he was studying. Usually, she learned, he came on Sundays around noon.

That's tomorrow, she thought.

When the entire occasion was finally over and she went to bed, she felt extremely excited for the next day.

Falling in Love

In the morning, soon after she woke up, Arjun was the first one she encountered. She was surprised because she hadn't thought he would arrive so early. He looked at her curiously with an embarrassing smile on his face.

He's very young, she thought, *I'm almost twice his age.*

He was dressed entirely in western clothes: fashionable jeans, a tight, short-sleeved T-shirt that highlighted the outline of his torso.

He nodded and muttered a "Hello."

"Hi," she replied shortly.

They stood in front of the each other for a long minute without any word spoken, and then both spoke immediately at the same time.

"So—"

"Are—"

They went silent again, embarrassed.

"Sorry, what did you say?" He placed a long, beautiful finger on his lips, as if declaring his intentions to remain silent while she spoke. Or was it to tell her to keep silent?

A long moment passed. Both faced each other, completely silent, waiting for the other one to speak.

To her relief, Ravindra came in, joyful and happy as usual, salvaging the embarrassing situation. He announced that breakfast was ready. They laughed, happy to get out of this tense situation. Ravindra looked puzzled; he was unable to understand why the breakfast announcement derived such a roar of laughter from them. They smiled in their private secret and followed Ravindra to the dining room, where all the residents of the house were present. Vera, with her hawk eyes and her sharp observation, caught that the two had something going on.

"I see you've met," she said, observing them carefully.

"Informally," said Arjun, glancing at Yael.

He's gorgeous, Yael couldn't resist thinking.

"Well," said Vera, "This is Yael. She's originally from Israel…"

Arjun jumped up to reach out his hand to greet her, western style.

"Now, young man, I haven't finished my introduction," Vera warned him, with a slightly amused tone, but still firm.

Arjun pulled his hand back, hid it behind his back, and then out again toward Yael, and pulled back once more. It seems he was playing with the gesture, but he did it so gracefully so that even Vera couldn't resist his charm. Her hardness faded and she smiled. She turned to Yael.

"This is Arjun, the son of Master Buphendra …" she said, emphasizing the "Master."

Perhaps she's warning me, Yael thought.

Vera went on, amused. "He came especially for you!"

Yael was surprised, a puzzled look on her face. *It can't be that he had already expressed an interest in me, and so openly*, she thought, blushing.

"After breakfast, you'll work together building the web site," said Vera.

I'm supposed to work on it with him? Yael's stomach fluttered a bit.

Now, after being properly introduced, Arjun reached out with his hand to greet her again. She squeezed his hand tightly.

Maybe it's too hard? She analyzed her grip, trying desperately to hide her attraction to him.

He didn't sit with them to eat. He had to go, and told her he would meet her in the evening after dinner, and left. Master was also absent. He was called to settle a dispute between two families.

In light of Master's absence, it was a golden opportunity for Yael to learn about Arjun. She was interested to know why he didn't sit with them. She was told that he had already had breakfast at his grandmother's house.

It was appeared to Yael that everyone sensed the interest she had in him and she was careful with her questions. She felt her mind was very unsettled knowing that in the evening she was about to spend time with him. During the day and dinner time, she found it extremely difficult to concentrate on any conversation that was going on around the table.

After dinner, he showed up and asked her to follow him. She trailed behind him up the stairs to the second floor. At the end of a long corridor, he led her to more stairs, and at the end of these stairs, there was a door leading to the attic. He opened the door to a small room that—much to her surprise—held an up-to-date computer. The computer stood on a table that looked rather shaky. Arjun removed several garments and fabrics that were lying in a jumble on a heavy-looking iron bench standing in the corner. He lifted it up with his sturdy arms and placed it in front of the table.

He invited her to sit. The bench was big enough, but for very thin two people. In the absence of another chair, she sat on the edge of the bench, as inviting him to sit beside her. He politely declined and she wondered whether it was because she was a foreigner, or a woman. He stood behind her and bent over to turn on the computer. As he bent, she got a whiff of his scent, a mixture of some Indian oil in his hair, a very pleasant contrast to the other typical scents of India. He smelled wonderful.

The ponytail of his hair was falling on his shoulder, and she relished the sight of his thin but muscular arms. She thought it would be very difficult to concentrate on the task which she didn't know much about to begin with.

He started to talk about what they should do. She found it more difficult to read him than to read boys from her culture. Usually, she felt if a particular guy had an interest in her, by the way he looked at her, his words, and his body language. It seemed to her that, although Arjun kept a distance, he occasionally looked at her like a man looking at a woman.

From time to time, she asked questions that were more personal. He always replied laconically to the point that he appeared unwilling to reveal details about himself. His answers were accompanied by an embarrassed smile. They were in the room for about an hour and he stood the entire time. When she asked him for perhaps the fifth time if he wanted to sit down, he finally obliged and sat beside her, being

220

careful to maintain enough space between them. As a result, it seemed that his right side was completely in the air.

As soon as he sat down, she realized it had not been such a good idea since he was even closer and she found herself imagining him under his jeans. Being physically close to him and his intoxicating scent had completely confused her. His face was too close to her and when he talked, she was even more aware of his almond-shaped eyes, his smooth brown skin, his full lips, and the beauty of his youth. She feared he would notice that she was as attracted to him as a fly is to fire.

She rose from her seat in the middle of his sentence and said, "Let's have a short break."

Surprised, he looked at his watch.

"Well, I have to leave in another half hour," he said apologetically.

"Two minutes," she said, "I need to go to the bathroom…"

Without waiting for his response, she rushed down the stairs, straight to the bathroom in her room, and tried to wash away her excitement by spilling cold water on her face. She felt heat all over her body. He had simply captured her heart, and not only because of her weakness at the sight of Indian men, but because of his youth, the way he carried himself, his shyness, embarrassment, and his beauty. He was such a refreshing alternative to the tough and aggressive Israeli men—the ones who always knew better.

"Arjun, Arjun," she whispered to herself, "What will happen with you?"

Realizing how she was acting, she caught herself. *Are you completely nuts? What is it with you and this young Indian guy? What do you want from him? Do you really want to sleep with him?*

The answer was clear, and she rushed to wash some more water over her face. She tried to regulate her breathing through breathing exercises from the yoga classes. She spoke a few words of reproach at herself—words of reason—and when she felt a little more in control, she went out of her room, climbed the long stairs heavily, passed the hallway, and approached the staircase to the attic.

221

Why it is that we must sit in a room so far and isolated from the rest of the house? Is it to make it more difficult for me? She took a deep breath and entered the small room. She found him standing with his back to her, flipping through what appeared to be a book or pamphlet. He sensed her presence and immediately turned around.

"The computer is frozen," he said.

She avoided looking at him and walked resolutely toward the computer, determined to demonstrate control over her mind and emotions. She concentrated heavily on the problem.

"The computer lost its connection to the Internet," she explained. He kept silent and, for the next half an hour, he remained standing, as if realizing that sitting next to her would distract her mind. She didn't look at him even once while trying to concentrate on solving the problem. She finally was able to restore Internet connection and they made a little bit of progress. She proposed a sketch of how the website would look and was delighted to find out that, despite his young age, he had his own intelligent opinions as per the content.

When he told her that they had to wrap it up for the day, he leaned over her and bent to turn off the computer. She got another waft of his special scent again. She was relieved that their meeting had ended; she felt she had enough of a thrill for one day. They went downstairs and said good-bye. He said he had a major test in a few days, and that he would be back as soon as the test was over.

Power Position

As the days passed, Yael experienced first-hand what it is like to live in a culture where an authority ran her life. One morning, as she rose from her bed, she felt the annoying pain in her back one more. She looked for Vera—maybe she would be willing to practice Yoga with her again. But Vera was nowhere to be found. She went up to the roof, spread a mat on the floor in front of the meditation room, and began to practice the poses in the same order she had done them with Vera. After a few minutes, Patab came out of the meditation room.

Patab was one of Master's senior Ayurveda students. Seeing her practicing, he asked her what she was doing. She replied that she was practicing yoga. She noticed confusion on his face when he told her that he is also practiced yoga. Yael then realized that yoga practiced in the West was not necessarily the same as the original yoga practiced in India.

She was curious to know where he was practicing. He told her that he practiced with Ravindra's uncle. She wanted to know more, thinking it may be good for her to join. When she showed an interest in joining, Patab said she must first ask Master. Startled and curious as to why she'd need his permission, she decided to ask Master about it.

She approached him during one of his breaks between treatments. His response startled her even more. He was very angry that Patab was practicing yoga and he was not informed about it. He ruled that he would kick Patab out from his studies because he must not provide Yael with the information about his yoga teacher. His speech, carried out in an angry rant, was interrupted by Ravindra, who showed up to remind him of a patient. The patient had already been waiting for a long time. Master left angry, leaving Yael completely puzzled and disturbed. She couldn't figure out what the problem was.

Vera entered the room. She sensed Yael's distress and asked if something had happened. Yael shared with her the details of the occurrence and asked her what it meant. Vera explained that, for Master, not knowing something about the people who were close to him, particularly his students, meant that they weren't giving him the respect he deserved and he was not in control of everything that happened.

"But when I practiced with you, he even encouraged it," said Yael.

"It is not the same thing," Vera smiled.

"Why?" insisted Yael, but Ravindra entered the room and said that Master had asked that Vera would come up. He wants to consult with her about a treatment. Yael went out to the Ashram's garden, taking her notebook with her.

I haven't written since the fall of the towers. This past month has been very strange for me, but the months prior to this were actually even more strange, horrible.

Yael stopped writing. She couldn't continue. She felt an enormous pain in her chest and tears flooded her eyes. She put the pen down, sighing heavily. For a few minutes, she just sat staring off into the distance. Images from Namchi hotel's balcony resurfaced and all the money she threw away. Somehow, she knew it was related to what had happened. It was as if she was trying to throw her previous life away. By throwing the money she had pushed herself to a point of such despair so that she would no longer have the luxury of worrying, of trying to figure out, or feel guilty about the past. A state of mere survival.

But if this was the case, it hadn't seemed to work. She still couldn't put everything behind her and soothe her mind, couldn't detach herself from what had happened. Still, the major puzzling question remained: what had really happened there? in the park?

While she stared into the distance reflecting on her despair, Master appeared out of the blue and brought her back to the reality of the present. He wanted to talk about Patab.

To her surprise, he declared that he had made a mistake, and added that Patab was not obligated to inform him because "He is only a student coming to the Ayurveda classes and nothing beyond this; he is not a follower," so therefore there was nothing wrong about him talking about it with her. She felt that he himself was not decisive about this and, as if by talking to her, he was trying to justify things to himself and convince himself that it was okay. He finally admitted that he was surprised by the fact that Patab was practicing yoga and eventually ruled that he would not punish him or kick him out of his studies. Yael wondered how much—if at all—his decision had been influenced by Vera.

His personality is so complex, she thought.

She sensed his immense abilities and his dedication to the people around him, his talent, and his vast knowledge, but also sensed his endless demand for others to please him, to show him respect constantly at their own expense. Yael was of the opinion that those who demanded respect didn't really deserve it. And he didn't practice what he preached—-he was angry when people were late, while he, himself, caused people to wait for him on a regular basis, whether it was his patients or visitors who were coming to see him. He claimed that one must not defame others in public and that they must be open-minded to other spiritual teachers, and yet, on a regular basis, he had defamed other popular and known gurus. Even if his arguments about other gurus were right, Yael wondered if it had arisen from competition and the fact that other gurus were more successful. He had to control everything that was going on. And it turned out that the past could be controlled as well, by providing his own interpretation of events, including twisting other people's personal experiences. Even when things were proven different, in light of his charisma and the great self-confidence he demonstrated, those around him diminished themselves in front of him and accepted his interpretations without questioning.

Yael tried to analyze what happened to people, especially men, who obtained positions of power. Not so long ago, before she parted from Iris who was her traveling companion, they were talking about memories from the time they were teenagers.

When they were sixteen, they went to the flea market one afternoon in the old city of Jaffa in Israel. In one of the alleys, they encountered one of the very appreciated figures at the time, a famous writer whose book *Don't Give a Shit* was perceived as one of the greatest social and political myth-breaker and targeted the most sacred cows of their country at that time. Identification with his message fit perfectly with the rebellion and convention-breaking of their teenage years, so when he had started a conversation with them and invited them to his nearby home, they felt much honored and were very curious to get a glimpse into the life of a spokesman for an entire generation. He led them to his house at a heavy pace, since the good-looking man from his youth clearly no longer existed. When they met him, he was already in his mid-fifties and quite repulsive in appearance, dressed in a white huge Galabia traditional Arabic dress that didn't hide his obesity.

It seemed even that his physical health was not good. However, as they sat in the foyer in his house, they enjoyed his wit and his sharp tongue. Yael welcomed the opportunity to challenge him intellectually, to sharpen her analytical ability, and to argue about philosophical issues. During the philosophizing process, she also enjoyed his arrogance and the effort invested on his behalf to impress them.

Then, when he suggested they move to "a more comfortable place" in his apartment, things began to sound suspicious. It didn't take too long to realize that her intuition was right. He led them to his bed using philosophical argumentation spiced with a thick hint that his invitation represented a modern social culture, anti-establishment, etc., etc. It was obvious he was using his knowledge and popularity to manipulate them. At the same time, she felt the situation was so disgraceful for him.

When he put his fleshy hand on the shoulder of her friend, Yael got up from her seat and announced firmly that they should be going. Realizing his grandiose plans had gone down the drain, he suddenly changed his attitude, left his kindness aside and become cynical, using a criticizing, mocking and despising tone. This was a man who insisted on forcing his position of power, and just like other men in power she had encountered, he was no longer the interesting great writer, only fat old and repulsive. He had become a disgraceful, pathetic "charity-case," as she liked to call it, which should be rejected in disgust.

Afterwards, they couldn't figure out how he even allowed himself to think of having sex with them.

"Why is he trying to sell merchandise he doesn't have? What on earth could he offer as a sexual object? And do all men think that women will be attracted to them even when they're repulsive, don't invest the least bit of energy in their appearance, and offer themselves despite being old, ugly and fat?" Her friend had commented as they left, disgusted.

What a fucked up world, Yael thought.

A Day at the Mansion

One day, Master invited only the foreign residents of the Ashram to his private house that was located in a more rural area distanced from the Ashram suburbs for the occasion of the arrival of his daughter from abroad. Mohan was not invited.

They had to take a car to get there and it turned out that they had to pay for the car, despite the fact that they had to carry things belonging to Master that he had asked them to bring. In addition, they had to stop and buy some shoes for John, since Master had liked John's shoes and simply taken them without paying. He also liked John's bag and told him with a smile that he was not borrowing it, but taking it.

Does he really have no respect or any sense of property? Does asking even exist for him? Yael was irritated.

John was left with no shoes, running around in sandals despite the fact that the cold winter temperatures had already begun. Moreover, Master had given specific instructions as to what gift they should buy his daughter when they were invited to his house. This only spread the sensation of his over-dominated control.

When they had reached Master's house, she was astonished to discover the wealth of the man whose Ashram was far from revealing anything.

Master Buphendra and his family had made their home in an estate surrounded by large fields that were filled with workers and laborers. The house looked luxurious and full of heavy gold furniture. It was three stories high and had marble floors and wide balconies surrounding each floor. She wondered why there was such a huge difference between his private home and the Ashram when he could easily invest more in the Ashram and turn it into a prestigious, luxurious place and possibly charge even more. But maybe the Ashram's modest appearance was done deliberately to encourage the local common people to come? Or maybe its simplicity was used to create an authentic appearance so westerners and foreigners would feel like they were experiencing the real India. Or maybe it was to hide the fact that he was flooded with money?

Arjun entered the room. This time, he was dressed in half-traditional clothes, wearing a celestial light blue Kurta tunic and airy pants in the same color but a slightly darker shade.

Celestial clothing for that heavenly looking guy, Yael thought, with slight thrill passing through her body.

His hair looked a bit messy and his father rebuked him for riding the horse with his good clothes. A woman entered the room, tastefully dressed and behind her, a younger woman entered. They were Arjun's mother and sister. The woman immediately noticed that her son was a bit messy too, but unlike her husband, she restrained herself and turned to greet the guests.

Yael found her pleasant and impressive. It was a family of good-looking, well-mannered people. The daughter had come to visit with her husband and her baby from the States where she was currently living. A few neighbors and close friends joined the occasion as well.

Yael found this event too similar to events in the West—a long buffet table was filled with beverages and snacks. A music typically heard in elevators was playing softly in the background.

The highest caste in India isn't much different from the West, after all, she thought.

Then, Master Buphendra suggested that Arjun would take them on a cruise in their private lake. Vera said she would pass on the offer. Yael, John and Susie were happy to join. All decided to walk to the lake by foot to enjoy the garden along the way. When they reached the lake, Arjun pointed to two wooden boats rocking in the pastoral view of the lake and garden.

The Other India, thought Yael, *without the noise, the fuss, and the muck.*

Each boat could carry three people. John showed signs of getting away from his wife and was clinging to Arjun, but Susie didn't give up and insisted they sat together. It didn't make sense for Yael to go out

229

on the boat with one of Master's servants, and so she found herself alone in the boat with Arjun.

He seemed very sure of himself and in his actions. This was his playground. In retrospect, Yael found it somewhat difficult to recall their conversation, but remembered it was very strange because it moved from thunderous silence to bursts of speech, particularly his. However, she felt something was formed between them and the tension in the air was actually pleasant. She was completely captivated by his charm. The way he rowed the boat charmed her, the way he looked at her, the way he softly tucked away his untamed hair from his face. He had a gentleness and softness mixed with power. When he rowed, it was as if the oars were an extension to his arms, caressing the water softly and firmly.

When they returned to the shore, Arjun got slightly hurt when tying the boat. His facial expression did not indicate he was injured. When Yael got closer to him, she saw that his finger was bleeding. She grabbed his hand and looked for a piece of cloth to stop the flow of blood. Their eyes met. Then she could see the pain in his eyes. The physical closeness to him was hard to bear, almost painful. There was softness in his eyes and wildness behind it. He was, without a doubt, the most attractive guy she had ever met.

They returned to the mansion. When all of the Ashram's guests parted from one another and from the mansion's residents, Arjun told her he would arrive to the Ashram the next day to continue working on their project. Their eyes smiled to each other as if they held a shared secret.

When she climbed into bed that evening, she felt an excitement for his unexpected arrival the next day. It pleased her to turn her thoughts to him, and she began to fantasize about ruffling his hair until it untied and flowed down his naked shoulders... She tried to picture his naked body lying in bed, how he would arouse her by tracing imaginary lines on her breasts, stomach, and genitals, how he would excite her, and how, when she would get to the point when she couldn't bear it anymore, he would enter her body like an ocean wave. Then, they

230

would rock together while she tightly wrapped her legs around him, with her hands sometimes caressing and sometimes kneading his arms, shoulders, buttocks... All the while his lips searching for hers.

Yael let herself give into the fantasy as her hand met her body and the thrill built until it reached its peak, and then she slowly drifted off to sleep.

Desecration

She woke up late the next morning and went to the dining room. Everyone seemed to have disappeared. On the table, there was a plate with a hard-boiled egg, bread, cheese, and some fruits. It had to have been Sabitri. Sabitri had arrived early and, as usual, left food for the Ashram's residents when she could not stay.

It looks like everyone's already eaten and left, thought Yael.

She ate slowly, trying to figure out where they had all gone. Then she felt someone watching her behind her back. She turned around quickly.

It was Arjun. He was holding a glass of lemonade in one hand and in the other, a pot. Their eyes met. He lost his grasp, the glass slipped from his hand, and the lemonade spilled everywhere. Embarrassed, he bent down to pick up the glass. Yael quickly grabbed a rag and threw it on the floor. With her foot, she pressed the rag down and tried to dry the spill with her foot. She wanted to do it as quickly as possible so his embarrassment wouldn't increase but still, she loved the thought of her sight being the reason for his shakiness.

When they were done, she asked how he was. He stammered a bit. Once again, she could see the glint in his eyes of a man looking at a woman.

Encouraged, she smiled back and they headed to the attic. The thought that they were alone in the house disturbed her calm. What would stop her now from fulfilling her fantasy? She wondered as she sat down at the computer.

Again, he stood behind her like he had done the last time, keeping a safe distance. Without looking at him, she felt he showed signs of discomfort.

So did she. This discomfort had become a real nuisance. They couldn't complete sentences, had no ability to focus on the goal, and both avoided looking into one another's eyes.

Silence. Discomfort.

Now, right now. Maybe this is the time to implement all I've practiced in meditation, she thought. *It's all in the head, Brush it off. Breathe deeply and don't let it control you. Why the hell does no one enter the room and break the moment, like in the movies?* But no one came. The house was empty and they were alone. He leaned over her again and typed something on the keyboard. Yael heard him clear his throat. Uncontrollably, she turned her head to him. Their eyes met. She fell deep into his eyes with a magnificent feeling of levitation. She didn't understand how it happened, but in a split second, her lips were inside his and his were on hers.

For a long moment, nothing else existed on earth—not the journey, not her life in New York, the towers, the murder, Israel, not her family, her friends, and her own identity. All were swallowed and forgotten in the magical sensation.

But then it brutality ended. He broke away from her and ran toward the door, turned back to her for a second, looked as if he was struggling with himself, and his gaze said it all.

He had done something forbidden. She got it.

That anguished glance, filled with pain, would haunt her.

He stood for another second at the door and left running.

She remained seated for a few moments, agitated. She felt responsible for what had happened. She was the one who had started it. She knew she wouldn't be seeing him any time soon.

She went downstairs and out to the garden and wandered, trying to rationalize it and convince herself that no harm was done and that he wanted it as much as she did, that it was a natural thing. If his culture condemned this natural instinct, maybe it was an opportunity for him to re-examine the validity of his culture and its values and to check what he will be willing to take from a modern culture.

He was the son of an admired master who was a spiritual leader of hundreds—if not thousands—of local and Western devotees, but maybe it was the time and place to stand up to his authoritative father. Then a surprising thought crossed her mind,

Was his attraction simply part of his urge to go against his father?

233

She remembered the words of Master Buphendra explaining that his son had his own opinions, and that he was stubborn and that he, Master, had no influence on him.

She wondered how it was to grow up with such a father

Was Arjun drawn to her as an act of rebellion against his father? Did he regret it? Would he tell his father about it? If he did, what could it mean? Was there a danger for Yael?

Suddenly, anxiety overwhelmed her. *Why am I always, always getting into trouble? Damnit! Eyal was right; I always go to places I shouldn't go, do what I shouldn't do. What mess did I get myself into this time?*

Foreigner in India

The day after her kiss with Arjun, Yael got up nervously and was relieved to hear that Master had gone away on business. Arjun didn't show his face. She decided to heed Vera's suggestion and accompany her to the girls' shelter where Vera was doing volunteer work. She hoped it would get her more involved in the local community life.

The girls' shelter was located in the poor area of the town. They took a Rickshaw on a twenty-minute ride, later stopping outside of the gate. As they approached, the sound of giggles and shouts greeted them. They entered a big courtyard. In its center, a large gray, simple looking five-story building with small windows loomed into view.

The remaining of what was probably once a basketball hoop—a rusty, stripped net hanging on a chipped pole—stood at the right corner of the courtyard. On the opposite corner, there was a torn net stretched between two polls about fifteen feet apart from each other. A few girls were playing with a feather ball—it was a game she remembered from her childhood. Finding it hard to believe it was still being played, Yael watched the girls. Two of them were holding a torn bat and ten other girls used their hands to hit a small rubber ball instead of the designated feather ball.

"In the absence of the real thing, you improvise," said Vera, laughing at Yael's astonished expression. In the third corner, a few girls were playing Hopscotch, jumping rope, and tag—all the basic games she used to play as a child and was almost sure they no longer existed in the modern world.

Noticing Vera, the girls dropped what they were doing and clung over her from all sides. They circled around her, their faces grinning, as though craving attention and words from her. The youngest among were fighting over a hug.

After few joyful minutes with Vera, they turned their attention to the foreigner with her: Yael. They looked her up and down. She felt that the girls related to her with curiosity tinged with suspicion, but the fact she came with Vera seemed to be granting her some credit.

Accompanied by enthusiastic chatter, the girls circled Vera and Yael and all entered the building. A heavy-bodied, white-haired Indian woman, wearing glasses and a white sari, received them at the entrance. She spoke fluent English. She and Vera greeted each other.

Vera introduced Yael. The white-haired woman was principal Shakti, and she ran the place. She seemed to be ignoring Yael and Yael began to wonder how she could be of use, if at all.

"Yael is here to help," Vera explained.

The principal looked at Yael. It was hard to decide if she was happy to get help or regarding her as a nuisance. She examined Yael as if she were trying to decide where she could fit.

"You said you needed help in Arithmetic, isn't that so?" asked Vera, as if she was reading her thoughts, and added, "Yael is an expert with numbers…"

Two girls entered the building, quarreling. The principal was quick to separate them. She asked why they were fighting in Nepalese. One of the girls spoke. Suddenly, the principal slapped the other girl's cheek. She gritted her teeth and tears formed in her eyes. With a serious expression, the principal sent both away. Lacking the familiarity with the culture and custom, Yael didn't dare to say or even think anything. From experience, she feared denouncing things too quickly.

The principal signaled for her to follow. They departed from Vera and climbed up a wide set of stairs. Screaming and shouting could be heard from upstairs. A group of girls thundered down the stairs, but when they saw the principal, they immediately silenced. They started whispering amongst themselves and replaced the stormy run with a slow walk.

Yael followed the principal through a long, wide corridor lined with doors. *Classrooms*, she concluded... She noticed that whenever the principal was spotted, the shouting stopped. *Someone manages things here tightly*.

The principal led her to a classroom where the formidable noise of about fifteen girls of various ages was heard. Noticing the principal, they immediately stopped their activities and –hurried to their seats at a run, frequently bumping into each other. Old, faded wooden tables and chairs sat in the center of the room.

This was not the way Yael imagined the scenario that she would be in. When she asked Vera if she could join her to the home shelter, she wondered what could she contribute with, but had never imagined that she will be led to a classroom. After all, she had never taught anything and had no experience with children at all. The scenario she imagined was more of one in which she would assist a student in a private lesson, one on one, and now, here she was, in front of an entire class. She felt an enormous fear.

The principal turned to leave; Yael felt the urge to stop her.

"What am I supposed to do here?" she asked in panic. The principal examined her again from head to toe and then back as if to say: "Who are you, anyway, that you're troubling me now with stupid questions? Don't I have enough on my mind?" and replied laconically, "Can you teach Arithmetic, or not?"

It was not the appropriate time to explain how she had envisioned her volunteering, and the shouting that came from outside the classroom had shortened the principal's patience even more.

Yael found herself saying, "Yes, yes, of course!"

The principal turned to leave, and Yael reprimanded herself. *So it's not what you'd pictured, sitting with a girl on the bed in her room, helping her with her homework and listening to her sad life story and how she had gotten here...*

She gazed at the principal's back moving further and said to herself, *you've volunteered! Do what needs to be done!*

Have that said, and with a growing anxiety, Yael turned her head toward the girls who were sitting in front on a row of worn wooden desks. She stepped into the classroom and stood behind the teacher's desk as if it will protect her from the unknown.

For an entire minute, complete silence prevailed in the classroom. The girls examined her with great curiosity. And then, all at once, as by a hidden signal, they all burst into laughter. All eyes turned toward her waist.

She looks down her waist—someone had stuck a sticker on her shirt as a joke, a comic of Superman. She knew that her reaction was about to go through a magnifying class. She felt her heart pounding hard. She tried to take off the sticker with no success.

Maybe I'll ask for their help and this will break the ice? She thought.

She looked up and asked, "Can someone help?"

Her question caused quite the opposite effect—it brought a renewed burst of laughter. The girls had seen it as a sign of weakness: the stranger who had arrived to teach them couldn't even handle a sticker.

That's definitely not it, she concluded and decided to leave the sticker there.

"Well," she said out loud, trying to apply an authoritative tone to her voice, "What are you studying now?"

Again, bursts of laughter erupted from all over.

A few more unsuccessful attempts to appeal to the girls in a mature manner and Yael realized that it was not going to work. The girls began laughing and shouting; some talked amongst themselves, some looked at her and giggled. *How to reach them?* Yael racked her brain for something creative.

She looked around the room. A chalkboard was behind her, and on its edge, a piece of chalk and a cloth. At the corner of the room, there was a broom and a bucket. An idea popped into her mind.

She went to the corner and picked up the broom, headed back to the chalkboard, and took the chalk and the cloth and put them on the teacher's desk. Some of the girls went silent and followed her with their gazes. She took off her shoe and placed it on the desk. All became silent and seemed intrigued. She examined them, their poor clothing, their dark hair tied neatly back adorned with colored pins, the amused expression on their faces, and smiles that didn't give away the difficult circumstances that had led them to the shelter.

"How many things do we have here on the table?" she asked.

238

Someone replied with a shout: "Four!"

Suddenly, without any warning, a shoe flew across the room. The girls giggled. Not a second passed, and another shoe flew off. The laughter increased, and a few girls rose from their seats. Yael tried to find out who was the girl that initiated the shoe throwing. Among the giggling ones, she was able to identify a relatively old girl who was tottering around with only one shoe. She called that girl to approach her, but the girl ignored her. They jumped and hop, taking off their shoes, throwing them at each other. Yael attempted to silence them in vain. In her despair, she decided to sit and wait thinking, *how long this fuss can last, anyways?*

Again, a shoe flew across the room, but this time, it hit the window. The glass was shattered. They all fell silent.

Yael was in shock. They turned a quick glance at her, checking her reaction, as if deciding how to proceed.

She sat motionless. *They must answer to that,* she thought. *If they think I would lose my temper just because of that, they're wrong. I must show restrain so they understand that this isn't the way to do things, that they aren't making any impression on me or exciting me.*

She was wrong. When they saw she wasn't responding, they increased their shouting and the throwing of the shoes continued. Now, books and bags were added to the party. Yael, realizing her mistake, thought fast and hard how to change her strategy, but suddenly, all the commotion stopped.

What happened? She wondered.

They all looked up over her shoulder. She turned her head. The principal stood in the doorway. Her face was stern, "It was here where the glass got broken?" the principal asked.

Yael wanted to defend herself, to say that she wasn't just sitting there helplessly, but it was too late.

The girls remained silent. The principal turned a questioning look to Yael.

Yael replies dryly, "Yes."

"I see!" the principal said with an angry tone, and ordered the girls to sit quietly until she returned. She marked for Yael to follow her out the classroom. No sound was heard. Outside the classroom, at the door, now in complete silence, the principal showed her the way out.

"Thank you for your services!" She said bluntly.

Yael had begun to explain herself, but the principal interrupted her, and with a dismissive gesture with her hand, said, "You do not belong here!"

Delusion of Truth

"Sit down, Yaeli." He didn't call her "Lalush," and something in his tone made it clear that bad news was to be announced.

"Come over, Spike," she gathered him in her lap, hoping to find comfort before hearing the news. Yael had just gotten home a few minutes ago, still on a complete high from Special Training. Eyal cleared his throat, clearly not able to find the words to begin. Yael grabbed his hand with a quizzical look. He rubbed his forehead and stated without a warning.

"Jeff is dead."

"What?!"

"Jeff is dead." Eyal repeated "He's been murdered."

"What do you mean?! When? Where?"

"Just before you left..."

"How? What happened? Where?"

"In Riverside Park, apparently..."

Her heart skipped a beat. Spike felt it, and jumped off her lap. Her throat choked up.

"Riverside Park?" she asked in almost a whisper. "When?"

"Just before you left."

"When before I left? A day before I left?"

"Yes. How did you know?"

Yael's heart started pounding. "How did you hear about it?"

"They said in the news," Eyal noticed her agitation and looked at her quizzically.

"Where in Riverside?" she pressed.

"I don't know exactly. Why?"

*There's no way...*She thought and dropped her head into her hands. *Could it be?*

"Try to remember, Eyal! Where exactly in Riverside?"

Eyal made an effort to remember but with no success. He couldn't understand why it was so important to her.

Yael explained.

Eyal remained silent, shocked, digesting the information. And then he got angry.

"Why didn't you tell me this before?"

"You weren't here…"

"You could call, couldn't you?"

"The next day, we were already on the way to Special Training and in any case, well… I wasn't sure that was what I'd seen… that it really had happened…eventually…" She shook her head from side to side, refusing to believe.

Eyal became even angrier.

"You could still have called!"

She held her head. *How could it be?*

Eyal was silent for a moment, and then managed to grumble, "Yael, how is this always happening to you?"

"What always happens to me?"

"Things are always happening to you!"

"What, what things?"

"Everything! For instance, the break-in in our apartment."

"But you were here as well; it happened to both of us!"

"Yes, but it happened following the incident YOU had on the subway!"

Great, she thought, *and then it's my fault, of course.*

"I told you it was dangerous around here, but you don't give a shit what I say and get messed up in something over and over again!"

Yael looked back at him blankly.

"The thing on the subway, the lame, here at our apartment, now the park…," he paused a minute and went on, "… and in the past. You remember what happened to you in Israel?"

Yes. She remembered, but it was no longer one of her top concerns.

"I have to go to the police!" she decided.

"And what will you tell them? What did you even see? We've seen how the police functions here! I don't think it's a good idea to get involved with this."

"What are you saying? Not to go? Are you crazy?"

"I'm not saying not to go. I'm only saying that we need to consider it carefully and to think about what you'll say!"

"What do you mean, what I'll say? The truth! I'll tell them what I saw! God! I saw him minutes before, and he wanted to talk to me and I brushed him off. He was in distress. Maybe he wanted to talk to me about something related to his murder?"

"About what?" Eyal asked skeptically.

"I don't know about what, whatever was bothering him ... Maybe he got messed up with something?"

"What can an ordinary person, a nerd like Jeff, get involved in?" Eyal dismissed the idea with a growing skepticism.

"Where's the phone? We'll call the police. Or maybe I should go to the station..."

"Lalush! You're too excited, relax first! We need to think about what to do..."

She looked at him. He was beyond understanding. How could he be telling her to relax?

He began muttering, wondering aloud what to do, with no reference to her, as if she was not there. It seemed that he had lost it.

Yael rose sharply from her seat and Spike gave a howl. She had an idea. She'd call Daniel. She was about to dial, when the phone rang. Confused for a second, she then pulled herself together and answered the call. It was Daniel. He had heard the news and also thought about the night in the park.

"We've got to go to the police," she said.

"Yes, of course," He replied calmly.

"Where should we go?" she asked.

"I think any station will do," he said and, sensing the distress in her voice, added, "Yael, It will be okay."

"Yes," she assented, finding comfort in his words.

"Is Eyal there?" he asked carefully, knowing it was a sensitive question.

"Yes, he's here!" she replied, looking at Eyal, who didn't understand and was busying trying to figure out who she was talking to.

"Hold on Yael! I have a call waiting, I think it is Peter," Daniel put her on hold, but after a second got back on the line. "It was Peter. Okay, listen, we'll meet in twenty at the subway station on Ninety-Sixth Street. Can you make it?"

"Sure!" she said and hung up. She grabbed her bag.

"What are you doing?" Eyal asked, puzzled.

Yael made a dismissive gesture and searched for her coat. Eyal was clearly offended, but she felt his presence was overwhelming and made her more edgy. His cell phone rang. Barbara was on the line. He debated over whether or not to take the call.

"Take the call, Eyal! I have to go anyways," she rushed out.

Daniel and Peter were already waiting for her at the station

"A grand finale for Special Training isn't it?" she said tearfully, and apologized, "I'm so sorry!"

"Forget it! It will be fine," Daniel reassured her. He asked where Eyal was. She said she preferred that Eyal didn't join them. Daniel dropped the subject. Special Training had brought the three of them even closer. He sensed that things weren't perfect between Yael and Eyal.

The Ordeal

A tall, red-haired police officer with a hanging gut entered the room, holding a portfolio. He sighed deeply, threw the portfolio on the desk, and sat down.

"Good evening, Ms. Finkelstyn—" he mispronounced her name slightly, "I'm Lieutenant Thompson,"

"Finkelstein," she bothered to correct him. She always got irritated when people mispronounced her name or last name. It was a reminder of her being a foreigner. And then, without delay, she asked him if they knew who had done it. He smiled indulgently as if it were a somewhat naive question to ask, and said that they were working on it. He was clearly attempting to apply a confident tone to his voice.

He then separated the three of them. When asked why, he replied that each of them would be questioned separately.

His questions took her back to that day, the day of the murder. He asked her to take her time and calmly tell him everything that had happened that day since she got up in the morning until the evening. He turned on a recorder.

Yael wondered how long the interrogation was going to be. He sat down, waiting for her to start talking. She began to describe that morning, started with when she went to the park to relax before meeting Daniel and Peter. She said she often did it to get away from the madness of the city. He looked bored. The setting reminded her of job interviews with human resources personnel who always looked so uninterested when the interviewees talking about themselves. While talking, she wondered which details she should linger on and which she should skip. She finally determined she should focus on the dry facts without censoring information. Doing so, the story felt like more like a journalistic report. She thought it helped her to overcome the rising emotions.

The bored officer finally expressed an interest when she got to the part about meeting Jeff a few minutes before he was allegedly murdered. Lieutenant Thompson wanted to know, in detail, what had been Jeff's mood, his state of mind, what he had said to her, and what she had said to him. Yael pondered.

She clearly remembered that Jeff was not in a proper mental state; he had seemed agitated. She told her impression with precision, but, when she got to the part where she quickly ended the conversation with him, tears began filling her eyes. She was tormented by the fact that she hadn't complied and hadn't wanted to hear what had bothered him, even trying to avoid him. Lieutenant Thompson waited patiently for her to calm herself.

"You okay?" He asked, and when she was nodding in affirmation, he asked her to continue.

"We started running to the north side of the park," she continued.

Suddenly, Yael recalled that she thought she had seen Jennifer. She paused for a moment. Should she bring it up? Her heart shrunk. She made a quick rational calculation. Lieutenant Thompson expected her to continue; he had a puzzled expression on his face.

"What is it - do you recall anything else?" he asked for clarification.

"No," She replied abruptly, cutting her dilemma short.

Her voice shook slightly when she described what she assumed to be the act of Jeff's murder.

"I'd almost reached the bronze statue…"

Jeff's face surfaced in her mind—frightened, distorted, terrified. A cold shudder seized her. She tried to pull herself together. *Tighten your mind*, Sensei's words echoed in her head. She continued.

"…then suddenly I saw two figures from afar…"

"Were you alone or were there other people there with you?" asked Lieutenant Thompson

"No, just me."

"You saw figures. How far were they?" he asked.

"It's hard to estimate exactly…"

"Ten feet, thirty, forty?"

"I would say something like sixty feet,"

"Okay, not so close," clarified the lieutenant, "and then?"

"I saw two people..." she corrected herself, "well...no...actually, first I saw something glinting from the corner of my eye and then, when I looked, I saw two people."

"So the glinting attracted your attention?"

"No, no. Now I remember. I heard voices....yes, that was the first thing I noticed. I tried to figure out where they were coming from because I was there alone, and then I looked in the direction there were coming from, and saw a glint and two people..."

"You remember what they wore? What they looked like?"

"From the distance, in the darkness, I couldn't see anything."

"Okay, go on."

"One of them—the shorter one—was waving in his hand something that was glinting, and a thought came to my mind that it was a knife."

"Did you see clearly it was a knife?"

"No, I didn't see it clearly, but I think it was a knife. It was already getting dark and I wasn't so close..."

"Okay, go on."

Yael took a deep breath, "Then, it looked like the short one stuck the knife in the tall guy and the tall guy looked to be staggering back, as if he could barely stand...Actually, he staggered like he was about to fall even before the shorter one stuck the knife in him..."

Again, Yael felt a chill in her body.

"Can I get a glass of water, please?"

The officer walked over to a water cooler that was standing at the end of the room, took a plastic cup and filled it up. He handed it to her. Yael reached out to pick up the cup but felt her hand tremble slightly. She took a sip. *Tighten your mind.*

The lieutenant waited patiently. Yael took another deep breath.

"And that's it...I passed out."

"Just like that? So suddenly?"

"Apparently so. It was too much after a vigorous run."

"You passed out right on the spot?"

Yael made an effort to remember. "No. Before I passed out, I jumped into the bushes to hide and then I looked for them from there,

247

but I didn't see anything... the attacker was gone....I was afraid that maybe the attacker had seen me and was coming to look for me... and then I heard a rustle behind me and I passed out."

"And where was the tall one, the victim, before you fainted?"

"The taller one?" Yael tried to remember, *He calls him the victim and this was... well...it was Jeff, for god's sake!* She took another sip of water, "I don't know; I didn't see him. I guess he fell to the ground..."

"How long were you passed out?"

"I have no idea. I suppose a few minutes. Daniel woke me up."

"What happened then?"

"I told Daniel what had happened and we started looking for them for a few minutes, but it was dark already and we couldn't see a thing. I began to think that maybe I hadn't seen what I thought I had seen... I thought maybe they had just been two people who were playing, maybe they were practicing some kind of martial art, you know. There are some martial arts you practice with weapons... and they were done and had gone home...so we decided to leave and went back to look for Peter."

"Did you hear a gun shot at any point before or after you had passed out?

"No, I didn't hear any shot."

"Did you see one of them holding a gun at any point?"

"No, no gun." She wondered what he was getting into.

Lieutenant Thompson sighed as though he was not content with her answers. He wanted to know why she had only just arrived to report all this and where were she had been for the last few days. She explained that she and her friends were in Special Training in Massachusetts, which had lasted four days. She added that, like she said before, she wasn't fully convinced that she had witnessed an attack and therefore didn't report anything.

"In Special Training, you're cut off from the world. There was no media there, so we didn't know about Jeff being killed," she found it difficult to use the word "murder."

248

A policewoman entered the room. Lieutenant Thompson introduced her, "Lieutenant Jones will be joining us."

Lieutenant Jones, a relatively young Hispanic woman, moved her chair a bit further as if she wanted to have a better view, and sat down. Lieutenant Thompson then asked Yael to tell them about the nature of the relationship between Yael, Jennifer, Jeff, and Lorenzo.

"You and Ms. Parsons are close, I understand," he said.

She answered affirmatively. Again, the image of Jennifer's figure on that day resurfaced in her mind. Quickly, she removed the image.

"Jeff and Lorenzo are…" she paused, realized she was speaking of Jeff in the present tense, and corrected herself, "Jeff and Lorenzo were very close friends."

"How close?" He asked. His question made her shift uneasily in her chair. She sensed that both of the officers had noticed her discomfort.

"I do not understand the question," she said weakly.

"How close?" Lieutenant Thompson repeated the question, and added, "Did they meet every six months? One a Month? Once a week? Every day?"

This is starting to annoy me, she thought, *and now the real interrogations started.* Her discomfort increased. *Who is this Lieutenant Jones, anyway? Why is she here? Did she come to evaluate me psychologically?*

Yael looked at them and replied, "Sometimes once a week, sometimes more…"

"Was there anything romantic between them?" He shot the question without any warning.

Yael recoiled, taken aback. She shifted uncomfortably again. Thoughts rushed into her mind at the speed of light. *What are they trying to find out? Whether Lorenzo murdered Jeff in a romantic context? What is this nonsense?"*

"Of course not," she was irritated, "They were simply close friends and neither of them was gay!"

Both police officers looked at each other. *Where the hell are they going with this?*

249

"What do you think bothered Jeff that day?"

"I have no idea…"

"You didn't like him much, I take it?"

What, am I also a suspect now? The thought crossed her mind and she couldn't resist asking defiantly, "Am I a suspect?"

"Just answer the question!"

"I'm not supposed to speak without the presence of a lawyer now, right?"

"Now, now…" he calmed her like she was a little girl "…We're just trying to understand the nature of the relationship between Jeff and his close friends."

He's definitely treating me like this because I'm a foreigner. I don't really count, she thought and replied "I was not a close friend of his! He was a close friend of my close friend, as you know!"

"Okay."

"Listen…" said Yael, "…we just got back from a four days of vigorous and exhausting training—Daniel, Peter and I. Can we go now?"

"Yes, some Karate kids you are!" he looked at her as though he was trying to figure out what business she had with Karate. His voice sounded dismissive.

Two minutes of silence followed. It seemed like he was debating how to proceed. She wondered where it would all lead.

Lieutenant Thompson asked her to excuse him for a second and left with Lieutenant Jones, probably for a consultation.

The wait seemed very long. Yael wondered if, like in the movies, she would get into trouble and would become a suspect just for being there. Maybe she should have listened to Eyal's advice after all and considered her actions before doing them.

Lieutenant Thompson returned.

"Just one more question for today," he announced, "Except for your friends, did you know of any other people who Jeff was close to or had contact with or he was seen with?"

"No. I really don't know who his other friends were or who he was in touch with."

"Okay, we're done for today. We have your contact information. You will be probably called for more questioning in the future."

Yael rose from her seat. Her legs were heavy. The physical effort of the last four days had started to have its impact.

In the waiting room, Daniel and Peter were already waiting for her. Their questioning was obviously much shorter than hers.

They left the police station and agreed to meet the next evening to exchange information about questioning. Signs of fatigue were clearly evident in all three, and their only desire at that moment was to get home to sleep. They parted at the subway station.

The auctioneer announced the approaching station. It was hers. She looked around at the people sitting in the train, their bodies shaking with the bounces. They were trying to ignore the horrible chafing noise created when the train rubbed against the rails. She felt lonely. The foreignness and alienation had become higher now after the extreme sensation of togetherness she had had in Special Training. What was she doing back there at the police station anyways, and how did it come to be that she was just reporting a murder she had witnessed of someone she knew?

The train doors opened. She rose. Everyone rushed to get out. Someone in front of her got hit by another passenger's bag while he was rushing to get out. *Pedestrian accident insurance is needed here,* she thought, and looked directly downward so she would avoid stepping on someone's foot. Then, when she lifted her head up, she thought she had seen the phony lame. Her heart seemed to skip a beat.

It wasn't him, she reassured herself. *I am only imagining.*

When she got home Eyal wanted to know how it had gone, but she felt little desire to share it with him. "Eyal, I'm exhausted, physically and mentally. I just want to go to sleep…" She told him, and went to bed.

Haunted

"Tell me!" Eyal demanded.

"Fine. I was hanging out with some people from Special Training. For some reason, the practice had taken place in the park. I left and walked into some kind of a building, and looked out the window and saw a man walking in the park. Then someone else came out with a gun. He aimed it at the man, demanding money or something—I couldn't quite hear exactly what, it was too far. He shot him and ran away. I followed him to be able to report it to the police, even though I couldn't believe what was happening.

I went downstairs, looking for traces of the killer. A woman passed by, I think with a stroller and a child, and I asked her which direction she had seen the man run. She pointed, but for some reason I didn't understand. In fact, since the beginning, I wasn't responding quickly enough. Something was slow, hesitant in my responses, like some kind of an autistic.

I looked for Daniel and Peter, but couldn't find them. I've made my way to the crime scene. The victim was lying there, and I approached him carefully to see if he was really hurt. He was holding his hands to his stomach and I could see blood. I looked at his face, expecting to see blood in his mouth, like in the movies, and sure enough, some blood was spilling. He was still alive. He raised his head toward me as if he was trying to tell me something. I brought my face closer to him, and he whispered a name I couldn't really understand. I ran away, shouting for someone to call the police. Someone was in the public phone booth and there was a long line of people waiting to make a phone call, so I ran to my building. Bobby, the super intendment, was on the phone.

'I need to talk to the police urgently!' I shouted, and Bobby handed the phone over to me, startled.

'What number should I call?'

'Zero,' Bobby told me with a vicious smile. I dialed, and to my surprise, it was the police. *He hadn't lied*, I thought to myself.

As soon as the voice on the phone said, 'Police,' I became speechless. And that was it."

"This dream is probably related to what happened yesterday at the police station, isn't it?" asked Eyal. He continued, "Strangely enough you have linked it to the incident. Maybe now you'll be willing to tell me what happened yesterday there?"

"It just felt so real," she muttered, after a night of disturbing dreams and nightmares the morning after she had gone to the police station. *How will I go to work? I'm completely blurred.*

Eyal pressured her more to tell him what had happened at the station.

Yael tried to recall the conversation, but her subconscious was still seized by some sort of twilight zone in between sleep and wakefulness. Her words were confused and she still found it difficult to wake up completely and separate herself from the reality of the dream.

"I haven't told them I saw her in the park," she said without thinking.

"Who did you see?" asked Eyal.

"J..." She paused.

"Yael?" he asked for clarification.

She didn't feel capable of dealing with him right then. Her world was in complete confusion. She turned her back.

"I'm going back to sleep. I can't go to work today."

Eyal continued to demand an explanation. She longed for him to get up and leave.

Finally, she heard the click of the closing door as he left. She was extremely thirsty. She got up and went to the kitchen, drank a glass of water, followed by another, and then went back to bed. Her eyes closed, and she immediately fell back asleep.

Three black men were passing by under her first-floor window, and she watched them through the cracks. One of them realized that she was watching. She moved away from the window, but it was already too late. They were pissed off; it was a racist thing. A white woman had been watching them. They started to come after Yael. They suddenly transformed into women. Yael decided she would sleep away from home. She could see them looking for her. She had a dog. The three women saw a bunch of tennis balls in the yard outside of her building and appeared to reach the conclusion that Yael has a dog.

One of them said to the other, 'American dogs say 'Woof!' but Israeli dogs say 'Orff.' How do you explain that?'

They were looking for Yael and got closer and closer to her apartment. In a few more steps, they would reach her. They grabbed her. She had to fight them. She threw punched anywhere she could, and she managed to run away.

She ran into the building next door yelling for the police. A group of people took her to the top floor. There were iron bars in the hallway. They turned to the left into someone's apartment behind a large iron door.

These neighbors are well trained in hiding someone, *she thought,* they're definitely involved in something illegal.

They looked out the window to see when the police car would arrive. Nothing.

Someone here screwed up big time, *she thought to herself.*

Three figures were approaching. She tried to identify who they were. When they got closer, she could see that it was Jennifer, Jeff and Lorenzo.

So Jeff didn't die after all? How come they're chasing me? *She wondered.*

She took a snapshot of them with her camera and rushed to print the image but failed. Only the message: "Error: there is no image to print" flashed across the screen.

Yael slept until noon without a break. It was a slumber filled with dreams. She had to force herself to get up. *I must call Jennifer.* She had hardly sat up in bed when Spike, sensing she was not at her best, jumped up into bed with her. He had bet right. She didn't kick him out this time; she simply couldn't find the energy. He wanted attention. After several minutes of trying to return to the real world, she sat up straight and collected Spike in her arms. He purred. She got up and took a quick shower to wake up, got dressed and looked for the phone. She hesitated a bit, but then she dialed Jennifer's number.

There was no answer.

She then tried both the cell phone and the home phone. Nothing. An hour passed. She felt trapped at home, but where could she go? The park that was formerly her island of sanity from the craziness of the city was no longer an option after what had happened there. She couldn't even get near it. She called in sick to work.

All of a sudden, Yael felt the urge to speak with her mom. She made a quick calculation of the hours difference between NY and Jerusalem. Yes, she could call Israel if she wanted. Apart from the brief talk they had had just before she went to Special Training, they hadn't spoken for a while. But she feared that if she'd talk to her, she would break and wouldn't be able to pretend that everything was alright.

Reflecting back, it seemed that the past month, a very strange dynamic had begun, beginning with the rising tension for Special Training, together with the rising tension between her and Eyal, up to the grand finale of Jeff's murder. She had a strange sensation that something bigger was coming. She couldn't get it out of her mind.

What had Jennifer been doing at the park? Had she spoken with Jeff? Was his state of mind related to what he had wanted to talk to Yael about? If so, what had he spoken to Jennifer about? And why hadn't I said anything to the police? What was I afraid of? She felt she had to talk to someone. With so many thoughts, she couldn't keep it all to herself.

Then she knew who she would call: Iris, her childhood friend who had lived in Belgium for some time. It had been a long time since they had spoken. She dialed. Iris picked up, happy to hear from her.

When she told her about the recent events, Iris was in shock.

"What a strange month," said Iris, "The incident, the murder…"

When Yael gave her the details of that day in the park, Iris sounded puzzled.

"What a strange coincidence! Are you sure you saw Jennifer there?"

"I'm not sure, but she looked so much like her."

Iris tried to cheer her up the best she could. She urged her to keep on trying to reach Jennifer and to ask her about her whereabouts that day.

"What about you?" asked Yael, attempting to change the subject.

Iris was alright and getting on with her ordinary life. All was good. She said that she would like to travel in a few months. She needed a break from the routine.

"What about you? Would you like to join? It sounds like you need to get away from everything even more than I do."

Yael replied she couldn't think about it at that moment; it is too chaotic for her, but she promised Iris she would think it over when everything calmed down a bit. The conversation was concluded with the agreement that they would talk about it again in the future.

She was hungry. She made herself something quick to eat.

What was Jennifer doing in the park? She had been a wreck the day before when they had met in the coffee place. She had felt like she was losing Lorenzo, and it is obvious she accused Jeff for Lorenzo's deterioration...but no, no ... she couldn't have done it.. I've never seen her lose control, never! She thought.

She picked up the phone again aggressively, as if in doing so, she could kick away her disturbing thoughts. *I'm going to call her again.*

She dialed, secretly wishing that there would be no answer. After all, what would she even say to her?

There was no answer.

Yael tried to call Lorenzo, again hoping there would be no answer. A few minutes passed by.

There was no answer.

She couldn't sit quiet.

She called Jennifer again. Still no answer. This time, she left a message that she was back from Special Training and had heard about

Jeff. She asked Jennifer to call her back as soon as she heard the message.

She was expected to meet up with Daniel and Peter in the evening. What would she do until then?

Why hadn't I been willing to talk to Jeff? Why did I have to push him away? Maybe I could have saved him? Thoughts were running through her mind and wouldn't leave.

The phone rang. She was caught by surprise. Her mother was on the line. She had known that Yael was in Special Training and that she had tested for a black belt.

"So how was it? Did you get the black belt?"

"Yes, I got it," Yael said weakly, and then, without warning, she burst into tears.

Her mother panicked.

"Yaeli! What happened?"

Yael pulled herself together quickly, wracking her brains as to what to tell to her mother without giving away everything so she wouldn't be too worried.

"I can't get a hold of Jennifer and I'm so worried," she managed feebly.

Her mother calmed her down and assured her that everything was fine and that Jennifer would call her back soon. When Yael hung up the phone, she sat a long time, staring at nothing, and then she got up and decided to go out.

She wandered the streets aimlessly, thinking about Jennifer. *If she doesn't get back to me, I'll go to her house and wait for her there!*

She walked and walked past apartment buildings and street signs and lost track of time in the blur of the city. By the time she got her head back on the ground, she realized she was already far enough away from home that she wouldn't be able to make it back on time for her meeting with Daniel and Peter unless she took the subway. She walked to the next closest station, and her heart skipped a beat.

This time it really is him.

A few feet ahead of her, the phony lame—now clearly walking normally—was right ahead of her, going down the stairs. There was no doubt about it: she recognized his stature, his physique, and his walk. *I've got to call the police - maybe they'll be able to catch him.*

She couldn't see his face. His back was to her. She stopped, waiting until he was a sufficient distance from her so she wouldn't be spotted, but then questioned herself. *How long am I going to stand here and wait?*

She went down the stairs carefully and searched for him, but he was already gone. The train arrived.

Hints

The view of Columbus Square stared back at her from the window. It was almost July, and New York was becoming hot and humid and filled with tourists. Many tourists could be spotted catching a ride in the square on kitsch horse carriages with drivers wearing gaudy uniforms with their strange hats.

I can't believe the madness of this city, thought Yael, looking through the wide window on the seventh floor of the reception of the escort agency where Joy, her friend, worked. Columbus Square, one of the most crowded junctions of the city, the juncture between bustling Broadway that splits into Columbus Street and West Central Park, stared back at her. The park started here. The steps around the huge statue in the square were host to a blend of pigeons, pedestrians, tourists, and homeless people.

Joy came out of the kitchen with two cups of coffee in her hands and went into her office. Yael followed her. The offices of the escort agency advertised a modeling agency. The actual offices included only the spacious reception area overlooking the square and three small rooms: one for Joy, the dispatcher, one for the company's owner and manager, a woman in her sixties who once used to be an escort, and a third office for customers who preferred to sneak in discreetly without being seen, meet in private, and flip through the pictures of the escorts in the photo album.

Joy was a literature and psychology student at NYU. She was on summer break. Having the job at the agency served her well. She had begun writing short stories inspired by events that had occurred at the agency. Both escorts and clients had provided fascinating material. The blanks in the stories were filled by her imagination, and the psychological sting was derived from her studies.

Joy's parents had immigrated to Israel from Canada when she was twelve with her older brother. She had made an extraordinary effort to re-integrate. It was not easy – she needed to learn a new language, new accent, leave her refined behavior behind, and get to know to a different culture. She became a foreigner at the age most of her girl friends were forming their identities as young women. But her efforts were fruitful and she had managed to integrate well. Her parents, however, failed to adapt themselves to the new mentality, and after five years decided to return to Canada. Joy told them she intended to stay another year to complete her high school graduation and then she would join the army like her friends.

Her parents had protested and threatened to not allow it, since she was still underage. But Joy was not going to be torn apart from her life again and was determined to stay. Ben, her older brother, decided he would stay for another year as well, and he would be her guardian. Their parents returned to Canada and Joy stayed with her brother. When she reached the age of eighteen and joined the army, her brother also decided to return to Canada. She remained alone, a soldier without any family nearby. But after finishing the army and traveling all over the world, something was missing for her. During her travels, she had been intrigued by the Big Apple and decided she would study in New York and then would be able to easily visit her family on a regular basis.

"So, have you recovered a bit?" Joy asked when they sat down. She handed the cup of coffee over to Yael.

"Yes, better now," Yael took a sip of coffee.

"What's happening with Eyal? Anything new?" she asked, knowing their breakup was difficult and painful. He had slammed accusations at her that she has been distanced, had never contributed to their mutual life and didn't make any efforts to preserve their relationship.

But his biggest accusation against her was, and she still remembered his burning words: "You're not built for being in a relationship at all. You require so much freedom. Sometimes, it seems to me you don't need anyone but yourself!"

Then he added and fired the last arrow, "You are cold!"

As soon as he said these words, everything seemed to pass by her and leave her untouched. It was the beginning of the end. Since then, their relationship had rapidly been deteriorating, especially since Jeff's death.

"We're still apart and cut off," Yael said decisively, set the cup down on the table, and added, "And this is how it's going to be." She didn't continue.

That day she told Eyal she was leaving. She moved into her own apartment and tried to return to a routine life. However, she felt like she was acting like a robot. All of her actions seemed to be made by someone other than her and her connection to reality had begun to crumble. She woke up in the morning, went to work, wore the mask of an important financial consultant, and in the evening another mask of a Yogi or Karatika.

"So you haven't gotten back to normal since the murder..." muttered Joy carefully, trailing off.

Yael was silent. No, she hadn't. Everything had changed since the murder, even her Karate. One day, Zoe stopped her before she was about to harm her opponent for real. Yael had taken a punch from someone of a lower rank. Blood had risen to her head and she began to take out her restrained rage on him.

Even though he was heavy and could absorb her punches and kicks, he panicked from her eagerness to hit him. Zoe, who had noticed what was going on, stopped her.

After class she asked her to stay, she wanted to know if everything was alright. Yael, with a frozen expression, said that yes, this was just a one-time slip. Zoe looked at her lengthily, debating whether to take her word for it, and finally sent her on her way without a word.

The organization will not accept violent psychos! Yael remembered Zoe saying often. Zoe already had had to distance a guy who had crossed the lines, causing irreversible damage to one of the trainees.

Is this is what I have become? Yael asked herself.

"Why didn't you go away for a while? Didn't your friend from Belgium suggest a trip?" asked Joy.

Yael turned her gaze to the window. A fancy red carriage harnessed to a beautiful white horse was passing by the square. Her gaze focused on the horse's harness, a device that only allowed the animal to look forward.

"She did," She affirmed, but she didn't elaborate.

"What's been going on with Jennifer lately?" Joy changed the subject, interested.

"Nothing," said Yael with a tone of anger in her voice, "I was looking for her and searched for her everywhere, and I wasn't able to talk to her."

"So you haven't seen her since the murder? Which is what...over a month now?" asked joy, surprised.

"Well, you could say that. You see, she finally sent me a text message that she'd be gone on business and she apologized for not returning my calls. And this is after I had left her a million messages..."

"So you haven't spoken to her, either?"

"No, she and Lorenzo disappeared as if they were swallowed up by the earth," said Yael, and she let out a deep sigh.

"Well, you know it's summer now after all, and the city is emptying out. Everyone's going away for a long vacation. Jennifer and Lorenzo probably went away after what had happened with Jeff and she'll call you when she's back, I'm sure," Joy tried to comfort Yael.

"The city's full of tourists now, which makes me feel more like a foreigner than ever before," Yael added.

"You really should go away," insisted Joy.

"I can't go now!" Yael protested, "I've got to wait to hear what happens with the police investigation," she explained.

"But why do you have to be here for that? You weren't even that close to him; even his close friends have gone away." Joy questioned.

Yael gazed through the window.

"I've been going round and round, trying to figure out what happened, and I can't get anything..."

"What do you want to find out?" asked Joy, puzzled.

"I feel like I'm not being told everything and I'm only allowed to see part of what happened. It's driving me crazy."

"Who isn't telling you everything?" worry edged into Joy's voice.
Yael was silent.

"So how is it in the new apartment?" asked Joy, changing the subject again.

"It's okay. It's a small studio apartment, but all mine!" She didn't care to get into any more details. Moving into her own apartment was related to breaking up with Eyal.

Joy was silent. She understood that it was better not to dig too deep at this stage.

"Say, what about male escorts? Do you have any?" Yael asked, curious.

"Why? Are you interested?" Joy smiled.

"Actually, maybe yes. With this break up, I have to admit; I miss getting laid and have no desire for a new relationship..."

"We do have male escorts. There are also female customers, you know," said Joy.

"So how many male escorts you have?"

"There are only a few, not as many as the female escorts. Some are willing to be with women only and some are willing to be with both men and women."

"Oh, so there's some who are not willing to be with men?"

"Yes, of course. We also have women that are not willing to be with women..."

"Crazy world, isn't it?" said Yael, reflecting.

"In the land of endless opportunities there's a little bit of everything. It's not only in the business world, but also in personal life," reflected Joy.

"After all you've seen in this place, nothing can surprise you, right?" Asked Yael.

"I see and hear such stories, that's for sure. It'd be very difficult to surprise me at this point," said Joy half sighing, half smiling.

"Say, are the men who do that with men necessarily gay?" Yael was interested. She felt the subject was a good distraction from the loop of disturbing thoughts she had been experiencing.

"No, absolutely not. There are those who want to increase their sources of income because of the relatively low demand by women customers and higher demand by men, so they're willing to do them as well."

Yael took a sip of coffee.

"You realize that if we were born in the future, say, another hundred or two hundred years from now, it'll be quite ordinary for women to have male escorts as well, no?"

"Obviously," agreed Joy, "you can already feel a growing trend…"

"Can you always tell who does it from which reasons?" asked Yael.

Joy thought a bit.

"Not always." She reflected again, and then continued, "We have a relatively new guy who's only been here a couple of months. He's a real stud, without a doubt, and so charming. As for him, for instance, I can't say for sure."

"There's no doubt your job is way more interesting than mine."

"What's new with you at work, by the way?" Joy asked.

Yael began to talk about her job. Joy, never particularly interested in the financial world, let Yael elaborate, clearly hoping that if Yael talked about something less personal, it would provide her a time-out from her torched soul. Joy pretended to listen but actually was using the time to go over the weekly schedule. From time to time, she picked up a name of a person she had heard in the past, such as Kristen or Max.

"Max…Yes! Of course I remember. He was the guy who Anna's been with and had some funny stories about him," said Joy as she looked down at the work arrangement.

Then Yael mentioned Chris Khan. She elaborated, since he was a new, promising client, and his split identity was very intriguing. Something about what Yael was saying about him seemed to catch Joy's attention.

"Yael! Wait a minute!" She raised her voice in interruption.

Yael stopped, looking puzzled.

"Did you say Chris Khan? Wait a minute..." Joy jumped up as she had been bitten by a snake and grabbed a black binder from a shelf full of binders and flipped through the pages.

"Bingo," she located a page, "Chris-Daoud Khan?" she asked again.

"Chris-Daoud Khan," said Yael, surprised. "How did you know?"

"Incredible!" Said Joy, shaking her head from side to side, "I'm not allowed to show it to you, but it's him." She pointed to the page.

Yael jumped to the binder. On the client's page, there were records of a number of client meetings for Chris-Daoud Khan. Under the "Escort" rubric, the name "Mike" was written.

"A male escort? That's hilarious. Chris-Daoud Khan is gay? Wow!" Yael was surprised.

"Looks like it," said Joy, and continued, "Mike or Mikey, as the clients call him, is the alias name of the new hot guy I told you about, and he's Chris-Daoud Khan's favorite!"

"Interesting..." said Yael, adding, "...just think of the huge load this man carries: half Muslim, half-Jewish, an American and Saudi as well, and now he's also gay?!"

"And why wouldn't he be gay with all those split identities?" said Joy.

"Well, come on Joy; show me a picture," Yael pleaded.

"What? Whose?"

"Mikey's," Yael said, assuming it were obvious.

"I can't," Joy sighed. "I feel like I've already broken too many confidentiality rules for one day."

"Oh, come on...its so exciting..."

Finally, after repeated pleas, Joy complied and pulled out a large binder wrapped in a photo cover featuring cigars, the photo album of the male escorts. She flipped through it, looking for the picture of Mike. Yael stood behind her, peering, and occasionally exclaiming in admiration when looking at the attractive pictures of the escorts.

Suddenly, her phone rang. Without turning her gaze away from the album, she rummaged through her bag, searching for the cell phone, and pulled it out. She continued gazing at the album and didn't bother to check who was calling.

"Hello," Yael answered abruptly.

Joy pointed to an image.

"Here, this it Mikey! A piece of art, isn't he?" she whispered.

Yael's heart missed a beat. Staring up at her from the album was a picture of Lorenzo.

"Hi Yael," Jennifer's voice was heard on the line. Yael was unable to speak.

"He's an Italian originally," whispered Joy.

A shiver crept down Yael's spine—that same shiver she had experienced so many times before during that past month. Reality, once again, was falling apart.

"Jennifer?" she stammered in a trembling voice, "I can't talk right now. Can I get back to you?" and she hung up the call.

Joy, noticing Yael's shock, looked up at her.

"What happened? Do you know him? Why did you hang up on Jennifer?"

Stamping

"July 26, 2001." Lieutenant Thompson wrote down in his book. "I want you to listen to what is being said." He pulled out some kind of voice recording device from his bag and placed it on the table.

Yael observed Jennifer.

She was once so put together, so proud and strong... and now she looks like a wreck, Yael couldn't help but think.

Lieutenant Jones entered the room, holding a chair for Lorenzo. She set it down next to him. He was standing with his hands crossed in front of his genitals in a defensive posture. Since the murder, the light in Lorenzo's eyes also seemed to have extinguished, and he, too, seemed ashamed. He dragged the chair farther away from the table as if he feared that what was about to be heard would bring a disgrace on him. He sat down heavily. All his beauty and vitality have vanished. He had lost weight, and an emaciated frame bent under dark-circled eyes.

It has to also be the drug addiction treatment he's going through... Yael thought.

Lieutenant Thompson pressed the "Play" button. A conversation between two men could be heard. Yael immediately recognized one of the voices. It was Jeff's. The second voice sounded somewhat familiar, as well...

That sounds like ... wait...it can't be. Yes; it is! It's Chris-Daoud Khan!

Yael listened to the voices being played back.

Jeff was heard first.

I'm telling you one more time to let go of him!

You don't scare me, Chris Daoud-Khan replied.

Well, I'm letting you know that if you continue, I'll make it public; I'll drag you down! Don't make me go there! Jeff's voice cracked slightly during the last sentence.

I'm a decent man, but don't force me to take measures against your threats, Chris Daoud-Khan replied smoothly.

I said what I had to say! Leave him! Forget all about him! You have two days! Jeff's voice cracked heavily.

The call disconnected. One of them had hung up.

Lieutenant Thompson pressed "Stop."

"Did you identify the speakers?" Lieutenant Thompson half stated, half asked.

"I don't know who is talking to Jeff," admitted Jennifer.

"You want to tell her?" The lieutenant turned to Yael, and then he looked at Lorenzo, "Or maybe you volunteer, Mikey?" he asked sarcastically.

Jennifer looked surprised. She turned to Lorenzo, then to Yael, and then back at Lieutenant Thompson with a puzzled look.

The inevitable has finally happened. I wouldn't have been able to hide it from Jennifer for forever, thought Yael.

No, she couldn't bring herself to tell Jennifer. She knew that Lorenzo's condition was only deteriorating every day and that Jennifer was fighting tooth and nail for his survival.

When he finishes the treatment he'll tell her he's an escort, she hoped.

"Chris-Daoud Khan," she said in a weak voice.

Lorenzo shifted to the side. His eyes cast downward, not daring to look at Jennifer.

And then Lieutenant Thompson explained everything, all of the painful facts, without hiding a single detail.

Lorenzo had recently been employed as an escort to finance his use of drugs that had only increased. While Jennifer and everyone thought he was going through drug addiction treatment, he was actually making money at the agency.

"Do you have any idea regarding who the two—Jeff and Chris-Daoud Khan—are talking about?" asked Lieutenant Thompson.

Yael anxiously watched Jennifer's reaction closely. Her face expressed pain, but gradually a cold and blunt expression took over. Her body seemed to stiffen as well.

After a long silence, Jennifer asked how they got a recording of the conversation between the two. Obviously, they had been tapping one of them. But who?

Lieutenant Thompson smiled with satisfaction as if to say, "You don't really think I would answer that question, right?"

He then asked Lorenzo to leave the room. He would remain at the station for questioning.

Yael and Jennifer were requested to wait. Someone would be arriving soon. Lorenzo and the two Lieutenants left the room, and Yael and Jennifer were left alone.

"Why don't you seem surprised, Yael? And how do you know who that is?" Jennifer asked, a slight alarm underlying her words.

Yael debated whether to tell her she knew Chris-Daoud Khan was using the escort agency, because then she'd have to tell her she had known about Lorenzo, too. She wriggled in her seat and mumbled a shaky explanation involving work.

Jennifer, who couldn't easily be fooled, seemed to catch on to the fact that Yael was hiding information from her.

Jennifer's gaze was harsh, and Yael realized she had made a mistake. She should have told her back then, the other day while she was staring at Lorenzo's picture in the escort album. She clearly betrayed her friend. Jennifer averted her gaze as if to say she had nothing further to add.

Yael looked down, feeling even more eager to tell Jennifer her darker secret, her greatest burden: that she had seen her in the park that day. But she can't bear doing it.

An officer entered the room. Yael and Jennifer were separated. Each were questioned separately and gave a brief testimony regarding the recording that was played back to them, and they were then released for the time being.

269

Yael was on her way back from the police station. On the subway, she reflected on what had just happened. Since the murder, Jennifer had distanced herself from Yael and from all of her friends, including her own family. Jennifer's sister even called Yael one time to ask if she knew how Jennifer was doing. Her sister said she couldn't get a hold of her and she wasn't returning her calls. Yael had replied that she was sorry, but she also couldn't get a hold of Jennifer.

"It's probably a temporary situation that will pass," she said, trying to encourage both Jennifer's sister and herself.

Jennifer's betrayed expression in the police station hovers in her mind.

On a Quest

"Hi Daniel, how are you doing?" Yael asked eager to hear his voice on the phone. She had missed him. Off from his tutoring job at the university, he was away for the summer break and wasn't even aware of the on-going police investigation.

"I'm fine," said Daniel, adding, "I got your message and here I am. It sounded important. What's going on? Any news about Jeff's murder?"

"Can we meet?" she asked. It has been almost two agonizing weeks since the last police interrogation. She'd rather speak with him face to face about it.

"Sure! In the Coffee Place, twenty minutes?"

"See you there."

When she approached the Coffee Place, memories from the last time she sat there with Jennifer began emerging. *She was in a pretty bad state of mind,* Yael reflected to herself.

She arrived early and found a table that was relatively far from the rest. She sat down and waited. She wondered what she would tell Daniel; everything was troubling. Jennifer's betrayed expression at the police station hadn't left her mind.

She felt a hand on her shoulder. It was Daniel.

He looked great. Clearly going away had done some good for him. *I wish I could get away from it all...* she thought, and stood up to hug him. He lingered with his embrace.

They sat. He seemed to immediately sense that she was troubled. He remained silent, waiting to hear what was on her mind. Yael began telling him about the recording the police had played at the station. She revealed what was said in the recording, but she couldn't find the courage to tell him she had known about Lorenzo prior to the police interrogation. She found herself sharing partial information hoping he might add more or raise some thoughts of his own that would distance Jennifer from her alleged involvement in this entire thing.

271

When Daniel couldn't offer any break through or information, but merely expressed his surprise at all he had heard, she found herself drawing him to talk about his niece. She wanted to know what Jennifer had done before she became a photographer. Daniel said Jennifer never spoke much of her work. He said that when she was very young, she worked for one of the governors as an assistant. After that, she was always doing something that was related to the Arts and supported herself working as a waitress or a bartender—nothing really serious.

The waiter approached asking for their order. Two people that were sitting in the other corner were having a loud argument, and Yael and Daniel had to raise their voices so the waiter could hear them. Yael recalled the fight that had occurred when she was there with Jennifer.

"Jennifer was Dan 5 when she last practiced, right?" Yael asked after the waiter took down the order and left.

"Yes," confirmed Daniel, "Why?"

"Why did she leave the discipline?"

"I'm not sure exactly, but she's also specialized in other martial arts."

"Really? What kind?"

"Some that are considered hidden. It's difficult to find people willing to teach them, and they're not taught in conventional places."

"Like what? What's taught?"

"Special techniques to bring down opponents," he said, "but I don't know much about it. She always kept it somewhat secret and was not willing to tell what she learned and where she'd learned it."

"Hmm," muttered Yael, thoughtfully.

Daniel was interested to know how Yael was coping after breaking up with Eyal, but, as always, he was very cautious asking her about her personal life. For some reason she, too, felt uncomfortable talking about it with him. She found herself diverting the conversation to talk about Jennifer again, this time about the men in her life. Yael wanted to know if Daniel had met any of her former boyfriends and how it had been with them. She succeeded in asking casually without coming off too suspicious. She emphasized the fact that Jennifer was dear to her

272

and that the fact that she had cut off all contacts made Yael worry about her.

Just as they were about to part, Daniel turned to her.

"You don't think Jenny had anything to do with Jeff's murder, do you?"

Astonished by his question, she realized that Daniel couldn't be easily fooled. She knew it was time to tell him. Even so, she was determined to do everything in her power to prove Jennifer hadn't been involved.

Hunting for Clues

The next day, Yael went to the police station. This time, she came uninvited. She looked for Lieutenant Thompson.

The police officer on duty at the reception desk asked her what the purpose of her visit was. Yael explained that she was involved in an investigation related to a murder, hoping this would pave the road to a meeting with the Lieutenant. The police officer didn't look too impressed.

She probably hears about a few murders every day, thought Yael.

The phone rang. The officer took the call. Yael waited impatiently. When she hung up, the phone rang again. Yael prayed it wouldn't ring again after the officer hung up for the second time.

"Were you summoned?" the police officer asked and added, "Is he expecting you?"

"No," said Yael.

"Well, then, you can't see him," the officer replied curtly.

The phone rang again. Yael waited, her impatience growing. As soon as the police officer put the receiver down, Yael spoke up again.

"How can I get updates about any developments in the investigation?" adding, "The murdered guy was a close friend of mine," as if this fact might justify her uninvited visit and change the officer's attitude.

The police officer appeared more impatient.

"If you were involved in the investigation, the Lieutenant has your details and will contact you if there are any developments he would like to share with you," she replied coolly and cynically.

Realizing that she couldn't get any further by using such an approach, Yael pleaded.

"Please, can you ask him to call me if there is anything new?" and quickly pulled a piece of paper and a pen out from her bag and wrote down her name and Jeff's full name. When she added the word "murder," she felt a pinch in her heart. She handed it over to the officer.

The phone rang again, but Yael remained standing there. This time, before taking the call, the officer instructs Yael with a very firm—almost threatening—voice to leave. Two police officers and a man in handcuffs entered the station while scattered segments of conversations could be heard on their radios.

Yael, realizing she had no other claim to be there, regretfully left the station, empty handed, with a bitter disappointment.

Another week went by, no one had called from the police, and no progress seemed to have been made. While getting ready for work, Yael felt tormented. The anticipation was unbearable.

She and Jennifer continued to be cut off. The feeling of alienation was growing. To Yael, it seemed like no one was left— Jenny was ignoring her, Jeff was dead, and Eyal was out of her life.

She had been having troubles sleeping at night. She went over and over everything in her mind, seeking a way to make any progress and to get more information about what had happened.

And then, one sleepless night, after a long hour, an idea popped into her mind: Chris-Daoud Khan. He was the answer.

In the morning, she made her way to her office, planning on asking Kristen about his current whereabouts and how to get a hold of him. She remembered he mentioned he would be moving his offices before summer, and it was already mid August. Much to her disappointment, Yael found out that Kristen would be away for a few days.

The days of waiting for Kristen's return felt interminable. Finally, when the day of her return arrived, Yael was anguish to get to the office. On the subway, she reflected over what she would say to her. She would have to fill Kristen in with some details and she would have to give her a good reason why she wanted to contact Chris-Daoud Khan on a personal level, which was not a common practice in the business world.

As soon as she stepped into the office, she asked if Kristen was already back. She was told Kristen was in her office.

Yael walked toward Kristen's office and stopped by her door. She took a deep breath. Kristen had always put Yael on edge a bit just by being close to her, and the idea of having to ask her for a personal favor involving an important client made Yael even more nervous. Yael wondered if she would be sympathetic and would cooperate with her. She hoped she would, since otherwise there was no other way she would be able to make any progress with her own private investigation.

She knocked, and hearing Kristen's voice saying "Yes!" she opened the door.

Kristen was behind her huge desk and was on the phone with a client. She signaled for Yael to come in.

Yael stepped in and remained standing. Kristen gestured for her to sit. Yael sat down and waited. As always, she pretended to be listening to the conversation like a disciplined employee who had a lot to learn from her skilled boss. But in reality, it all went through one ear and out the other. Yael's mind was solely concentrated on the matter she had come for. Eventually, Kristen hung up and, as always, avoided the small talk and got immediately to the point.

"What's up?"

Yael clears her throat and mentally decided to follow the plan she had prepared for how to persuade Kristen to allow her to contact Chris-Daoud Khan and give her his confidential contact details. She hoped reveal as little as possible and, only if there was no other choice, to reveal more.

She started by asking if there was any progress regarding Chris-Daoud Khan becoming the firm's client. Kristen replied that she wished there were, but he still needed to get back to her with an answer and usually such "heavy" clients didn't make a decision quickly; it sometimes took months, sometimes even more.

"Why the interest?" Kristen asked.

Yael asked if it was customary to contact him to snoop around a bit regarding his state of mind. Kristen said that it would all depend on the circumstances and the actual customer and that as per Chris-Daoud Khan, the last time she spoke with him on the phone he said he would contact her.

"With heavy potential clients like him, you don't call again. The initial work was done and done quite nicely, I should say; now we wait."

Yael moved ahead to stage two and mumbled something about Chris-Daoud Khan having some information about her friend's death and that she would like to get a hold of him.

"Would it be possible?" she asked weakly.

Kristen looked puzzled.

"What it is about? Is it your friend who was murdered?" she seemed interested to know.

Yael confirmed it was. She added that she knows she was asking a lot.

Kristen asked to know more. Yael revealed slightly more information, telling her that, apparently, Chris-Daoud Khan was in contact with her friend before he died. Kristen wanted to know why Yael felt compelled to talk to him, and why she didn't trust the police to do their job. Yael struggled not to reveal the real reason for why she wanted to talk to Chris-Daoud Khan, but instead said that another person was involved and she must speak with Chris-Daoud Khan to get a hold of that person. Although it wasn't customary, Yael knew that if Kristen wanted, she could break the rules and allow Yael access to Chris-Daoud Khan.

But things didn't work out so smoothly. Clearly not satisfied with Yael's reasoning, Kristen firmly turned down Yael's request. Yael knew that Kristen sensed she was not telling everything and the conversation ended somewhat bitterly.

Yael rode back on the subway that night frustrated. Kristen's refusal had ignited a spark in her to take matters into her own hands and, after few more sleepless nights, she decided she would find out how to contact Chris-Daoud Khan on her own.

As expected, some short research revealed that neither his private nor his company's phone numbers were listed in the phone book or in 411, but the more she thought about it, she realized that in any case this was not a conversation for the phone and that it must be done in person.

The next day, Yael was the first to arrive at the office. Although she knew that if she got caught it would mean the end of her career, she snuck into Kristen's office and went over her files. She managed to locate his file and was surprised to find out much more information about him that hadn't been in the folder she first took home. She wrote it all down. She was delighted to find out that according to the most updated information, his offices were still located at the Twin Towers where she had been before. Kristen was known for keeping the most updated and accurate information about clients. Yael made a decision. The next day before going to work, a Friday morning, she would make an attempt to see him there.

The Twin Towers

On Friday morning, Yael was on her way to the twin towers, eager for the meeting with Chris-Daoud Khan.

As she sat on the subway, she wondered how she would be able to bypass the tower security guards. She was wearing her best suit, which was usually kept for the more important clients; her business cards were stuck deep in her most luxurious executive suitcase. All appearance items that would assist her in passing the guards.

"World Trade Center," the voice of the subway announcer was heard.

Yael collected her executive suitcase and stepped down on the platform. She felt tremendous excitements mixed with fear, as if the entire fate of Jennifer depended on Chris-Daoud Khan's words.

She approached the tower. The security guard observed her, and she understood from the look on his face that he approved her entrance. Her appearance was convincing and she managed to pass him without a problem. She was then invited by the elevator operator to step into the elevator, which climbed up to the forty-seven floor where Chris-Daoud Khan's offices were located.

As she reached the reception desk on the forty-seventh floor, Yael immediately noticed that something has changed. She asked the receptionist about Han Oil Ventures. The receptionist looked at her suspiciously, but Yael's sharp appearance and the expression of determination on her face did the job again. The receptionist replied that the company was no longer here. They had relocated.

Although Yael was surprised and began feeling deeply frustrated, she managed to conceal it well, and with a flat, casual tone, she asked, "Do you happen to know where to?" adding, "I would really appreciate it," with a warm smile.

The receptionist sighed as if it was a huge trouble making the effort to find the address, and she opened one of the long reception desk drawers, searching for the record of Han Oil Ventures. When she found it, she then dictated the new address to Yael. He had moved to

Franklin Street. Yael left. It was too late to get to his new office since she was already late for a meeting back at her own. She would do it first thing Monday morning.

At the office, she tried to avoid Kristen. Since she was acting against her orders, Yael decided she'd rather not have to face her.

On Monday morning, Yael headed out immediately to Chris-Daoud Khan new office on Franklin Street. She dressed up in her best clothes again since she wasn't sure the security measures in the building that revealed itself to be also a very luxurious one when she got there. It didn't have the prestige accompanying the Twin Towers, but still, it was impressive and Yael wondered whether the rental fee was really substantially lower enough to justify the move.

Why then he relocated? That is strange, she thought. Soon, she would find out…in addition to few more things, she hoped.

At the front desk in the building lobby, she stated the purpose of her visit. She was then directed to the twenty-seventh floor.

The golden letters of Han Oil Ventures illuminated aggressively when she reached the reception desk. Realizing whom the receptionist was, Yael had higher hopes. It was the same receptionist who had been in his previous office. Encouraged, she approaches her.

Using the correct amount of formality and informality, Yael smiled and asks for Chris-Daoud Khan. The receptionist looks surprised,

"Do you have a meeting scheduled with him for today?" Yael was about to render the answer she had prepared ahead of time, which was that they had met before, and she was out of the country for a long time and she had lost contact and wanted to meet him again, but she didn't have the chance until now.

"Chris-Daoud Khan is overseas," the receptionist said to her surprise.

Yael quickly pulled herself together, refraining from revealing her great surprise. She was interested to know where he had traveled to. The receptionist, who had finally recognized her, asked if she had seen Yael before in the office.

"Yes, I'm from World Financial Solutions, and Ms. Kristen Stewart and I had a meeting with him about four months ago," said Yael, increasing the informal dosage in her smile. The receptionist, clearly convinced of Yael legitimacy, was willing to share the information.

"He actually went to Saudi Arabia to visit his sick mother," she said, and then she lowered her voice as if she was giving away secretive information, "His brother actually asked him to come over, stating it was an emergency."

"Oh! Sorry to hear that," said Yael sympathetically, adding, "Do you know how long he's going to be away?"

"About three weeks, but from there, he's flying to India. It'll be a while before he's back to the States."

"Are you sure?" asked Yael.

"Definitely," said the receptionist with a confident tone, "I booked all of his flights!"

"Do you know where in India?" asked Yael, although she had a pretty good idea where to. She recalled that he mentioned the state of Sikkim in the north of India in their meeting, where he went to a particular place for a medical treatment.

"Well, I booked the flight to New Delhi, but I think from there he traveled to the north. What a shame! You just missed him. He left yesterday!"

On her way to work, Yael felt so frustrated by the fact that she had just missed him. In her heart, she blamed Kristen for holding back information that, if would have been received earlier, would have allowed her to see him before he left. Another disturbing thought went through her mind: *Why was the information Kristen had on file faulty?*

I'm becoming obsessed with this whole issue, she thought, asking herself why she wouldn't just let go when it seemed that everything was working against her.

But she couldn't let go. Until she found out what really had happened on that horrible day, especially with Jennifer, she wouldn't be able to move on with her life as if nothing had happened.

281

On the Edge of the Abyss

She returned to the office after being at Chris-Daoud Khan's luxurious offices. The day passed slower than ever. She was constantly trying to avoid Kristen, seeing her responsible for not being able to get in touch with Chris-Daoud Khan on time. On the subway heading back home, disturbing thoughts had risen into her mind, and she reflected on the latest occurrences. She was haunted by Jennifer's betrayed expression at the police station and was very angry with Kristen. She felt her work was no longer a source of enjoyment or interest.

And again, an overwhelming sensation of loneliness took over her. Everything seemed so alien. What did she have to do with that city, anyway? With the culture? With the people? Betraying her best friend who she might even suspect of murder? Looking for a gay Arabic oil tycoon who might have information about the murder? The noise of the subway, which always bothered her, now seemed like the pound of a huge metal machine throbbing and hammering with no mercy. She felt restless. She couldn't keep on sitting. The train felt like a mobile prison.

Yael got up and walked toward the head of the train. The first car had a window overlooking the tunnel, so maybe it would ease her feeling of suffocation. She had to get there. She crossed between the cars, and the train stopped and people get in as she continued pushing her way through. A woman called her a "rude bitch" as she pressed past.

She continued car after car. She passed a beggar on the way, a devoted Christian singing praises, an orthodox Jew, one after the other of a long line of diverse faces and shapes. The train seemed endless.

Finally, she reached the first train car. Someone was already taking the position near the front window. She looked over his shoulder, at the dark walls of the tunnel and the sudden loud noise as a second train in the opposite direction violated the darkness, passing by with a roar. She looked through the train's side windows—fleeting images of people appeared in the window frames, seen for a split second and before vanishing. As the train entered the station, the image of a figure standing on the platform was broken off and re-appeared in the window, in a flash similar to the scene of Roman Polanski's "The Tenant." The feeling of strangeness and alienation emanated through the same visual images, giving the sensation of something distant, anonymous, disjointed and weird.

The front window was free. Yael took her position there and glued her face to the window, staring at the dark tunnel apparently leading nowhere. And the train kept on forging into the tunnel's darkness, like a ride at an amusement park, but this time, the witches and demons were real.

How has New York become this? She thought to herself. *A sleepless city soaked in slumber. People, even my own friends, as well as myself...all of us have become foreigners. There's something about this city and the madness of the people here that's like being in a deep sleep, a comma, and it cannot be real. What happens to those who are unaware of the boundaries to sanity? In the end, a friend turns into an enemy, a lover to a hater, the faithful to a traitor, and the weak into a killer. Now, every bit of progress turns out to be going backwards. For some reason, this is inevitable.*

I can't stay in this city any longer. I must leave, leave it all, Yael decided.

Collapsing

"A plane crashed into the Twins!" Robert yelled at her as he passed by her office's door.

What's he going on about? Yael thought.

It was 8:55am, the morning after failing to get a hold of Chris-Daoud Khan. Yael, unusually, came to work early. She had arrived at 8:00, after a sleepless night full of disturbing thoughts and feelings of hopelessness. She had tossed and turned, checking the clock every few minutes in anticipation for the morning to arrive.

"Everyone! To the conference room!" Robert yelled again. His panicked voice sounded hysterical.

Yael rushed with her colleagues to the conference room.

"What happened? Is everything okay?" frightened voices buzzed back and forth.

"A plane crashed into the Twins. It's unknown what plane, what it was carrying, how many people were on board, and how many casualties there were."

"Are you kidding?"

"No, not kidding at all," replied Robert feverishly, "Turn on the TV, damn it! Where the hell is the remote?"

Kristen entered the room, looking troubled. She pulled out the remote control from a drawer and turn on the TV.

"These disturbing images depict one of the Twin Towers on fire. Although many reports remain unconfirmed, a plane crashed into the tower at 8:46 this morning. In these moments we are checking with our sources and are trying to find out what has exactly happened..." The voice of the anchorwoman trailed off while a still photo of one of the towers unharmed was displayed on the screen.

"How can it be?" A wave of questions hummed through the colleagues, who were gathered in the conference room in front of the giant screen. Slowly, horrible images of the burning tower started to be revealed. They began making speculations about the accident. From the street outside, the sound of police and fire sirens could be heard.

The anchor turned over to a senior news caster on CNN who said that it was probably a passenger plane.

"The plane," he stated, "looked as if it were struggling, and was flying straight into one of the towers." From where he was standing, he could not be sure whether the north or south tower was hit.

"Switch to ABC—let's hear what they're saying," Kristen said frantically. Robert grabbed the remote and switched stations.

ABC was broadcasting a more or less similar picture of the towers with smoke rising from one of them.

"It seems that more and more fire and smoke are at the edge of the tower and firemen are getting organized down below, but it does not appear that an effort was made to..." the announcer trailed off.

Suddenly, as the anchor continued, the live image of a burning tower was being interrupted by a second airplane flying at a crazy speed and colliding into the second tower. A huge burst of fire exploded into the air.

The anchor remained silent for a moment, apparently unaware that something else had just happened. After a few seconds, his cries are heard.

"Oh my God!"

An additional voice was heard in the background.

"Oh God, oh God!"

Their startled reaction mixed with the cries of everyone in the conference room. Kristen tried to hush everyone so the report could be heard.

"It seems as though there was just a second plane," a male anchor began.

"I saw no plane!" Another anchorman interrupted.

"I saw an airplane," an anchorwoman confirmed, flustered. They began going back and forth trying to understand what had happened.

Several minutes passed, and one thing became clear: the World Trade Center was attacked.

The thought pounded down like a lightning bolt against a dessert. The commotion and tumult on the streets screamed past in sirens and alarms.

"It sounds like a terrorist attack," a voice from the side of Yael stated.

One of her colleagues clasped her fingers and said anxiously, "God! Are we also in danger? After all, we're so close!"

A tangible wave of nervousness passed through everyone. Kristen tried reassuring everyone everything was okay. Max, however, looked anxious. Everyone was captivated by the television screen, glued to the horrific images of flames and smoke above the buildings.

TV commentators reinforced the assumption that it was a terrorist attack. A few more minutes passed. Still watching TV, exclamations began to be heard throughout the room.

"God! What is this?"

"Are people jumping down from the towers?"

"No, it can't be!"

Several more minutes passed and many started calling their loved ones to check if everything was okay, sharing feelings of shock and astonishment.

A TV broadcaster came on, delivering a short and concise report:

"According to our reports, at 8:46 this morning American Airlines flight 11 crashed into the northern tower of the Twin Towers. At 9:03, a United Airlines plane hit the southern tower, and at this hour we are getting reports that a third plane was hijacked and on its way to Washington. The White House has been evacuated and there is a high preparation of security forces, police, and army in the area. All flights still in the air have been forced to land at the nearest airport; there is no opening of the NY Stock Exchange. People have also been evacuated from the Sears tower in Chicago."

"The world has gone mad," Amy, one of the colleagues, exclaimed.

"God!" cried Robert.

"Mom, I'm fine," Yael managed to get a hold of her mother. It was already afternoon in Israel and her mother, knowing that Yael worked close to the twin towers, had been trying to get a hold of her for almost an hour without success. All phone lines were busy.

"We are probably still in the midst of an integrated terror attack..." The anchorman added.

"Mom, wait, wait! They are announcing something..."

"A third plane, American Airlines, has just crashed a few minutes ago into the Pentagon..."

"Mom, did you hear that? Now a third plane has crashed into the Pentagon," chills ran up Yael's body.

"Good Lord. What's going on? Yaeli, why do you stay at work? It's dangerous to be in that area, no? Why don't you go home?"

"No one here is going home and besides that—you heard—this is probably an integrated terrorist attack, so being at home is not necessarily any safer!"

"You have no shelters there?"

"We're finding out right now," said Yael, trying to calm her mom down, "Don't worry; we're fine, I got to hang up now!"

"Promise to call me every hour," her mother pleaded with her.

"Okay, Mom, I promise I'll try, but there may be a problem with the lines."

"Okay, Yaeli. Bye honey! Please be safe."

"Bye, Mom, Don't worry!"

Yael hung up. *It's probably not easy to be so far away and hear about all of this while it's actually happening live,* she thought.

If her mom had known she had been in the World Trade Center just the day before, she would have had a heart attack.

Thank god she doesn't know.

Another twenty minutes passed, plagued by difficult scenes from both New York and Washington flashing across the screen. The commotion from the World Trade Center could be heard in the conference room.

Yael's cell phone rang again. It was Eyal.

It had been about three months since they had last been in touch. His concerned voice asked if she was alright.

287

"I'm fine, thanks," she said, her phone shaking a bit against her ear. "The tower is collapsing! The tower is collapsing!" Someone yelled.

"Eyal, wait, wait! Are you seeing this? The tower is falling down!" On the big TV screen, the south tower looked as if it were being peeled and eaten from the top down like a banana. Floor after floor disappeared as if they had never been there as the tower crumbled to the ground while a heavy black shroud of smoke, dust, concrete and iron twisted around it. And just seconds ago, there had been a skyscraper standing in that spot…with people.

The TV anchors, shocked by the terrible image, were having difficulties finding words. Images popped up from cameras in the street showing crowds of people running in all directions, panicking, crying, as huge clouds of smoke, falling from above and mixed with pieces of metal and concrete, threatened to swallow them.

It looks like it's the end of the world, thought Yael.

The TV anchor asked viewers to pray for the people who had just perished in a split second.

Kristen was talking with Jane in the corner and then began making number of calls to find out if they should leave the office and, if so, to where.

"I would like to have your attention, everyone!" She almost shouted as she hung up her phone, "We are being asked to evacuate the building!"

"Eyal, we need to evacuate the building, so thanks for calling. Everything is fine with me. Is everything alright with you?" Yael debated whether or not to add Barbara's name at the end of the question. Two weeks after they had broken up, Eyal started seeing his colleague. After another two weeks, they were already going steady and had moved in together.

Yes, he reassured him, everything was fine with him, and he was just worried about her. Yael knew he had never really gotten over their break up. He was so shocked, so hurt. He had his entire future planned with her.

288

Yael had to hang up and she reassured him they'd talk soon. She felt a burning sensation after the conversation with him. The memory of a life she had once loved and lost.

She recalled the harsh words he had fired at her just before they broke up. *You are cold!*

However, the damage of his words was felt a week after they were said, when she was sitting on a bench in Central Park staring at the mixture of squirrels and pigeons in front of her. Both the squirrels and pigeons were busy looking for something to eat on the ground. A little boy ran toward them and the pigeons began flapping their wings.

If only she could talk with Jennifer, she had thought, but it seemed that she had lost Jennifer forever when she had realized Yael knew about Lorenzo at the escort agency all along and had told her nothing. It had been six weeks since she had seen her at the police station. They were not in touch.

I need her so much, Yael thought while sitting on that bench, and then Eyal's words hit her and she burst into tears.

Kristen called everyone to evacuate the building. The entire area of downtown was filled with smoke and debris. The mayor had given a direct order to evacuate the southern part of the island.

How are we going to leave now and detach ourselves from the TV, without updates?

Kristen urged everyone to leave. Yael picked up her bag and walked with the others toward the elevators. People from the neighboring offices who had also responded to the mayor's orders to evacuate joined them. A great commotion could be seen at the elevators. Mixed statements of shock, astonishment, anxiety, and fear were made by everyone. No one could quite digest what had happened. Strangers had begun comforting each other, people who had never spoken before were sharing what they had heard, and the entire crowd became united.

"Maybe it's not good to take the elevator. What would happen if there'd be a sudden power failure?" someone asked anxiously.

"You want to go down thirty-one floors by foot? Please, the door is there," replied Max.

He's taken that personally since it wouldn't be easy for him to go down thirty-one stories with his weight, Yael thought to herself.

Jane said it would be okay in the elevator. "There's an emergency generator in case of power failure," she reassured.

"And if that also doesn't work?" someone else insisted.

"The probability of that is low!" said Kristen decisively. The elevator doors opened. She instructed all to get in and waited for everyone to enter, entering last.

It took the elevator two long minutes to reach the ground, and a sigh of relief could be heard throughout the entire elevator as the doors finally opened.

Downtown, Uptown

The building doors revolved and Yael reached the street. There was a strange smell in the air. The wind brought scraps of smoke and metal into the air. People on the street could be seen running in all directions. The city was in panic.

Yael joined the stream of people that entered the train, confused as per what exactly she had to do. Should she go home? But she'd go crazy in the apartment all alone…

Her cell phone rang. It was Daniel. He wanted to make sure she was okay.

"What are you going to do now?"

"I don't really know…" she admitted, feeling completely lost.

"Listen, I just left work now…" he said, "and I'm heading home. Would you like to come over to my place?"

Yeah, sure," she found herself saying, "Maybe we should call Peter to come over as well?"

For some reason, she realized, she feared being with Daniel alone. She couldn't say why. After all, they had known each other for some time.

But we've never truly been alone together, Yael thought. *To be alone with him in his apartment…in his apartment….is a bit scary.*

As she walked to the subway station, she called Joy to ask what was going on with her. A few days ago, Joy had gone out of town to see friends in Boston and Yael couldn't remember if she was due to be back that day or the next.

"I was supposed to come back tomorrow…" said Joy, "but in light of everything that happened, I'd rather wait and see how things develop."

Yael reached the subway's stairs. The commotion that had always characterized the city had only grown. People were seen emerging from all directions to the subway station as if it were rush hour when in fact it was only a few minutes before noon.

I guess everyone was instructed to leave the southern area of the city, she thought.

The subway was delayed. The subway announcer reported train service disruptions and asked people to be patient.

Unlike usual, people –were making eye contact. Total strangers were seeking comfort from the terrible tragedy. Yael found herself listening to random conversations around her:

"A plane crashed in Pennsylvania," said a guy while listening to his cell phone.

"What now?" says another guy in response, "Is this the end of it, or more attacks are expected? And where will the next ones be?"

Well, it's probably really the end of the world, Yael thought cynically. *Is this really even happening? Is this a nightmare?*

"Oh my god! What will be next?" another woman exclaimed in response.

It seemed to Yael that people's hidden fears were resurfacing. They were anxious. The routine of their lives had been so brutally shattered.

The subway finally arrived, completely full. Yael had to struggle to squeeze herself in. The train doors closed.

Nervousness and tension were apparent on peoples' faces.

Yael got off on 86th Street and walked toward Daniel's place. Here, in uptown Manhattan, the attack seemed more remote and the atmosphere was more quiet, as if the island had been divided into two parts.

She walked to his apartment.

"Hey Daniel," she managed a weak smile as he opened the door for her.

"Hey Yael," said Daniel with a sad smile, "Come on in."

She followed him through a narrow corridor that opened to a large, simple looking, bright and spacious room. At the far corner of the room, there was the kitchen area. On the other side, a bright couch and an armchair sat, and in between them, a round small wooden table was placed.

The TV screen in front of the couch was displaying horrifying images over and over. Yael found it difficult to decide where to sit.

"I talked to Peter," said Daniel, as if sensing she was nervous about them being alone, and added, "He will come soon." Yael sat down on the couch.

"Want anything to drink? Coffee, maybe?" he asked.

"Yes, thank you."

Daniel turned toward the kitchen. The TV anchor was introducing several military officers so they could convey their interpretation of who was behind the terrorist attacks. Conflicting reports were being received from the field. It seemed no one knew exactly what had happened, what was happening and what would happen in the next hour.

Daniel handed her the coffee and remained standing. She felt that he was also debating where to sit. The armchair looked far—too far. He sat next to her, on the couch, leaving a safe distance between them.

They watched the news, shocked by what was happening, when a commercial interrupted the reporting. Daniel protested that even with a horrific event, they were commercials. Yael agreed.

"Everything seems to have deteriorated since Special Training," she said, adding, "Like this was the last event before the world collapses. First Jeff, and now this attack…"

"You know," she continued, "In Israel, you grow up with terror daily. It becomes a routine event, and then you arrive to a place so far from your homeland and you think the new place will be a place where you can manage a routine life, grow and develop, improve and get better and then you find out that it's everywhere, there's no escape—it's a crazy, dark world."

"This is why you left Israel?" asked Daniel.

"No! Not at all," she hastened to deny, "I came here to see how it was to live in the 'future.' You see, beyond the fact that my roots are somewhat here, New York had always represented progressive futuristic society for me that Israel and other places will eventually become, but in many years from now. For me, this place has always

293

been a model of how our future life will look in all aspects—cultural, technological, and social." She checked his reaction, wondering if he understood what she meant. He looked a bit puzzled. *He grew up here so maybe this is why he can't relate to the fact I get excited about the city,* she thought.

Daniel lingered with his response and then, to her surprise, said, "I thought you came for Eyal."

Silence. It was too direct for Daniel.

She shook her head. "No! The fact that Eyal was here helped, it made coming here a little softer..." She paused slightly and continued, "... then we became a couple. But I really came here out of curiosity. I had to come to see how life is over here."

Daniel tilted his head and asked, "And how is it?"

Yael looks away, reflectively. Images and sounds passed through her mind: the airport, the first appearance of the city, trains, huge roads, police and fire truck sirens, beggars, skyscrapers, money changing hands, saxophones, subway tunnels, darkness, light, noise, commotion, people, Jennifer, Lorenzo, Jeff, Eyal. Her gaze turned back to the TV screen. The picture of the twin towers—the embodiment of the authority of a world superpower—and nothing was left. Horrific images of people jumping from the tower to their deaths flashed across the screen, the images of people fleeing from the black cloud of dust, fire and metal threatening to cover them…

She looked at Daniel and replied, "Not so great at the moment."

She could feel tears welling up in her eyes. His gaze softened. He moved toward her.

A ring came from the intercom. They both jumped up in panic. Daniel leapt to the intercom as if bitten by a snake.

"Hi Peter; yes, come on up, we're here."

Passed a finger below her eye, wiping away one single tear.

Toward Black Skies

The city seemed to be on hold, busy salvaging what could be saved. The early stages of estimating the destruction had begun. People were being evacuated from the southern area of the city by boats. Large groups of people, weeping, full of dust, were walking east on Canal Street toward Manhattan bridge.

Detached, Yael wandered the streets in the radius of her home. If only she could talk to Jennifer now, Yael pined. She would know what to do and how to help. But Jennifer wasn't to be reached and there was no way of knowing if it was because she still didn't want to be found, because she had disappeared due to her work, or because of disaster. Yael found herself wandering, doing nothing, distressed. Even Joy couldn't be reached.

A horrifying restlessness took over and Yael wondered where everything was leading. In the past, she used to go to Riverside Park, near home. *The same one where Jeff was killed,* she thought. There, she could relax and escape the noise and madness of the city. But since the murder, she hasn't dared to go near. She wandered in circles of the streets like a caged lion: back and forth, back and forth, aimlessly.

At night, the police set up barricades on 14th, Houston, and Canal Streets. Tired from her directionless walks, she spent a long night in front of the TV. Fatigue eventually overwhelmed her and she fell asleep while images of the attack floated over and over again through her mind...

She was in the office. Kristen pointed to the skyline through the window and, to her astonishment, the Twin Towers were being built at an amazing speed, as if there were a huge, invisible machine building them.

"You see?" Kristen said, "Anything can be fixed!"

"But this is impossible."

"If you will it, it's no dream," she replied profoundly.

Yael turned to her, surprised to hear her quoting a famous founder of Zionism. Kristen began to laugh, and, right before Yael's eyes, a

blonde beard sprouted around her chin…but the famous founder—
Herzl—had a black beard…

Yael woke up the morning of September 12, and wrote down her dream. Since her breakup with Eyal, she had begun recording them. She glanced out the window. The city was paralyzed. The majority of the city wouldn't be going to work that day. Everything south of Canal Street was evacuated, and whoever wanted to cross Houston Street to the south would be required to prove residency there.

The city has become two districts, she thought. *And what's there for me in this world of pause after the attack?*
She decided to document all that was happening. She opened the notebook where she had recorded her dreams, turned it upside-down, and started from the last blank page.

Black Skies—A Diary

Wednesday, September 12

I don't hear sirens anymore. They stopped late last night and, apart from a steady flow of equipment and emergency vehicles making their way south, the streets are quiet and empty, as if this weren't New York. Not even a single horn can be heard. It's strange. I always missed the silence, and now it's here, loudly, and I hate it. It is a heavy, dark silence, the kind associated with disaster, death... black skies.

I stayed hooked to the TV for so long that my eyes started to burn. I just couldn't anymore. I went down to the street. The shops were all closed. Garbage trucks were everywhere. I was debating whether to go to Riverside, but I still can't bear it. I didn't know what to do, so I went back to my building, but instead of going home, I went up to the roof. I wanted to see any evidence, any sign of attack, with my own eyes. I looked to the north—it was a pleasant fall day—and then I looked south. There were black skies. I went back home feeling useless, helpless. Those bastards forced a new world order upon us.

Thursday, September 13th

A cloud of smoke is still hanging over and covers much of the southern area of Manhattan. Discussions regarding the air quality are now on the agenda. Is it safe to stay here? The wind has changed direction and a layer of smoke and soot covers the entire area. Bridges and tunnels are still closed, as well as the area below 14th Street. The work of clearing the ruins and the attempts to locate and recover bodies continue.

What should I do today? It's so frustrating being simply useless. All life has stopped. My quest to find Chris-Daoud Khan is gone, and with that, the attempt to clear Jenny. All is on hold now. It's an impossible situation. I've decided to go to the park, to force myself, so I went there and the memories of Jeff and that night resurfaced. Despite all of my efforts not to, I started to cry. I cried about not having paid attention to Jeff's pleas for help; I cried about the fact that his death didn't upset me as it should have at first, I cried about the shock. I cried that I lied to Jennifer, that I hid facts from her, because I've betrayed her, and now she won't talk to me. I cried for the Twins, the people, the chaos, everything.

Friday, September 14th

At night, the rain cleared most of the dust from the area, but made the extraction and evacuation efforts very difficult. Access finally was permitted to the area below 14th Street. There was supposed to be a Karate class tonight, but we've all been called off until further notice. Michelle, who apparently had been in the World Trade Center during the attack, is missing. She had gone to look for her husband who worked there. He is missing too. After hearing about him I don't care that he is missing one bit, but Michelle...I hope it will turn out she is okay. What a horror.

I'm heading downtown. A mass of people is there with their cameras. People stand behind the police barricades and take as many pictures as they can while trying to get as much information as possible from police officers. Vendors are jumping at the opportunity to sell shirts with military prints, firefighters, and police posters.

People who lost their loved ones hang ads with their pictures on trees, phone booths, bus stations, or fences, anywhere they can.

At night, a fog descends. It illuminates with the emergency lights that flash where the towers one stood.

I came home late last night. I couldn't sleep. I turned on the computer and started to write. I decided to document all that had happened to me since I arrived in NY, but I'm going backwards in time, beginning with the collapse of the Twin Towers, Jeff's murder, Special Training, Eyal, my job interview, Jennifer. I reunited with Jennifer on the second week of my arrival. Maybe I'll make a story out of it, using Jennifer's exquisite photos, and will design kind of a nice web site, embedding the story with the pictures, and send it to her as an act of reconciliation? Then maybe she'll agree to talk to me? But maybe I'm being naïve. It'll probably take more than that to get her to talk to me again.

The Twin Towers are constantly reminding me of my quest to talk to Chris, reminding me it was the only thing that might shine some light on the incident. I find myself calculating where he is now. Is the police looking for him as well? The receptionist said he went to Saudi Arabia for three weeks, so he should still be there now and should be traveling to India in about two weeks.

At night I had that dream again: Jennifer and I were walking around, and suddenly a storm began. It threatened to sweep everything - people, objects, buildings. I felt confident enough to stay where we were but my friend wanted to move on and she left the place. A local told me rooms can be rented nearby. If I didn't hurry, no rooms would be left. The storm was getting stronger and had begun to sweep up everything. People, signs, bins, carts, and children, even parts of buildings were swept away in all directions in a strong, painful din. A huge commotion could be heard from the pained cries of people bumping into objects in their path, carried by the storm. Children were torn from the arms of parents. With great effort, I ran toward the building next door. I had difficulties opening my eyes because of the dust, sand the angry blasts of air. From afar, I recognized two multi-story buildings: the Twin Towers. Chris was there. I had to find him. I started running but was going nowhere. It seemed like I was stepping in the same place. Protecting my face from flying objects, I managed to reach the towers' entrance with great effort and asked if he was renting a room there and if any remaining rooms were left to rent. People were running in all directions and no one paid attention to me. I shouted at them, but no one was listening. The wind's intensity rose, increasing the chaos around. If I didn't hold onto something firm, the wind threatened to sweep me away... Gosh! What a dream!

A wild idea just came to me. I'm going to call Iris in Belgium. I'm going to suggest we travel east together, to India.

I just called Iris. She was actually delighted to hear my idea. She won't have a problem taking a couple of weeks off from work, but anything more than that would be problematic. I told her where I wanted to go and why, saying all we needed was a couple of weeks. She encouraged me and said she'd be happy to join. She asked about my work and if I could take a vacation, because, after all, in the State's we don't have as long of a vacation as in Europe. I could usually get about four days, and now after my office was closed because of the attack, it would be unthinkable to go away, but I told her I didn't give a damn anymore and that if it would come to it, I'd quit without a blink. We agreed we'd try to look for tickets to India as soon as possible.

Saturday, September 15

It's very hard to find flights now for anywhere. Everything's in chaos. The cling to nationalism is intensifying—alongside national shirts and various props, flags are hung everywhere. At night, candles were lit in the street corners in memory of those who were killed. Sometimes a flower or a bouquet is laid down. Passersby ensure that new candles are placed. It seems that the probability of finding survivors is very little. The nation is in pain.

Streets on the south are opened gradually. Despite the presence of the police, it seemed there was no logic or order in tagging areas where people are permitted to walk as opposed to areas off limits. Army's helicopters continue to circle above the ruins.

My yoga studio finally reopened. I went. A teacher had arrived from India as the studio's guest right before the attack. I can't help but think the poor guy had terrible timing. However, I was captivated by his charm. Something in his behavior overwhelmed me. He was a fairly old man, slender, and with a pleasant, relaxing presence. It seems to

300

me like he came from another world, another rhythm, another life. After class, all practitioners remained seated and he told us a bit about the way of life in the place he came from. The lifestyle there sounded very different from the one here. We also talked about the attack and how to cope with disasters. He spoke against violence. His words reminded me of the Dalai Lama's non-violent way of thinking, or "turning the other cheek," as Jesus had said, a phrase I always found puzzling since it seemed to me it implies weakness. However, the way that this thin little Indian man talked about it, it didn't seem like it was coming from weakness.

I came home late. It's night now and I sit by the computer. I'm making progress with the writing. I like the aspect of investigating the obvious and, in the process of looking into things, finding out that they're not all what they seemed. I'm beginning to reflect that maybe I should turn it into something more concrete; maybe I should change the direction of what I do, maybe become a journalist, an investigative journalist. It's so more creative and interesting than what I do now.

In the last week, I got around to thinking a lot about my work. In light of everything that happened in these past few days, my job seems more and more bullshit to me.

Is it a coincidence? Just this evening, I got a message from the office that on Tuesday we're going back to work.

Sunday, September 16

With all this nationalism right now, suddenly I feel I belong more than ever. Since everyone here is in shock and so shaken by what had happened, the differences between outsiders like me and the rest has minimized. All share the fear, the agony and anger of what had happened and we all have our concerns for the future. But I'm still not really part of 'America.' But isn't everyone in New York a foreigner? I guess so, but there are foreigners and then there are strangers—it seems to me that I'm both.

Police check points appear all along Canal Street. Residents in Chinatown have initiated a distribution of the nation's flags to passersby. Last year, at this time, we—Eyal, Jennifer Lorenzo, me, and of course, Jeff—celebrated the Feast of San Gennaro festival in Little Italy. I remember streets filled with processions, food booths, pony rides and celebration.

Now, all you can see is the pile of timbers dismantled from their stands. The streets are empty—no festival, no mirth, no joy. In some parts of the area, however, it looks like business is going back usual. Small flags are hung on the wall of the fire department station on Houston Street, along with pictures and names of the firefighters who perished in the midst of the attack and after it. By the wall, a crowd of people gathers with flowers.

In the afternoon, at a collection point at Pier 40 on the West Side Highway, I brought two packs of items. We were all requested to bring required items such as batteries, drinking water, cough medicine and some other stuff. A pretty big crowd has gathered there and every time either a police car or a rescue vehicle had passed by, everyone cheered. T-shirts with imprints of USA and pictures of the flag were hung for sale for ridiculous prices. On Canal Street, T-shirts reading "I survived the attack on America" were for sale. Some of them were imprinted with the image of the plane colliding into the south tower.

I returned home late again and sat by the computer. I haven't been sleeping much at night. I slept really badly the last two days, and woke up with back pain. I went to the Yoga class with the Indian yoga teacher again. It was excellent. I entered the class with a terrible back and head pain, and the practice saved me.

Joy is back in town tomorrow and I should go with her downtown to check her apartment. She lives not far from the where the Twins stood. You could have seen their peaks from her apartment window.

I'm calling Iris in Belgium again soon. She's already reserved a seat on a flight to India and will soon buy the ticket. I'll have to let her know by tomorrow if I can get a flight or not. From here, it seems impossible to get a flight anywhere.

Monday, September 17

Barriers were placed on Canal Street again. The southern part of the island has become a maze of open and closed streets. Joy came to town and we went to her apartment for the first time. She lives on Liberty Street. Can you believe it? What a name for a street at a time when the 'Nation of freedom' is under siege. We arrived to a closed area but managed to get in thanks to the fact she lives there. Her apartment was intact, but everything was covered with black dust.

We went up to the roof and from the 14th floor; we could see the ruins of the towers. Through a smoky fog, we could even see the broken glass of the Winter Garden in the inner central courtyard of the Twins. A huge American flag is still hanging, torn. Dozens of rescue workers could be seen from afar, working with cranes and forklifts. The roof was full of dust and of burnt torn papers of financial reports, index cards and documents of the well-known companies that were housed in the buildings. The National Guard also has demonstrated a heavy presence.

It was the first day trading in the stock market resumed.

On Wall Street, women and men in their business suits can be seen wearing masks for blocking the dust particles, navigating their way through barricades and military vehicles.

Someone stopped us right in front of the Stock Exchange building and asked us to take a picture of him.

"Make sure that the flag is shown in the picture," he said, adding, "and the man with the mask, the policeman, the church behind, and the stairs of the federal hall, where George Washington stood. The Judgment Day, religion, politics and money all together, you know!" He said passionately. I was struck by the cynicism.

303

Joy will sleep over at my place tonight. It's not pleasant to be downtown at her apartment. Tomorrow I'll go back to work. Not looking forward.

(Don't) Look Back

It was to be Yael's first day back at work. She was about to take her usual route—starting uptown, taking a subway, making her way downtown, stopping at the local deli, getting a croissant and a coffee, and continuing to her office. It would have been automatic despite the collapse, but nothing felt normal.

Everything had changed, from the settings of this city, the changes of the subway routes, the streets, the remains of soot and smoke, the on-going sirens and, and, along with all these, the collapse of her private life. Deep down, she felt an enormous confusion, a pain that refused to heal. She approached the building where her office resided, feeling discomfort and unease. The feeling was intensified as she entered the building. In the elevator, she was already fully aware of the fact that she was back to work and the daily routine was about to return. The elevator doors opened, and memory flashed before here of the day they had all gone down the elevator together. It had been a day in which they feared the terror would spread across the globe and a horrifying new order would take over.

Yael reached the transparent glass doors of her company. Vain golden letters were imprinted on these doors reading World Financial Solutions. *Such a pretentious name*, she thought.

It was clear to her she doesn't want to be there. She entered the office and suddenly felt nauseous. A pain in her stomach became overwhelming. Maybe she should turn back and run out? But the receptionist already was nodding at her.

"How are you, Yael? How have you been?" she asked with a sweet, artificial voice, and without waiting for a response, added, "How awful! Isn't it?"

The voices of her colleagues could be heard from afar.

"This client is looking for a safe investment and now with the uncertainty in the market after the attack..." Robert's voice could be heard.

"We have to show a united front in front of our customers!" Jane interrupted him.

"People, let's try to coordinate positions..." Max's voice was heard.

Nothing has changed, thought Yael, *the world keeps on turning, and the bullshit continues.*

She walked into her office. It seemed alien. She sat on her fancy office chair with heaviness and stares at the black monitor. Her finger was about to reach the power button, but she stopped. What was the point? Her latest conversation with Iris just the previous day resurfaced.

"There's no way I can get a flight from here!"

"Then what should we do? Should I cancel mine, as well?" Iris had asked. But then her following thought had made the difference.

"Maybe I should book you a flight from here..."

Yael, still with her finger pointing to the power button, hesitated for a moment. Then she picked up the phone and dial 125—Kristen's extension. The phone rang and rang but there was no answer. She was about to hang off when suddenly she heard Kristen's voice on the line, purposeful and businesslike, as usual.

"Good morning, Yael. How are you?"

"All right, thank you, and you?"

"Fine. A busy schedule after all recent events…"

Yael paused.

"Yael, is there anything you need specifically?" Kristen's managed with an underlying impatience, "I'm very busy…"

"I need to talk to you," said Yael weakly.

"Something urgent?"

Is it urgent? Yael reflected on this question. *Or I could simply leave without telling her*, she thought.

"Yes," she replied more firmly.

"In ten, my office?"

"Yes, thank you."

How on earth was she going to pass the next ten minutes? She knew they would feel like an eternity. She recalled the last time she was in the office: the day of the attack, the collapse. Only a week had passed, but it seems as if it had been a year. She looked out the window. The skyline—empty of the Twins—only reinforced the feeling that nothing was the same. At least not for her. It was time for another place, another time…another life.

She got up and walked to the bathroom. On the way, she ran into Robert, who as usual, thundered a greeting.

"What's up? How was the week? Tough, huh?" he continued mumbling, as if talking to himself. She knew he wasn't really expecting an answer, so she nodded her head, hoping this would end the flow of chatter, and then she continued to the restroom. The strong artificial smell of perfume—frequently sprinkled across the ladies room—greeted her.

Everything here is so exaggerated, so extreme, so noisy. When it's a bit warm, they freeze you. When it's cold, the heating is stifling. When in the restroom, they bomb you with perfumes. When they speak, it's always loud. When they drive a car, it has to be a huge one. Salaries are huge, buildings are huge, the nation is huge. Uncle Sam is larger than life.

She washed her face and stared at herself in the mirror. Even her own reflection looked different, as if something was not quite familiar about her face.

"Come in! Come in!" Kristen waved to her while holding the phone in her other hand. She covered the handset, "Just finishing," she whispered to Yael.

Yael sat down uncomfortably.

I wonder how she'll take it, she thought, while looking at that woman, Kristen, whom she had so much respect for. The respect had been replaced by more mixed feelings. Despite all the respect, she felt toward Kristen, she couldn't escape the feeling that Kristen, too, wasn't much more than a product of her environment and so the way she lived, in the end, was no different from everyone else. Like the rest, she just wanted to excel, earn a respect, money, status, career, and control… lots of control.

Kristen finished her conversation.

"We'll have to roll up our sleeves to get ready for the customers. It's going to be a difficult time now!" She said to Yael as if predicting the dissonance of Yael's next words. Kristen sighed and leaned back in her chair. "So what is it? I don't have much time."

A short and purposeful question to an answer that is going to be totally the opposite, thought Yael.

"I want to take some vacation time," she said, instead of the "I quit" she originally intended. *You're such a coward*, she immediately reprimanded herself.

"But why it is urgent to talk about it now?" asked Kristen impatiently.

"Because I need some down time now. I need to travel,"

Kristen raised her eyebrows. "What do you mean by now? These days?" Kristen examined her protégée carefully.

"Yes. I have a flight booked to leave in less than two weeks."

There was a knock on the door. Max's head peered around.

"Kristen, you should join us, we have to coordinate positions in front of the shareholders…"

"I'm coming," replied Kristen impatiently.

Max's head disappeared. The door closed.

"I don't understand. You have a flight in less than two weeks? What do you mean? Where? For how long?"

"India, for a couple of weeks, maybe more. I'll need the option to extend it if needed," said Yael stiffly. She paused for a second and added fuel to the fire, "But I also need time off to get organized before the trip." She knew that the last words were a way of saying *I quit.*

Kristen examined Yael lengthily as if she were trying to decide how conclusive Yael's position was. Yael sensed the disappointment of the one who had nurtured her and had so much faith and trust in her.

"Got it," Kristen finally said, clenching her teeth, looking angry, "You're making a big mistake, Yael. I hope that's clear to you!"

Yael was quiet. She didn't see any point in trying to explain. Everything she'd say would be misunderstood. *Kristen, after all, is the product of the 'winner's culture,'* she thought. Now, in Kristen's eyes, Yael had just turned from a potential winner to a loser. No more was left to be said.

"Put your resignation letter on my desk, and you are invited to leave today," said Kristen stiffly. She got up abruptly and left the room angrily, slamming the door behind her, leaving Yael seated alone, stunned at her reaction. She did not anticipate Kristen would be so angry. Everything had happened so quickly and, in a way, left her with a sense of disappointment that Kristen had given up on her so easily. *She didn't even try to convince me to stay, not even on*ce. On the other hand, she felt a huge relief. Finally, she had made her decision.

She went to her office quickly, trying to avoid any familiar faces. Luckily, everybody was in an important emergency meeting. She quickly typed her letter of resignation, printed it, went back to Kristen's office and left it on her desk. She went into her office to see it for the last time. She looked through the window at the gap where the Twin Towers once stood. The skyline seems empty, vacant. The void seemed to mirror her private one. All the important people in her life were gone and now, too, her job. She turned her computer off and stepped out her office. Feeling like a thief, she managed to sneak out again without bumping into anyone.

I can't say goodbye, she thought, *After all, everyone will look at me like a loser anyway. Maybe some day I'll return to explain things a little. Maybe...*

Crossroad

"You don't belong here!" the voice of the girl's shelter principal was echoing in her head. *Where do I belong, if anywhere at all?* Thought Yael on her way back to the Ashram, her face sunken.

She went to the attic, determined to upload the web site to the Internet without any assistance. She managed to make some progress and had completed a draft design of the site's front page. She stuck to the design agreed upon with Arjun. She thought she succeeded in implementing the message Master sought to convey: treatment for any problem, a stay in the Ashram at the discretion of Master, and total devotion on behalf of the patient to treatment and to the therapist. She uploaded the pictures of the Ashram she had taken with John's camera a few days earlier.

The site, she thought, was cleverly designed, meeting the needs of marketing, and user-friendly. She felt content that, at this point, it could be said she had earned some of her bread. She could then turn her attention to the deeper layers of the site where the details were.

Reading the content, she soon discovered that her sense of alienation was creeping back in her. The culture, the Ashram, India, the people—all seemed so foreign to her. A sensation of longing for her family and Israel overwhelmed her. For a while, she simply sat there, in front of the new, nicely designed website she has created, while memories of Israel flooded into her.

Starting all over again there, she thought, *would feel more like home… right?*

She kept on sitting there for about an hour until a decision was made.

Dear Mom and Dad, she wrote, *I'm fine, but I lost my belt with all my money in it…* She fabricated a story and asked if her parents could find a way to send money to her since she had decided to leave India and come back home. She was short and ended the message by sending her regards to all.

Two days passed, and Arjun still was nowhere to be seen.

Master hadn't returned from his business trip, either. Yael was relieved he wasn't back. She didn't know how she would react upon seeing the son she felt she had violated and how would she deal with his father's reaction if he found out.

It was morning. She went down to the kitchen. It was very quiet. It seemed that, apparently, all of the Ashram's residents were out that day, running some errands.

She went to the attic and continued her work on the web site when a reply from her mother came in, asking for her exact address. Cash would be sent to her and be delivered by someone by the name "Yoni." Yoni was expected to arrive some time in the next two days.

When Mom worries, she thought, *she'll turn the world upside down to find a way to help her daughter; a daughter that always seems to get into troubles…*

Knowing that the money was on the way made Yael confident enough to make her decision final. She sent her friend Joy in New York an email saying she was not coming back, and that she was ending the lease of her apartment and if she, Joy, could take some of Yael's personal stuff out of the apartment, it would be great. Then, she sent another email to her landlord, saying she was leaving the country and that after her friend Joy Mayer picked up her personal stuff, he could lease it to someone else.

After sending the emails, she felt a huge relief. She finally put the New York chapter behind, and could move forward with her life.

In the evening, everyone returned. It turned out they had all gone shopping together since Susie had wanted to buy a new Salwar and John still needed a pair of shoes. Vera decided to join them. Mohan was nowhere to be seen in the past few days. At dinner, when everyone sat down at the table, Yael asked about him. It turned out there was an emergency with his family and he had to leave. She expressed her sorrow and regretted she would no longer enjoy his company.

"What a nice, luminous man, Mohan," she said.

All agreed.

Two more days passed in which she divided her time between helping Sabitri and making final improvements to the Ashram web site. During these days, she could quell the annoying thoughts related to Arjun and Master. The huge excitement from kissing Arjun had decreased a bit and the knowledge that she was going to leave soon filled her with peace and serenity.

In the morning, when all were seated for breakfast, a young man entered the dining room. He had curly blonde hair, and very nicely built body. *Pretty hot*, Yael had thought to herself. He turned to Vera—clearly perceived by him as the authority figure—and asked in English with a heavy Israeli accent if someone by the name Yael was staying there. Vera pointed toward Yael.

"Yes, it's me!"

So this was Yoni, who had arrived from Israel, carrying money for her. Vera invited him to join them for breakfast and they all showed interest in the new guest. It was his first time in India and he was planning to go through Sikkim to Nepal and do some trekking in the mountains. He looked tired since he had just landed the previous day and had spent his time on flights, dirt roads, trains, and more to get to the Ashram.

Vera, half asking, half ordering, said to Ravindra: "We do have a place for this nice man in the Ashram, yes?"

Ravindra affirmed that the room Mohan stayed in could be arranged.

Yoni reassured that he wouldn't be interfering by staying there, but it was apparent he was happy he didn't have to look for another place to stay. While he waited in the Puja hall as Ravindra was arranging the room for him, he couldn't keep awake; weariness overtook him and he fell asleep on top of his backpack.

At dinner time, after he had showered, slept and recovered, he appeared to be a very laid back, funny guy. He and Yael very quickly found a common ground and their conversation continued even after dinner. Like her, he had lived in the States for several years. He had an Israeli mother and an American father. He was very interested in the

312

treatments carried out in the Ashram, wanted to study alternative medicine, and was particularly interested in Indian medicine. When he asked her what she was doing and how she had gotten here, she avoided the question, and instead elaborated on the Ashram's web site she was currently building, how she was enjoying it, and the fact that she was considering writing as a profession. Yes, thanks to this place in particular and to India in general, she had realized she was not happy in her profession at all and she had no intentions of going back to it. Of that she was certain.

When got late, they said goodnight with a smile, and retired to bed.

Before falling asleep, Yael thought about how having money again had already made her feel more strong and independent. She no longer owed anyone anything. *Now*, she thought, *I could face Mater even if he finds out about this thing with Arjun.*

The next day, Yoni made sure to be present while she was working with Sabitri and even volunteered to help when it came to lifting heavy things.

He is looking good, this Yoni, she couldn't help but think. He was the complete opposite of Arjun: fair-skinned with blonde curls rolling down to his shoulders, the unshaven bristles of a beard, cool blue eyes reminiscent of the sea she missed so much. Compared to Arjun, he was tall and big, but nicely built. *He looks athletic, she thought, but like most Western men, he lacks the flexibility and feline grace th*e Indian men have.

Sabitri, who sensed that Yoni was "dancing" around Yael, kept on smiling as if it were obvious to her that the new guy was trying to catch Yael's attention.

At dinner, both made an effort not to have conversations in Hebrew. All felt the two were clicked and everyone's faces, without an exception, wore the same expression of unconcealed satisfaction from the alleged connection. During dinner, somewhat bitter thoughts went through Yael's head. *If all would have known about the mutual attraction between me and Arjun, would they also have been so happy? How would they have accepted it, if at all!?*

Indeed, she discovered she still had concerns about the whole thing.

Entertainment

After dinner, Yoni suggested they spend some time together, perhaps look for a local club to hang out. Yael thought it would be a good idea. Maybe it would distract her mind from disturbing thoughts: throwing away her money, the charged kiss with Arjun, the unbearably patronizing behavior of his father. She felt she was walking on extremely unsafe ground and running away from all this was very appealing, especially when her companion was a man like Yoni. She wondered if it was a coincidence that such a charming guy was sent to her.

Little did she know it was no coincidence at all.

Yael wondered to what extent she was willing to risk things and how much she should choose to play it safe. She pondered this to herself as she was dressing up for going out, when a knock on the door interrupted her thoughts. Yoni's voice sounded through the door.

"Are you ready?"

She opened the door "Yes, I'm just taking a jacket since the evenings are a bit cold here."

She felt his curious eyes wandering, examining the room as though he sought to learn more about her. She wondered how much her possessions scattered in the room could say about her. His gaze lingered on the bed. Then another difference between Arjun and Yoni hit her again: the former wouldn't dare to knock on her door, moreover to look directly at her bed.

They went to a club that Vera had recommended. In fact, it was the only club in town.

"There's alcohol there, bands playing live music and karaoke," Vera had said.

"Sounds good."

They stopped a taxi that then brought them to the main street in town. Following Vera's instructions, they entered a building and went down the stale stairs. The entrance was made of one-sided glass preventing those on the outside from looking in. They were surprised by a guard who immediately opened the door for them as if foreigners were the most welcomed guests. A waiter or a local host led them to a small hall and a table in front of a stage over which a disco ball dangled, emitting a kaleidoscope of lights around the room.

"We're back to the seventies," said Yoni, a bit amused.

"Where were you in the seventies? Not near being born, no?" Yael was curious to know his age.

"Hey!" He responded indignantly, "Maybe I'm a little younger than you, but not much."

"Really?" she laughed, "And how old are you, sir?"

"In three months, I'll be twenty four. And you? How old? Twenty seven, eight?"

"No, I'm in the second half of my thirties."

"Get out of here!"

"Yes!" She laughed.

"Well, it doesn't show," he concluded the subject, clearly unaffected.

A waiter approached and handed them menus. After determining what to order, they looked around, observing the people. A number of tables and seating areas were inhabited by small groups of Indian youth. There were also several mixed small groups of boys and girls. Most of them wore Western clothes. There were only a few couples seated and they weren't demonstrating intimate contact. For some reason, she liked it. Relationships in the Western cultures used sex as a commodity, a showcase product. *The Western world has a lot to learn when it comes to modesty and being humble...*

She shared her thoughts with Yoni. To her surprise, he agreed with her. Was it because he was interested in her, or did he really think so?

Pictures of Bob Marley decorated the wall behind the stage. Two locals came on stage, a singer and a guitarist. The guitarist looked like an Indian version of Bob Marley.

"They are really hot for him here," laughed Yoni out loud, trying to overcome the loud volume of the music. He tried to persuade her to order an alcoholic drink.

"I'd rather not," she shouted back.

He didn't give up. Finally, she relented and ordered a fruity, diluted drink with a bit of alcohol. He ordered a drink with more alcohol and asked her to try it. She found it difficult to refuse his inviting smile. *He's so cute and attractive*, she couldn't help but think.

When he offered her another drink, she refused. She was not an alcohol drinker and the drink she had just finished already showed a considerable influence. She had always considered herself a very down-to-earth person and lacked for alcohol. When she desired erosion of the senses, it happened naturally and it seemed to her that the heavy alcohol drinkers were paying a high price for numbness. She didn't buy their claims that certain senses were being sharpened. She felt the same for drugs.

Yoni, however, proved to be a serious drinker.

"In the end I'll have to drag you back," she said.

"Remove any concern from your heart! I'm far from being drunk, I'm just having fun," he said, laughing.

You're lucky you're so cute, she thought.

Yoni had tried to draw her to tell more about herself. He was especially interested in her work and her friends in the U.S. She didn't want to talk about it and made up some accuses. He insisted, and even tried to press her to speak. It was awkward. She found his insistence quite puzzling since she didn't quite feel like it was coming from wanting to get to know her better. She did mention something about maybe changing to a career in journalism, but the way he questioned her about it wasn't adequate in her view. Finally, when he didn't let it go, she had to tell him off firmly.

"Don't ask me again, because I won't say anything. So let's just enjoy the evening."

Yoni accepted the order and the rest of the time passed pleasantly. They were amused with the entire club scene, the karaoke, Bob

Marley's songs and the youth gesturing toward each other. Everything seemed different and interesting. Yael felt at home in the company of Yoni, like she was coming back to her roots as time passed, her true self. All that had happened with Arjun seemed so distanced and foreign now.

When the bill arrived, Yoni wanted to pay. Although it was nothing in terms of US dollars, she refused.

"Finally, the money came." She said, and continued, "You have no idea how it changes my feelings and how it was to be with no money for so long…Now, since you've delivered it to me, it would give me a great pleasure to pay, and I would like to treat you".

She was also curious to see if he would accept her offer, a kind of test she often did to guys she met to see how open-minded the man was. Fortunately, he agreed,

There are definitely advantages to being with a modern Western man, she thought.

He then made an attempt to get to the bottom of why she had been left with no money. She told him she couldn't tell him since she herself didn't know what had happened. Again, he seemed too eager to know, almost suspiciously so. Eventually, she dismissed him by saying, "It's a complicated story; not now!"

They took a taxi back to the Ashram.

Yoni's presence is symbolic and very meaningful, she thought. He had brought her back to her culture, to her Western mentality. By having money again, she felt he had brought her back what she had lost when she let go of those bills: a sense of power, strength, and security. She was no longer subject to the mercy of others, especially Master.

When they had reached the Ashram, it was clear to both of them that they wouldn't be spending the night apart. He accompanied her to her room, and when she opened the door and moved to allow him to enter, he walked in without hesitation.

As he leaned over her naked body and swept her to a place beyond reality, his entire body pleasured her. But then Arjun's image appeared. For a moment, Yael wasn't certain if the experience was a dream and Arjun's image was actually the reality, or maybe it was the opposite. Before they fell asleep, she told him that he had to get up early and sneak back to his room before everyone was awake, since their sharing of a room wouldn't be perceived well by the Ashram's policy. He nodded understandingly, and they sank to sleep, curled up.

When she woke up in the morning and Yoni was no longer in her bed, she had a vague memory of him kissing her lips while the rooster crowed. She also recalled him saying something about having to leave for a few days, and that he'd be back to say an appropriate goodbye before he continued his trip.

Collision

In the evening another Puja ceremony to honor the gods was about to take place, Sabitri arrived and was busy in preparation while gently giving instructions to Yael, who assisted her. Spending more time with Sabitri, even though she could not communicate with her through language, had made them close.

Master, who had finally returned from his journey, entered the hall from time to time, yelling, throwing sporadic sentences here and there—being, as usual, more of interference than a help. He did not seem to be in a good mood. Yael wondered if his business trip had been successful. But there was a good omen in the fact that he was behaving as usual: it led her to believe that he didn't know anything about her and Arjun. Arjun, on the other hand was still nowhere to be seen.

Cleaning and organizing the big room where the Puja was supposed to take place was intense. Sabitri left a bucket of water near the area where incense burned. When Master entered the hall, he ran into the bucket and dirty water was spilled everywhere, messing up the entire Puja area she had just cleaned. Instead of apologizing, he raised his voice, cursed in a local language and, despite the fact Yael could not understand what was being said, it was clear that Sabitri was offended. Yael's inability to bear the way Master treated everyone, and especially Sabitri, had intensified and her mind was troubled by how to talk to him about it.

In the evening, it was time for the Puja. A surge of people started to flood the room along with their offerings. Yael was surprised to see that Sabitri, unlike usual, was staying for the Puja; she was accompanied by a man who Yael had never seen before. The man was close to Sabitri during the entire evening. Yael wondered if they were a couple. Yael watched Master receiving the offerings and blessing the people, and again, although it was an interesting ritual to watch and it was obvious that people were enjoying it, she felt annoyed watching Master being elevated to an almost god-like level by the people.

After the ceremony, when people began to disperse, an old man approached Sabitri with a suitcase in his hand. He handed the suitcase to her with luminous face, and she, with a big but modest smile, bowed her head gratefully several times but refused to accept it. An old woman joined the man and grabbed Sabitri's hand firmly. She put the suitcase in her hand, not allowing her to detach. A number of people had gathered around.

It seemed that Sabitri had won respect from the couple, but Yael did not know the reason. Master, standing nearby with a pile of gifts, was greeting people who were leaving, accepting all the offerings they had brought. Noticing what was happening around Sabitri, he walked toward the gathered group. People stopped their interaction with Sabitri and all eyes turned to him. It appeared that he asked what was going on, and his eyes were shifted from the old couple to the suitcase Sabitri held in her hand and back to Sabitri. Because Yael did not understand what had been said, her senses sharpened, and she watched what was going on closely. She felt something was about to happen.

Master seemed unhappy about something, even though he was lavishing smiles at everyone. Sabitri put the suitcase on the floor and then, suddenly, he picked up the suitcase, turned her upside down, as if he is studying it carefully, assessing her worth. He looked quite pleased with the quality, and appeared to start to flatter the donors. He began to speak passionately. All attention was now diverted to him, and Sabitri was pushed aside.

Only a small number remained from the large group of people who were closer to Sabitri: the elderly couple, the man who had been sitting by her side all evening, and a small number of people who Yael was unsure of regarding their relationships with Sabitri. After a few minutes, without any warning, Yael was amazed to see that Master had taken the suitcase and disappeared.

The act seemed to have come as a surprise to the people who were gathered there, as well. They started to whisper amongst themselves. It was clear it was not appropriate. Sabitri looked embarrassed. Yael felt a deep distress. She had to understand what had just happened here.

321

Vera seemed to be engaged in a deep conversation with an Indian woman who looked like she was from the upper class. She sought Ravindra but he was nowhere to be seen.

Someone approached the woman that was talking to Vera, and Yael jumped the opportunity, approached her and asked whether she had seen what had happened and if she has any idea who the couple was and why they brought Sabitri a fancy suitcase. Vera said that the two were the parents of Sabitri's sister-in-law. Yael remembered that Ravindra had told her that Sabitri used to take care of them when they were sick and that her brother's wife had been diagnosed as mentally ill while her brother, as Vera reminded her, got messed up with the law.

Vera could not say for sure whether the gift was from them, but at least it seemed they have decided to give Sabitri the gift in a respectable situation of the Puja in front of other people to emphasize their appreciation.

"But Master took the suitcase from her!" Yael couldn't hide the criticizing tone in her voice.

Vera, with her sharp perception, looked at her with a firm gaze and answered laconically "Don't judge too quickly only by sight. You don't really know what's going on."

Yael stared at Vera and studied her facial expression carefully, debating whether she had a point or is she was only protecting Master out of blindness. Vera had a strong personality; she was not the type of person that would follow anyone blindly.

Vera turned to go. Yael held her arm. Vera turned her head to her quizzically.

"If you thought Master was making a mistake, would you have told him?" Yael asked.

Vera observed Yael again, as though trying to find an appropriate answer.

After a brief silence, she said, "After the consequences were weighed considerably."

While Yael processed her reply, Vera turned back to the Indian woman she had previously talked to and continued the conversation. Yael turned around and bumped into Sabitri.

Sabitri's eyes said it all. Although she didn't understand English, her face expression revealed she understood that the conversation was about her.

"Master took the suitcase?" Yael asked.

"Ah ha," said Sabitri, adding the typical Indian head shake that indicated "yes."

"A gift, a suitcase for Sabitri, no?" Yael tried to communicate with her using a basic English.

By Sabitri's reaction, Yael had the feeling she had understood the question. However, she looked embarrassed. Yael twisted her wrists in a gesture of a question. Sabitri looked even more embarrassed.

Outside, the boom of thunder could be heard. Ravindra and Kutan entered the room, hauling in wood from the garden. Ravindra smiled as usual, and said, "A big rain is coming..."

Suddenly, Master came in, grumbling something about people while pointing to Ravindra and Kutan. He reprimanded them for not finishing their work and said it was about to storm as his devotees returned home. He placed an extra emphasis on "my devotees." Then he turned to take some of his stuff out from the Puja's incense area.

Without much of a delay, Yael stood behind Master, to his back, and hurled the question at him.

"Where's Sabitri's suitcase?"

Master turned around, completely surprised.

"What did you just ask?" He questioned, as if he hadn't heard her.

Yael decided she was no longer cutting him any slack, "I saw that you took her suitcase! Why?"

Master looked at her as though he refused to believe what he had just been asked.

With a cold, harsh stare, he said loudly: "Do I owe you any explanation?"

323

It was too late for Yael to withdraw. Everyone in the room stopped what they were doing, and there was an awkward, uneasy silence.

"Not to me, but maybe to her?" Yael replied, standing her ground. Another silence.

Master looked at her for a few long seconds with a harsh stare, as if he was debating what to do and how to respond.

"Go to sleep," he muttered and turned his back to her.

Yael felt a burning insult. He didn't even bother to properly address her opposition. She looked around. No one was looking in her direction. All hurriedly returned to their matters, were lowering their sight, and trying to look very busy. The group was quick to leave.

Yael realized she had to leave the hall.

She went to bed and had troubles falling asleep. Although she felt that justice was with her, she couldn't escape the feeling that things didn't turn at all the way she had anticipated. But what did she really expect? That he would willingly submit to her criticism? That he would admit he was a jerk with delusions of grandeur?

The next day, she left her room with a small fear that she would encounter him. After the previous night's confrontation, it probably wouldn't be a pleasant encounter. She was relieved when she heard that Master Buphendra had gone away again. No one knew to where.

She looked for Vera. In her distress, she wanted to know more about the story of the suitcase and Sabitri, but Vera couldn't be found anywhere the entire day. Yael tried to understand from Ravindra what had happened with the suitcase, but he refused to cooperate. She asked Ravindra if he knew where Vera is, but he didn't know.

After dinner, she bumped into John, who, as usual, made his way to the meditation room on the roof. She tried to extract a piece of information about the previous evening from him as well, but he didn't know what she was talking about. She asked him if he knows where Vera was.

"She's in the local library," he said, "helping a number of Indian girls with their educations. She won't be back too late, since good

Indian girls are not allowed to stay away from home late," he said, winking.

Men, Yael thought cynically.

She sat in the garden and waited for Vera. She went over what had happened the day before in her head and through the events that led to the conflict and the confrontation with Master. Something was not quite right. She was looking forward to getting a hold of Vera. This time, unlike in New York, she would not give up and would get to the bottom of what really had happened.

After an hour, Ravindra came and said that Vera wouldn't return tonight. She would be staying overnight in the library.

Yael felt despair.

Brightening

Vera welcomed her at the entrance of the library with total surprise.

"Vera, I have to know what's behind Sabitri's suitcase. Please, will you tell me?"

Vera hardened her face expression. Apparently, she did not like the question, but the surprise of seeing Yael at the library overwhelmed her.

"You came this far just for that?" she asked.

"Yes." Yael looked tormented. Vera's facial expression had softened.

"If so, then you deserve an answer," she said, and added "Let's sit."

She sighed deeply and sat down, pointing Yael to a seat next to her.

"It was many years ago, or so I heard. Sabitri's brother got in trouble doing some gambling and some other criminal offenses and Sabitri had to raise a lot of money to bail him out of his debts while his life was at risk because of his creditors. Sabitri was a newlywed and pregnant. With only a minimal education, she worked as a cleaner in some kind of a government institution."

"Where was her husband? I know he was a soldier who died about a year ago in the Gujarat riots..." said Yael.

"Yes, it was a very difficult time," Vera continued, "At the time, they were so poor, with no means, and they also had to support her husband's parents who were sick. On top it all, her brother's wife was diagnosed as mentally ill..."

"Yes, I heard," said Yael sadly.

"Sabitri's husband worked in the south of India to earn as much as possible; at that time he was not yet in the army. In any case, all these troubles had landed on Sabitri. At that time, her husband's parents were Master's students..."

"What do you mean students?" Yael interrupted her.

Vera smiled, "You have a Jewish Rabbi, right? We, the Christians, have priests, and Indians have a kind of mentor and spiritual guide who advises them in all sorts of problems and when dilemmas arise..."

"Got it," said Yael, "Followers you mean."

"You may call them so." Said Vera with a smile.

"Okay," Yael urged her to go on, "And?"

"In their plight, they turned to Master for advice and help. Master, as you may not have already known, also has a huge influence in this region and can pull few stings, besides being a teacher and healer for this community. Some suggest he's also quite close to India's political elite figures," Vera explained.

"Okay," said Yael, making an effort to show she wasn't impressed.

"So in any case, the parents of Sabitri's husband have been loyal to him for many years..."

"What do you mean, loyal to him?" Yael interrupted her.

"Indian gurus indeed dominate areas, but sometimes there are situations where a particular geographical area has more than one guru or master. This splits the community and..."

"There is also a war between gurus?" Yael interrupted her again.

Vera looked at her suspiciously, realizing the tendentious nature of the question.

"Well, yes. Of course there is. But you must understand that each Master has his or her own view, and even though all are Hindus, there is pluralism in this religion, contrary to popular Western religions. Gurus, depending on the caste they come from, when embracing one god or another, are free to emphasize a particular aspect of their teaching as well as the way they conduct their matters in the community and with people..."

"Who did Master embrace?" Yael was intrigued.

"Master is, as you already may or may not know, of the warrior caste. This caste is considered to be one of the highest in India, and as such, he prays to Hanuman god, or as Westerners tend to call him, 'Monkey face.'"

"Yes, it really does look like a monkey, with a tail," agreed Yael.

"Yes," confirmed Vera, "Hanuman is described as almost divine in his nature and with human capabilities, especially in everything related to physical strength. Hanuman is able to change its shape at will and to leap in the air for great distances. The long tail is characterized by great intensity and he was always the object of many legends. Many Indians in various temples give offerings to Hanuman before they give them to the other gods. In Hinduism, Hanuman is a living god and thousands of villages dedicate shrines to him. He is a god who is identified with physical strength and admired especially by athletes and wrestlers."

"I see," said Yael.

"One of the legends…" Vera went on with her story, with sparkling eyes as if she was herself one of Hanuman's devotees, "… that Master enjoyed telling is the tell of Ravana, the king of Ceylon, who had abducted the wife of Rama, Sita, and put her under heavy guard in his palace. Hanuman went looking for Sita. He went to the mountains of Chandra, jumped beyond the passages leading to the palace of Ravana, and when he reached the palace, he wandered disguised as a cat and found Sita in the garden. He promised her that he would rescue her soon. He gave her Rama's ring as proof he was his friend. But Hanuman was captured and brought in front of the throne of King Ravana. In his audacity, he rolled his tail and sat on it, so his seat was higher than the seat of the king. Every time Ravana raised his chair, Hanuman raised his tail, and, as a consequence, his seat height as well. Then, he managed to set his tail on fire and escape. While jumping and bouncing from house to house away from his captor, large parts of the capital city of Ravana were burnt by his burning tail. After all the damage he caused, he returned unharmed to Rama and told him all that had happened. But unfortunately, during the battle against Ravana, Rama's brother and other warriors were seriously wounded and the healers needed healing herbs desperately to treat the wounded. The herbs only grew in the far mountains. Hanuman went to get them, but when he got there, he didn't know how to identify which were required. Having no choice, he lifted up the entire mountain and brought it to the battlefield. After the healers used the herbs they needed, he returned the mountain to its original location."

"Nice story," said Yael, "It's no surprise, then, that Master follows this Hanuman god," she said with a cynical tone.

Vera smiled. "You know what Master's name—Buphendra—means in Hindi?"

Yael shook her head. "What?"

"King of kings!" said Vera.

"Very appropriate," Again, Yael didn't make any effort hide the cynicism in her voice.

Vera smiled and took a deep breath.

"Now, where were we?" she paused to recall, "Yes... Well, pluralism in the religion allows each Guru to pick up certain characteristics and adjust his or her teachings to each individual. Therefore, among the master's followers, there are those who have chosen him because they believe in the same gods and there are those that, when they follow his guidance, chose to accept his gods.

"Who competes with master here?" Yael interrupted defiantly.

Vera shifted with discomfort in light of the question; Yael knew that Vera's charismatic personality allowed her to be a true student to Master and, at the same time, not to get too excited by criticism for his weaknesses.

"Guru Kiran Singh," said Vera.

Yael was astonished. *That's the Guru Chris-Daoud Khan went to see for a cure!*

Chris had stayed in his place of treatment, and that was where Yael had last checked on him and found out he had just left for Saudi Arabia. Everything that had brought her there seemed so far away.

"Kiran Singh?" she repeated his name, as if confirming she had heard it right.

"Yes! He is a man of many deeds, but Master says he's a fake since he claims to have supernatural powers. Master says he also caused the deaths of some of his believers."

"And what do you think? Is it true?" Yael asked, continuing, "Do you believe him? Maybe it's only a competition in which everything is kosher, and Master uses stories like that to spar with him?"

329

"Look," said Vera, "we, the foreigners, have no way of knowing exactly what happens because we don't live here; we didn't grow up in this culture and we don't have the tools needed to reach intelligent conclusions. We must rely solely on our intuition and common sense. We come here with our set of values from a distant and very different culture, looking through Western spectacles, and use Western standards to judge."

"It is so true..." muttered Yael, more to herself than anyone, "But let's go back to the story of Sabitri and the suitcase..." she said.

"Well," continued Vera, "Where were we? Oh! What old age does to you...." she complained.

"I hope I'm like you when I'm your age," said Yael.

Vera laughed, not hiding her pleasure from the compliment, and continued, "Her husband's parents were loyal disciples of Master for many years, and therefore, when the disasters happened, Master instructed them to send Sabitri over to live at his home. He then promised he would take care of all her needs. In addition, he tried to pull some strings to release the brother from his debts, including, they say, spending money out of his own pocket. Sabitri herself went through a complicated pregnancy and Master treated her during it. She became like a family member. A year ago, after the death of her husband, Sabitri got closer and closer to her husband's close friend from the army who had comforted her in her grief... and perhaps even more than just that. Sabitri also got very close to his sister and they became friends.

"This friend from the army and his sister are students of Guru Kiran Singh, and eventually Sabitri joined them for the meetings and ceremonies he conducted. Of course, she hid it for a long period of time, but then, about two weeks before the event with the suitcase, Master found out about it. You can imagine the magnitude of his anger. He had given and done so much for her, had taken her under his wing, treated her, took care of her brother and, as far as he was concerned, it was a huge betrayal. He claimed that the fact that she had hidden it and lied to him bothered him more than the actual act, but I

330

think..." Vera's emphasized her last words, "He was also hurt by the act itself."

"Hmm... the picture begins to clear," said Yael, reflective, "but I still don't understand. Did he take the suitcase to punish her?"

"Here, now I'll get to the suitcase," Vera stopped her before she could continue, "On that evening in the Puja, the parents of her brother's wife came with her late husband's friend and brought a gift for Sabitri from the other guru. It's not acceptable for a Guru to give a gift to his student unless she has done something extraordinary for him. Not only did Guru Singh give her a gift, but he also asked that it would be done in public in a Puja conducted by Master Buphendra and the gift be handed over by Guru Singh's disciples—the parents of her brother's wife. In addition, the man she was seen with, her late husband's friend, is also Singh's disciple and was there that evening by no coincidence. His job was to spy on what happened and report back to Singh on how things went. It was, without a doubt, a demonstration of power by Guru Kiran Singh in public, and as far as Master Buphendra's concerned, a kind of humiliation. Sabitri was merely a toy in the hands of the other guru, and was also caught in her betrayal. Incidentally, your words to Master on that occasion only increased the drama."

Yael lowered her head and was silent.

"Well," said Vera, "I hope this helps you."

Yael raised her head, still silent, absorbing what was had just been said.

"Things are not always what they seem," said Vera emphatically, adding, "Don't let the truth get away from you. Strive hard to look for it, even if there are difficulties."

Yael pursed her lips. She had realized the magnitude of the mistake she had made. She had insulted the father and violated the son, his virginity, his innocence and his culture. She felt that her actions had had destructive consequences, and this all happened after they took her under their wings when she was penniless. She felt ungrateful. How would she redeem her deeds?

"You're still young," added Vera, laughing lightly as if trying to ease the severity of her last words, "And now, excuse an old woman, but I must retire to bed."

Yael went back to the Ashram, absorbed in her own thoughts

She realized that she had absorbed herself in the local life and culture while wanting to leave the past completely behind, but Vera's last words got to her. "Don't let the truth get away from you. Strive hard to look for it, even if there are difficulties."

An image of Jennifer resurfaced in her mind.

"Ground Zero,"— A Diary

Tuesday, September 18

I resigned this morning. I went home and immediately called Iris to tell her. The ticket she had ordered for me is now confirmed. I will be leaving from New York in less than two weeks. I'm getting so excited to get away from this place, to get out of here and finally talk to Chris.

I went to Liberty' Street, to Joy's apartment, to help her clean. We worked a good few hours. There was so much soot and dust, and the smell is still there. I told Joy she was welcome to sleep over until the smell went away, but she doesn't want to; she'd rather be at home. After finishing with the cleaning, we went wandering around in the area. The demand for flags is increasing. Stores advertise that they're out of stock. Memory rallies are held in town squares. The smell of scented candles mixes with calls for war. In one of the squares, a statue was unveiled: it's a firefighter kneeling with one hand supported on the ground and the other to his knee, covering his sad face. I just got back home, in the evening, exhausted, and it just truly hit me that I've resigned.

I can't take in all that's happened in recent months. It's too much; I have no strength left.

I'm going to sleep.

Wednesday, September 19

I spoke with Joy on the phone to check how her first night was near Ground Zero. It turned out that making a local phone call behind the barricades was free only up to three minutes. Joy had a birthday and she planned on having a party tonight despite it all. However, she didn't feel it would be appropriate to have a big party, so she just invited a few people to a small neighborhood bar, south of Canal Street. At night, on the way to the bar, we weren't allowed to cross the police barrier, and one of the bar staff had to get to the checkpoint to vouch for us.

From different vantage points, you can see the big piles remaining from the towers filled with concrete, metal, and glass. The smoke coming out from these piles has changed to a light gray now and it is sparser. In one of the Indian restaurants, I saw a sign: "Salam Bombay salutes our heroes."

I thought: "India! Here I come in a bit!"

The uneasiness about Jennifer has only intensified. Joy persuaded me to call her. There was no answer. I left a message.

Thursday, September 20.

The rain today ruined the posters and the ads down in Union Square, the ads and lists of photos of the missing people. The streets close, re-open, and close again. The constant presence of the police had already become routine.

Jennifer hasn't gotten back to me.

Friday, September 21

Memorial services are being held. The clearing of the rubble continues, the supply continues to arrive, the media continue to look for spicy stories, and everyone is sharing this feeling of anticipation for something. But what?

I called Jennifer again and left her a message to call me back.

Saturday, September 22

The garbage trucks are still clearing the rubble, and it seems it's never-ending; the more they clear, the more there is. Most streets have

334

already been opened for free movement but most of the shops are still closed, and windows are shattered. Downtown, dust and ruin are everywhere, and access is limited. The presence of the National Guard, the Secret Service and the Red Cross is heavily felt.

The smoke and the smell coming out of the rubble piles reach north whenever there is a northern wind. There are stations scattered throughout the city for receiving supply for those who are busy clearing the debris.

Jennifer still hasn't returned my call.

Sunday, September 30

I haven't written in a whole week. I just didn't feel like it. It's official now: Michelle died in the attack. There is clear evidence that she was one of the people who had jumped from the burning building. I cannot imagine the horror she went through. I can't even cry anymore. I feel detached from all that is happening.

There are two days until the flight. A pungent smell of the smoke still reaches here; it gets worse at night when the north wind is blowing. It seems to even reach my building, which is more than a hundred blocks north. The pile continues to burn, memorial ceremonies continue and their number grows. Evacuation work continues, but hope for finding survivors is fading. It's estimated that about 3000 people were killed. Railway maps are continually changing, announcing route changes. The elections for the mayoral office were postponed by the mayor, and now posters for opposing candidates are everywhere. Journalists are everywhere, interviewing activists, passersby. Relatives are busy recording moments of hope, fear and grief.

Many of the flags that were lowered to half-mast are back to the top today.

I feel like a tourist in my own town.

Still no news from Jennifer.

October 1

It's the day of the flight. I tried to talk with Jennifer one last time. Once, in the good old days, every time I thought of her, she would call, and now I've called her so many times and left so many messages... and nothing. Where is that telepathy we used to have? After all, I feel like I can't travel when things are unresolved between us.

On the other hand, what will I even tell her if we speak? This time, I left a message that I wanted to talk to her about the day of the murder and that it was related to her. This will make a difference. She won't be able to ignore that; she has to call me back now.

The Hours Before

It was only a few hours before the flight, and finally Jennifer's voice, dry and cold, could be heard on the phone.

"Hello, Yael."

"What a surprise." Said Yael, adding, "It's very hard to get a hold of you these days; I guess you got back to me because of my last message," she said her last words somewhat hesitantly.

"Yes, I'm a little surprised. You said in your message there was something to do with the day of the murder?" The questioning in her voice was obvious.

"Yes." Yael took a deep breath. "Jennifer, listen… it's been on my conscience ever since that day, and I can no longer keep it in."

There was silence on the other end. Yael could feel that Jennifer was waiting in suspense.

Yael took another deep breath and spilled it out, "I saw you a few minutes just before the murder over there, in the park!"

Silence.

"Jennifer?"

More silence.

"Jennifer?"

Jennifer's voice was finally heard, hesitant.

"No way…"

"I know it was you. God, what on earth were you doing there?"

Jennifer kept silent for a long few seconds, and then with a deep, quiet voice asked, "What did you say to the police?"

"I said nothing."

Silence. And then in a very harsh tone that sounded almost commanding, Jennifer demanded, "Yael! This never happened! You never saw me there. Put it behind you!"

Yael, overwhelmed, couldn't find the words for a response. She remained silent, speechless.

"Yael, I have to go. Can I trust you?" Jennifer softened her voice.

"Trust me with what?"

"That this matter is closed! That you won't bring it up to anyone." She paused for a second, and then added, "You don't really believe that I had something to do with Jeff's death, do you?"

"I don't know what I think anymore," said Yael despairingly. Jennifer's response struck her.

"If that's what you think, you'll put yourself in a mess you won't be able to get out of!"

Yael found it difficult to decide if it was said out of warning, as a threat, or a concern. Jennifer's tone of voice was so harsh, so cold, and so detached, like it was someone else, not the woman she knew, not her best friend.

Jennifer hung up without warning. The phone dropped from Yael's hand. She remained stunned.

What the hell's going on?

Confrontation

Yael got out of bed heavily. A feeling of exhaustion took hold of her. For some reason, the mere mention of the guru's name that connected her back to Chris-Daoud Khan threw her back to the dark place she was desperately trying to run away from. Slowly, she dragged herself to the dining room. It looked like everyone had already eaten, and she found a dish left on the table for her.

She ate slowly, almost unwillingly. When she finished eating, she took the dirty dishes and walked slowly to the sink. She felt, however, that she was neither asleep nor fully awake. Thoughts of the events over the past few days continued to trouble her mind—Arjun, Sabitri's suitcase, Chris Daoud-Khan… and then it went further back, to the past. New York had come back to pursue her, not letting go. She had no redemption.

"Master wants to talk to you," the bewildered tone in Ravindra's voice was apparent as he surprised her from behind while she was watering the plants. She froze, and pulled herself together.

"Okay, when I'm done."

Ravindra insisted. "I think he meant now!"

Yael turned to him. The sheepish grin on his face was reminiscent of the smile people wore when they attended funerals and were not sure how and what to say to the mourners.

"Okay," she said, put the funnel aside, and followed him up the stairs.

They entered into the room where she had first met Master. He stood there, dressed in orange clothes behind a desk, his back turned to the door.

"Master…" Ravindra tried to capture his attention with a faint, awed voice.

Master waved with his hand, instructing Ravindra to leave, which he did with no delay.

He's probably right to run as quickly as hell, thought Yael, gathering all her strength so she would be able to face what was to come.

"I am Master Buphendra," he said without turning around.

Yael, puzzled for a second, lost in some kind of déjà - vu of her first day in the Ashram. She kept silent, waiting for what was to come.

"And you?" he turned around, his face sullen.

Now it's just me and him… she thought.

"I did not hear your answer," he insisted.

"Yael Finkelstein!" Again, like on her first day there, she felt the need to specify her full name.

"No, I did not ask you for your name. Try again! You?"

Silence.

"Master Buphendra is more than just a name," he said, adding, "It was achieved with great effort!"

Yael kept her mouth shut.

"And what about you? What have you achieved?"

More silence.

"Why are you here?"

"You called me."

"Why are you here?"

"You wanted to talk to me!"

"Why are you here?"

"You are angry with me and want to put me in my place!"

"That's better. Try again."

"I was angry with you and wanted to…"

"To put me in place?" He interrupted her with a cynical, derisive tone.

"Well, actually—yes!"

"Okay. Now we can start! Why did you get here? To this place?"

"Sabitri brought me."

"Try again."

"Because I was left with no money."

"Again!"

340

"This place was my salvation."

"You wish to be saved?"

"I've already been saved."

"Is that so? How?"

"The money I received a few days ago when you weren't here."

"Hmm… I see…" he said, paused for a second, and continued, "What is your salvation?"

Her answer was slow to arrive. Yael tried to figure out what he was getting at. "I don't understand."

"Is it your stay here, or the money you got?" he asked.

"The money is my ticket back to the world!"

"So," he smiled strangely, "where is your salvation, then?"

She was quiet. She knew he was right. From the very start, the money was not her salvation, but rather the opposite. When she threw away her money, she felt for a brief moment that she was free from her past, but she didn't dare to admit it to him.

"You had a chance and you blew it!" He slammed the harsh words at her.

She looked at him in horror. Jennifer's image came into her mind. *What's he referring to, damn it?* She thought, looking at him with a questioning expression.

Then Kristen's image popped into her mind. *You're making a mistake*, Kristen's words echoed.

He looked at her intently, stood up, and turned toward the door.

"Master—" She called after him. He turned.

"I apologize for what happened with Sabitri."

He was silent for a few long seconds, and then repeated, "You had a chance, and you blew it."

She looked at him in horror again. Why was he repeating it? Was he referring to Chris? Maybe, in his own mysterious way, he had found out why she came to India and who she was looking for? And maybe, he was referring to Jennifer after all…

"Once there and once here!" He added.

341

She couldn't help but slam a question back at him. "Where is there?"

He glared at her silently. "Don't apologize to me; apologize to her," he said and turned his back to her again, walking toward the door.

Who does he mean? She wondered.

"Master," she said, raising her voice, "Apologize to whom? Sabitri?"

He kept going as if he hadn't heard her.

"Master!" She yelled loudly, taking herself aback.

He stopped.

"Are you saved?" she asked.

He froze. It looked as if he was debating for a second if and how to reply. Then, without a word, he left the room.

A Turn

She went downstairs. Ravindra and Kutan were busy preparing an herbal steam sauna for one of Master's patients. Yael was distressed from the talk, so she sat few feet away from them, far enough so they wouldn't start a conversation with her, but close enough so she'd be able to see them. Watching them was something she did often during the time she was at the Ashram, when she needed to soothe her mind. However, she then came to realize that watching them was no longer doing the trick. It didn't relax her or calm her down, but rather made her even more agitated. Now, in light of recent occurrences, the scenes of the Ashram, the people, their actions, the place, the pace, and the culture—it all seemed foreign to her.

To make matters worse, Master's words continued echoing in her head: *you had a chance and you blew it.*

She agonized again. *What did he mean? Maybe if I wouldn't have dismissed Jeff on the day he was murdered there in the park, I would've known what had happened... I did have the chance and I blew it. My arrogance!*

Apologize to her, echoed anew in her mind.

What's become of her? Why did she distance herself so much from me? Did she guess what I felt? Did she suspect anything? Maybe I should have been upfront with her from the beginning. Will she ever speak to me again? Ever?

Apologize to her, echoed in her mind.

Yael became angry. *No! He's wrong; it's not me that needs to apologize to Jennifer! She has to clarify what had happened and apologize to me for misleading me...For disappearing on me... for ignoring my calls, and even threatening me...*

Things are not always as they seem... Vera's voice entered the picture. *Don't let the truth get away from you; strive hard to look for it even if there are difficulties.*

Then it hit her. *Jennifer's hiding something deeper. How was I so blind as to not see it before? I must go back to New York and find out what this is all about, but this time... I won't be so helpless.*

She looked at Ravindra and Kutan completely emerged in their task. *Each additional day here is useless; there is nothing left for me to seek here*, she determined.

Now she knew exactly where her salvation would come from. She had to solve the mystery. She couldn't escape it anymore. She had to continue to search for the truth. It was time to go back to New York.

Masks

It was the morning after the confrontation with Master. Yael was called. Yoni was waiting for her outside in the garden. He was about to leave India and continue his trip. He had come by to say goodbye.

He approached her. Agitated from the talk with Master and her recent decision, Yael rushed out, happy to see a friendly face. She spread her arms to give him a hug only to realize that something was holding him back. He seemed distant, very distant.

"Hi."

"Hi."

"So you're leaving..." she said, examining him.

"Yes," he replied curtly.

She looked at him, expecting him to say something. Sensing it, he added, "It's time," and released a fake sigh.

She kept silent, unsure of how to proceed.

"And what about you?" he asked while looking away, pondering.

"I'm going back," she said heavily, "I don't belong here."

He suddenly looked alert. "Back where?"

"Tel Aviv."

"You belong there?" he asked.

She paused slightly. "I don't know; I'll have to see..." she said weakly, adding, "But before, I'll be passing through New York."

He looked at her, a questioning expression on his face.

"I've got some unfinished business there that I must resolve," she said resolutely.

"Like what? Work?" although he seemed curious, his voice was still cold and distant.

"No, I'm not going back to work," she said, "it's actually a personal thing."

"A personal thing?" Now he seemed even more curious, something completely inconsistent with his previous coldness. He pressed on.

"What? Friends? A girlfriend?"

She was surprised by the fact that he said "girlfriend—" there was something very awkward about the question.

"Yes, something like that..." she said, not elaborating.

"What, something happened to a friend or a particular girlfriend of yours?" he sounded very eager.

This is really weird, she thought.

"Yes, but I don't want to go into it," she said stiffly.

"Ah," he backed off, realizing she wasn't going to elaborate, and changed the subject. "And you're going to change directions, like you thought? To journalism?"

"Yes, I'll start a new life. I'm not going back to my old work."

"Got it! Well then, good luck," he said coldly.

She stood still, waiting to see how he would say goodbye. He approached her, and she reached her arms again toward him, but his facial expression stopped her once more. Then he inclined his head toward her and whispered in her ear.

"Yael, listen well. When you get back to New York, you will be summoned for the investigation. Do not tell the police you saw Jennifer on the day of the murder!"

Yael backed away, in shock. His words—words that had seemed to come from a horror film—left her speechless.

He pulled his head away from her and whispered, "I'm sorry." Then he inclined his head toward her again, let his lips touch her cheek in a slightly cool kiss, and turned to go.

Yael grabbed his shirt, a painful questioning look on her face.

"Who are you? What's your story? What's going on here?"

"I'm sorry; I can't tell you any more than this."

"What do you mean? What can't you tell me?"

"I'm sorry; it's a matter of national security. Just forget it; forget you saw Jennifer!"

His gaze was harsh, but his eyes looked soft.

"Yael, for your own sake... don't get involved..."

Yael even thought she heard a pleading note in his voice as he said it, and turned to leave. Then he disappeared.

346

Tracing

"Mom, what's up?" she waited for a reasonable hour to call Israel.

"All is fine here." Her mom said, and added, "And what about you? Did you get the money we sent you?"

"Yes, Mom, thank you," Yael replied gratefully. She wanted to ask about Yoni, but was uncertain how.

"Yaeli, what are you going to do now? Are you going back to New York?"

Yael didn't want to tell her mother that she had actually decided to return to Israel, not before tying up all her loose knots.

"Yes, Mom. I am." She said.

Her mother was silent.

"Yaeli, what is bothering you?"

How does she know? Thought Yael, *She always senses in my voice when I'm going to ask something...*

"Mom, tell me how this guy—Yoni—got to you? How do you know him?"

"I didn't know him, Yaeli. I saw him only once when he came to take the money. He's a friend of the son of friends of our friends, something like that, who was just about to leave to India, so it worked perfectly."

"But how had these friends heard that I lost the money and that you want to send me some?"

"I'm not sure..." her mom admitted, adding, "Actually, your Dad spoke with them."

"Well, then let me speak to him," said Yael eagerly. She could hear her mother calling to Yael's father. Soon, maybe she would be able to understand the meaning some of the mystery. An excitement took hold of her.

"Yes, Lalush? How are you?" her father's voice came on the line.

"Dad, I'm fine. What about you?"

"Nothing new, just getting closer to God every day," her father joked, as usual.

"Dad, how did the guy who brought me the money get to you?"

"Ohhh!" Her father said, emphasizing the fact he was trying to remember, "Do you remember the Kleins, our friends?"

"Yes," said Yael.

"Their friends said that someone was traveling to India—I believe it was their son's friend."

"But how did they know you were looking for someone to take the money?" she didn't hide her eagerness to know.

"Why is it so important, Yaeli?" her father asked, and she could hear him turning to her mom saying, worried, "Hey, Dvora! She didn't get the money!"

"Dad, Dad!" She interrupted him, "I got the money; everything is all right!" Yael hurried to soothe him, adding "… I'm just curious to know how you got to this guy."

"Well," said her father, calmer, "I don't understand why it's so important." He paused and continued, "But the guy actually got to us. He called and introduced himself as the son's friend and said he was going to India and would be happy to take the money for you. The Kleins confirmed that he was indeed their friend's son and that's it."

Yael realized that she wouldn't be able to figure out Yoni's involvement in the story. She had to talk to the friends of the Kleins, but how would she do that without drawing any suspicion? Without having to reveal what had happened? Then an idea sparked in her mind.

"Dad, I need to talk with these friends of the Kleins," she said while trying to find a good excuse for it, saying, "Yoni, the guy, left today and he forgot here a ring that looks very expensive to me. I want to talk with the Kleins' friends to get in touch with their son so he could get me in touch with Yoni."

"Oh, so this is what it's all about?" her father seemed to have fully relaxed, "You don't want us to ask?"

"No, no, I want to talk to him personally. I didn't really have the chance to thank him properly for bringing the money…"

"Do you want to talk to them from India, or when you return to New York?"

"Now, if it's possible."

"Well, wait…" He quickly briefed Yael's mom and got back to the phone. "Mom is calling the Kleins now. She'll ask for their friends phone number. Maybe we'll be lucky and she'll get a hold of them."

"Shula? Hello," Yael heard the voice of her mother over the phone, and then heard her asking for the phone number.

"Ah, I see, okay, I'll tell her," she heard her say before hanging up.

"Yaeli, here's the number," said her mother, "But the chance you will be able to get a hold of them is very low, since they're all traveling abroad now."

Yael sighed. She was disappointed but determined. She wrote down the number, repeated it carefully to ensure she had it right, and thanked her mother.

Upon hanging up, she immediately dialed the new number, but, as her mother warned her, there was no answer. She tried several more times throughout the day, but with no success.

Back

Yael was at the airport, impatiently waiting to board. Since she had bought her ticket, she had been eager to leave India and get to New York as soon as possible. She had almost begged the travel agency to board the next coming flight. Fortunately, while she was in their office, a seat had become vacant for a flight the next day. She didn't think twice and bought it.

She couldn't get the recent events in the Ashram out of her mind. Things were even more confusing, and her head was a mess of thoughts running back and forth restlessly. First, there was the awkward conversation with Master, and shortly after, the even more bizarre, and unsettling meeting with Yoni. What did he have to do with Jennifer? How did he know about everything? Did he know all that happened? And where did he show up from all of a sudden?

Her thoughts were interrupted by the flight attendant announcing boarding. Yael joined the long line winding in front of the gate. The line was populated predominantly by Indians and Pakistanis. *Do all these have an entry visa to the U.S.?* She wondered.

Finally, she was on the plane. A welcoming Indian flight attendant instructed her where to sit. She asked for an aisle seat. It was going to be a long flight, and she would have to get up several times to allow her body to stretch.

She sat down, allowing her mind to drift by watching the passengers boarding the plane. Just before getting to the airport, she attempted to call the Kleins' friends one last time. It was another failure.

Two Indian women sat in the seats next to her. One was older and the other was a young teenage girl—the woman's daughter, determined Yael. The mother was wearing a traditional sari and she looked to be from a lower class. Her daughter, on the other hand, was dressed in a Western style and looked quite literate.

Curious, she took another look at the girl. The girl sensed she is being watched and looked back at Yael. Yael immediately turned her gaze away.

It's not only the clothes; there's something about her appearance, her expression… her behavior indicates that she is educated, Yael concluded while turning her head to the other direction. She felt the girl looking at her curiously.

The old woman sitting beside Yael seemed troubled a bit and her gestures indicated nervousness. Yael thought that she was probably wishing, like everyone else, that the boarding would end and the plane would take off. But there was a delay and it was unclear why.

The captain's voice could be heard over the speakers, "Dear passengers, welcome to American Airlines flight 292. I'm David Gordon, and I will be your pilot today. Unfortunately, we are experiencing a slight delay, but please remain seated and we will be on our way shortly."

The old woman turned to the girl with a questioning look. The girl started translating, but stopped when she heard the announcement being repeated in Nepalese. A translation was no longer needed.

It was evident that after hearing what had been announced, the mother was feeling even more nervous.

After several long minutes of waiting, the plane finally took off.

New York is getting closer, after all, thought Yael, feeling excitement. However, the excitement blended with fear and doubts.

But why am I coming back, anyways? Why return to the unknown? Just for the purpose of finding out what had really happened? I almost don't have anyone there. The place has changed; nothing is the same. A deep sadness and concern overtook—her—what would happen when she got back?

It was dark outside the plane. Minimal lights illuminated the aisle, and weak glimmers lit up the overhead passenger storage compartments. Yael shifted back and forth from sleepiness to wakefulness. Images of past events in New York were going through her head. The images that had led to India: the scene at the club, the park, Jeff, Jennifer from afar, running, murder, finding out about Jeff's murder, the search for Chris.

She woke up from her half sleep. Something was happening nearby. Signals of distress were coming from the Indian woman, the mother. Yael, with her vision slightly blurred, opened up her tired eyes.

The woman was shifting nervously in her seat. Her agitated body movements were gradually intensifying. She put her arms up, and her eyes rolled back as if she was not entirely conscious. She started slapping her thighs, raised her arms up and again, and slapped her thighs once more. She began to unbutton her blouse buttons under her Sari. She continued mumbling words in Nepalese.

Her daughter, who had probably also been sleeping, woke up in alarm. She asked Yael to excuse her, hopped over her, and rushed to the back of the plane.

She probably went to call for help, thought Yael. The woman's distress continued. It was alarming. *I must do something right now*, Yael thought.

Where the hell is the daughter with the help? Yael thought back to what the seniors had done for the trainees that had problems during the Kiabadachi practice. She knew what to do.

She gently turned the woman's head toward her. The woman's eyes kept rolling back as she fluttered in and out of consciousness. With two fingers, Yael gestured for the woman to look into her eyes.

Seconds that seemed like minutes passed, and the woman refused to focus, but Yael wasn't giving up. She raised her voice.

"Look into my eyes!" She repeated several times, aiming her two fingers toward her eyes. It seems that despite being unable to understand the language, something succeeding in penetrating the woman's floating consciousness. Her eyes stopped rolling.

Two flight attendants along with the daughter arrived and although the woman was not heavy, the flight attendants had difficulty picking her up. Fluttering in and out of consciousness had apparently added some weight. They carried her to the back of the plane. The daughter trailed behind.

Yael tried to sleep but couldn't. She wanted to know what had become of the mother. She rose from her seat and walked to the back of the plane. There, surrounded by flight attendants, the woman was lying on a mattress on the floor. A pillow was placed beneath her head and she was covered with a blanket. Her daughter was beside her.

Yael asked how she was doing.

"Everything is fine now, apparently, just a panic attack!" said one of the flight attendants, and asked Yael to go back to her seat.

Yael returned to her seat and attempted to fall asleep. This time, all the images from India began to float through her mind. Her goodbye from Yoni hovered last and a sharp pain went through her head.

When she would reach New York, she would have to get a hold of the Kleins' friends and trace who Yoni was and how he was related to Jennifer.

Morning Dew

"What are you going to do now?" asked Joy as she got ready to go out.

"I'll start searching for job and school in Israel," replied Yael.

"Journalism, you said?" asked Joy.

"Yes!" Yael responded while thinking, *I must get a hold of the Kleins' friends. I'll call again as soon as Joy leaves!*

She had landed late at night the day before. When Joy offered her a place to stay in her spare room, Yael jumped at the offer.

"It shouldn't be so long until I'm ready to go back to Israel," she said, and told Joy about her plans to change her career. She avoided telling her that the main reason she wanted to stay there was to find out what Jennifer was doing in the park that day, why she had threatened her, and how Yoni knew Jennifer.

Yael watched Joy wrapping up her things while she sat at the table and had her first New York coffee. It is winter and it was drizzling slightly outside. They had just finished their breakfast.

"You just got here," said Joy, "Give yourself some time to rest and to get back to the pace over here!"

Yael raised her eyebrows, as if saying, "I can't rest."

"Sit back on the couch and relax; watch stupid soap operas a bit. Take your time. What's the rush?"

"I was sitting back long enough in India, for almost two months," she said, shaking her head, "It was a major head cleaning and straightened things up in my mind," she paused slightly and corrected herself, "Well, some of the things, not all."

"You see, you said it yourself: some, not all. You need more time!"

Yael remained still, playing with her fork and shifting the remainder of her breakfast from one side of the plate to the other.

"In any case, the fact you've discovered what you like to do most is huge. I wish I would have found it!" Joy tried to cheer her up. "Sounds much more interesting than what you did before… one hundred and eighty degrees…" She smiled.

"Everything has changed, Joy. And all in such a short time, as if my entire life turned upside down."

She looked out the window. Once, when they were still standing tall, she could see the Twin Towers from that very window. Joy noticed Yael's gaze.

"Yes, everything has changed..."

"It's probably not so pleasant getting a daily reminder of the disaster," said Yael.

"Not pleasant? It's horrible! It's still fresh!" Joy sighed. They were silent. There wasn't much else to say on the matter.

Joy pulled herself together.

"But life goes on, and I'm late." She grabbed her bag, threw a light jacket on her shoulders, turned to Yael and said, "Bye, dear! Good luck with your searches."

Yael smiled at her.

"Bye! And thanks, Joy"

"Oh, forget it!" Said Joy, and the door slammed behind her.

Yael immediately jumped out of her seat, grabbed the phone, and dialed the Kleins' friend's number. She prayed they'd pick up.

No answer.

She sighed and sat down for a moment helplessly, and then began to clear the table. She couldn't help noticing the huge breakfast they had. The image of the small breakfast in Sabitri's tiny home resurfaced. *What a difference.*

Since she had landed, she couldn't avoid comparing. The catalyst pressure to do and achieve more and more had managed to overwhelm her after only a few hours.

Joy was right. Why couldn't she just sit back a bit and move on at a slower pace? Maybe she should try?

She laid down on the couch, looked for the TV remote, and turned it on. After almost two months in India with no TV, watching the images of tiny people on the flickering frame was too strange and felt weird, unnatural. Now, more than ever, it was boring, so she started zipping through the stations—news, politics, various reports, fashion, soap operas.... She fixed on the shopping channel. A vacuum cleaner on a special sale was featured with very low payments. *Really fascinating.* She thought cynically.

She continued to channel surf. A stupid comedy was being aired on the movie channel. Then a commercial for a sports car popped up.

Who needs that, anyway? The presenters are pretty and caked in makeup. They don't even look real. The entire Western world lives in a movie, she couldn't help but think.

Again, people and events from India fluttered into her mind: Ravindra and Kutan lighting a fire in the yard, preparing herbal steam stew for the sauna of an American woman.

She turned off the TV. The deafening siren of the fire truck came from outside, bringing her back to reality. Since the attack on the Twins, sirens continued to be a reminder of that horrible day and the following two weeks during which those sirens were constantly in the background. They meant more casualties, more fires to put out, more debris to remove.

In the next hour Yael had already started searching for a job. She also began looking into potential Journalism schools in Israel. She was content. She managed to make few important phone calls and even schedule an interview with a company in New York that apparently had an affiliation with a company in Israel.

Once again, life is moving in fast-forward, she thought.

She needed some air, so she grabbed her jacket and went outside. Autumn was over and winter was in the air, bringing with it a wind of change. She walked around the streets aimlessly, feeling the excitement of the new life she would soon have, but also reminding herself that she wouldn't be able to move on before speaking with Jennifer.

She looked at her watch. She should call, but she'd rather do it after resolving Yoni's issue. She dialed Jennifer's number from a public phone so the caller ID couldn't be identified. She was just curious to see if there would be an answer and planned to hang up as soon as she heard her voice, but there was no answer and no voice mail.

Did she change her number?

Tangle

"Did you have any contact with Ms. Jennifer Parsons from the day of the murder?" without preamble, Lieutenant Thompson had fired the question at her.

Yael was on the subway on her way back from the police station to meet Daniel, reflecting on how she had done in the investigation.

She had lost her cool for a moment when the question had been asked and felt like she was going to be caught, but she quickly pulled herself together.

She answered with a lie—she said she didn't. Yoni's image was floating in her mind when she thought of her response. She felt it hadn't truly been a lie, because seeing Jennifer face-to-face like she was desperately hoping for hadn't happened, but she refrained from telling if she had seen her or spoken with her on the day she flew to India.

Why now, six months after the murder, I am summoned for a questioning again? And why the interest in Jennifer? Is it possible she's a suspect?

Only two days have passed since she returned from Delhi, and she was still experiencing culture shock. Apart from the astronomical number of people in both locations, New York and Delhi, everything was so different: the people, the culture, the colors, and the smell. The mechanical noises and the scent of the subway tunnel hit her. Her heart didn't like what her senses perceived. She didn't feel like she was back home. The city felt more foreign than ever.

She saw Daniel sitting at the table in the Coffee shop where they had decided to meet. Her heart ached. She had feared meeting him a bit. It had been so long, and he seemed like he belonged to another world to her, another time… she wasn't sure what she'd feel when she saw him.

Upon seeing her, he rose from his seat and greeted her. He seemed to hesitate over whether to hug her or not. He examined her carefully to take the toll of recent events on her and the journey she had made, note what had changed about her, and whether or not there was still some spark between them.

Seeing him face-to-face gave Yael the sudden urge to burst into tears. She rushed to hug him so he wouldn't be able to see the moisture building up in her eyes. She would have wanted to share everything she had been going through in India with him, but the focus of their meeting was the murder and the police investigation. India would have to wait.

"This time, in the investigation, it seems that suspicion has been moved to Jennifer," she said as they began to analyze the new developments.

"The case definitely isn't closed," said Daniel. "I was also called for a questioning when you were in India," he added.

They continued examining the facts using every piece of information each of them had.

Then he asked about her trip in India. Yael shared a bit of the details with him, but she didn't tell him everything. She didn't mention Yoni at all. She felt she couldn't tell him about Yoni without telling him about the romantic aspect of their relationship, and for some reason she didn't feel comfortable talking about it.

Their conversation quickly shifted back to the murder. The news, as described by Daniel, was that Chris-Daoud Khan was no longer a suspect. He had a solid alibi—he claimed to have been with Lorenzo, and the latter confirmed it. The surprising part was that this meeting was a private one. There was no record of the meeting by Joy at the agency. Paradoxically, the fact that Lorenzo was with Chris-Daoud Khan removed all suspicion from Lorenzo himself, as well.

"The suspicion definitely has shifted to Jennifer now," Daniel sighed.

It was obvious he didn't feel comfortable with the fact that his niece was a suspect. According to the questions he had been asked, he understood that several contradictions and shortcomings had arisen in Jennifer's investigation. He knew that his niece had claimed that she was busy with a photography project of the Puerto Rican parade that was held downtown that day.

She couldn't have gotten uptown on time, killed Jeff, and returned, Yael thought to herself. Horrified by the thought that Jennifer had something to do with it and that the option was crossing her mind again, she was quick to ask Daniel what he thought would happen next. Daniel said that the police were checking another lead for another factor that might be involved in the murder.

"What do you mean another factor?"

"I don't think they don't know for sure, but I think it seems to them that even if Jennifer was involved, she didn't act alone."

"Hmm," Yael muttered, wondering what he might mean.

A waiter approached their seats and put two cups of coffee on the table. They remained silent, waiting for him to leave.

"Say, we have talked about it once before, but remind me—Jennifer was Dan 5, right?" Yael asked when the waiter left.

"Yes," Daniel confirmed.

"And why did you say she left, again?"

"I'm not sure exactly, but she had also specialized in some other martial that are considered hidden," he said.

"Oh, that's right. The ones with the special techniques to bring opponents down instantly," she added.

"Do you really think that she broke contact with you just because you didn't tell her about Lorenzo?" asked Daniel.

"Why else?" she asked, scanning Daniel suspiciously.

How could Yael know that Daniel wasn't involved somehow for sure? But she immediately eliminated the thought from her mind. However, she still didn't know how much he knew about her conversation with Jennifer just before she had left. She assumed he didn't know she had seen her on the day of the murder, but how could she be sure? *Since this thing with Yoni, everyone is a suspect.*

Daniel looked thoughtful. He appeared to be truly struggling to understand what was happening.

"I don't know. I really just don't know." He answered her question with sadness in his voice. He looked sincere.

Am I developing paranoia? She wondered to herself, and was almost tempted to share her heavy thought with him and tell him she had seen Jennifer on the day of the murder... but no, she had to first solve the mystery surrounding Jennifer, and Jeff's murder.

"Where are you staying now?" Daniel asked, changing the subject.

"I'm at Joy's, temporarily," she replied.

"If you need to, you're welcome to stay over at my place, you know." He seemed sincere in the invitation.

"Thank you, Daniel. For now I'm fine," she tried to be equally sincere in her response.

"Are you sure?" he looked worried.

"Yes, really, thank you," she replied quickly. Her heart ached again, and she couldn't help but think to herself, *this is so not true. I'm not fine at all.*

"What are you going to do now?" he asked.

"A brand new start," she answered, and elaborated. "A new direction, a new job, new life..." She stopped as if trying to figure out what that actually meant.

She didn't mention her plans to move back to Israel.

Daniel was silent, waiting. His silence had always allowed her to find out how she really felt about things.

"I lost everything I had," she said, "I'm looking for something I can feel I belong to, I suppose."

"You didn't lose everything," Daniel said with a gloomy smile, "I'm still here."

Yael looked at him closely, as if trying to figure him out.

"You're a good friend, Daniel. I'm so sorry you have to be in between me and Jennifer in this story. It's probably not easy for you."

"Try to talk to her," he said.

Yes, she thought, but *will that unfold the mystery?*

"She doesn't answer my calls, you know," she said.

"See her face to face!"

"But she doesn't answer the phone," Yael replied, "Is she even still around?"

"Yes, she is," said Daniel.

Yael was silent for a moment.

"Then I don't understand why she doesn't answer the phone."

"Well, then, go to her house! Ambush her!"

A Twist

There was a short ring, followed by another. Finally, Yael had managed to get a hold of the friends of the Kleins.

"Hello, I'm Yael, the daughter of the Finkelsteins, the Kleins' friends..."

They explained that Yoni was their son's friend from the army, but they really didn't know or remember how their son knew she had lost her money. However, they were happy she got it.

"Didn't you ask your parents, Yael?" they were interested to know, taken aback by all her questions. She asked if she could speak with their son, since Yoni had left a ring behind.

"Our son, Roy, is currently not available. He's on a diplomatic mission outside of Israel," she was told. They gave her his phone number.

"Where is he?" she asked.

"Venezuela."

She thanked them and hung up. What a disappointment. The conversation with them had left her in the same darkness, but maybe it was better they didn't know anything since Roy, their son, would probably have more answers.

Immediately, Yael began to dial his number, but paused before finishing. For some reason, she was nervous to talk to Roy. He might be the one to untie the mystery, and she was uneasy about what she might find out. She put down the receiver.

She stayed in Joy's apartment, pacing back and forth in the little room like a lion in a cage. She took a deep breath and, mustering as much determination as she could, she began to dial again, somewhat hoping there wouldn't be an answer.

It rang, followed by another ring, and another. She felt slightly relieved; clearly he wasn't picking up. And then it stopped. Her heart stopped as well.

The voice of a young man with an Israeli accent greeted her. It was Roy.

He sounded surprised when she said her name. However, strangely enough, he immediately knew who she was. He didn't ask how she had managed to get a hold of him.

To avoid arousing suspicion, she first asked for Yoni's number. When he asked why and she told him about the lost ring, she could tell he didn't buy the story. He said he didn't know how to get a hold of Yoni since Yoni was traveling in India.

He said he would be happy to take her phone number and in case Yoni called, he would deliver the message and her phone number.

Yael had the feeling he was just saying that to lead her on. He started to sound impatient, and she sensed a slight nervousness in his voice, but she wasn't willing to let go, and when he was about to end the call, she quickly fired the question regarding how he had known she had lost the money.

There was a slight hesitation, and then he told her his parents had mentioned it to him. Since he knew Yoni was on his way to Sikkim in India, he had suggested him to be the courier.

"But your parents said they heard it from you!" Yael wasn't going to let him off the hook so easily despite her position.

"Well," he said, his voice sounding more aggressive, "they don't remember it right, and I'm sorry, but I really have to go now!"

Yael hesitated for a second, debating. She was clearly getting nowhere with him, but she sensed he was lying. But why? She decided to insist.

"I think they remember it correctly. So tell me—how did you know?"

He hung up.

Yael became absolutely sure he was hiding something. She paced the room, struggling to get into the bottom of it. After a few long minutes of going over all that had happened in her mind, she grabbed her coat and bag and rushed outside, determined and angry.

She knew it was time to target the one who appeared to have all the answers. It was time to see Jennifer.

An Ambush

While standing at her surveillance post in the street opposite Jennifer's building, Yael couldn't help but wonder how she had gotten to that point.

From where she stood, Jennifer's window could be clearly seen. It was 8:00 pm and Yael knew that Jennifer would usually be heading to the gym at that time. They often used to meet before or after her workout.

She intended to confront Jennifer face to face, like Daniel had suggested.

I can no longer bear this mess; I need to understand what's going on here!

Long minutes passed and Jennifer was nowhere to be seen.

Damnit, thought Yael, did she go out already and I missed her?

She had already been standing there for a while. How long could she keep it up?

And then someone left the building.

It was immediately apparent it wasn't Jennifer.

Maybe she isn't home... But the light is on in her window! Maybe she's sick or something and won't be going to the Gym?

She continued waiting.

Minutes passed, and still there was no sign of Jennifer. Yael debated what to do.

She made a decision: she would go to Jennifer's apartment, ring the doorbell, and, if necessary, enter by force.

And just as the thought entered her mind, the light went off in the window. Yael held her breath. Several more long minutes—*or where they seconds?*—passed, and there she was. Jennifer was leaving her building.

Alarmed, Yael hid behind a wall, unable to muster the courage needed to approach her. Jennifer walked briskly.

Yael, hesitated for a moment, and began following Jennifer, keeping a safe distance. The gym was close by, about two blocks from Jennifer's apartment.

Before she knew it, they were there. But Jennifer passed the gym as if she had no intention of entering. Walking fast, she continued for three more blocks and then stopped suddenly.

She stood in front of an ordinary-looking building and looked sideways. A very fat man came toward her. They nodded to each other. The man handed her a large manila envelope and continued to walk. "

What the hell is she involved with? Yael wondered.

Jennifer continued to walk with the envelope in her hand. For a brief second, she turned her head back.

Yael jumped aside quickly, hiding behind a pillar.

Is she on to me?

Yael glanced around the pillar. Jennifer looked as if she was debating in which direction to continue. Several seconds passed, and she continued walking, crossing the street. A car went by, blocking Jennifer sight for a moment.

The car passed, and suddenly Yael realized that she had lost sight of her. Jennifer has disappeared as if swallowed by the earth.

Yael spotted a subway entrance located exactly where Jennifer had disappeared. Assuming she went down to the subway, Yael tried to cross the road, but it was quite busy. She started to get upset, fearing she would lose track of Jennifer.

She crossed the street quickly and went down to the subway station, looking carefully for Jennifer. The platform was almost clear of people and there was no sign of Jennifer. It seemed the train had recently stopped, and Jennifer disappeared with it.

Frustrated, Yael went back up the stairs to the street. She decided that rather than confronting Jennifer, she would continue watching her until something was revealed.

She didn't know what she expected to discover, but something told her there was more to it that met the eye.

Deception

It was early in the morning, and Yael was again at her surveillance post watching over Jennifer's building. It was cold, very cold. There was a heavy drizzle. Yael wrapped her jacket tighter around herself. She had been waiting for around twenty minutes.

Finally, Jennifer came out. Yael went after her, careful not to be exposed, but this time, she maintained a closer distance. She wasn't going to lose her again.

Jennifer took the subway to 42nd Street on the East Side and walked toward First Avenue. Yael was behind her, extremely careful not to be revealed.

Jennifer approached a building that looked extremely secure. Yael attempted to read the sign, but it was too far. Jennifer entered. Yael approached the building. She could make out the sign: "The Federal Authority for Immigrants Affairs".

What in God's name does Jennifer have to do with that? Maybe something related to Lorenzo? Yael didn't have much time to hypothesize, because, before she knew it, Jennifer had left the building and was heading straight in her direction, as if knowing all along that she had been there.

Yael remained stunned, rooted in her place.

What will I say? What's my excuse? Thoughts ran chaotically through her head.

Jennifer approached her calmly and without any preamble.

"Come!" She ordered in a commanding voice, and started walking.

Yael followed her without a word. She was too stunned to do anything else.

They entered the building. Jennifer swiped a card. The security guard performed a search over Yael's body and her bag while Jennifer waited. Yael collected her bag, and Jennifer walked toward the elevators. Yael trailed behind. The doors opened. Jennifer didn't look back, and they walked into the elevator without a word. Jennifer pressed the third floor button, still not looking at Yael. Yael didn't dare to ask. She knew that something was about to happen, something that would probably shed some light on the truth. She felt butterflies in her stomach.

They got out in an artificially lit corridor. A tall young man passed them. He nodded toward Jennifer and scanned Yael. Jennifer opened a large door and instructed Yael to enter.

Yael entered a small room in which a desk was positioned in its center, surrounded by a few chairs. Jennifer instructed her to sit. Jennifer remained standing. It seemed that she was waiting for something or someone.

A long minute passed. Yael still didn't dare ask what was going on, sensing things would soon be clear.

A man entered the room, the same man that had previously nodded to Jennifer when he passed them in the hallway. He closed the door behind him, sat in front of Yael, and leaned forward with his elbows on the desk.

"Yael, right?"

Yael watched him, trying to figure out who he was.

"Yes, and you?" she asked sternly.

"Thomas." He smiled, "You can call me Tom, though."

In Hebrew, Tom means innocence, and you sure don't look innocent to me... Yael couldn't help but think.

"Do you know where you are?" Thomas asked.

"The Federal Authority for Immigrants something?"

"No," he said, pausing slightly for emphasis, "an FBI division."

He leaned back and examined her as if trying to see the impression this new piece of information left on her.

Yael turned her head to look directly at Jennifer. Jennifer's expressions remained unmoving. She bent down and whispered loudly at Yael.

"I asked you not stick your nose in my business, but you just couldn't help it, could you?" And then surprisingly, she smiled.

Yael, completely puzzled, remained silent.

"What do you know about Chris-Daoud Khan?" Thomas asked suddenly.

"I'm not saying anything about anything until you explain to me what's going on here!"

Yael felt a rush of bitterness and confusion. Here she was, for reasons not known to her, trying to find her own information, and all they were doing was asking her questions. Then Yoni popped into her head.

"Yoni! Is he also linked to you?"

Jennifer and Thomas looked at each other for a second and, without saying a word to each other, they asked her to excuse them and stepped out of the room. Several minutes passed and Yael could hear them speaking through the door. She couldn't exactly make out what they were talking about. She wondered why the question about Yoni had made argue over a response.

They returned. Thomas sat down. This time, he leaned back and claps his arms together. Jennifer put her elbows on the desk and finally began to explain.

"I've been with the service for a long time. My job is to expose people suspected of being involved with Muslim terrorist groups," She paused for a brief second, allowing Yael to digest what had just been said. "It has been known to the Bureau for a while that Chris-Daoud Khan was a closeted gay with a particular fondness for Western immigrant men." She paused again. Yael could sense that Jennifer wasn't very comfortable saying it. She continued.

"When the FBI discovered that Lorenzo—" she paused again and took a deep breath.

Thomas took over.

"When the FBI discovered that Lorenzo was seeing Chris-Daoud Khan—" he paused and glanced toward Jennifer. Jennifer's gaze was on Yael, but her face remained expressionless other than a slight movement of her bottom lip.

So Jennifer hadn't known about Lorenzo, after all, Yael thought.

Thomas continued. "We hoped to recruit him, too..."

369

But didn't they know, thought Yael, *that Lorenzo's is an addict and has a serious drug problem that Jennifer was desperately trying to solve? Hadn't she told them that?*

"Jeff had become an unexpected disruption when he discovered the relationship between Chris and Lorenzo and threatened to expose Chris. The chance Lorenzo had to get closer to Chris-Daoud Khan would have been lost forever."

"So what? You murdered him?" Yael asked boldly.

Thomas didn't appear alarmed by her question.

"We had offered Jeff a job on the West Coast, but he refused," he said, completely ignoring her question.

"You offered him a job on the West Coast?" Yael repeated, puzzled. "Just like that? Why would he leave?"

"We offered him a job with higher prestige, a higher salary, a house, everything," said Jennifer.

But what he wanted most of all, more than anything, you didn't offer him: Lorenzo! Yael thought bitterly to herself.

"And...?" she asked.

"He refused," said Thomas.

"So you murdered him?" Yael threw back, appalled.

Jennifer and Thomas looked at each other. Thomas looked back at Yael.

"No."

"Then what happened to him? Who killed him?"

"That, we don't know. The Police are still investigating," he paused for a second and continued, "Jeff was involved with drug dealers so might be that things got complicated there."

Yael looked at Thomas and Jennifer alternatively, trying to read whether they were telling the truth in their eyes.

For some reason, Vera's words at the Ashram popped into her mind: *"Things are not always as they seem..."*

"So Yoni worked—or still works—for you?" she asked.

"Jonathan? Oh, yes. "We tried to warn you through him not to dig too much into it, but you didn't listen," said Jennifer. She leaned back to allow Yael some time to process what had just been said.

They must have been monitoring my emails to know I needed the money, thought Yael, irritated. She was furious that her privacy had been violated, but she didn't say anything.

Job Offer II

Thomas leaned toward her.

"Now, what do you know about Chris-Daoud Khan?"

Yael thought for a moment.

Yes, she had met him, and she had gone over his confidential file, *the one that Kristen had,* and had even taken notes of what was in the file. He had seemed to be quite a complex character to her, a difficult man to attach a label to, and somehow, she had felt he liked her. Thomas and Jennifer seemed to like that last bit.

"What about his big brother?" Thomas asked.

His older brother was even more of an enigmatic figure to her, she admitted. The younger Chris-Daoud Khan did actually lie in the shadow of his big brother, Muhammad, while the latter ran the business. Thomas seemed satisfied with what he heard.

"We need your help," he said suddenly.

"Meaning?"

"We want you to return to your job and get closer to Chris-Daoud Khan. We need someone from the inside, and even better you" —he put an emphasis on *you*—"will have an insider's, professional view of what's going on. We have suspicions that some of his businesses were used, apparently without his knowledge, for money laundering to get weapons to Muslim terror organizations, including Al-Qaeda."

He leaned back again.

"So the attack on the Twin Towers was also connected to him?" Yael asked, incredulous.

"Yes, but again, we don't believe he's aware of it," Thomas said.

"If really is, how can he not know about it?" Asked Yael, unable to hide her surprise.

"His brother. He's the one involved in this, and they're business partners. His brother uses some of his businesses as a pipe to transfer codes, money and maybe even weapons. We must crack it and get to the bottom of this, and we think we can do this if you'll help us," said Thomas, assertively. He pressed on.

Yael was shocked by the proposal.

"Do you think you can get your job back?"

Yael seemed to hesitate for a moment.

"We can always pull a few strings," he looked toward Jennifer.

"I don't know what to say... I'll have to think about it," she replied, still in shock.

"What more is there to think about, Yael?" Jennifer glared at her.

Yael shook her head, overwhelmed. *This can't be true, she thought. This has got to just be another dream...*

They looked at her. She could feel their examining gazes.

She looked back at them. She found it extremely difficult to internalize all that was happening. Disturbing thoughts began to run through her mind. Had they already thought about recruiting her in the past? Maybe they even planted her in the company in order to recruit her a year and a half later? And Jennifer was the one who got her the job! *Oh god! Jennifer! It was such a huge deception on her behalf.* It was all overwhelming.

Thomas, now attempting more direct approach, leaned forward and said, "Think of it – three thousand innocent people met their death in the September 11th attack."

He looked at Yael fiercely, waiting for her to respond. Yael, still in a state of shock, could only think about being deceived all that time.

"Think about the people you know that were lost. Think about Michelle—didn't she deserve to live more? To have a better life than the life she had? After she had finally reached a state in which she was no longer under her husband's threats?"

How on earth do they know that as well? This is horrifying, thought Yael.

"You have an opportunity to do something important here! Something useful."

"If you can pull strings at will, why only now? Why haven't you approached me before?" asked Yael angrily, "Maybe something could have been done to prevent the attack?"

"His brother is watching all the time," Thomas retorted. "We had to be very careful and couldn't afford to get you in before the time was right. Having you start to snoop around too soon would have raised suspicion."

Yael was silent. The pieces were all starting to come together. She recalled Chris saying his brother had forced him to relocate his offices, leaving The World Trade Center before summer.

His brother knew about the attack to come.

"You're perfect for it," Thomas nodded as if to emphasize the fact. "And besides, he likes you and feels close to you, being half Jewish and all." He paused for a second, "And most importantly, it seems he trusts you."

Yael was still silent. She looked at Jennifer.

Thomas, appearing to interpret her body language as a sign she was in a dilemma, signaled Jennifer. They looked at each other for few seconds and then, without saying anything, they stepped out of the room.

Revelation?

A few minutes passed by. It seemed like an eternity. Yael was left alone with her thoughts.

I would never in my wildest dreams have anticipated this. Vera's words came to her once more: "*We, the foreigners, have no way of knowing exactly what is happening because we don't live here; we didn't grow up in this culture and we don't have the tools needed to reach intelligent conclusions. We must rely solely on our intuition and common sense…*"

Thomas returned. He watched her carefully as if trying to evaluate what impression it all had made on her.

"Take a day to think about it," he finally said, "but know that we're short on time. The further we get from the day of the attack, the harder it is to bring these terrorists down."

He reached out and shook Yael's hand.

"We would be happy to hear a positive response, you know how important this is and you are perfect for it."

Yael rose from her seat, still shaking his hand, speechless.

Jennifer stepped in again. Thomas nodded toward her and left.

Yael's legs felt heavy. She sat down. Jennifer sat down opposite her. Both were silent.

After a few long minutes during which Yael reflected on all that had happened, she looked at Jennifer, realizing that she couldn't be angry for what she had thought of her.

"I owe you an apology," she said genuinely. Master's words came into her mind.

Jennifer nodded gently in acceptance. She even seemed to smile slightly, but there was still something in her face indicating that she was different. She was no longer the Jennifer Yael used to know, not the one before Jeff's murder. Yael couldn't decide if she seemed different because Yael knew who she really was, because of the past events, or because their friendship was about to undergo a drastic change if Yael decided to join the service.

"Yael, think about it positively. Think about the priceless reward of revealing the terrorists. Think about the Twins. Haven't you said that you feel useless and want to make a difference? To be involved in something bigger? This is your chance to make things better; the world will be a better place without those terrorists," she paused for a second, "And there are excellent people here. We're like a big family, we really are," she emphasized.

How am I always getting into the most bizarre situations? Thought Yael.

Jennifer, as if reading her thoughts, continued.

"This hasn't happened without any reason. It happened because it had to happen!"

"What had had to happen? My life here? My job? My friends?" Yael shot back, staring at her. "All were a big lie!" She added bitterly, "And now I got mixed up in all of this!"

"Yael, my dear," said Jennifer softly, "I know you're upset and in shock right now, but I have known you for some time now, and you didn't get involved without any reason. Your struggle to find the truth despite all obstacles shows that you've changed and want to be more involved. Now you have a real opportunity to do so, to be part of the culture here! You can belong!" She paused.

"You'll do great, I know it."

Yael was silent.

"Think it over," urged Jennifer.

Yael remained silent, thoughtful.

Jennifer rose from her seat. For Yael, there was still one question remaining, a question that she knew she would never get the chance to ask if she didn't ask then.

"Jennifer," She got her attention firmly.

Jennifer turned around to face her.

"There's one thing I need to ask you."

Jennifer looked lengthily at her. She seemed to predict what the question was going to be.

"No! I had nothing to do with it!" She said firmly, staring directly at Yael.

"But you were there. Weren't you? It was you I saw!"

"I was there, yes. And I knew that he was going to be there. I came to talk to him and warn him to stay away from Lorenzo."

"So what happened?"

"He was about to buy drugs in the park. I actually tried to stop him, for his sake and for Lorenzo's sake..." Jennifer sighed. "It didn't work. He went ahead with it. I feared for him, but I couldn't risk sticking my neck out for him because of the sensitivity of this whole thing and Chris's involvement..."

"And...?" Yael urged.

"We think he was murdered by a crazy drug dealer; that's it. We don't really know. The police don't either, but that's what it looks like."

Yael breathed a deep sigh of relief.

A Vision...

They walked out from the FBI headquarters. Jennifer led the way. She accompanied Yael all the way to the subway station.

At the entrance of the station, just before departing, they stood in front of each other in silence.

I have more questions unresolved, thought Yael.

Jennifer, as if reading her mind, said, "All in good time, all in good time." She hugged Yael gently. They departed. Yael's eyes followed her friend until she disappeared back into the building.

Yael's gaze lingered for a moment, and just when she was about to turn to the subway, her eyes caught a familiar figure who seemed to be going out of the building. This figure was limping.

No. It can't be...

Suddenly, it dawned upon her. Had the apartment break-in also been staged? There was something strange about it, almost unreal.

Would she just have to join to find out?

Yael attempted to focus her eyes on him, but he was too far away to see clearly. The limping figure stopped a cab, got in, and disappeared into the city.

Closure

She was with Daniel. They were going out after seeing a movie.
There had been a fair number of jokes that she didn't quite understand,
and Daniel filled her in during the movie. He comforted her when they
got out.

"Never mind! You really have to be born here to get it, and even I
didn't understand them all..."

"It's okay," she said, smiling back at him. She wasn't as bothered by
her lack of understanding as she used to be. "Shall we go for a drink?"

"Yeah, sure," Daniel smiled back, "I'm so glad that everything is
finally settled with Jennifer and that you two are back in touch."

"Yeah, me too," she agreed.

They were about to turn down the street, when suddenly, she
thought she saw a familiar limp across the street.

Him again? She thought, aggravated. He looked to be watching her.

"Hey, Daniel, do you see the guy across the street standing there?"
She turned her head slowly in the direction of the phony lame so he
wouldn't notice she was drawing attention to him.

Daniel turned his gaze slowly, understanding that a low profile was
required. "Yes."

"I think he's been following me since even before I went to India."

She didn't tell him she suspected he might also be the one who had
broken into her apartment.

"Really?" Daniel questioned, somewhat concerned.

"Yeah, I'm pretty sick of it. Every time I see him, he's somewhere
else. At first, I saw him uptown near home, and not so long ago in the
center..." She paused for a second, "Actually, I'm not sure if it was
even him in the center."

Daniel looked at her with questioning eyes.

"I want to confront him!" She said suddenly.

Daniel snuck another glance at the guy, attempting to estimate how
dangerous he was.

"Are you sure?" he asked, worried.

"Yes! I'm simply sick of it. I need to know what his story is!" She didn't elaborate beyond that, having a sneaking suspicion that he might be linked to the service.

The determination in her voice indicated that she was not going to back off. Daniel suggested they go together. Yael insisted on going alone. *If this guy really has something to do with the service, Daniel shouldn't be nearby.*

They agreed that Daniel would watch from a safe distance and if she was in danger, he'd come immediately.

Yael walked up to the phony lame with determination. Only one thought went through her mind with every step. *Is he linked in any way to the service?*

The man didn't move, as if he was standing and waiting for her. She stopped in front of him and looked at him carefully. *Is it really him?*

She looked directly into his eyes. His light blue eyes were cold and empty. There was something impenetrable in his gaze, and she couldn't quite figure out who he really was. *They train their people well,* she couldn't help but think.

A long moment of silence passed. Yael felt like she was in the moment of a battle depended on assessing the enemy before something happened. There was no change in his face, no expression. This frozen state began to raise a fear and suspicion in her.

"Who are you?" she asked firmly, "Why are you following me?"

Every muscle in her body became alert and ready for any possible attack he might initiate.

He remained silent, unmoving.

She repeated the question.

Silence.

Daniel approached from behind. Seeing them standing opposite each other without moving and without saying anything had alerted him, and yet, typical of his cautious state, he stood aside, on guard, waiting for things to occur. He didn't intervene and let her continue.

She asked the phony lame for the third time.

"Why are you following me?"

He moved his gaze to Daniel and, for a split second, it seemed he didn't quite understand what was happening. Then, without warning, his face twisted, his mouth opened, and he let out two short barks. "Orff! Orff!"

Both Daniel and Yael stood still, astonished. As soon as she recovered from his surprising reaction, she attempted to figure out if his voice, although barking, sounded familiar. He rolled his eyes up to the skies, completely disconnected with reality, and hurried away, continuing his bark, leaving both Daniel and Yael puzzled.

"Another crazy New Yorker," commented a passerby who had overheard the barking.

"But his upper lip was torn a little," Yael muttered to herself.

It was the last time she ever saw him.

Sky Line

Yael and Kristen waited for Chris-Daoud Khan in his luxurious offices on the twenty-seventh floor of his Franklin Street location. The view of Manhattan was spread outside his window. It was December 11, exactly three months after the fall of the Twin Towers.

Yael recalled the last time she had been there looking for him, just before her journey to India. From that very spot, the city looked like a huge monster with many arms. Streets branched out and meet at accurate ninety-degree angles as if built by a gigantic machine. The symmetry, straight lines, and constant construction of huge buildings lay before her in incomprehensible, inhumane dimensions.

She thought about all of the transactions being formed at every moment of every day. The stock market was climbing, finances were rising, money and properties were changing hands. From his office, everything seemed to be driven by financial wheels. Turmoil of events, commotion, people, cars, galleries, restaurants, buildings, and shops looked up at her from the concrete jungle, an organized chaos like the swinging boxes in a closet.

How can such a small island take so much abuse? She wondered to herself, imagining the giants of construction digging deep into its ground, pounding into its flesh and paving new roads, sidewalks, and buildings. Only the scattered clods of dirt served to remind of an earth that no longer existed; it had been replaced, covered by a mask of gray and concrete. It was a new world, a world whose sole purpose was to provide its citizens with their growing needs: pipes, cables, canals, electricity, steam, sewage.

Some day, something will happen. Yael thought back to her earlier predictions.

And something had happened, taking the lives of three thousand people with it.

Yael had trouble halting her flood of thoughts and feelings as she stared out over the city. *Why has New York become what it has become? And for what?*

382

It was a city that one could only face half numb, comfortably numb, and asleep. Otherwise, it was too much. What had become of those who didn't know the city's limits? Its strength rested in its somber solitude, a solitude that—even though it shone—did not illuminate.

Chris-Daoud Khan walked in smiling, interrupting her flow of thoughts. He seemed truly happy to see her.

"Glad to see you're back," he said, shaking her hand warmly.

"Oh! We're very happy to have her back," said Kristen, adding softly, "If only she would have told us about her aunt's death and the extremely difficult circumstances after it had happened..." She shook her head, wearing a convincingly sad expression.

"Yes," he agreed, turning his gaze to Yael, "I was told you were very close." He added emphatically.

"Yes, we were. Thank you." Yael offered him a weak smile.

"Family is very important," he added.

"Indeed it is!" Yael agreed. "And how is your brother?" she immediately added, "Well, I hope?"

"He's alright," Chris-Daoud Khan replied. He looked at Kristen. He seemed as if he wanted to say more but was holding back from elaborating because of her presence.

"Well", said Kristen "I'll leave you two to your business!" She smiled at Chris-Daoud Khan. He smiled back.

"Yes! We are going to be touring the gas plants today of my brother's company."

"Splendid!" Said Kristen, smiling at Yael.

"I'll walk you out..." he said to Kristen. He turned his gaze to Yael, "... and get the chauffeur ready for us."

Kristen nodded to Yael and left with him. Yael watched Khan showing her out.

What a stab in the back, she thought.

For a second, sadness started to fill her, but she had been told by the service that in the beginning it wouldn't be easy.

All of this is just a huge deception, she thought, *I was deceived, and now I deceive others.*

383

The thunder of a plane's engine could be heard. Yael looked out through the huge window, searching with her eyes for the plane.

There, in the distance, the skyline could be seen, lacking the Twins, reminding her, in fact, why she was there.

Epilogue

The storm was strong and had begun to sweep up everything in all directions. I had difficulties opening my eyes because of the dust, sand, and the angry blasts of air.

A local told me rooms could be rented nearby. This time, plenty of rooms were left.

He said that we were all big family now.

From afar, I recognized two multi-story buildings: the Twin Towers. Chris was there with his brother. While protecting my face from flying objects, I was led to the towers' entrance by the local. He left.

People were running in all directions so I could find Chris and his brother without anyone paying attention to me.

The storm faded slightly away.

Made in the USA
Charleston, SC
29 May 2015